THE NIGHT SHE FELL

BY JENNIFER SOUCY

To my love.

You may be my hero,

but I'll always protect you from the monsters.

PROLOGUE

WHERE THERE'S SMOKE...

The girl dreamed of fire again.

Red, orange, and gold flames billowed, racing like hell clouds across the ceiling and down the walls. The crackling tongues hungered, licking over everything in its path. Hot, but not the good heat of Mama's kitchen—the girl's favorite room, where yummy meals and snacks were prepared just for her. The flames weren't pretty like Mama's candles, which she always lit before singing those old songs. This fire snapped like a wolf, toothy maw clacking as it streamed closer to the bed where the girl slept, eager to gobble her up.

Oh no, please... I'll be good. Don't get me!

She awoke, hands in the air to ward off the sentient fire that didn't exist outside her nightmares. Everything was cool and dark—safe, like before. *It's only make-believe, silly.* But the fire had been real once, real enough to take Daddy away.

Mama, she'd make the bad dream disappear. She could fix anything, telling the darkness and monsters to shoo and leave her baby alone. Beautiful Mama beneath a veil of long, black hair, with eyes sweet as caramel candies—the girl's favorite treat. Mama only made those for the best and most deserving children, even silly Tay and boring Denny, but she didn't love them the same.

I'm her best baby. She said so.

Mama would sweep the girl in her arms, showering her cheeks with kisses. Her strong, brown hands were always scented with garlic and herbs from the garden, fresh and green. Maybe she'd sing for the girl, too, one of those nice ballads in the Old Tongue. The girl practiced those songs every day with Mama, learning so she might make Papou and Yaya proud. Songs from the women in their family—long dead, but still here—who watched over all good girls. At least, that's what Mama said, and she never lied.

Glassy eyes met hers from across the pillow, reflecting a twinkle from the nightlight and reminding her she wasn't alone. Leona stood watch, unafraid of bad dreams or monsters. Her stitched pink mouth hadn't moved with a warning, so all must've been well. The girl cuddled with her best friend—made special by Mama—and whispered into the triangle ear, "Wasn't real, only a dream. Right, Leona?"

The stuffed cat didn't answer, but her expression remained calm. The girl's thumping heart slowed. Normal sounds emerged from the dim room: the hum of the heater, a brush of branches tapping on the window, the ocean waves beyond, and...something else—closer and in her house—a string of murmurs occasionally broken by damp whimpers.

"You hear that?" she asked Leona, still receiving no response. The cat stared at the bedroom door, and the girl looped her fingers through the purple collar. "We can look, but be quiet. We don't wanna wake Mama."

She inched the door open, sneaking along the hallway and daintily hopping over the shadows. A row of nightlights lit a path in case she needed to use the bathroom, but plenty of gloomy spots remained to threaten her safe passage. The sounds grew louder, rolling down the hall from the kitchen—a room no one should be using at this time of night.

Harsh whispers crackled beyond the borders of the white door, hissing softly as a snake but with rough edges, crunching gravel like when the girl walked across the driveway. Words from another land, another life, but she'd recognize that voice anywhere.

Her grip on Leona tightened, holding the stuffed cat before her like a shield. She nudged the door open. Her nostrils flared from the oily smoke, eyes widening at the rows of flames dancing within the cage of the cast-iron stove.

Mama stood over a steaming pot, her special one made from the same black metal as the stove. The puzzling dialogue continued as she added handfuls of ingredients from a pile on the kitchen island. But who was she talking to? Her hands shot into the air, palms up, as more angry words poured forth to mingle with the scorched steam.

"Bind, *desmévo...* Great Hekate, hear my cry. *Timoró*, grant me justice...*dikaiosýni*, for your daughter who was so wronged, the daughter who loves you."

A pop sounded from the pot, gouts of steam and muddy liquid splashing, then sizzling on the hot metal. The girl buried her face in Leona's soft neck, but not in time to hide the cry that leapt from her mouth.

Mama spun around. Her black curls stood on end, quivering and alert as Medusa's snakes in the girl's storybook. The eyes were new and strange, two all-black holes sinking into her skull. Bruised lips pulled back, revealing rows of gleaming teeth—more like fangs, tinged red from the stove's fiery light.

She screamed as those eyes met hers, the sound muffled by Leona's head while the door swung shut. The girl stumbled back, thumping into the wall. A monster had taken her mama.

She ran from the rapid footsteps and the hungry, alien face—recognizable still, which was even more horrifying. Was Mama gone forever, taken by a big, bad wolf who wore her skin like a costume—a trick to swallow up nosy children?

The girl's small feet slapped the floor, drumming through the suddenly oppressive house. She screamed when powerful hands snatched and spun her around.

"Baby, no—don't be scared. It's only me." The voice was normal again, skin and bones sinking to reform the beautiful shape she knew and loved. Similar but not quite right; the purplish-red marks on her cheeks, lips, and neck hadn't disappeared.

"Mama, you're hurt." The girl raised a shaky hand toward the gruesome chain of bruises, purple as smooshed irises—her favorite flower.

"I'll be okay, baby. I can fix this." Her rich voice thickened, threaded with the same anger she'd displayed in the kitchen.

"Who hurt you?" The girl trembled, gulping back more tears. "Will he hurt me, too?"

"No, sweet girl. No one will ever hurt you. Don't worry. Mama knows how to make bad men pay." She lifted the girl off the ground, cradling her. "Come now, it's time for you to sleep."

Back in the bedroom, the girl was tucked beneath the quilt once more. Cooler in here, thanks to the picture window which wasn't stout enough to fully block the brisk autumn wind. Better than the kitchen, with its oily hellfire stink. The girl clutched Leona and stared at the woman she loved more than anything. Her eyes were back to normal, molten caramel sweating with unshed tears.

"I didn't mean to spy. I'm sorry. I had a fire dream again. It was a bad fire, like the one that took Daddy."

"No, I'm sorry." Mama stroked the girl's hair until her tight muscles melted like butter. "I shouldn't have woken you. I tried to be quiet."

"You looked scary, like someone else," the girl said, fighting against her drooping eyelids. "Like the witch from my storybook."

"Shhh... Sleep now, my baby."

Before her eyes finished closing, a funny thought struck the girl. "Mama, are you a witch?"

The hand paused, gently cupping her cheek. Mama leaned closer and one diamond tear shook free, losing itself in the crease of her wounded mouth. "Go to sleep, Cori. I'm here, and we'll both be safe—I promise. We'll talk about this another day, okay?"

The girl nodded, a smile blooming on her rosebud mouth—watered by her mother's kiss and another stray tear. Everything would be fine. Witches weren't *really* real, and even if they were, Mama could never be an evil one. A bad person hurt her, but she'd fix it.

Cori believed her. No one would hurt either of them again.

No one was stronger than her Mama.

ACT I

AGNÓTIS

"My love for you was greater than my wisdom."

—Euripides, *Medea*

CHAPTER ONE

The nutmeg scraped across the miniature grater; one, two, three—perfect. A lovely finishing touch for the spell of good fortune. Another day, another lesson. Maybe this time the spell would actually work. If nothing else, Mama and I would have an awesome coffee with our breakfast.

I dipped the straw carefully against the inner edge, stealing a sip. This might've been the best latte yet—fresh-pressed espresso, luscious steamed oat milk, and a flawless maple leaf design. The sales pitch unfurled in my mind, a speech for the elite Greenwich ladies taking a break between shopping and spa rounds: *A dash of freshly grated nutmeg in honor of fall... Pair this dairy-free, hand-crafted beverage with a delectable paleo pumpkin cookie baked just this morning.* Yes, these would sell like crazy.

"Mama, try it. I did everything like you said." I crossed the kitchen, cradling my creation and setting it beside her. She glanced from her task, squeezing homemade pumpkin buttercream onto the cooled cookies. How'd she make buttercream without dairy? Another type of culinary magic, but one I had at least a chance in hell of mastering.

"Let's see how it came out. After all that baking, I could use a pick me up." Mama smiled, wiping her hands on her rust-colored apron. She held the saucer, sniffing the cup's contents. Her fabulous caramel eyes widened in appreciation of both the delicate design and the aromatic steam. She swallowed a hearty dose, assessing the flavors, and slowly nodded.

My fingers twisted in my apron pockets, foot tapping as I awaited a favorable response. This time, it had to be right! Her eyes softened with pity, and she took a second dutiful gulp.

"Well?" But I already knew.

"It tastes wonderful, baby, but it's just a regular latte. I'm sorry."

"Dammit! I did everything you said." I turned away, already set to grind more coffee beans. "Let me try again. Maybe I got one of the words wrong."

"No, I watched you. Everything was just right." I flinched from her comforting touch, irritated she always tried to make each failure seem like no big deal. "Why don't you set these cookies in the display case. If you hurry, I'll let you finish the soup."

"Why bother? If I touch it, I'll ruin whatever you did to make it good." Best to keep moving, hop back on the proverbial horse. If I dwelled too long on another failure, I'd never try again. Although why I kept trying made less sense than ever.

"Coralena del Prado, you quit that," Mama said, using the stern tone she saved for her regular employees. "How many times do I have to tell you..."

"...it'll happen when it happens," I finished the same, tired phrase for her. "I know. I've been studying for years, Mama, but it's no good. I'll never have your magic."

I didn't fight her this time when she took me into her arms. I should've been embarrassed, leaning over my mother—who had once towered above me—to accept the loving hug she always doled out whenever I was sad or scared. If Monica were here, she'd tease me without mercy. *Aww, little mama's girl...* But I didn't care about that now. Fifteen years of study, scrutinizing my mother's every move, memorizing herb lore and spellwork—all for nothing. I would never unlock the *pharmakis* gifts she swore lived in my blood and bone, flowing in an unbroken line for hundreds of years only to end here, with me.

What a ridiculous fantasy, studying magic to become a witch like my mother. Maybe none of it was real; a goal built upon girlish hero-worship, an illusion woven like a pretty ribbon through an impressionable mind.

No, denial was a halfhearted sop to my damaged pride. I'd seen my mother's power firsthand: the teas and unguents she crafted for our friends; spectacular meals she created at home and in our restaurant; and a terrifying moment from one grim night, long ago, when she appeared to summon fire. She had a gift—magic, sorcery, or whatever one wanted to call it—one it appeared she'd failed to pass on, no matter how much I tried to coax it out through fruitless practice.

"You worry too much. Trust me, Cori. A mother always knows when her child is special. Your time will come."

"Yeah, whatever." Her steadfast belief was nice but didn't really help. Mothers always said such things, maybe more often if their children failed to surpass expected benchmarks. "Let me go set up the front. You know, in that same *special* way I always do."

"Go on, but you'd better cheer up," she sighed, passing me a tray of flawless pumpkin cookies. "Smile and be polite for the *Vasílisses*, or else they'll show you how a wicked witch really behaves."

"Of course, Boss. Can't upset their majesties." I suppressed a smile at our private nickname for the wealthy women of Greenwich—The Queens. She used it on purpose, certain I'd thaw beneath her humor.

Mama had a way with people, especially charming to those she despised the most—and they adored her more than anyone, never seeing beyond her gratifying smiles. She effortlessly balanced deference and pride with genial warmth. The society ladies ate it up at lunch, as did the friends and family they dragged back for dinner service. Appeasing those families had earned us this building and some modest success, allowing our restaurant to thrive for fifteen years.

Cornucopia, an unassuming gem in Connecticut's wealthiest city, was nestled near the end of the world-renowned shopping and dining district on Greenwich Avenue. We owned the entire building outright, priceless real estate gifted from my parents' former bosses, the Colburns. The restaurant filled the ground floor, and we lived in the comfortable space above. They loved us, these flowers of New England royalty, gushing over the cozy ambience and traditional dishes inspired by Mama's authentic

Mediterranean heritage.

Mama always avoided telling the full tale of how we gained such a lavish gift. I'd been too young to remember much of our life at Cypress Point, the Colburn family's massive fifty-acre waterfront compound. We lived in the small cottage at the edge of the property until Daddy died, my first home and the only dwelling we shared as a complete family.

They felt bad after your father died in the stable fire. The building was a generous workman's comp settlement, that's all. I doubted that was all, but it didn't matter. No gift could replace the handsome, kind man who danced along the hazy edges of my childhood memories.

The tray of cookies emptied, framed just right in the polished display case. The lunch crew would be here soon—Monica and her little brother, Marcus. Their chatter always brightened the restaurant, making each monotonous shift pass easier. Our weekdays were often busy, but it wasn't a challenge when we maintained the same crew and routine for years.

With Halloween approaching, the holidays were back—our second annual peak season and maybe a chance for some excitement. Otherwise, it would be another day of pleasing people to prove, once again, that we belonged in Greenwich just as much as the rest of them.

***

"Princess alert, incoming!" Monica hissed, a fleck of spit hitting my cheek.

"Ewww, damn! Say it, don't spray it." I wiped myself as she giggled, elbowing my ribs.

Almost every day, the same trio graced us with their outward perfection and annoyingly predictable routine. Although, sometimes the girls invited similarly privileged guests to join them. They breezed through the doors wearing stylish yoga outfits, perfect messy buns, and glowing tans—Instagram-ready and gorgeous, even after their afternoon workout.

Bronte Colburn led the pack, a blonde and blue-eyed porcelain angel. Waverly Nguyen followed, her lips set in a perfect pout as she studied the screen of her limited-release iPhone, probably preparing to bitch about something. Opaela Dinesh bounced behind—last, but loudest—already whining about her thirst.

"I got this crew, don't you worry." Monica tossed me a sassy wink. "You wanna follow with a water carafe?"

"For all the good it will do." Our water was never good enough, inspiring the Princesses to begin their meals with a disappointed tirade. We had no plans to change our standard complimentary beverage starter, despite the unsolicited suggestions they pulled from their tight asses.

Lemon water, still? Ohhhkay...but that's so basic, don't you think? What if you infused it with something else—anything else? Obviously the ingredients have to be naturally sourced and organic, otherwise I'll break out all over!

I spent years in school with this trio, who conveniently appeared to forget our shared sentence at the same institution. Maybe I was easy to forget, entrenched in the family business while they shared exotic vacations, memorable parties, and Ivy League educations with the rest of our former classmates.

The girls took it upon themselves to push two tables together, chattering loudly as scattered sets of ladies murmured to each other with a mixture of approval and dismay. Even the super elite had cliques, each with their preferred standards of decorum—a pleasant thought, imagining this pack of barracudas gnashing on each other's tails.

"Ladies, welcome back," Monica announced with an exuberance I recognized as her fake voice. She only talked like that for the worst customers, saving her irreverent wit for me and Marcus. She never dared speak so boldly in front of our mothers—a smart strategy. They wouldn't have found the humor in either her phony service voice or earthy sarcasm. I wouldn't mess with our mothers, either.

"Yeah, so I'm dying for some of Theresa's special tea. Will you tell her it's for me? Thanks," Bronte said, fanning her face with a linen napkin. She paused when I approached with the lemon water carafe, a saccharine smile fixed on her lips. "Oh hey, Cori. I didn't see you there. Can you ask your mom about the tea? She'll know what I mean. And give her this list, please. My mother has an order she needs me to bring home after we eat."

"I want some special tea! Anything will be better than boring old tap water." Waverly covered her glass as I attempted to pour.

"You can't be serious? Has this always been tap water?" Opaela cried, tearing her eyes away from her phone. "No wonder my tongue always swells when we leave here."

"Girl, nothing on you is more swollen than those thighs. You need to take it easy on the calories today if you want to look your best this weekend," Waverly said with a stinging cackle.

"I'll take this back and get your tea started." I grabbed the folded note from Bronte's outstretched hand, throwing Monica a warning glance. Her dark cheeks flushed, but she risked a smirk and an eye roll for me. I couldn't help but add, "By the way, the water is imported from Iceland. You might want to visit your allergist again and get that checked out."

I couldn't help but take a bit of pleasure from another of Waverly's cackles. At least one of them had a sense of humor, even if the three of them were as out of touch as visitors from another planet.

The paper poked my palm, and I opened it to read the new order. It wasn't unusual, these requests for Mama's specialties. Bronte's mother, Aspasia Colburn, had always been a steady customer. The local ladies swore by her teas and recipes.

We also catered special events, hence why Mama had partnered years ago with Dora, Monica's mother, for help with the workload. Despite our string of mockery behind the rich folks' backs, Monica and I loved working those events. We'd gaze at one-of-a-kind, million-dollar homes in all their glory, pretending for only a few hours that we also belonged in the proverbial lap of luxury.

The dulcet tones of New Age music in the dining room cut off at the kitchen doors, where a wave of heat and sound assaulted me. Mama's pots bubbled on the stove, and an array of meats sizzled on the grill. Marcus attempted to mimic another mumble-rap anthem playing on the radio in the dish pit.

"Let me take over for a minute. Bronte Colburn is here with a special order, and she's absolutely *dying* for some of your tea," I said with a dramatic flourish, palm to forehead.

"I'm nearly done, baby. Turn the kettle on and grab the yellow cannister from the shelf—two scoops of Sunflower Dream. Let it steep for five minutes before serving," she said, steady as a battle-hardened general. It took a lot to push her over the edge, another of her qualities I envied.

I could usually hold my comments and frustration in, but it was more of a struggle the older I got. Twenty-one years in Greenwich, a fly suspended in amber, stuck in the family restaurant but consistently failing to unlock the one skill I yearned to master. Anyone would have some issues swallowing that fate with aplomb.

"What's so special about this, anyway? She acts like you invented it just for her," I grumbled, preparing a tea service. Three cups, though; if two of the girls were drinking tea, the third would follow suit.

"I did, actually," Mama chuckled, dabbing her brow with a small towel. "She had terrible hay fever as a child, and I made a special blend to help. I'm surprised she remembers after all these years."

"Yes, she made sure everyone in earshot heard about her special drink. So, here's the list. We need a birthday cake for Friday, a bunch of your fall-blend tea, and 'Tonic.' What does that even mean?"

"Just something I've made for years for Aspasia, sort of a beauty remedy." She plated the seared meats on special platters prepped with a sample of Greek salad, seasonal fruit, and quinoa. "I'll pour the water for the tea and bring it out. Take these to table 4, please."

With a platter in each hand, I returned to the dining room. Monica continued to explain the menu to the girls. Every single time, the same song and dance—and these girls had been coming here for years. So picky! I'd never grill a random server in such a way, especially over quality food made from scratch. What happened to trusting a skilled chef and being grateful for whatever they painstakingly crafted?

The older ladies in their lightweight woolen dresses beamed, duly appreciative of their colorful plates. They asked for a set of extra napkins, which I grabbed while Monica finished her tedious task. As I turned to leave the table again, I smothered a groan at Bronte's delicate but insistent wave. *Christ, what now?*

"Do you think my tea is almost ready?" Her patronizing inquiry ended with a whine that set my teeth on edge. "Planning for my birthday party has ravaged my immune system. So much goes into making twenty-one memorable, wouldn't you agree?"

"Oh, I don't know. We didn't do much for mine, but I'm sure yours involves much more work," I answered mildly, recalling my birthday in February. Mama made an amazing cake, and I received several thoughtful presents from our family and friends. After, Monica dragged me to Stamford for a night of drinking and dancing. Who could've needed or wanted more than that?

"There she is! You grow more lovely every time I see you," Mama proclaimed, emptying her tray with a speed and grace I hadn't been able to duplicate yet. Hot tea kettles always made me nervous—worse when the flimsy tray wobbled, endangering her antique cups and saucers. "Your birthday is coming up. Twenty-one, it doesn't seem possible."

"Thanks, Theresa! I told Mother I must have one of your cakes. I figured if I'm indulging, it should be with only the best." Bronte stood and kissed Mama's cheek. "What do you recommend? You know I love chocolate, but maybe we could do something not quite as heavy as a regular cake?"

"I have just the thing," she replied, pouring out tea for each of the girls before passing me the empty tray. "Opera cake. It involves a fair bit of work, but nothing less grand will do for such a special birthday."

I bit my tongue, dismayed at the half a day of prep and baking such a cake would require. Mama only made it once or twice a year, usually during December. Over a dozen paper-thin layers of almond sponge cake soaked in espresso and Frangelico, buttercream filling, and topped with chocolate ganache... What a pain in the ass, a gift this spoiled girl would accept as her due with little more than a shrug.

"That sounds divine! I knew I could count on you." Bronte smiled and hugged Mama again. Her expression faded when her gaze landed on me. She glanced toward her friends—oblivious and on their phones throughout the conversation—before adding, "The family party is Friday, just a casual affair, but we're all heading to a new club in the city afterward. It's called Inferno. You should totally come with, Cori."

"I don't know. We stay pretty late on Fridays. I might not get out in time," I said, grateful for an honest excuse. As if I'd attend one of their mindless parties. I could only imagine the kind of people who'd be there. They'd either ignore me or mistake me for an employee, asking me to refill their drinks and fetch snacks.

"No. Cori has work all weekend, and she doesn't go to the city." Mama's warm tone turned brittle, something I'd never heard when she talked with one of her valued customers. She appeared to remember herself, patting Bronte's cheek then waving at the table of girls. "Well, let me finish your lunches, then I'll pack your mother's order. Enjoy the tea, my dears."

I followed on her heels, unwilling to get trapped in a vapid conversation with the Princesses. In the kitchen, Monica and Marcus laughed over some joke, probably making fun of how Bronte and her friends ordered. Likely all off-menu dishes, heavily modified for this or that diet requirement or specious allergy.

"Why did you jump in? I had it handled," I demanded, but Mama ignored my irritation in favor of adding a fresh round of chicken to the grill. "I didn't want to go, anyway, but you make it sound like I'm not capable of deciding for myself."

"Bronte's a good girl, but I don't want you socializing with them. And I'm not comfortable with the notion of you partying in New York City by yourself."

"Why not? In case you forgot, I am an adult." I glanced to Monica and Marcus for backup, but they immediately found new tasks. They wouldn't stand against Mama—fair, since she was their boss. Mine, too, but I wasn't afraid of being fired. I'd have to die to escape this place. Even then, she'd find a way to drag me back from the Other Side.

"Bad things happen when people like us mingle with those types. We're not like them, even if sometimes we forget while living in their world." Mama knocked the extra marinade from her tongs with a series of sharp raps. "But they never forget. We're the help, an expendable commodity."

"Believe me, that's something I never forget, either. And next time, let me speak for myself." I stomped back to the dining room to see if there was anything I could clean or organize while cooling down.

Why was I so mad? So what if Mama jumped in? I was refusing them, anyway...those insufferable pains in my ass.

But hadn't something in me considered saying yes? A night in New York City, dancing in a fancy club I'd never have a chance to visit otherwise. They probably only let in the most fabulous, connected people. That almost sounded like fun.

I never went anywhere. Cornucopia devoured most of my time. We were only open a few hours for lunch and dinner but, with prep and cleaning, we worked an average of twelve hours a day. That didn't include paperwork, orders, inventory, and shopping. Six days a week, with Mondays off; work, eat, sleep, rinse and repeat. No time for college or much else. Occasionally Monica and I escaped to the movies or the beach in the summer, but we rarely ventured beyond our zip code.

Mama's interference bothered me the most. She'd practically forbidden me from going—worst of all, she did it in front of those smug princesses. I may have been a failure at spells, but that didn't mean I was incapable of managing the rest of my life. My recipes were passable, even if they lacked her unquantifiable dash of mysticism. I may not have been as accomplished as her, but I wasn't a total buffoon either.

The other lunch guests trickled out, trapping me at the cash register while they paid their bills and purchased the last of our pastries to take home. We rarely had leftovers, as if Mama had a sixth sense for making just enough without going overboard.

Every day we featured something new, which kept the regulars coming back to see what we'd offer next. That was the only way to operate in a town of pampered people who grew bored easily, every desire granted so often they tired of even the finest things. Mama's rotating menu, dependent on her mood and what looked best at the market, never allowed for complacency.

Monica sidled up after dropping off the food for Bronte and the girls, tugging my ponytail until I met her sideways grin. "Hey, snap out of it. Your mama didn't mean any harm. It's normal for them to worry about us, right?"

"Yeah, I know, but she's been this way since Dad died." I instantly regretted the words and the connection they formed. "I get it. She doesn't want to lose me too, but can't she let me live a little?"

"You, Miss Goody Two-Shoes, are definitely safe from danger. Nerdy ole bookworm... My grandma takes more risks than you." She laughed, smothering me with an impulsive hug to dull the edge of her ridicule. "Hey, I wouldn't mind partying at a fancy nightclub. We could tell our mothers we're spending the night at each other's houses."

"Seriously? What are we, sixteen?"

"You got a better idea? Come on, Cori. I dare you! Go get the info from Bronte—quick, before your mama comes out with that order."

Glancing through the porthole window, I couldn't see her salt-and-pepper head by the stove. She must've been packing the Colburn order in the storage room.

I grabbed the full receipt before approaching their table. Despite the complaints and lengthy ordering process, the girls' empty plates sparkled—a testament to Mama's skill. No one could refuse her meals after one taste.

"Your order should be right up, but I wasn't sure how you all wanted to split the check." I set the receipt on the table, then stacked the plates on my arm.

"It's on me today, girls. You can get me back tomorrow," Bronte said grandly. Not that Waverly or Opaela protested. It was easy for Bronte to be generous. She wasn't spending her money, just adding it to the family credit card like a good princess. "Here you go, Cori." She placed a heavy black card on the receipt holder.

"By the way, what time is the party on Friday? Will there be a list to get in?" My casual question belied the tension holding my neck rigid as I resisted peeking over my shoulder.

"Is your mommy going to let you come out and play? She agreed to extend curfew for one night?" Waverly cooed in a baby voice while Opaela brayed with laughter.

"Shut up, you two—honestly." Bronte struggled to hide her own amusement beneath the business-like instructions. "Yeah, there's a list. Here, I'll put my number on the receipt. Text me to confirm and let me know who you're bringing as a date. I'll take care of everything."

"I hope you have a fairy godmother to bring you a decent outfit. They are super strict about their dress code," Opaela piped in, sweet as canned frosting.

"I'm sure I can manage. Some of my rags are nicer than others," I replied dryly, taking the check back from Bronte with her number. *Save it for later.* Out and about in New York City, I wouldn't have to restrain my tongue from retaliating against their smart-ass comments.

"You'll be fine. Just show some cleavage and leg. That's all the bouncers care about," Bronte advised, then playfully smacked her friends. "Thanks, Cori! See you soon."

"Can't wait."

That would show Monica. *Goody two-shoes, my ass.* I'd prove her wrong when we were in the city, dressed in our finest and fending off admirers. A night on the town, away from the unsatisfying realities of Greenwich... That'd be a dream come true. Even Cinderella escaped to hang at the ball, so why couldn't I?

CHAPTER TWO

Hangers clattered as I raced through the discount rack, each plastic rattle making me more frazzled. Nothing. How was that even possible? This was the third store and our last opportunity. We had to head back to Greenwich soon and prepare for dinner shift. Our second trip to Stamford Town Center had to succeed. The big party in the city was tomorrow. I refused to let the Princesses see me in anything less than my best. Unfortunately, I'd never taken the time to purchase a best of anything.

"I am totally getting this, it's perfect! What about you?" Monica strutted from the fitting rooms wearing a pink mini-dress slashed with red satin; a stunning choice, complementing her model's figure and lustrous umber skin.

"There's nothing here. Maybe I should just stay home?" I rested my head against the metal rack.

Dozens of dresses, but none would help me fit in with them. Dammit, why did I care? I didn't even like those girls, but my pride wouldn't settle for a half-assed attempt. We'd already exchanged texts. How badass would it look if I backed out, too scared to show my face at one stupid party?

"God, you're so emo!" Monica pushed me out of her way before attacking the multitude of outfits for something suitable. "Spoiler alert: none of these dresses will be as fine as what those girls wear. Hell, you think Bronte Colburn even buys off the rack? Her clothes are probably hand sewn by virginal French nuns under a vow of silence, for Christ's sake! It doesn't matter what you wear but how you wear it—ya feel me?"

"Easy for you to say. You didn't have to endure twelve years of school with these people. On a good day, they ignored me." A line of haughty faces blurred past, same as when our paths crossed in the halls. It wasn't fair to say I had no friends in school, but most were transient—buddies for a few months before inevitably moving on to bigger and better social connections.

Even Nolan, my first and only boyfriend, couldn't hang. We started off as friends in middle school. Our friendship experienced a growth spurt during senior year, ignited at homecoming, then died a wasting death during his freshman semester at Yale. For one brief, idiotic moment, I'd thought I loved him. Then came The Talk—more like a series of gripes he couldn't let go, and I accepted with reluctant despondence.

We never see each other.

Are you ever not working?

You know I can't visit when I have to study.

And the Grand Finale: *Hey, Cori… How 'bout we try seeing other people?*

Technically, we were still friends—if one counted the infrequent chats on social media or the rare times he stopped by the restaurant during holiday breaks. I used to believe we understood each other, both of us outcasts among our affluent neighbors. Nolan came from money, too, but nowhere near the level of Bronte Colburn and her crew. We liked the same bands and movies, laughed over the same jokes, and our relationship had been passionate for a time.

He was my first...everything. I'd once hoped he would be my last, but it wasn't meant to be.

I wasn't ready to give up. Hell, I was twenty-one—too damn young to accept the spinster title. I had wanted Nolan to be the one, but he wasn't. Oh well, time to move on.

I grew lonely over the weeks and months after The Talk, a period that stretched into almost two years. Maybe I was ready to try again, find a decent man—but definitely no one from Greenwich. I ran into enough of them at work, fortunately sinking beneath their notice most of the time. Occasionally, one of the little princes had a bit much to drink and slipped their number in with the credit card receipt. Ugh, I wasn't that desperate. I'd rather spend my life alone instead of chasing one of those weak, pampered babies.

Goddess knew Monica had no trouble finding companions; as a self-proclaimed pansexual, her dating pool was virtually endless. Not to mention, with her brazen confidence and sultry good looks, she could've grabbed the attention of a stick. She was simply better at the game— naturally outgoing, delighted by any opportunity to meet new people.

It would've helped if I found more—or any—activities away from home. I didn't want a Greenwich version of Prince Charming. What did guys like that know about real life and hard work, chasing a lifelong wish for something more, spending countless hours honing their innate talents to create something original?

My spells were a disaster, not that I'd dare share that info with anyone. I'd dreamed for years of cooking like Mama, succeeding at the common tasks anyone might learn, but my passion was to excel at magic. That gift continued to elude me despite the promise passed through our bloodline for countless generations.

Could someone complacent in their privilege—whose future was guaranteed, living comfortably being served by others—ever understand a fundamental desire, a hunger, to build a true and lasting legacy?

"Are you even listening to me?" Monica shook a handful of dresses in my face. "Take these into the dressing room, and you'd better give each one a shot. Move your ass."

"Fine, whatever. You don't have to be so pushy." I huffed, fighting to shut the curtain.

"Then don't make me push! Try acting for once like you're down for an adventure," she said from the other side, fingernails tapping away on her phone. "And you need to let go of your grudges. News flash: high school is over. Who cares about Bronte and her little friends? Why do you dislike her so much, anyway? Didn't you play together as kids?"

"Please, only until we were five. That doesn't count." Little Bronte had been a friend—Tay, who played dolls and co-hosted tea parties with me. Denny, her older brother, ignored us—a typical boy, uninterested in the whimsical games that little girls loved. I barely remembered those moments; if Bronte did, she cast the memories aside long ago.

In grade school, Bronte and her pack of nasty followers mercilessly teased me, but even then, they lacked imagination. Their taunts were obvious and superficial—my clothes, shoes, whatever. The attacks grew more subtle as we aged, but I stopped caring about their opinions, so the barbs were easier to ignore.

Monica continued hopping from subject to subject while I stripped. "Too bad we won't get a slice of that cake. I love your mama's opera cake. Maybe she'll make one for my birthday?"

"For you, she might," I agreed, discarding the lavender taffeta when it wouldn't fit over my shoulders. "One of these days, I'll make cakes just as good. You'll see."

"Girl, your food is already off the chain! I don't even know why you talk like that."

"It's not as good as hers. Maybe it won't ever be. Mama's one of a kind."

"That's a matter of opinion. You need to stop trying to compare yourself. Worry about rockin' your own thing instead." Monica always cut to the heart of the matter, brutally honest and perceptive, but her support never wavered—the perfect best friend. Then she gasped, shocked as a coma patient jolted back to life. "That son of a bitch! Guess who's on his way back home for the weekend? He just tagged Bronte and Inferno. I swear, Nolan is such a dumbass."

"Oh, great! I haven't seen him since August." I sucked in, fighting with the zipper of a leaf-green silk confection. Not bad, and the little pink flowers embroidered along the hem were kinda cute. "What do you think about this one?"

When I pulled the curtain back, Monica was nose deep in her phone, eyes wide with outrage. She glanced up and slammed her mouth shut. Plastering on an artificial smile and using her customer-only voice, she enthused, "I love it! Get that wild mane under control, and you'll outshine all those basic bitches. Don't even give them or Nolan another thought.

You'll totally have your pick of hotties."

"What are you talking about? I'm over Nolan." I twirled the short skirt, smiling as it belled outward.

"Nothing! I mean, it could totally be a typo. Come on—let's change so we can get back to work." She tugged on the curtain, but I stopped her, tilting my head until her darting eyes reconnected with mine.

"What's a typo?" I nudged her calf with my toe. "Hey! You'd better spill it. You're such a crappy liar."

"I checked out Bronte's timeline, and," Monica took a deep breath before pushing out the rest, "it kinda looks like Nolan's her date for tomorrow. That's why he's coming down for the weekend."

I yanked the curtain shut, blocking her hesitant sympathy. I stared at the lovely dress in the mirror, but its allure faded. Bronte's would be more beautiful. She'd be a vision, as usual, someone I had no hope of competing against. The golden girl with the soft curves, rising like Aphrodite on a clamshell from the sea of her peers. It wouldn't even be a contest; ordinary me, playing dress up in my bargain-bin evening wear with a girl like her—a goddess in the making, gifted from birth with every possible advantage.

I exited the fitting room, the lackluster dress drooping over my arm. "We should go. There's a lot to do before dinner shift."

Monica changed back into her street clothes, too. The smile fell, but her gentle touch reminded me she was on my side, no matter what—a comfort I'd appreciate later, but it was wasted now. All I could see was Nolan bending as his sparkling eyes closed, happy and honored to kiss Bronte's candy-pink mouth.

Son of a bitch, indeed. The hell with them both.

***

"Coralena, pay attention! You have to keep stirring." Mama appeared out of nowhere, prying the whisk from my hand.

The chocolate seized, thickening like cement in the double boiler. So much for the ganache. "Sorry, my mind must have drifted. Can we save it?"

"Get me some vegetable oil, quick." She turned off the burner, lifting the bowl from the sizzling pot. "It was too hot for too long, plus you forgot to stir. You know chocolate is delicate. You can't take your attention away for a second."

With a few drops of oil and several rapid strokes, the mixture relaxed into silky smoothness—appetizing again and probably delicious. She also boosted it by muttering a string of incomprehensible Greek words. Unfair that she had an advantage I didn't, even though she swore it would happen for me one day.

I hated those two words—one day. They nagged me for as long as I could remember: *one day you can do whatever you want, one day you'll unlock your magic, one day that perfect guy will sweep you off your feet.* The hell with "one day." I was ready for something to happen right now.

"Can I help you spread the chocolate?" I turned my gaze to the double-tiered masterpiece on the prep table. Twenty layers of cake and cream, the smell of coffee syrup beckoning from across the room. All it needed was the topping, then the final touch—curls of white and dark chocolate sprinkled over top.

A visual masterpiece, and no one but Mama and me knew of the bonus magic she activated with each key ingredient. Nutmeg for prosperity, Almond for beauty, Vanilla for peace, Chocolate for love and protection—which I nearly ruined. Maybe on purpose? Did Bronte Colburn really need Mama's spells for an even easier and more enjoyable life?

Mama dipped her pinky into the ganache, sampling it before deciding. Her nose crinkled, lips drawing back in distaste. "Oh my."

"I'm sorry, Mama. I'll get more chocolate." She stopped me, checking to make sure we were alone.

A flicker of excitement in her lively eyes sent a similar quiver through my chest. "It's not strong, but I can sense it. The chocolate absorbed your bitterness. That's what ruined it, not your technique. Your magic must be awakening!"

"Really? Oh please, let me try again," I begged, impatiently tugging her apron.

She laughed, her coarse hands patting my cheeks as she stretched to kiss the tip of my nose. "No, you won't touch this cake. I can't have you accidentally cursing Bronte. Her mother would never forgive me. But tomorrow, we'll try again with something else. It's happening, my girl. Didn't I tell you?"

"Yes, you're so smart," I agreed with a playful eye roll, taking the bespelled chocolate to the sink while she prepared a new double boiler. So tempting to save it for posterity, even if it was ruined. My first spell, and I hadn't even been trying! Maybe things were turning around.

***

Dinner service was wrapping up at last. Tonight, I hummed along to Marcus's appalling playlist instead of bugging him to put on anything else. Steamed coconut milk wafted over my skin as I poured, crafting a perfect maple leaf on each cup. I accented the leaves with a drizzle of homemade caramel, adding a dash of Mama's spice blend.

"Beautiful job, Cori! As pretty as the trees themselves," Cristina said, clapping as she studied each step. "Even Papou couldn't have done better."

"How's he been? I'm sorry I haven't been to visit in a few weeks." Our shared grandfather had lived with her since Yaya and Theía Arianna passed away. Mama was the baby of the family, and the one who inherited Yaya's Gift. Mama's much older sister, Arianna, gave birth to Cristina when Mama was only six. The pair were more like sisters than niece and aunt. As a result, even though she was my older cousin, Cristina acted more like a fun aunt.

"Same as always. You know how it goes." She shrugged, backing out of the kitchen doors with the lattes. "What more can we expect after what he lost?"

Poor Papou. He never recovered from the stroke that knocked him down within a month of Yaya's passing. Thankfully, Cristina and her husband, Adam, had plenty of room in their Stamford home. In return, Mama let Cristina work dinner shift to make extra money and escape her family duties for a few hours.

Over the years, Mama created a variety of healing concoctions to bring Papou back to us, but nothing worked. His wrinkled face and vacant eyes never moved, grayed lips barely twitching as he sipped her many potions. They'd been in love, him and Yaya, married for over fifty years. Who could overcome a loss like that?

Mama overcame it, though. I asked her about it years later, as the splendors and fears of true love began drifting through my teenage brain.

You weren't like that after Daddy died. Did you love him less?

I had to stay alive, baby. You were so young, and you needed me. Without you, I wouldn't have made it.

In a musing tone, she added, *The Old Tongue has words for all kinds of love. It differs, of course, based on the relationship—spouses, family, or friends. Agape is the most special, the root of our magic and the devotion we express toward the Divine—in our case, Hekate. She loves us all in return, but she also expects us to love ourselves, for we're her blessed children. She'd patted my cheek, sharing a heartening smile. All love has a power, and it's more than just romance. Love gives us a reason to live, drawing us out of bed every morning and sustaining our souls through the hard times. One day, you'll understand.*

One day.

"Boy, you better turn that racket down. I can't hear myself think," Dora complained, breaking off her conversation with Mama. She was an older version of Monica, barring some extra lines and a cap of snug curls instead of the sleek extensions favored by her daughter; almost identical, until Dora rattled off her stern commands. I loved her to death, but when she got riled up... Well, I was glad my mother wasn't as strict.

"Ma, it's the best part!" Marcus complained, waving a soapy hand in my direction. "Cori likes it, too, don't you?"

"Don't drag me into this. I have customers to check on." I waved him off, pausing by the door. "Mama, how much longer for the soufflés?"

"Five minutes. I'll bring them out. You get moving." She waved her spoon, then resumed her gossip session with Dora. What a pair, those two—best friends since Stamford High, partners in Cornucopia, and closer than family. Lucky for me, I genuinely adored Monica and Marcus. Our mothers wouldn't have given us a choice other than carrying their friendship into the next generation.

My section shrank as another table finished, a handsome older couple savoring the last drops of their wine. "Everything was fantastic, Cori, as usual," Mr. Santini said, never letting go of his husband's hand as he passed me a credit card. "Please send our compliments to Theresa."

"Of course, gentlemen. We always appreciate your generous feedback." I glanced back to the kitchen, then to my adjacent table. Another couple—tourists, they'd confessed—but they seemed to enjoy their first time with us. I didn't want a late dessert to spoil anything. "She should be out any second, and she'd love to catch up with you both."

The kitchen doors burst open to reveal Mama with a mini caramel-apple soufflé in each hand. As she strolled past me, the front door also opened to admit a laughing and tipsy trio. Goddammit, Nolan and Bronte with some other jackass.

I fled to the cash register, pretending the transaction required all my attention. Maybe if we ignored them, they'd take the hint. Unfortunately, Monica saw everything unfold and raced to greet the newcomers. She could take them, for all I cared, or give them to Cristina. I wouldn't wait on my ex-boyfriend with his new fling—especially not *that* fling.

Of all the fucking people to choose... Seriously, Nolan?

"My goodness, look at this stranger! I can't believe my eyes." Mama waved to the trio, then returned her attention to our first-time guests, ensuring they were satisfied with the desserts. Next, she glided to the Santinis, kissing each man's cheek while murmuring a few pleasantries. Finally, her arms widened to embrace the tall male accompanying Bronte and Nolan. A skilled hostess, she never failed to balance multiple tasks with an easy smile.

"Tessa, you haven't changed a bit." The stranger's husky voice filled the space in a slow, elegant pour, like Mama's favorite single-malt scotch. He was older than me, but somehow familiar—breathtaking with his cap of artfully disheveled dark-blond hair, confident stance, and blinding smile.

"Liar! But look at you, a grown man now—and so dashing in this suit. Hardly the same boy who was skin, bones, and scabs after all your wild adventures." Mama tore her gaze away, waving me over. "Cori, come here! You may have been too young, but do you remember Hayden? Bronte's brother? The three of you watched cartoons while I worked."

Is that Denny? My mind fixated on his childhood nickname, even though he was undeniably a man now and going by his proper name. Wow, the years made a big difference...

Something thumped in my chest when the dazzling man faced me—sapphire eyes and a glowing complexion, similar to Bronte but hardened by a wider jaw, larger nose, and a glint of golden stubble. He studied me, smiling with a fond remembrance I didn't share.

Hayden Colburn. Anyone in Greenwich would've recognized the name, the only son of Alastor and Aspasia, and Bronte's big brother. She often mentioned him to her friends, bragging about his accomplishments and exploits. He'd often been a source of gossip for the ladies of Greenwich, perpetually pining for any eligible bachelor worthy of their eminence. I faintly recalled the distant boy from my brief sojourn at Cypress Point, deliberately isolating himself while Bronte and I played. He was a man now, who called my mother Tessa—a nickname only Daddy and our family used.

Who the hell does he think he is, calling her that?

"Nope, I don't remember." I flashed an artificial smile—*sorry, not sorry*—and gathered the Santini's receipts. Mama released an exasperated sigh, but Hayden's lips twitched.

"Well, that's humbling," he said to Mama. They both laughed, resuming their chat about shared memories, which probably didn't include me. Whatever—I'd only been five, and he never made an effort to bond with me. If he was anything like his sister, whatever connection we once shared wasn't one I cared to resurrect.

I offered the Santinis a distracted farewell, dropped the check for my soufflé couple, then steeled myself before facing the newest table. I couldn't ignore their presence any longer without revealing a glimpse of my true emotions. No way would I give Bronte the satisfaction.

Bronte and Nolan held hands while chatting with a stiffly polite Monica. They were dressed up as if coming back from dinner; casual for them, but the tailored cut of their outfits indicated a price tag likely equivalent to our monthly auto payment. Bronte's designer dress clung to her like a second skin, the wispy material and color too amazing to be real. If this was her choice for a casual night out, what would she wear tomorrow? Something made from starlight itself?

"Hey, Cori!" Nolan waved as Monica left to get their drinks. Bronte's penetrating gaze fortified me as I made my way over—was that a spark of jealousy, perhaps? Still, I cursed each step and prepared any excuse to slink back into the kitchen and stay there.

"Hiya. Wow, I didn't expect to see you. What are you doing in town?" The questions were for Nolan, but Bronte's smirk told me all I needed to know—as did the hand creeping possessively up his thigh.

What a bitch! Whose idea was it to come here, anyway?

"Yeah, it's Bronte's birthday, so I couldn't miss it. We're seeing each other now." Nolan's smile shifted to his date, petting her manicured hand. "I hope you're coming tomorrow night. We haven't hung out in months. You look...healthy."

"Of course she'll be there—won't you, Cori?" Bronte asked archly, leaning against his shoulder. The repeated invitation sounded cordial, but her expression rang with a cocky challenge. This whole party was starting to stink. I envisioned entering the club and being doused in pig's blood. Did she only invite me to torment me, one more in a series of mean-spirited games?

"Wouldn't miss it." My reply matched Bronte's sweet trill. I smoothed my apron, hiding my hands in the pockets as they balled into fists. "Did you guys eat already? It's a bit late for dinner."

"We wanted dessert. I told Denny about my birthday cake, and he insisted on a preview," Bronte said, waving her brother back. "Would you mind checking on your friend? Last time she made me a latte, I swear she used half and half instead of coconut milk. Can you be a doll and make it for me, Cori?"

"You could do with a normal latte. You're too skinny, Tay." A rush of spicy cologne tickled my nostrils as the seat beside me filled with Hayden's sprawling form. Another one, so careless with his one-of-a-kind suit. Did they have live-in dry cleaners at Cypress Point, or did the help donate their masters' fine clothes to Goodwill after one use?

"Thicker may have been popular when you were my age, but the influencers say it's swinging back. Thin is in again, bro," she tittered, cutting her eyes my way.

This bitch... She's pushing it tonight.

I inched back, flushing as Hayden's admiring gaze drifted from my face, then skimmed over the curves hiding beneath my uniform. "Healthy never goes out of style," he affirmed before turning toward his sister. "Don't believe everything you read on Instagram. Or do you just scroll through the shiny pictures and click the pretty hearts?"

"Fuck off, old man. I'll educate you, don't worry." Bronte smacked his arm, then scrolled through her phone to point out her favorite examples of supreme femininity. My cue to go, thankfully—just in the nick of time.

In the kitchen, Mama chatted with Cristina and Dora while warming the last slices of bread pudding. "Hey, I thought we were eating that after our shift?"

"I'll make some more tomorrow. Our guests haven't had this in a long time," Mama said, gesturing with her spatula. "Will you finish those lattes for me and add some whipped cream and chocolate shavings?"

I complied while the ladies enthused over Hayden's good looks. Even Dora appeared impressed, rarely compelled to peek out at the guests who dined on the food she helped Mama create. Monica breezed through the kitchen doors, toying with her long braid to appear casual until her mouth stuck to my ear, unleashing all she'd been holding back.

"Those bastards! Can you even believe he's acting so cool, coming in here with another girl on his arm—and one of the Princesses, at that? Puh-leeze! What a pathetic, ass-kissing loser."

I appreciated the whispered fury she mustered on my behalf, but my heart wasn't in it. Nolan appeared happy to have Bronte hanging on him. Had he ever looked at me like that? Hard to remember after so much time apart.

The milk swirled beneath the steamer, and my eyes closed while Monica rambled. I tried to recall what Nolan's lips tasted like. They'd been soft and inhibited, but not his tongue; that was rough and plunging. Our best time was that party after graduation when we made out after a few too many drinks. Heavy hands drew me close, skimming over all the right places. We grappled in the limited space of his back seat, tearing at each other's clothes. I shivered, recalling the panting moan he made right before he—

"Cori, enough! They're lattes, not cappuccinos." Monica tapped my arm, impatient.

"Damn—good call, thanks." The steamer squeaked to a stop, and I slowly filled each mug of espresso. Swirling and spinning the carafe, I didn't realize until the last cup that I'd fashioned a series of heart-shaped flowers on a layered field.

"That's spring, not fall! Get it together."

"Don't worry, just grab your tray. They won't know the difference." I finished with the chocolate shavings, sprinkling them like stars in the sky around the flower. The design was too pretty to hide with whipped cream, but a dash of cinnamon and vanilla-bean powder would balance the flavors again.

"Let me get these out before your mom sees your new artwork." Monica set each beverage on her tray, then sauntered away.

"Cori, help me with the dessert bowls?" Mama called.

I grabbed one in each hand as Dora finished her decorations, laying a scoop of spiced peaches and a flourish of sweet cream over the decadent custard and brioche base. Mama blew out a trio of smoldering cinnamon sticks, adding one to the center of each serving. Picture perfect—only the best for the Colburns, as always.

In the dining room, I noticed my last couple appeared ready to go. I sent a smile their way, hurrying to drop my plates and move on. Bronte cried out, hands flying to her cherry cheeks. "This is just what I needed, but wow! I must've been colder than I thought. This latte is burning me up."

"I may have steamed the milk a bit long," I said blandly, stringing a line of curses in my head as Mama's eyes narrowed.

"Did you make it, Cori? It's awesome! And the flower design was cool as hell," Nolan said, halfway through his own cup. "You got really good at these, way better than when we were kids."

"Yeah, I don't know what got into me. I made so many autumn leaves the last few weeks I thought they were ingrained, but I guess not."

"Here's your dessert, kids—my top-secret bread pudding recipe. I don't make this for just anyone." Mama patted Hayden's shoulder, but he failed to notice.

He was staring at me again, concentrating hard enough to see past the thin fabric of my white Oxford blouse. "Truly delicious, thank you," he said, saluting me with his mostly full cup.

"Um... You're welcome." What was up with that? And why wasn't he drinking faster it if he liked it so much?

Oh, who cares? My table needs me.

I left Mama to her entertaining. My other couple smiled anew after a round of sincere apologies, thanking me for the service. I quickly cashed them out so they could move on with their night. After, I fled into the kitchen to find Monica laughing against Marcus's shoulder.

"Cori, what did you put in those lattes? Bronte's pretty little head almost popped off!"

"Caffeine probably ain't allowed on whatever crazy cleanse she's promoting now," Marcus said, sliding to the full sink of pots and pans when he caught his mother eyeballing him.

"What do you know about her diets?" Monica demanded, drying her face.

"I follow her Instagram. So what?" Marcus grinned at the extra round of laughs he drew from his sister.

"More cleaning, less playing! I'll be finishing that Netflix series tonight if it kills me," Dora commanded, her tone inspiring us all to find a task.

Cristina tugged my hand, drawing me closer to the storage room and away from the others. "Is it really happening—your magic? After all these years?"

"I think so, Tina. Something's happening, that's for sure."

I must've done something to the coffee when my mind wandered, sending vibrations to ingredients which already held their own magical properties. We used our gift to give Nature's elements a nudge, activating their innate powers and guiding them toward a specific purpose—a partnership and the essence of witchcraft, according to Mama. Milk by itself wasn't anything special, but when combined with the other ingredients it made for a potent aphrodisiac—especially if I accidentally added a dash of my own passion while daydreaming about Nolan's kisses.

"Praise Hekate! Yaya's magic will survive for another generation." Cristina hugged me, bouncing in my arms. "No offense, but I was starting to worry."

"Me too," I confessed, peeking around to make sure no one else heard our private conversation.

Mama pushed through the kitchen doors, her thunderous gaze settling on mine. "Coralena del Prado: cooler conference, now!"

Shit.

CHAPTER THREE

"What are you playing at, *katergáris?*"

Uh oh. Not a good sign if she's whipping out the Greek.

"It wasn't a trick, Mama! I honestly didn't realize what happened until it was too late."

"*Min Káneis Kakó*—Do No Harm. What is so confusing about that?" Mama blazed while repeating our noble oath, enough that the cooler suddenly didn't seem so cold. "It's our first rule, the core of who we are. Your power comes with a certain responsibility, Coralena! I will not have you endangering others."

"I didn't endanger anyone. It wasn't a curse. Sort of a love spell gone wrong," I admitted, avoiding her glare. "Don't look at me like that. It wasn't on purpose! It's not like I'm used to my magic actually working. You always say intent matters the most. I didn't realize random thoughts were potent enough to cast a spell. I'll be more careful next time, I promise."

"See that you are." Her finger jabbed my upper arm. "Our customers keep us in business. We may own this fancy building, but we couldn't pay the taxes and other bills without our regulars—the most important being Aspasia and her children. Despite the rest of the family, they are innocent and decent people. You'd do well to adjust your attitude."

"What does that even mean? Despite the rest of them?" My voice rose, but Mama shushed it with a hiss.

"You worry about keeping your magic under control. These first few months are delicate. You'll be highly vulnerable to your emotions, like puberty all over again—lucky us." Her faint smile subdued the anger, restoring her customary kindness. "You have a good heart, baby, but you have to take extra care. Any time you harm another, you risk damaging yourself three-fold. Some acts could destroy you forever."

"What do you mean? Like I could die if I hurt someone—even if it's an accident?"

"No, it's much worse than that." She hugged me, a comfort likely meant for the both of us. "You might lose your immortal soul, the best and purest part of you. The Universe does not differentiate whether a harmful spell was cast by accident or on purpose. Hurting others is a crime, do you understand?"

"Yes, Mama, I'll be careful," I replied, chastened by her warning. "So even my thoughts and emotions can act on their own? Is that normal for a witch?"

"Not necessarily," she said, guiding me back into the temperate kitchen, "but it is normal for a human."

***

During our break after lunch, Monica and I loaded our dresses and shoes into her car. We planned to change on the way, touching up our hair and makeup if needed. At the latest, we should make it to the city by midnight—a pair of reverse Cinderellas, sneaking out to join the ball for its peak and beyond. If we were careful, our mothers would never find out.

"This looks cute, but not too fancy—like we just randomly decided to try something different. What d'you think?" Monica held a hand mirror, checking the back of her hair from every angle in the full-length on my bedroom door.

"Sure! If anyone's suspicious about why we look so nice on a regular Friday night, we'll tell them we practiced some YouTube tutorials for fun. Except," I snorted, finishing the curl on my left eyelash, "who cares what they think?"

Fridays were steady but not crazy, the opposite of normal restaurant rules. Most of our regulars hit New York City for weekend date nights. And why not? With the best cuisine in the world less than an hour away, who wouldn't take advantage of such an opportunity—assuming money was not a problem?

We both decided to go curly, braiding and pinning our hair into elegant twists for dinner service. After, it should be easy to free then fluff when we arrived in the city. We might not be going with the fanciest clothes, our hair and makeup applied by professional artists, but we'd hold our own against the Princesses.

"This is gonna be great." She hugged me from behind, accidentally choking me. "Time to cast off that loser—and good riddance! Nolan... God, you could do so much better. We'll find you some super-fly hunk with a real pair of balls, instead. And I might find my own princess to deflower. I'm in a girly mood, so why not?"

"Christ, just don't let it be one of the regulars. I got an earful from Mama last night about making sure we take good care of them for the sake of the business."

"I'd take excellent care of some of them. I swear, Waverly was checking me out the other day. And you were getting checked out hardcore, too, by Bronte's tasty big brother."

"Oh, please! He may be a Ken, but I'm no Barbie," I scoffed then paused, gauging her reaction in the mirror. "And he's way too old for me, right?"

"Girl, he is only twenty-nine. Yes, I stalked him online. His profile was ancient, though. Probably hasn't updated it since college—NYU, by the way. And he's a man with experience. Who wouldn't want to learn what tricks he picked up over the years? If you don't want to hit that, I'll take care of him." She performed a full-body shiver, topping it off with a lewd wink. "Don't worry, I'll share every single dirty detail."

"Waverly, Hayden... You can't take everyone for yourself," I chided, ushering her from the room so we could return to work. "It's only polite to leave some hot ones for the rest of us."

"Join me on the Pan Express, and your horizons will expand to infinity and beyond." She paused to make a silly kissing face. "Don't worry, Cori, I'll always share with you. What are best friends for?"

"Awfully generous, sis. Now, let's get downstairs before our moms send out a search party."

***

Moments after the doors were unlocked for dinner, the man I'd just been daydreaming about swooped through the entrance.

"Sorry I'm late, but I'm here to pick up my sister's cake," Hayden announced, casual in a plain sweater and jeans. The crisp afternoon breeze painted rosy blooms on his fair cheeks, contrasting with his sparkling teal eyes. "Hey Cori, how are you? Or do you prefer Coralena now?"

"Huh?" I snapped back to reality before his fathomless gaze swallowed me whole. "Oh, most people call me Cori still. Mama only says Coralena when I'm in trouble."

"Interesting. I'll be sure to save that for a special occasion." His rumbling laugh caused the hairs on the back of my neck to curl. "Could I trouble you for a latte to go? I need a pick me up if I have to live through two parties tonight."

"Sure, I'll be right back. Any preference for flavors or milk?"

"Surprise me."

Did he just wink? Goddess, save me.

My expression must've revealed my flustered emotions because Monica squealed when I entered the kitchen. "Is that who I think it is?"

"Will you grab the cake for him, please! I need to make a coffee, something special," I blurted, fanning my cheeks and forehead while deciding where to begin.

"There he is—finally!" Mama said, striding out of the walk-in and spotting Hayden on the other side of the porthole door. "Marcus, will you carry the cake to Mr. Colburn's car? It's in the cooler, already boxed and labeled."

"Sure, Miss Theresa." Marcus untied his rubber apron, smirking at both me and Monica. "I bet this guy ain't even all that."

"Don't you go bothering anybody, boy, or that'll be the last prank you pull," Dora called from the stove, ringing the simmering pasta pot like a bell. "And girls, you better act like you got some sense. Don't you dare embarrass us or yourselves."

"I don't know what you're talking about," I muttered, setting brew on the fresh shot of espresso. His cheeks were like apples, but with those ocean eyes...maybe a nice salted-caramel latte?

I gathered the ingredients, choosing half and half for full flavor. A swirl of homemade caramel along the inside of the cup, a zesty dash of cinnamon, and... What next—cardamom? No, I already got in trouble for one accidental love charm. I didn't need to get caught stoking unbridled lust.

I poured the warm milk, garnishing the top with a couple of Mama's candied-apple slices, a sprinkle of ginger, and a pinch of Mediterranean sea salt.

Health and healing, luck and power, magical enhancement—a bit of love, but that was unavoidable with the standard latte ingredients. It wouldn't last, anyway. Mama always said spelled food wore off with regular digestion. Tonics, decoctions, and tinctures were different—far more potent and intended to last for longer periods.

This was just a generic well-wish for a pleasant evening on the town. He must be joining Bronte at Inferno, and I hoped he had fun. I know I intended to once Monica and I got out of here. *To a memorable evening for all of us.*

I glanced over my shoulder. Everyone was busy doing their own thing. Good. I didn't need Mama sensing I'd practiced again.

Monica leaned against the display case, shamelessly flirting instead of working. He didn't seem to mind, either...typical. She was crazy to suggest he liked me. Another player, flirting for the fun of it.

"Here's your coffee," I said tartly, planting the paper cup on the counter. "It'll be $6.50 plus the cake."

"I already rang him up, no worries." Monica pinched my waist before spinning toward the dining room to our first table. "See you later, Hayden!"

"This looks amazing. Apples on coffee, though?" He raised a skeptical brow at the floating slices of candied fruit but ate one, anyway. Pleasure surged through me at his contented groan. He grabbed the next slice and devoured it, too, licking caramel off his fingers. "Well, this is definitely a surprise. I guess I should trust the expert."

"Mama always said I was precocious," I replied wryly, sliding him a paper napkin and a lid. "I hope you enjoy the rest of your coffee and the party."

"I'll see you later, won't I?" he asked, taking a careful sip. His eyes drifted closed, a small smile spreading along with his satisfaction. *Hell, yeah—I definitely made it right.* "Your friend promised you were both coming out."

"Yes, but shhh! Not so loud." I peeked through the portholes, but the coast was clear. Mama was gabbing by the stove with Dora and Cristina while they continued to prep. Even her freakish hearing couldn't pick out my words over the normal kitchen clamor.

"Mommy doesn't let her little lamb stray too far, I take it?" He passed me a slender black and red business card that he'd kept tucked in his hand during our conversation. "Text me when you arrive. First drink's on me—a tip for the coffee."

"I don't really drink." *Dammit, of all the...* I wished my brain would stop, think, and do its freaking job before volunteering the most idiotic truths to just anyone.

"I won't tell if you don't," Hayden said in a stage whisper. He paused before leaving to add, "Thanks again for the boost, Coralena."

The door hadn't fully shut behind him before Monica was back, tugging on my sleeve. "Oh my God, girl! I swear, if you're not hitting that later, then I am—and no apologies. That is too fine a man to waste."

I examined his card. The thick script perched between two slender trees, curving into an arch. *Cypress Lounge, NYC: Hayden Colburn, Proprietor.* A business number and address were printed in the bottom corner, but his cell was scrawled in pen above it. "What is this place? You ever heard of Cypress Lounge?"

"Nope, but I'll Google it later. Hell, I'll google anything he wants! Come on, let's get this night over with so we can see what's waiting for us in the city."

A solid plan, but suddenly our evening out seemed like one step in a longer game. Why was this man flirting with me? I'd made him a couple of coffees with a dusting of magic, but nothing drastic and certainly not long-lasting. What type of man had little Denny Colburn become, and what did he want with me?

I dropped the business card into my apron pocket, light as a feather but landing with the weight of a tossed gauntlet. My move now, and I suspected he wouldn't wait long for a reply. Tonight... I'd think of something. His ultimate goal intrigued me, but I wouldn't be won over by just a handsome face and a fancy name. I had my pride, after all.

CHAPTER FOUR

"Damn, look at this line! It's too cold to bother with this shit," Monica chattered through her teeth. We had brought coats, of course, but left them in the car half a block away. The parking lot's first available spot was on the fourth level, and it cost $30 until dawn. My enthusiasm was fading fast, and our big night out had barely begun.

"Wait, I got an idea." My fingers flew over the phone, already texting the latest contact I saved. He said the first drink was on him, after all.

"Who is that—Bronte?"

"Even better," I said, refreshing my screen as my heels tapped against the chipped asphalt. "Come on, let's get closer to the door."

By the time we crossed the street and made it halfway past the admittance line, my phone buzzed with a new notification—a martini emoji, a positive sign. I stuffed the phone back into my clutch as Monica dragged us toward the head of the line. A pair of bored bouncers shuffled in place, looking anywhere but at the rows of restless wannabe clubgoers.

"Hey, we're here for a private event for Bronte Colburn," Monica declared, puffing out her chest.

"Name?"

"Monica Harper and Cori del Prado."

He scrolled through a list on his phone, shaking his head. "Nope. Back of the line's down there."

A hot flush swept across my body. Dammit, I should've known it was too good to be true. Bronte Colburn, inviting us to her birthday? Another prank, which she and the other princesses were likely giggling about while we froze our asses off on the sidewalk.

"Check again," Monica said, her sweet veneer flaking away.

"It's not gonna be there." I retrieved my phone, quickly unlocking it. "Bronte either forgot, or she's fucking with us. I'll text Hayden. Maybe he can—"

"You finally made it! I was about to give up," a voice from behind called out. The man who strolled from the side door was not the same one I saw only hours before. Suited up again, hair slicked back, shaved and polished... This was a mirage, something I expected to find shimmering over a desert horizon instead of strolling the dirty, chilled streets of Manhattan.

"Our knight in shining armor!" Monica impulsively hugged Hayden, maybe a few seconds longer than necessary. "Your sister conveniently forgot to add us to the list. Can you bring us in with you?"

"Nothing easier. Come along, ladies." Hayden extended his free hand, his eyes gliding from my head to toes, then back. The slow, curving smile said it all, causing a new geyser to flood my cheeks. I took his hand, gulping when he squeezed before tugging me along behind Monica.

"You can reenter, but they're not on the list," the bouncer said. A wall of fat and muscle, he revealed not one twitch of sympathy or a likelihood for bending the rules even once.

"Maybe check one more time, if you don't mind? We recently updated the list. These ladies are old family friends. Surely, we can work something out." He let go of my hand, dipping into his pocket. The bouncer's deadened gaze flickered with interest as a folded bill transferred into his meaty paw.

"Yeah, must've misread. Go on in." He stepped back, unhooking the red velvet rope.

"That's what I'm talking about!" Monica said, darting through a pair of black curtains.

Hayden grabbed my hand again, hurrying so we didn't lose my dingbat friend.

"Do I even want to know how much you gave him?" I called over the thumping bass, which galloped down a hallway illuminated by black lights.

"Don't worry, I still have enough left to buy you the drink I promised. If we run out, I'll grab some cash from Bronte as a punishment." He leaned in when we reached the ID checkpoint, lips tickling my ear. "You look beautiful, by the way. The green matches your eyes."

"Hey... Hello? I need to see your ID."

I shook my head, fumbling through my clutch. The surly man with the flashlight must've asked more than once, but I didn't want to apologize and risk annoying him further. He grabbed my right hand, stamped it, and waved me in.

"Cori, hurry!" Monica waved from the edge of the dance floor, but her presence didn't register.

A room the size of a football field sprawled ahead. LED screens on the ceiling and floor displayed swirling stars, speeding on a flight toward a distant galaxy. Onyx pillars towered, shimmering with digital flames. On the far left, a sea of colored spotlights rotated above a pyramid dais topped by a DJ and his group of scantily clad dancers. On the right, a roped-off staircase led to the balconies above. Hayden led me in that direction, only stopping to grab Monica.

"This is unreal, like we're in a music video," I said, trying not to shout in her ear.

"What? Who smells like onions?"

"Never mind." I laughed. It didn't matter. We were here, and the fun was on its way. I didn't even care anymore that Bronte never added us to the list. None of it mattered when the end result was more than we dared to dream during our fantasy discussions all week.

This bouncer didn't stop our ascent. Maybe Hayden's presence was enough. Slow and steady, I held my breath until we crested the spiral staircase. The scene from above was even more amazing, a bird's-eye view of a surreal dream. The mass of writhing bodies moved as a cohesive unit, seemingly choreographed beneath the spinning rainbow of lights and synthetic flames. I longed to join them and lose myself.

"Fitting name for a club, Inferno." Hayden tossed his arm over my shoulder, shattering my reverie. "For a horde of the damned, they seem to be enjoying themselves."

"Let's dance!" Monica tugged my skirt, the starry ceiling reflected in her ecstatic eyes.

"First things first," he insisted, waving for us to follow. "The VIP area is back here, and we have every drink you can imagine prepared by a private bartender."

Beyond the next set of flaming columns, the party indeed awaited. Bronte and Nolan danced in the middle of the crowd, red-faced and drunk, soaking in the cheers of their friends while swaying to a beat that most certainly wasn't coming from the DJ. I shifted my gaze, embarrassed by the bawdy display.

Hayden cleared a path by the end of the bar, waiting to place our order. Monica elbowed me until I followed her pointing finger. She sent a little wave to Bronte and blew a kiss to Waverly, who promptly began hissing into her friend's ear. A frown marred Bronte's flawless visage, deepening when she saw who escorted us to her special party.

"Ladies, any preferences?" Hayden asked, pulling more bills from his pinned roll.

"Something sweet!" Monica said at the same time I said, "Nothing too sweet."

He rolled his eyes and spoke to the bartender. I couldn't hear the conversation, but something from one of Mama's police shows nagged me. I grabbed Monica. "You don't think he'll put anything in the drinks, do you?"

"Girl, he already won me over. He can save the roofie!" My face must've reflected the horror her statement inspired, but she squealed with laughter even when I smacked her arm. "Damn, Cori—relax! It's Friday, and we're in New York mother-fuckin' City. This'll be the best night of our lives!"

"I'm so glad you made it," Bronte said flatly, slinking over with Waverly by her side. "Better late than never. How did you manage to sneak away?"

"They must've relaxed the dress code," Waverly sneered, examining my gown with a malicious glint in her eyes. "How adorable...spring flowers during autumn—a bold choice from such a little mouse."

"Where did my dear brother run off to?" Bronte stumbled, champagne sloshing from her glass. "He gets distracted so easily. You should ask his former fiancée. He almost made it to the altar with that one. Oh well, he should be fine now. He's moved on plenty of times over the summer. That man would charm anything for the fun of it."

Her words sank into my gut, heavier and more resistant to dismissal than Waverly's unimaginative insults. A fiancée? They must've been serious to try for marriage, and summer wasn't that long ago. Maybe he craved another distraction during his recovery.

Well, he'd be in for a rude awakening. I wasn't that inexperienced to fall head-over-heels for a couple of smooth pickup lines and a free drink.

"Found some more champagne," Nolan announced, filling Bronte's glass before squinting at us. He gaped upon recognition, lips snapping shut beneath his new friends' glares—daring him to say anything remotely complimentary. "Hey Cori, Monica. You guys look...nice."

"You stupid bit—" the words steamed from my tightening lips, stifled by my wily friend's interruption.

"Thanks, Nolan. You don't need much when you're already working with spectacular natural assets. Imagine, we look this hot after a whole day of actual work." Monica snuggled with me, cutting her eyes over Bronte and Waverly's rumpled finery and smudged makeup. "Not all of us have cushy trust funds. Some of us succeed on wits and talent alone. Oh—by the way—happy birthday, Bronte!"

Bronte's champagne flute rose, ready to splash across the shrinking space between our groups, but a hand dipped in to snatch the glass away.

"All right, kittens, back to your corners. We're here to celebrate, remember?" Hayden kissed Bronte's cheek, the diplomatic smile vanishing as he whispered terse instructions into her ear. She huffed and walked away, her drunken posse following without a word.

"Sorry, man, but they had it coming," Monica said without a drop of genuine remorse in her flippant apology.

"I'm aware of the circle I was born into, no apologies necessary. Actually, maybe one more is due." Hayden glanced at me with a faint grimace. "I've been informed—more times than I cared to hear—that my sister's dating your former boyfriend. I'm sorry, Cori, but he's obviously an idiot. And Bronte should be old enough to behave better. So why don't we drop all the drama and have some fun." He handed each of us a crimson drink garnished with an orange peel, then retrieved his glass—an amber liquor, served neat. "Negronis for you, ladies—a little sweet and a little tart. Somewhat appropriate, I thought. Now, run along to the dance floor before you make me referee again."

I appreciated the words, unsure how to respond to his unexpected support. Instead, I sniffed my cocktail. Did roofies have a scent? As I took my first sip, Monica drained her glass. "Hey, this isn't a race!"

"Hurry up. I need to dance. Thanks for the drinks and everything. You're a sweetheart, Hayden." She dragged me away while I tried to gulp the strong, citrusy beverage. I needed at least one stiff drink to give me the courage to join that hellish tangle of bodies.

"My pleasure. Go have fun, ladies." Hayden raised his glass in farewell before rejoining his friends.

So that was it? Dammit. Figures Bronte would make things awkward. He was older, probably uninterested in talking to girls his sister hated. Or Bronte had told the truth, and he was recovering from a bad breakup. I understood, even if Nolan and I had parted on amicable terms—well, he thought they were amicable. I never intended for anyone—especially Nolan—to learn the full extent of my hurt and disappointment. Tonight was damn sure not the time or place. I spotted him in the crowd, my gaze skating away with disgust when I caught him trying to stuff his tongue down Bronte's throat.

The sensual heat from the cocktail and the smooth electronica beat overtook me, dashing my regrets and second-guesses into fragments. Monica found a prime spot up front, in the shadow of the giant pyramid stage.

Dancing in a world-class nightclub in New York City wasn't the same as shimmying with friends at a school dance or flailing alone before the bedroom mirror, but Monica and I happily accepted the challenge. Most of the people around us slithered bonelessly, entrancing as snake charmers. A few were drunk and out of their element, but they didn't last long enough to ruin the enchanting spectacle.

The dancers appeared different upon closer inspection. Unlike the mob of lost souls suffering eternal damnation beneath our VIP perch, this group personified the fiery passion of life—an irresistible, Dionysian celebration we were delighted to join.

Monica and I held hands, taking turns leading each other in spins to warm up. I gripped her waist, helping her stretch back nearly to the floor. She shot up, spinning again before seductively wrapping herself around me. We slid closer to each other, probably resembling one woman with multiple arms—Kali, maybe, out for a wild night among her ardent worshippers. We shared a private smile, sensing a growing number of interested eyes following us.

She shouted in my ear, the words nearly smothered by the pounding music. "Hell yeah, Cori! We got this."

We bumped our hips, laughing and twirling in a fair imitation of the bulk of the crowd. After only one song, a pair of guys wandered over. Their dress shirts hung open, limp from sweat, revealing gold chains and ridiculously hairy chests and hands. Their once-neat pomaded hair melted into greasy locks over empty eyes and grins full of mischief. Monica glared at the small figure grinding against her leg. She pushed him, dragging me deeper into the crowd. They tried to follow, stumbling in their Gucci loafers. I waved them away in another attempt at silent-but-stern rejection.

We resumed our dance. This time, our backs pressed together as we faced outward. My eyes popped open at an insistent tug on my skirt, narrowing upon discovering the return of our cast-off admirers. A queasy smile slid along his dripping face. I raised my hand to knock his own from my waist, but that was unnecessary. Someone else yanked him up, then shoved him to the side.

Hayden's rigid eyes and razor-sharp scowl convinced the smaller man to hunt elsewhere. He threw up a middle finger before stomping off. In a flash, Hayden's forbidding countenance tempered into the same charming smile from our previous encounters. His cool hand captured mine, drawing me into his arms.

Lips brushed my earlobe before his mild admonition sent a shiver along my overheated skin. "You should be careful dancing like that out here. God knows who you'll attract."

I stood on tiptoes, pulse thudding in my throat as I copied his move. "You mean someone like you?"

He replied with a wink of perfect teeth and a nonchalant shrug, sliding his hands down my fluttering ribcage before they settled on my hips. We moved together—slowly, at first, then picking up the pace. His smoldering gaze caused any additional words to evaporate in my mouth.

I stepped back when the song changed. Fueled by my one drink, I found just enough courage to dance for him. My body took over, detangling the rhythm from the upbeat melody. Brazen only moments before, his expression grew bemused—captivated, as if I held him hostage. I understood. His attention made it impossible to focus on anything else.

He moved forward, eliminating that blip of empty space once more. How satisfying to be pursued by someone I desired, an enticing and enigmatic man who simply wouldn't quit. I wasn't sure what was happening between us, but my will to resist was disintegrating fast.

I turned, swaying against his long frame. One hand stretched up to weave around his neck, and I yielded when he guided my backside flush against his pelvis. He stirred behind me, and I smiled, pressing back harder. His hands clenched, probably wrinkling the hell out of my skirt. The slow, grinding motion and persistent dance beat spurred me on. If only we were alone, the things we could've done...

When I opened my eyes, Monica stood before me. She waved and winked before backing away. I reached out, suddenly nervous to be alone with Hayden, but she pranced toward a silver-clad, androgynous beauty. Their eyes linked, taking the measure of the other, a silent assessment which resulted in the pair gliding into the thick crowd.

Before I could protest Monica's desertion—or worry that she was on her own in the endless sea of bodies—I was spun to face my dancing partner. The naked hunger in his eyes caused me to stumble, thrown off guard. I wasn't free for long. My hesitation invited him to close in again. He placed my hands on his shoulders, then embraced me. I gasped as his fingertips stroked my bare lower back, the skin rippling beneath his unexpectedly intimate touch.

My breathing grew choppy as the air between us vanished. He must've felt my heart thumping against his chest; there wasn't enough space between us to slide a piece of paper. The vein at my temple spasmed when his lips grazed it, moving toward the wealth of curls that probably drooped within the humid ring of dancers.

We moved with the song, but at a different tempo than the crowd—people who soon faded, as if they'd never been there. We danced for one song or a hundred songs; I lost track as time melted around us.

I fingered the waves of hair above Hayden's collar, then stopped to trace the thick muscles lining his shoulder and chest. A flash of blue caught me—heavy-lidded eyes swimming above mine, both intent and indolent. If I held onto any wisp of a doubt, it fled. He wanted me but appeared willing to wait—a cat toying with a mouse until the poor thing's heart burst from heightening anxiety.

But did I want the same thing?

I wanted something. I just hadn't decided on what yet.

He drew a series of lazy circles along my spine, the feather-light touch battering my will. Each looping whorl sent a quiver through my abdomen, as if he were already inside me. It stopped, then a finger skidded along the low-cut waistband of my dress. Plucking at the fabric, he dipped just beyond the thin barrier, causing a jolt that made me trip forward.

My lips parted, and I braced against his broad chest while my eyes drifted shut. His mouth caressed the shell of my ear, maybe preparing to speak. Unnecessary, as I swore the music stopped; no other sound, sight, or sensation existed except whatever he was doing.

"Thirsty, Coralena?"

The double entendre wasn't lost on me. All sorts of witty responses bobbed along the surface of my brain, sassy or flirty comments Monica would've been proud of and encouraged me to share. I only nodded, forgetting how to communicate in a more meaningful way.

"Let's take a break."

Excellent idea. I needed a breather. Being with him was far more intoxicating than any watered-down club cocktail.

CHAPTER FIVE

We stopped by the bar for a new round of drinks. I drained my glass, watering my arid throat. A stray ice cube squeezed past my esophagus, awkwardly stuck until the last of my cocktail washed it down. We each got a refill before moving on, a drink I swore would be my last of the night. I didn't trust myself with more liquor around a man this alluring.

What was his deal? There had to be an angle, some reason he relentlessly pursued me above all others.

Unless it was simply an urge for sex, which fascinated more than offended me. Nolan had been my only lover. I foolishly gave him my heart and virginity after months of pursuit—wasted gifts, in the end. Even with him, I never felt in danger of losing myself. Pure lust wasn't something I had much experience with, until now. No wonder people went crazy over those who inspired such an erratic emotion.

Funny, I regularly chastised Monica for giving in to every pretty face without deeper analysis. She enjoyed them for a moment, then grew bored or frustrated when they didn't rise to her high standards. Eventually, she moved on to the next adventure while lamenting she never found a true connection. She didn't let the failures hold her back, always hoping to find an ideal partner.

Most people turned into fools over love, a predicament I often mocked in the past. Was I really any smarter than them?

No, this was different—lust, pure and simple. I could slake it, if I chose. Hayden and I were both adults. Who would dare judge our choices? As long as I didn't involve my heart in the animalistic cravings of my body, then he couldn't hurt me. Problem solved.

He tempted me, lulling the sensible part of my mind with his visceral masculinity and each deliberate, skillful touch. What attracted me the most was how much this striking man wanted me, a feeling he didn't bother concealing. Not that I was undeserving; I was as pretty as any girl in this club, with way more going on in my head than those trite Princesses.

But it didn't make sense. I was a regular girl, nearly a decade younger than him. How'd I snag someone like Hayden Colburn, a successful businessman who had his pick of the most accomplished women in the city?

Maybe he was another rich, lazy asshole who preferred an easier conquest. Guys like that probably believed those of us in the lower classes were desperate for their attention, awed by fabulous wealth and distinguished social connections. That special type of scumbag would view me as the perfect victim—inexperienced as hell, a high-school graduate and humble restaurant worker. Well, he'd better brace his ego for a dose of disappointment. I'd rather be alone for a lifetime than entertain even a brief affair with someone like that.

Anyway, I had magic to protect me—unreliable as it was, right now.

Wait... What if that explained everything? No, magic didn't operate independently to bewitch others. Or did it?

That would make the most sense. Maybe it was the coffee I made earlier, or my surging pheromones. Was that enough to spawn some sort of spontaneous love spell? I should've flown beneath his notice even on a night like this, dressed in my best. What did he really want?

"Cooling off?" Hayden asked, resting against the brick wall of the courtyard. Yet one more surprise from the labyrinthine Inferno—a sprawling dance floor, luxurious balconies, and now an enclosed courtyard garden for smokers or anyone seeking a break from the blaring music and lights.

"Yeah, much better. Thanks." I sipped on the icy drink. Either it was stronger than the others, or my senses were heightened by a combination of desire and dehydration. "I'll be switching to water after this, though."

"Lightweight," he teased, finishing his drink and setting the glass on a nearby table. "Your big night out, and you're already hitting the brakes?"

"What do you know about my big night out? I might go out all the time." I shrugged to hide my annoyance, draining my glass and setting it beside his. A dumb move to further intoxicate myself, but it was a refreshing beverage. The tartness kept me alert even as the alcohol sought to dull my inhibitions, which had sunk fairly low after our erotic dance.

"That's not what Monica says." He feigned interest in my necklace, rolling the pink flower pendant between his fingers. I watched, riveted by his delicate examination. "She said you never do anything except go to work, read, and listen to lame emo music."

"So that's what the two of you were doing when I made your coffee. Talking shit about me?" I scooted back with a light laugh, a poor cover for the mix of embarrassment and delight.

He'd asked my best friend about me.

"You were gone for a few minutes. We had to talk about something." He inched closer, angling his broad torso to block the breeze cutting through the roofless space. "It was worth the wait, your coffee. Maybe you can visit my restaurant sometime and show me your secrets."

"Cypress Lounge—in honor of your childhood palace, I assume?" I stammered as he traced the embroidery along my waistband, slender white fingers creeping along like a curious spider.

"A palace you were born in, same as me. I remember your parents bringing you home. I heard you crying at night from across the yard. Your poor mom must've never slept." I froze, only able to roll my eyes toward his face, wary as a deer when a distant twig broke the forest's silence. "You really don't remember me?"

The distance between us shrank, enough that the whiskey on his breath thawed the icy tip of my nose. Humor glimmered behind his light irises until something darker bobbed then sank into the depths. He must've wanted more, yet he restrained himself. Or he got his kicks by flooding my autonomic system, waiting for the inevitable stimuli overload. My skin tingled in anticipation of his next contact.

Who was I kidding about resisting him? In this moment, surrender was all I could think about.

"Remember you? I don't... No, I was too young. I mean, I remember a little but not much. After what happened..." I knew the words he expected to hear, but I was unable—or unwilling—to dig that far back. "It's hard for me to think about those years."

We'd left Cypress Point when I was five, a few months after Daddy's death. Most of my early memories were blocked, likely a safety feature of my subconscious—a system wise enough to defend a child's mind from such a traumatic loss.

"I'm sorry. Felix was a good man." Hayden retreated, hands dropping to his sides. "I shouldn't have brought up the past."

My clearest memory of those days resurfaced, a shiny lure offering more if I dared to bite. Mama in the kitchen, the stream of Greek and English curses flying like bats from a belfry into an inky sky. Her fury had terrified me, but my fear reined her in. She promised that night to share her secrets and, soon after, she did—all but the reasoning behind casting a dark spell on someone who had hurt her. I nagged her about it as a kid, but she always evaded. Eventually, I let it go. After all the pain she'd endured, I didn't want to force her to remember more.

"It's okay. It happened, and there's no way to change it now." I wrapped my arms around myself. A sudden chill gnawed at our warm bubble of intimacy, crushing it with the pressure of a too-real conversation.

"Do you want to head back inside? You're shivering."

"In a minute. I should check on Monica soon, but it is peaceful out here. I like it."

"Come here." He opened his arms wide. "Shared body heat. We can't have you sneaking back home with a cold."

"Right, that wouldn't do at all." I chuckled at his ploy, but it was an offer I couldn't refuse. I yearned for the closeness we shared during our dance, tempted to see what might follow. Something more had to happen. We weren't done yet—at least, not according to my increasingly fuzzy brain.

I burrowed through the opening of his suit jacket, running my hands over his solid stomach, fighting to hide a smile as he trembled beneath my touch. My hands linked behind his back, and our chests met once more. A tremor rolled from my abdomen to the tips of my extremities, the energy transformed into a spark which caught and kindled between us. A small moan of pleasure slipped out, causing me to flush at his sudden, smug smile.

"You're right. It's much nicer out here." He brushed a spill of curls from my jawline, stepping forward until my bare back pressed against the cold bricks.

I warmed again from the gentle touch trailing along my collarbone, leaving patches of goosebumps in its wake. The tiny bumps spread outward as his fingers traced the silk strap biting into my skin. A tantalizing pause, as if they considered traveling down the line toward my plunging bodice. My nipples stiffened, poking through the thin fabric. I regretted not purchasing a proper bra for this dress, opting to go without in case the straps showed. The alternative, it seemed, was far more revealing.

He watched me, those intrepid fingertips waiting for their next move. Waiting for me.

Alcohol spurted through my constricted veins, thumping with the new song trickling from the club—a sexy salsa number. His blue eyes darkened, clouds obscuring the sun, as his tongue swiped over his parted lips. A tongue I imagined sliding against mine, or somewhere else.

"Hayden, you should..." I lost my train of thought before it left the station. A warning, a plea, an invitation... I forgot which command I intended to state, but I also didn't care about his possible reply. My mouth widened as I surged forward, capturing the lips that hovered a breath away from mine.

A wave of heat and muscle blasted me back, the coarse wall scraping my shoulders. My hands clawed a path up his chest, tangling in his thick hair. *Would we? Wouldn't we?* Those questions had taunted me ever since he first entered my restaurant, but now the mystery was solved.

His plunging tongue fought against mine, smoke-imbued from the whiskey. I tilted my head, inviting more of him inside. He traced the curve of my right breast, engulfing it with his palm and gently squeezing.

Another moan rumbled when his thumbnail flicked the aching peak, then circled its base. Each rotation expanded, setting off seismic shocks that left me reeling—worse when he stopped, moving to the other breast.

His other hand gripped my thigh, dragging my leg over his hip. I flexed to hold myself steady while he positioned himself, grinding to match the rhythm of the song. It was too much, too hot in our steamy alcove. The October night became an August afternoon blazing beneath the midday sun.

Two sets of breath hissed upon our separation. Our final kiss lingered; a farewell nip along my bottom lip caused my hips to buck against his rock-hard pelvis. His hand flattened on my heaving chest, rising to rest on the pulse pounding in my throat. I faded in the aftermath of that explosive moment, dizzy from the sensations as he stroked and kissed my nape.

"Coralena... Will you come home with me?"

His breathless question barely needed to be voiced, yet the offer was there, dangling between us. I yielded to another kiss, arching beneath his wandering hands and daring to explore with my own. What more could he do to me? Or what might he let me do to him? The possibilities made my head whirl.

He stood upright, poised for an answer. I nodded faintly, and he released my leg so I might stand on both feet again. It took longer than it should've for my wobbly legs to stiffen. Damn, what had he done to me?

"I have to find Monica." I smoothed by hair, cool fingers resting on my overheated face before straightening my outfit. The fidgeting reminded me I was awake, not lost to a dream.

"Let's go. I'm sure she hasn't wandered far." The bland statement sounded condescending when accompanied by such a cocky grin. He was enjoying this, my momentary befuddlement. Unfortunately for him, my mind sharpened with each determined step. If he thought I was down for the count, he had another thing coming. He may've leapt ahead after that scorching interlude, but our little game was far from over.

The stifling air of the club wrapped around us like a hot towel, the music spiking with a screech that fortunately occurred seconds after my phone vibrated. A new text, as if she knew I'd be on my way.

M: *Restrooms by the entrance.*

Easy enough to spot, even in my current state. Hayden held my hand, allowing me to guide him this time. Something I sensed wouldn't always be the case if his dominance out back was any sort of a hint. What the hell was I getting myself into?

Monica waited for me with the androgynous silver dancer. I was inclined to say female, based on a pair of shapely hips, but I didn't want to presume. Whatever the dancer had going on satisfied Monica, and that was good enough for me.

"There you are! Cori, meet Dany. Dany, this is Cori and Hayden." Monica grinned, taking in our appearance. Yeah, she already sensed something had happened. I'd have a lot to explain later. "They're shutting down soon. Let's get some food."

"I own a restaurant, in case you forgot. Plenty of food and drinks if you'd all like to check it out. And my apartment is right above it," Hayden said, looping his arm around my waist as if fearing I'd flit away.

"I'm game," Monica replied, tearing her nibbling lips from Dany's ear before turning to me. "Cori?"

I glanced between their cheerful faces, increasingly nervous at the thought of a prolonged evening with Hayden, which might stretch beyond sunrise. An evening with the two of us, alone, as Monica and her new friend obviously sought some privacy.

Mama will kill me.

"Yes, let's go."

***

The tension decreased in the Lyft to the restaurant, an impressive three-story corner building in the East Village. Hayden rode in front with the driver, keeping up a sociable conversation focused on the World Series; the pair lamented another year without a Mets victory. Chatter I couldn't join in, even if I was so inclined, as the high leather seats made too effective a barrier.

Nor could I chat with Monica and Dany, who spent the ride whispering and kissing. The fuzziness from the alcohol burned off under my frustrated isolation, inviting common sense to return with a flourish. What on earth possessed me, agreeing to hang out in a strange man's home?

Well, his place of business too. The building stood apart from its humble neighbors, sheathed in a rippling shell of black slate with an arched granite doorway. A faint design was etched into the stone, subtle slices sprouting along one central trunk—was it a type of leaf?

"Twin cypress trees, just like home," Hayden said, leading me toward the entrance. "My mom liked it, anyway."

"What can we eat? I'm starving!" Monica said, shivering again without the coats we never took the time to recover from our car in the overnight parking deck.

"I'm a vegetarian, just throwing that out there," Dany added in a low, musical voice.

"Don't worry, there's plenty to choose from." Hayden ushered us through the open door before rushing to the nearby alarm system. A few beeps, a click of the locks, and we were safe.

What a space. Cathedral ceilings vaulted over a cozy dining area already set for tomorrow's service, a polished chrome and wood bar gleamed beneath the yellow emergency lights, and a wrought-iron staircase spiraled from the middle of the room. The crimson walls appeared dark in the muted lighting, contrasting priceless white marble floors accented with an array of Turkish carpets.

"It must look amazing with all the lights on," I said, ambling toward the staircase. "What's up here? More seating?"

"For now, but I have an idea for something different." He seized my hand, taking me with him to the kitchen. "I'll give you the tour later. Your lovely friends are starving."

"Cori, you know what I like," Monica called while dragging a very willing Dany toward the bar. "We'll make drinks while you get the food ready."

"Okay, sounds good. And yes, Dany, vegetarian for you. I got it." I sent them a small wave, stilling the reminder before it left their lips. Vegetarians always gave at least two reminders of their preferences in case one missed it the first time.

The kitchen was fully loaded with every modern convenience, the space easily the size of the dining room—bigger, if one accounted for the walk-in cooler and freezer. A mountainous four-burner gas stove with a flat top and charcoal grill filled one wall. Contraptions loaded with pans and utensils dangled overhead, and an L-shaped stainless steel workstation filled out the rest. I was pleased to see, like Mama's kitchen, this one also lacked a microwave.

"Do you have pasta?" I turned the front burners on, placing copper-accented pans on each to warm.

"What were you planning on making?" Hayden tugged me until I began turning, then pinned me against the cold flat top. "Not that it matters. You're my guest. I should be cooking."

"Do you know what you're doing?" I asked haltingly, my control fizzling when his forehead rested against mine. His breath feathered my skin, generating an itch that I yearned to scratch.

"I know a little bit, enough that I don't hear any complaints." He stole a kiss from my lips that still hummed from our interlude at the club.

"Oh no you don't. I'm not drunk anymore, so you can't take advantage." I somehow laughed, even though his flirting drove me mad. I pushed him away, corralling my wild thoughts. "Fine, you can be my sous chef. Start boiling water for pasta, and I'll grab some stuff from the walk-in."

"Yes, Boss. Right away." He saluted, then slapped my ass before I fled. "And, in my defense, you hardly seemed like a helpless victim. I didn't do all the work. If I recall, you kissed me first."

I darted around the reinforced door, hiding my blush in the breezy cooler. This was real. I was in Hayden Colburn's restaurant in the middle of the night. Trapped, miles from home, my only ally already surrendered to her own spontaneous romance.

Be careful, think! Don't screw this up—whatever this is.

A silly game, that's all it was. I shouldn't take it seriously, but I accepted an invitation into my opponent's home. He'd be at his strongest here. A thrill of danger shot across my limbs, but I shook it off while gathering a series of ingredients. If he wanted to play, I could do that. Plenty of helpful tools filled this cooler, fresh herbs and more. I hadn't tried my burgeoning magic on real food yet—drinks and sauces were lighter and easier to enchant—but now seemed an ideal time for a little experiment.

A wholesome shield of protection or a surge of spicy lust? *Maybe a combination of both. Why not?*

No, I had to take it easy. I may have cast the first spell with two potent coffees, but what he did to me in the club had a magic of its own. If I added more accelerant to this fire, the resulting blaze might spread beyond my control. Was I ready to take such a risk? I suspected he was, and that scared the hell out of me.

CHAPTER SIX

Garlic, basil, and tomato: all three offered protection against evil, among other factors, fortifying the mind and body with a blessing from Hekate herself. A sprig of rosemary for spell enhancement and mental clarity, something we all needed tonight. Fresh cream and salted butter, additional endowments from the Mother, formed a lush base to bind everything together. As a bonus, the flavors would be perfect. Despite a few tricky side effects that might fuel more than one type of appetite, this would weave a multilayered shield for us all—assuming I didn't get carried away again.

It didn't help to have Hayden so close, scrutinizing my every move. I nearly knocked the pan off the burner when he sneaked behind me, deftly tying an apron around my waist.

He laughed when I cursed, fetching a new spatula when mine fell to the floor. "Relax, I'm helping. Be a shame if any oil stained such a nice dress."

"You sneak up on me again, and I'll fix you. How about that?" I grumbled, returning to my pan. He hugged me from behind, planting a swift kiss below my ear before pulling the top of the apron over my head. The whole time, I couldn't move—eyes closed, breaths becoming something akin to panting. What was that smell?

"Garlic's done, don't you think?" he murmured, still smiling when my eyes popped opened.

"You're a nuisance. Stop distracting me!" After giving him a semi-kidding shove, I tossed the cherry tomatoes and basil into the pan. My nerves sizzled along with the sauce components.

Time to focus again. I added the remaining ingredients, just in time for Hayden to finish the pasta. The necessary words rolled through my mind, layering to overwrite the vivid images from earlier. I wouldn't think about us in the club, how he took control of me on the dance floor and in courtyard, his mischievous expression when I downed that cocktail... And damn Monica! I said no more alcohol, but she forced me to take a glass of wine while I cooked.

Everything seemed to be conspiring against me tonight.

I removed the sprig of rosemary, blowing a wish across the steaming spines before tasting the sauce dripping from its tips. There it was: a telltale tingle, confirming a spark of magic nestled within the meal. A splash of curious passion—understandable, after such an evening—tempered with personal control and protection from harm. Whatever else happened tonight, it would be my choice and not Hayden ensnaring me with his more mundane powers.

"Interesting process you've got there," he drawled, drizzling olive oil over the warm noodles in each bowl. "You're a hell of a lot sexier than my usual chef. Poor Francisco, I've never seen him put such effort into a simple plate of pasta."

"Maybe you hired the wrong chef?" I teased, spooning the finished white sauce over the noodles before garnishing each bowl with fresh parsley and grated parmesan.

"I'm definitely rethinking my decision." He hefted three of the bowls, leaving me with one and my almost-empty glass of wine. "Let's move, otherwise Monica might pass out from low blood sugar."

"She was just being dramatic. She's not a fan of waiting when she wants something."

"Neither am I." His words were light, but they stirred me.

No, I'm in control. His charms wouldn't overwhelm me once I got this food down.

But resistance wasn't so easy, especially at the candlelit table Monica and Dany set up for us. Leftover bread, herb-infused olive oil, and a new bottle of wine awaited. They cheered our approach, digging into their plates as the porcelain hit the table.

"Cori! This is the best thing I've ever eaten," Monica cried through a mouthful of noodles.

"Damn, this is just what I needed. Thanks so much." Dany treated me to a sweet smile before diving into their bowl with gusto.

"I'm tempted to call Francisco, fire him, and make you the new head chef," Hayden said, passing me the bread and olive oil.

I appreciated the compliments, but opted to focus on my food rather than lounge on my laurels. It wasn't the first time I cooked for my friends and family. They'd always enjoyed my creations, but nothing I ever made held a candle to Mama. Her skills had been bolstered by decades of expertise. This simple dish wouldn't put her out of a job, but—for the first time—it was in the ballpark.

"Thanks, everyone. Let's eat before it gets cold." I tucked into my bowl, enjoying the simple pleasure of a meal with friends.

This was a magical night. Everything I'd hoped and more, enough to sadden me that our New York adventure would soon be over. Time to return home, sneak in, and pray our trip went unnoticed. Back to reality, where our experiences would file themselves into distant memories. Soon enough, a layer of dust would bury this one shining moment where we escaped our ordinary selves for just one night.

Every bite of food disappeared. Monica released a series of yawns, leaning her head against Dany's. The two appeared worn out as children after a full day of playing.

"You're gonna kill me, Cori, but I need a nap before we drive back home," Monica said, forcing her smudged eyelids up before they drooped again.

"We can take a taxi to my place, if you guys want," Dany added, covering their mouth to smother another gaping yawn.

"I have a two-bedroom apartment upstairs," Hayden reminded us. I rolled my eyes at the solicitous tone, too mild to conceal his far-from-pure motivations. "I insist you rest, then I'll drive you back to your cars when you're ready."

"How generous." I bit back an additional comment, useless as the offer only perked Monica and Dany up again. Convenient how things always worked to his advantage, but a man like Hayden was probably accustomed to getting his way.

"Safety first." He winked at me, then helped our companions stand. "We'll get you settled in for your nap."

I stayed behind, gathering the remains of our meal. "I'll be up in a minute. I just want to clean a little."

"Here we go... Nerd alert!" Monica declared with the last of her energy, snickering with Dany as they raced up the curved staircase.

"I heard that!" I giggled, too, but they were already gone. A strange sound, laughter in an empty room; it jabbed uncomfortably at the bruises left from a life of too much solitude.

By the time Hayden returned, I'd run the bowls, silverware, and glasses through the small industrial machine. I left the pot and sauté pan to soak, swearing to finish before his staff arrived. Nothing worse than starting a shift in a dirty kitchen. Poor Francisco; if he was real, Hayden's head chef deserved cleanliness and order before entering his domain.

"I'm not sure how much rest they'll get, but I set them up in the spare bedroom." Hayden gave me a disbelieving grin, leaning against the tile partition. "You're actually washing the dishes? No shit?"

"One always treats another chef's space with respect." I tossed my hair over my shoulder, shaking the excess water off my hands. "Plus, this was the first job Mama gave me at the restaurant. I'm an old pro at proper sanitization."

He grabbed a handful of paper towels from the dispenser and dried my hands. "Tessa is an excellent teacher. I learned a few things from her as a kid, but your skills far outshine mine."

"She let you cook with her when you were little?" I couldn't help but be surprised. Cooking was so personal for Mama. It wasn't something she often shared with others, apart from our closest friends and family. Maybe what she'd said had been true; some of the Colburns were bad, but not all.

Then who in that family didn't she trust, and why?

"I was always too curious for my own good. Eventually, she got sick of my nagging." He threw the paper towels into the trashcan before extending a hand to me. "But we weren't going to talk about the past, remember? Forget the cleaning. I'll give you the rest of the tour."

When we reached the dining room, I made him wait while I took off my heels. I sighed, stretching my bare feet against the cool marble. "That's so much better. I fucking loathe heels."

"I don't understand why ladies wear them. You're a pack of masochists," he said, urging me up the stairs first. "And your legs still look fine without them—more than fine, actually."

I shrieked, bounding ahead as his hand ran up my calf and behind my knee. "That tickles! You don't believe in boundaries much."

"You have no idea."

The second floor appeared even more spacious, decorated in muted tones of gray, black, and silver. The vaulted ceilings held rows of small lights—dimming, then brightening like captured stars. Elegant and low-key, the space demanded fantastic food and beverages to counter the understated design.

"Beautiful." I ran a hand over the satiny wall, stopping to stare over the treetops toward the iconic skyline. "It must be amazing, living here."

"It doesn't suck," he agreed, joining me at the window. "Well, most of the time."

"Please, what problems can a guy like you really have?" But my smile fell when his lips thinned and he turned away. The seconds that passed were unsettling, as if he'd abandoned me in favor of visiting a distant realm locked in his head. I nearly pinched myself to make sure I hadn't faded away.

When he returned, the lines of his face softened. He took my hand, guiding me toward a polished pair of elevator doors. "One more floor. After you."

"An elevator for only three floors, really? What other surprises are you hiding?" I ignored the chuckle, sweeping by him to lean against the wall. He punched in a special code, unlocking the ride to the top level and his home.

"You won't learn everything about me or my business in one night, but we have plenty of time for all that." With each word, he stepped closer to cut the distance between us. I backed into my corner, antsy over what his assurance implied.

The elevator doors opened with a ding, and I evaded him once again for the foyer. An open space stretched ahead, backlit by filtered white lights, inviting and airy as a seat in the clouds. A closed door lay to my left, and I paused when a soft moan escaped from the other side.

"I didn't think they'd fall right to sleep, but for the record, that's the spare bedroom. Are you thirsty?"

"A glass of water would be good." I set down my shoes, sinking into the cream-colored carpet blanketing the living area. A decadent and impractical touch, but otherwise the space was as minimalistic as the rooms below. Polished wood, white walls, chrome accents, tinted windows across most of the walls, and black suede furniture. Devoid of personal touches, the apartment appeared more like a hotel suite than someone's private home. Hayden's refuge lacked any sign of life or love, which saddened me.

I waited by the empty fireplace, noting the expensive TV screen but the lack of artwork or photographs. No stray socks peeked from beneath the plush sofas. The coffee table only held a plain lamp, no dirty glasses or in-progress books. One more door lay to my right, closed tight, but I suspected I'd see the inside soon enough.

"Come on, Cori. You must be exhausted." He passed me the tall glass of water, gesturing toward the unopened door.

The sip stuck in my throat at this newest surprise. The black hole of a bedroom pulled me in. More marble and brocade-covered walls, all dark as pitch. A massive king-sized bed was the lurid centerpiece, bedecked in black satin sheets and red velvet pillows.

Holy hell, it's some sort of sex den.

"Ummm... I don't know what type of girl you think I am, but I am not sleeping on that."

Instead of being offended by my declaration, his lips twitched in amusement. "There's always the sofa, if you prefer. I'm sure Monica and Dany would love your company, too—maybe more so after they finish their own fun."

"Grow up." I padded away, placing my glass on the night table. "I'm too tired to argue, but I will say, you really need to reconsider the message this room is sending. Who the hell chose the decorations?"

"Someone long gone from my life, who I'd prefer not to discuss." The tone turned my head, coarse but vulnerable beneath an expression as unforgiving as stone—unnatural after his cordial behavior throughout the evening.

"I'm sorry." The response was automatic but sincere. All too well, I recalled Bronte's comments about his former fiancée. The mystery woman had ghastly taste—in decorating, at least—haunting this room like a stubborn ghost, unwilling to find the damn light and move on.

"Don't worry about it." His jacket flew toward a hamper by another closed set of doors. A closet, maybe; the door on the far wall probably led to a bathroom. Random thoughts of additional rooms and color schemes fluttered away with the white dress shirt he unbuttoned, removed, and tossed with the rest.

Half-naked in his bedroom, blond hair tousled around a face that should've been sleepy but seemed more awake than ever, his fit torso illuminated by golden hairs trailing down toward... Yikes. My tongue curled in my mouth, an autumn leaf drying up and ready to drop. *Where's that water?*

"What are you doing?" I squeaked, grabbing my glass with both hands.

"Getting ready for bed, obviously. It's been a long day." His smile widened as I emptied half the glass in one long swallow. "Would you like a t-shirt?" I nodded dumbly, closing my eyes and counting as he entered the walk-in closet behind those double doors. I made it to sixty-three before a handful of cotton fabric bounced off my face. "Bathroom is over there in case you're shy."

"I'm not shy, I'm just not...whatever the hell you are." I strode away with my head high, ignoring the laughter that followed.

The bathroom was a relief after the constricting black and red of the bedroom; ivory walls bordered with golden wood, accented by brass fixtures and yellow lights. Grand but cozy, though its one extravagance was a sizable garden tub beneath a dual-head shower. Another mental image distracted me: the two of us in there, sprayed on multiple sides by warm water, bare skin slipping against each other...

Enough daydreaming, damn!

I removed my wrinkled dress, hanging it on a wall hook. It wasn't ruined after our adventurous night, but I should give it a rest if I wanted to wear it again. The t-shirt was soft and roomy, faintly smelling of sandalwood. The front was decorated with a flaming church and the name of some random metal band, not a style I would've guessed for him. I freshened up, washing my hands and face but carefully blotting both so I didn't stain the towel with traces of makeup.

My hair was a wreck, a haphazard nest of ebony curls poking in all directions. Raccoon rings from the supposedly waterproof eyeliner and mascara stained my bronze skin, making my bloodshot green eyes pop. The crystal carriage had definitely turned back into a pumpkin, but there was little I could do to fix it now—and why bother? If Hayden was truly interested, he might as well get used to me looking less than my best after a busy day.

Back in the bedroom, he sprawled beneath the garish comforter, patiently awaiting my return. Of course he intended to sleep in his own bed. Had I expected anything different?

Isn't that right where you want him, to get more of what happened earlier? The lascivious thought sent a last burst of nervous energy through my weary limbs. Great, now how was I supposed to fall asleep?

"Don't worry. There's plenty of room for us both." Hayden patted the empty expanse beside him. His wolfish grin drew me in, playful yet disconcerting. An observation hovered on my lips: *My, aren't your teeth sharp?*

"Don't you get any funny ideas," I warned, joining him beneath the covers but maintaining my distance.

He rolled on his side, propping that devilish visage on one flexed arm. "I have a lot of funny ideas, but I'll try to behave."

"I've never done this," I admitted, staring at the ceiling to avoid drooling over his tempting form.

"Done what, exactly? Tell me all about the things you've never done. I'm all ears."

"You're impossible, a dirty old man."

"I'm not that much older than you. And you're not a child anymore—remember?"

I turned and faced him, preparing to deliver a lengthy lecture—ground rules, restrictions, threats to his manhood—and instead found his incredible body only inches from mine. The one with all the muscles and no shirt, close enough that the faint sheen of stubble along his jaw and his upper lip glinted like Rumpelstiltskin's precious straw—a treasure I longed to touch and claim for my own.

"Why are you doing this?" I asked, emboldened by the last drops of wine. Or anxious that my magic may have set this in motion. Maybe his interest wasn't real, and I'd gone too far. If the emotions swimming in those beautiful eyes weren't genuine... "Stop teasing me, Hayden. It's not fair."

"Teasing you?" His brow furrowed until realization dawned. "The way you danced with me, kissed me... The way you're looking at me right now, with those big eyes. No one is that fucking innocent. You're lying in my bed, wearing my favorite t-shirt and nothing else. Cori, you've been driving me crazy all night."

"If all you're looking for is some quick, easy conquest—"

"I'm not." He brushed the wispy hairs from my forehead, running a finger down my cheek. "I wasn't looking for anyone or anything, but here we are."

"Dammit. You're really going to do this, aren't you?" My annoyance flared like a strip of magnesium, burning out and leaving behind an ember of insecurity...or was it a spark of hope?

"Do what?" he asked, somehow sharing my pillow now.

I rested my hand on his chest, the next words coming before I could stop them. "Please, Hayden...just don't hurt me, okay?"

The plea should've embarrassed me, but I felt stronger for saying it out loud. I clutched a last grain of control, although his proximity swept the rest away. I traced the edge of his jaw, fascinated as his Adam's apple bobbed in confusion, as if trying to recall how to breathe or speak. His discomfort was entertaining, a nice change from how unbalanced he'd kept me all night.

"I'd ask the same from you. Fair is fair, right?"

I didn't have time to answer his solemn statement. Hayden's tongue glided into my mouth, a key unlocking a small door. Something—someone—lived back there, and it was hungry; a hunger I hadn't felt in years, not since my heart received its first serious break. The pressure below returned as he nudged closer, and I welcomed him into my arms.

One hand shoved the blankets aside, securing my hips where he wanted them. I helped by wrapping my leg around his waist. His other hand tugged at the collar of my t-shirt—an unnecessary loan, after all—and I helped him drag it over my messy hair. He threw it over his shoulder, then gazed down at me. I should've been more shy—a demure lady, avoiding his blatant lust and cowering behind a veil of modesty. I wanted him to see me, though—to want me as much as I wanted him.

"All night, I imagined what you were hiding under that dress. You're more lovely than any fantasy, Coralena." My name tumbled from his lips with flattering reverence.

"We shouldn't—"

"Just let me touch you. I won't do anything you don't want." Desire thrummed in his eyes, constant as the rhythmic pulse connecting us below.

I wanted to say more—to command or beg—but the words flew from my head like a flock of birds scattered by a loud noise. My lips parted, but nothing came out except a string of wispy pants. I nodded helplessly.

In one swoop, he buried his face against my chest. The swirling tongue across my nipple inspired a sharp cry, and I arched up from the mattress. He divided his attentions from one to the other, stoking my ardor—oh, how it worked, causing me to rub against him like an animal in heat.

"Shhh, slower. If you keep moving like that, the fun will be over too quickly." One of his hands roamed, sliding down my torso then lower, stroking the damp fabric of my panties. "What do we have here? Eager little thing, aren't you?"

"Shut up and do something." I stole a kiss, sucking slowly on his full lower lip. He pulled away, smiling, as I succumbed to his sensual massage.

"Tell me what you want," he urged, the randy wolf peeking out and ready to play. "What should I do next?"

"Take them off," I groaned, the friction eroding my final ounce of resistance.

His fingers hooked into my panties and pulled. I helped, kicking until the bit of fabric flew and disappeared in the scattered covers. A breeze raced over my exposed skin, inspiring a shiver until he covered me with his body again. I toyed with the waistband of his boxer briefs, tugging them past one taut buttock. He laughed and took over, pulling them the rest of the way down.

"I shouldn't be the only naked one here." I shyly nuzzled his neck even as I peeked at what lay below, waiting for me to touch it if I dared.

"What next?" The question came in between a series of heated kisses along my neck, stopping at my heaving chest. His tongue flicked one puckered nipple, a tease to distract me from the fingers slipping inside— one, then two—an insistent knock I couldn't ignore. Without a peep, he demanded greater access. I didn't dream of refusing, craving each delicious invasion.

I'd never experienced such a flood of desire, even with Nolan at our peak. He'd never touched me like this, more concerned with groping his way to a hasty finish. Nor had he ever given me an orgasm, a pleasure I had to discover on my own, but I sensed Hayden could take me there.

"Kiss me." And he did, snatching the breath from my body. I escaped his needy mouth, whispering, "No, not there. Lower."

"Lower where?" He grinned, fingers flexing as I squirmed. "Use your words, Cori."

"Goddammit, you know what I mean." I fought back, my embarrassment delighting him even more.

"I suppose I could be gracious, for now. We'll work on making you bolder another time."

Another time? Goddess, I had to survive this time first.

My eyes closed as his weight shifted. I clenched the bedsheets, waiting for him to reach his target. His warm breath tickled, as did the stubble brushing the sensitive skin of my inner thighs. I quivered when his fingers parted me, making room to lick that hidden flesh in one determined swipe before getting to work. My hands sprang back, clutching the headboard. The persistent motions drove me to the edge, tearing another low cry from my throat as he switched to leisurely circles—slower, mocking my need.

"Hey!" I exclaimed at a light pinch, pulling me back from a decadent reverie. "Why'd you stop?"

"I want you to watch." He never broke eye contact while his wicked mouth sank again, delivering a kiss that tore a cry from my soul.

Heaven to be touched like that, but it wasn't enough. I lifted my hips higher, but he took his sweet time—slow and steady, as if I were something to be savored. So close, if he'd only focus; but maybe he wanted me to beg, to scream his name. I nearly did, aching for that elusive climax. Maybe my whimpers generated a flicker of sympathy. His tactic changed once more, relentless as his hot mouth finally delivered the mercy I craved.

My hips bucked, and I floated in liquid release. The increased sensitivity sharpened, and I skidded away to the head of the bed. He joined me with a lazy smile, stealing my whole pillow. Dizzy with disorientation, I refused to rest now. I touched his chest and the muscles banding his stomach, erasing his smug expression the moment I seized him with both hands. Fair was fair, as he'd said.

"What are you doing?" He tried to kiss me, but I avoided his mouth and moved lower, my lips mimicking the trail he'd made on my body.

"Whatever I want." I ran my tongue over the head, treating him to the maddeningly slow rhythm he forced me to endure. Smiling, I took him in further. His fingers buried themselves within my curls. He gave another moan, crying my name out. Up and down, soft then hard... I hummed my pleasure as he quaked, but he didn't allow himself to finish.

"I'm done playing with you." He dragged me up, claiming my mouth for a fiery kiss.

"What are the magic words?" I taunted, running that probing tip against me as his eyes fluttered closed.

"Please, Cori...you win."

"You got protection?"

He dove for the nightstand, rummaging and cursing. Tearing at the small foil package, he batted my hand away. I bit back a giggle, but my mirth fizzled while he deftly unrolled the rubber sheath along his impressive length.

"Just wait... Jesus, let me get it in before I explode." He eased inside. Both of us groaned at the snug passage, which eased after each languid thrust.

"Harder," I rasped, raking my nails across his damp chest before stabbing into his shoulders.

He lifted one of my legs, clutching it for support while driving into me. Our joining grew louder, more fervent as both of us energetically took from the other. Any louder and Monica would hear us, but I figured she'd be too distracted to care.

Time melted as we collided, a joining more intense than anything in my wildest dreams. Sweeter after two years of nothing but loneliness and unfulfilled wishes. This was true magic, the reason people searched their whole lives for someone special. A perfect match, even if only in this fleeting moment.

We both needed someone, but this was quickly becoming more than just a physical release. All night we'd explored, determined to discover what lay behind our polite masks. Maybe we found more than either of us bargained for.

Sweat dripped from his forehead, plinking onto my breast. I couldn't tell if it was from sheer exertion or his attempt to extend our union. No, the next series of rapid movements proved he was done holding back. He licked his fingers, then found the bud between my thighs, swirling in speedy circles. I thrust upwards and clung to his lower back, a move which pleased him enough to cry out in pleasure.

He slowed, but I sped toward a new climax. I squeezed my eyes shut, riding the surreal wave of heat and power. I'd never danced along such a precarious edge, thrilled as each marvelous spin sent me soaring higher, uncaring how far I might fall.

"You were amazing." Hayden collapsed onto the pillow, scooping me against him as we tried to catch our breath. "Thank you."

I didn't know how to respond to his clumsy sincerity. *Thank You?* Had I performed an adequate service, or was his humble gratitude indicative of deeper emotions he wasn't ready to reveal?

His insatiable lips lovingly caressed mine. Both of our hearts continued to race, a discovery I made while resting on his chest. He stroked my back, cradling me as if he couldn't bear to let me go.

What we shared was special, wasn't it? I couldn't have misjudged him so much. I wouldn't become anyone's tool, a temporary diversion, even if it meant never feeling this good again.

Please, let this be real. How I yearned for more of him, the endlessly appealing and endearing Hayden Colburn. *Don't let this be just for tonight.*

CHAPTER SEVEN

I'll see you soon, beautiful.

I brushed my fingertips along my lips, remembering our last kiss before parting—satiny as his sinful bed, velvety as a ripe peach, but indelible as an iron seal pressed into molten wax.

Yet all signs pointed to this being a one-night stand. Even Monica's enthusiasm appeared cautious regarding Hayden's future intentions. She was supportive, either exclaiming or quietly musing over the tidbits I revealed.

Whatever happened between us, something told me he wasn't lying.

The key turned into the lock, and I sneaked into the quiet apartment. Plenty of time to shower and dress before heading downstairs. I'd spent the night at Monica's. That was the only story I had to share. Easy peasy.

I didn't get far before realizing the jig was up. The sofa had become a bed, complete with one of Mama's blue pillows and a thick comforter. Empty tea cups and a silver scrying bowl sat on the coffee table. A cut-crystal vase brimmed with the ashes of scorched herbs.

Yep, we were done for.

Pattering steps raced from the bathroom. Her hair was still wrapped in a towel. I winced at the red rings around her brown eyes, sensing the storm was about to unleash. "How could you, Coralena del Prado?"

"I'm well into adulthood, Mama. I don't have to fill you in on every plan I make." I forged my stiff words into a thin shield, hiding my twinge of guilt. A useless gesture, as she must've smelled it from across the room. This wasn't our first battle, and I was familiar with her favorite strategies. I would not allow her to turn this around on me.

"That is not what I'm talking about, and you should be smart enough to know what I mean." She crossed her arms over her slender chest. "You lied! You told me you were spending the night at Monica's, but you were with *him*. Of all the... Did I not just tell you to stay away from that family? After everything I've taught you over the years, and you disrespect me like this?"

"It's none of your business!" The shout spouted forth like steam from a pressure cooker. This wasn't just from being chastised for my night with Hayden; it originated after too many years of being coddled and hidden away, only working and studying magic, never able to experience the world as other kids did. "I'm a grown woman, and I'll hang out with whomever I please. If you want to continue having me in your life, you will back the fuck off...with all due respect."

She recoiled as if I slapped her, eyes flickering with outrage before moistening. This was new, tears to inspire pity and even more guilt. I wasn't fooled. Mama was too strong for a loud voice and some foul language to shake her up. "Do what you want, then. You're right, maybe I protected you too much. It was hard not to. You're all I have left. I can relax, I swear, but you have to promise me never to spend time with anyone from the Colburn family."

"You're not making any sense." I paced away, warding off her hands that once again tried to deliver comfort. "Why should I stay away from Hayden? What's wrong with his family, besides being insufferable Greenwich snobs? You just said the other day that he was good."

"It's a long story, and it happened many years ago. Now is not the—"

"Now is *exactly* the time!" I pointed at the coffee table, littered with detritus from her spells. "You spied on me! I don't even want to know what you saw because that would be an even more incredible violation of my privacy. I will see Hayden. I'll do whatever the hell I want with him—and rub it right in your face—unless you give me a damn good reason not to."

"Sit down, and I'll explain," she coaxed.

"Just tell me. No more secrets." I set my jaw, waiting for whatever excuse was coming.

"You were only a little girl when we lived at Cypress Point, working for the Colburns," she began, taking her own advice and sitting on the edge of the sofa. "Your father was a maintenance man. I cooked and minded the children. It wasn't difficult. Bronte was your age, and Hayden was willing to help. Aspasia couldn't handle them both, and I sympathized. Turns out we were both from Athens. I was only conceived there, but she spent her youth in Greece. We formed a bond, you see, and we were women—all of which sealed our friendship."

"Okay, quit stalling. If you and Aspasia Colburn were such besties, then why doesn't she ever come in?" I countered. "She only sends the servants or Bronte to pick up stuff, like she's too good to grace us with her mighty presence."

"It wasn't her or the children. I told you they were innocent. But not the father, not their friends," she whispered, twisting the edge of her blanket between her fingers. "And maybe Hayden is no longer innocent. He was different when he came in the other night, carrying a shadow on his soul that wasn't there before. Although I hadn't seen him for years between boarding school, college—"

"Mama, tell me!"

"His father raped me, Cori."

The statement landed with a dull thump, meaty as a severed limb rolling across the carpet to lay between us. Before she spoke again, my legs wobbled. I tottered to the other end of the couch, sinking into the cushions.

"Alastor Colburn is a monster. He wields his own type of power, just like his friends—wealth, connections, and more. I suspected for years he had some dark secrets—your father did, too—but the Colburns seemed kind, at first. We were treated fairly for many years, almost as if we were part of the family," she continued, each word carrying all the emotion of a sleepwalker reciting their dream. "He somehow found out what I was.

Shortly after your father died, he took what he felt was his. Ritualistic, not even some random attack in a normal bedroom or after a night of drinking. He brought me to their private island in the bay where they performed their nasty ceremonies. I wanted to die—might've died—if it hadn't been for Hayden."

Another punch to the gut sent nausea rollicking through my abdomen and beyond...like motion sickness, but I'd grown stiff as a corpse. He'd touched me, put his mouth on mine. My ears burned with his treacherous words—promises, compliments, and irresistible sentiment—reeling me in, as I had feared, for some sick purpose.

"He knew what happened to you?"

"He heard my screams and took a small boat to the island. He couldn't act until his father and the others finished, but he found me afterward. He made me come with him, bringing me home to you." She reached out to hold my hand. I didn't fight her off; the nerves in my body were severed, dying with a muted fizzle. "That night, I had my revenge. A spell so dark, no one ever taught it to me. The words rooted in an evil which would've shamed my mother and grandmother if they saw our power used in such a way. A spell you walked in on, do you remember?"

Bind, desmévo... Great Hekate, hear my cry. Timoró, grant me justice... dikaiosýni, for your daughter who was so wronged, the daughter who loves you.

"Yes, I remember." How could I forget? That face, bruised and terrified—terrifying to witness. "You told me you were a witch. Then we left to start the restaurant because they gifted you..."

"Paid me off, yes, to stay silent," Mama finished for me, "but they didn't trust me. The condition was I had to stay close. That was fine. I could stay silent to protect you from their threats, and I couldn't leave the last of my family behind. Yaya was already dying. Nor did I want to cause Aspasia and her children any further pain or shame. The spell was my revenge. A binding, severing his manhood—a spiritual and physical castration. He'll never be able to hurt another woman like he hurt me."

"You said there was a ritual? How did he hurt you?" I stuttered over the question, wanting anything but the answer, yet compelled to ask. If she was brave enough to share one part, I had to prove I was brave enough to hear it all.

"Did you ever hear those stories, urban legends about the rich and powerful making deals with the devil? Secret societies?" she asked, and I nodded along. "It's true. Or one of them is true. I don't know their proper name, only what I picked up from their Latin prayers. Mammon, he is their Lord—a Prince of Hell, Commander of Legions, and Demon of Greed. I can't say if they truly have magic, if demons exist, or if it's all a manic delusion shared by these psychopathic princes of Earth. But they believe it's real, Cori. Anything is possible with enough belief fueled by the gratuitous amount of blood they used in their rituals."

"Oh Mama, I'm so sorry." I leaned into her embrace, accepting her support while wishing I might return the favor, beyond sorry that I hadn't known about the pain she carried until now. "I wish you'd told me. I could've listened, helped you."

"You help me all the time. Such talent, working hard to learn the old spells, carrying on the traditions of the brave women who came before us. I'm proud of you, my sweet girl. I never wanted your life darkened by my sins."

"Your sins? You didn't ask to be raped!"

"No, not that," she sighed, pulling me closer as fearing I'd somehow slip away. "I cursed another human being, broke the first and most sacred law of our people. It eats into my soul, draining my vitality as each year passes with the curse active. Maybe a worse punishment awaits, during this life or after I die. Even so, I renew it every year—at Aspasia's request, no less."

"The Tonic?" That mysterious item from Bronte's list. Mama brushed it off when normally she was eager to teach me some new recipe.

"She helps me keep him drugged—sedated, but functional. A penance she claims for herself, for being so in love with her husband once that she failed to recognize his corruption. He's a willing thrall to darkness... Cori, you can't imagine." She wiped her eyes, shedding tears for another woman after that woman's husband initiated her unimaginable suffering. Amazing, the wealth of compassion her battered heart could hold...more compassion than I'd ever muster for any of them.

"I'll kill him myself." I tried to stand, but she pulled me back down with a low cry.

I could find him, Alastor Colburn. Obviously, I was familiar with his main home. And like so many of the Greenwich elite, he worked in New York City; surely he kept another home or apartment there. I could find a spell, too, or make my own. If that failed, a sharp knife would also take care of him—a public service, ridding the world of such an animal.

"It's done! I already punished him. Cori, I won't have you compromising your own magic or soul in such a working. You must promise me, love. You're all I have, the only piece left of my precious Felix. Please, if not for me, think of your poor father who loved you so much." She wept freely now, burying her face against my shoulder.

"Shhh... It's okay, Mama. I won't do anything crazy." *Unless I have to, or a chance presents itself.* But that was unlikely. My only way into their world was through Hayden, and he was the last person I wanted to see again.

As if reading my thoughts, she said, "Please stay away from Hayden. What if he joined his father's cult, causing that darkness? Maybe it's some sick rite of passage for them, a sort of boys' club. When you were with him, did you sense anything unusual? Any magical vibrations, unusual decorations, or idols in his home?"

"No, nothing," I lied, kissing her cheek and smoothing her wet hair. "You can ask Monica. Everything was super fancy and expensive, but we both thought it lacked basic decorations. Not even pictures."

"But did you feel anything, Cori?" She pressed, whispering with urgency even though we were alone in the privacy of our home. "Your magic is starting to soar, and you should be sensitive to various emotional frequencies in others. If he's a servant of darkness, you would've sensed it. Even if he tried to hide it, some part of you would've been afraid or suspicious. Be honest with me, sweetheart. I won't be mad at you."

"It was just a one-night stand, nothing special. I never even planned on seeing him again." I rose, walking to the bathroom before she could unearth anything more. "I'm going to shower so I can make it to work. Will you be all right?"

"Of course, baby, take your time. Sleep a little more, if you need."

I didn't reply, shutting the bathroom door before collapsing onto the soft bathmat. My stomach rebelled, the nausea deciding to make its escape.

But nothing came up; my heart and soul were filled with sickness, not my body.

I'd just served so many lies to my mother. She'd only ever asked me to be honest with her. Even after that brutal story, I couldn't follow through. I couldn't face it, wanting to wash my hands clean of the whole situation. I wished I never met Hayden, never gone to Bronte's dumb party.

Did you feel anything...a darkness?

My body still tingled from his touch, and I was sore in places I barely knew existed before last night—or this morning, whatever. More than the sensations he'd drawn from my weak flesh, I was troubled by the feelings he spawned with barely any effort. I swore my heart had been hardened, but his caring smile, open generosity, the rousing touches and kisses...

We had sparked a darkness last night, both on the dance floor and in his bed. I'd felt it. His touch maddened me to the point where I would've given anything for more of him. Despite hours together, after everything we did to each other, it wasn't enough. Leaving him this morning hurt. I was unsatisfied, ravenous for more. I could've stayed there forever. That type of blossoming obsession couldn't be healthy. Was it him, or was it a sign that something inside of me was innately flawed?

Whatever happened between us wasn't only his fault. I encouraged him, thrilling with each new invasion and discovery. I might've fallen in love with him, if given time.

No, I hate him—now and forever.

He'd lied to me, then lured me into a situation where I was forced to lie to my own mother. Maybe it excited him, knowing the depraved and criminal connection between our parents yet keeping me in the dark? He knew what she had suffered and still put his hands on me... Ugh, there was something so foul about that it made me retch again.

(I'll see you soon, beautiful.)

Yeah, we'd see how that went. *I fucking dare you to come crawling here, looking for more. I'll be ready.*

ACT II

ENILIKÍOSI

"Stronger than lover's love is lover's hate.

Incurable, in each, the wounds they make."

—Euripides, *Medea*

CHAPTER EIGHT

I took Mama's advice and tried to sleep, but it didn't work. I laid in bed, ignoring the periodic ding from my cell phone, trying to think of anything other than last night. Of course, the opposite happened.

Although I swore to ignore the texts, I ended up peeking. Besides the obligatory *Lazy Ass!* text from Monica, the other two were from Hayden.

H: *Lunch rush sucks. I'm exhausted.*

And a couple of hours later.

H: *Can't stop thinking about you.*

Same here, asshole. I nearly typed the thought before blocking him for good. *Wait...*

What he did was unforgivable, an omission that wiped out the fact he saved my mother from possible death. That was a brave move from a kid. I'd begrudge him some credit. But to not tell me? It wouldn't have been a pleasant conversation but essential before beginning a relationship with the daughter of the victim he rescued from his father's Satanic cult.

I had promised Mama I wouldn't seek retribution or use my magic against Nature, as she'd done. I also promised I wouldn't see Hayden again—an easy vow, but I'd meant it. Could I really consider casting it aside?

Hell yes. I'd do anything for my mother, and she deserved a life free from further dangers.

Hayden could get me close to Alastor, a golden ticket into the Colburn home and their inner circle. He was clearly still interested, based on those texts. It's not like I had to sleep with him again. A flirtatious chase would keep him distracted from my true motive. Playing hard to get seemed to work in silly rom-coms. This wouldn't be any different. Except I'd sooner stab him than allow him to lay another hand on me, and that was only a snippet of what I wished to unleash on his despicable father.

It might work, at least for the short term. I had to build a plan and act fast. My lying was improving, but I didn't want this to become a new normal. A vile man raped my mother, hurt her, defiled the magic linked to her immortal soul. What kind of daughter would I have been to let that slide? What would my father have done?

Promise me...

I made a promise to him, too, every morning before he left for work. Papa, his breath a mix of cool mint and warm tobacco, whose moustache tickled my cheek when he kissed me goodbye.

Promise me, Coralita: be a good girl, and look out for Mama while I'm gone.

Yes, Daddy, of course.

Some promises must be kept.

***

Dinner was slow, and I almost wished I'd stayed in bed. The prep for Sunday brunch helped distract me, at least. There wasn't time to recall Hayden's smile when he joined us outside the club; his hands on me while I cooked, or his lips against my neck, my breasts, my...

"Too much heat, Cori. Those apples will scorch," Mama chastised, coming from behind to turn the burner down. "Caramelize, not charcoal. Pay attention!"

"Sorry, Mama." I shook the fog from my head, shifting my focus back to the filling for the mini-tarts.

"These girls think they know everything, staying out all night and making up stories about where they went. Y'all best remember, you can't hide nothing from your mamas," Dora said, already informed about our night out. She spent the afternoon riding me and Monica's asses as punishment, and she was right. I wouldn't be able to avoid Mama's keen intuition forever. I only needed a little longer, then I could enact my vague plan for retribution.

"I saw Bronte's dress on Instagram. It was so pretty!" Cristina said, stacking her dirty plates by the dish pit for Marcus. "I bet that was some birthday party."

"I'll be eighteen soon, so I better get an invite to the next night out in New York," Marcus added.

"I got you, Bro, don't worry," Monica said, overhearing the last part as she entered the kitchen with more dirty dishes. "But if Ma kills me for corrupting you, make sure my funeral's awesome. Try to get Bey to sing for me."

"Don't be giving each other ideas. Damn kids... What were we thinking, Tessa, inviting these little monsters into our homes to stress us the hell out for the rest of our lives?" Dora complained, and Mama just smiled along. Almost natural enough to cover the sadness in her eyes, but I noticed it before returning to my apples.

"These are done, Mama." I set the pan aside so the filling could cool.

"Would you get me some more butter? Then we'll pop that tray in the oven."

I nodded, breezing past the chattering crew toward the walk-in. A hand shoved me in, closing the door. "You told me you'd fill me in later. What happened?" Monica asked, eyes bright in a face bearing no traces of our sleepless night.

"Nothing, she just knew. She'd been waiting up and chewed my ass out." I grabbed two pounds of butter before trying to escape.

"Not that. I meant Hayden. Did he call, text, anything?"

"Yeah, just random stuff. Let me by."

"Random stuff? Are you fucking kidding me?" She laughed, barring my exit once more. "Come on, after all that? He couldn't keep his hands off of you!"

"You hear from Dany?" I asked, ready to change the subject.

"Course I have, and we're going to the movies next week. That's not the point!" The laughter faded, dragged down by a growing frown. "Didn't you have fun, Cori? You seemed so happy this morning when I dropped you off, floating on clouds and shit. Did he do something? Say the wrong thing?"

"No, it's perfect. He's a regular Prince Charming. Now let me get this to Mama." I finally pushed through to the crowded kitchen. I'd need to work on my game face. Between Monica and Mama, they'd sniff out anything suspicious before I could act.

We spent the next hour closing the front while everyone else cleaned the kitchen, and Mama baked her mini-tarts for tomorrow's service. Monica rambled on about our night, filling Cristina in on the details she craved. What was the music like, the outfits, the drinks? What did the inside of a real New York City club look like?

Like me, Cristina dedicated herself to our family and the business. She'd jumped into marriage at a young age, building a family with her high-school sweetheart. A simple and easy choice, one I almost envied. Even without magic, she minded her obligations to the family line, choosing duty over self. The same choice I was expected to make...one day.

My phone buzzed, and I closed my eyes while leaning on the broom handle. No more, I only wanted to finish work, sleep, and start with a fresh day tomorrow. *Go away, Hayden.*

But my curiosity won out. When the girls left to get the mop, I unlocked my screen to see whatever he had to say that couldn't wait.

H: *What are you up to?*

One more buzz and the screen filled with a new message, widening my eyes and inspiring a furious blush.

H: *My sheets still smell like you.*

***

Coffee hadn't been enough to keep me going today. Brunch was busier than usual with people out shopping for Halloween on Thursday. Monica pestered me anew about what to wear. We'd already begged off last month for the holiday, intending to go to her friend's party in Stamford. Once we closed for the day, I agreed to go with her to the Halloween store and finally settle on our costumes.

"You want anything from the grocer?" I asked Monica, taking a break since the restaurant was empty.

"Yeah, get me an energy drink. I need that pre-shopping boost. I swear, I feel worse today than yesterday. And I slept like the dead last night."

"Same here. Must be a delayed hangover." I forced a smile, ducking out the door. I'd slept plenty, but my dreams starred the same face in various stages of carnal ecstasy. Not the way to promote a restful slumber.

It didn't take long to walk around the corner and make my purchases. When I returned, a vehicle I'd ridden in only yesterday sat outside—black and sleek, low to the ground, stout—a modern version of a classic muscle car. Shit, this wasn't supposed to happen yet.

Back inside the restaurant, Monica abandoned her sweeping to laugh and whisper with Hayden. A gorgeous bouquet of flaming flowers filled his arms, brightening his muted clothes and leather jacket. They both stopped when I entered: Hayden, stunned in appreciative silence; Monica, mouthing *oh my God!* while bouncing silently behind him.

"What are you doing? You can't be here." I set my plastic bag on a table and glanced toward the kitchen.

"Huh? What do you mean?" He lowered the flowers, a pained flicker tightening his expression.

Of course, Mama chose that moment to crash our awkward reunion. She stopped in the doorway, wiping her hands on a towel. Whatever question she had trailed away, her easy warmth doused quicker than a bucket of ice water poured over an inviting hearth. She stared at me, an unspoken message clear in the unforgiving lines of her face and the way her hands wrung the life from that fragile towel.

"It's fine. I'll take care of it." I grabbed Hayden's arm, leaving him with no choice but to follow.

"Cori..." Monica began, but I waved her off.

Outside, Hayden shook himself free. The late afternoon sun lent a reddish cast to his blond waves, transforming it into a blood-stained war helmet. "This wasn't exactly the welcome I expected." He shoved the bouquet toward me, and I accepted it without thinking.

"What are you doing here?" I demanded, glancing over my shoulder to ensure no one followed us.

"I texted you all day yesterday, and you never responded. I thought an actual visit might interest you more." He tucked his hands into his pockets, pacing along the sidewalk. "Did I have too much to drink that night? 'Cause I was under the impression we had an amazing time."

My throat muscles constricted, filling with a backlog of heated words and accusations. Anger, hatred, and betrayal tainted the sensual moments we'd shared, a slow venom I yearned to inject him with so he would suffer as I did—but not yet. Time for that later.

Stick to the plan, stupid—now or never.

"Mama was angry I lied. She told me I shouldn't see you again." I had to walk a fine line between intriguing and insulting him—beguile him, pretend I wanted him too—whatever heightened his interest long enough to get what I wanted.

"I'm sorry. I didn't mean to cause you any trouble." He relaxed, tentatively stepping forward. "I can talk to her, if you like."

"No, I handled it. I'm a big girl, remember?" The nausea was back, splashing beneath the sickeningly sweet smile I plastered across my face. "But you shouldn't come to Cornucopia for a while. Let me work on her, assuming...you want to see me again, don't you?"

"I didn't race here after a busy brunch service for my health." He grinned, running a hand down my arm. I shuddered and stepped back, using the flowers as a barrier. "Maybe a little for my health. I can't stop thinking about you."

"Me too." It was the first honest admission he'd coaxed from me since his unexpected arrival. "Look, we can plan something soon. I want to see you again, but I promised Monica we'd go shopping for Halloween costumes today."

"What are you going as? I've never seen anyone attempt the sexy chef before." When he stepped forward this time, I couldn't back away. His stupid car stopped me, leaving only a breath of space between us.

"I don't know...maybe. I haven't decided." I held still when his hands slid to my waist, the light touch burning through my layers of clothes.

"Come with me instead." His voice poured through my ear, sweet as warm honey over baklava. "I was supposed to go to my family's house for their annual masquerade, but I'd rather do anything else. I can pick you up on Thursday night. We'll go wherever you want."

A party at Cypress Point, hosted by his parents. Alastor would be there, maybe joined by a few of his nameless friends—all the people who assaulted my mother. I might not get a better chance, perfectly timed while I was still fired up for vengeance. Only four days away... Surely, I could string Hayden along through texts for four measly days. Then I'd unleash my anger, feeding him the accusations my mind continued to stockpile as future weapons.

"Yes, that sounds great." Another truth reshaped my cautious expression into something I hoped resembled joyful anticipation.

"Get over here," he murmured, leaning in for a kiss. His hips pressed against me, igniting a desire which filled my mouth with bitterness.

Play along! Don't be a dummy.

Goddess, I hated him. That warm, soft tongue swam through my mouth before embracing mine. His fingertips massaged my lower back, the heat melting us together even further below. I'd hurt him, break him for doing this to me. I wanted him, even while imagining his face collapsing beneath my fist.

"You need to leave before she comes back out." I jerked my head, trying to recapture my breath. My grip tightened on the bouquet, hard enough a few stems cracked.

"I'll pick you up on Thursday, Coralena. I can't wait to see your costume."

"Yeah, it'll be a big surprise."

...for both of us, asshole.

CHAPTER NINE

Three days didn't leave a lot of time to craft the perfect murder weapon. On Monday, our day off, I volunteered to go on a supply run to the Farmer's Market in New Haven. I also stopped by our favorite pagan shop for a sack of dried foxglove. A little farther, I found a gardening store with a few foxglove plants for sale.

"They won't flower 'til spring, in case you didn't know," the old man said, adjusting his cap in the bright sunshine. "Awful pretty when they come in, but poisonous. Be careful if you have pets or kids."

"It's just to keep the deer away." I flashed him a smile, hastening to the car before I incriminated myself.

Three days to soak the dried and fresh leaves, milk what sap I could from the live plants, then boil it all and strain the solids. With the proper prayers, and a few more ingredients for additional potency, I'd have a powerful natural weapon.

Digitalis was a common ingredient in heart medicines; in excess, it caused heart failure. Without a doubt, it'd be detected during a toxicology screening, but digitalis was also known to build up in one's system and cause accidental overdoses.

Alastor Colburn was sixty-six, according to my Google searches. Healthy and handsome, British by birth—and somewhat of a recluse over the past decade—he'd suffered a mild heart attack two years ago. It was entirely possible he continued to take some sort of medicine, but I didn't want to raise any flags by asking Hayden. The presence of digitalis in his system might be attributed to the heart attack and recovery meds.

I counted on that, anyway. Or, at the very least, I hoped when I murdered him no one realized it was my decoction that sent him over the edge.

My goal was to avenge Mama. It wouldn't change the past, but maybe she'd enjoy the second half of her life more if she didn't live in fear of the villain who'd pursued and captured her long ago. I loved my mama, and I wanted to share those years with her, but I had to take care. Vengeance would be bittersweet if I succeeded but wound up in a jail cell, ruining both of our futures.

Some called poison a coward's weapon, but I wasn't left with many options. I had zero martial skills, never owned or used a gun, and what if he had bodyguards? Hell, if he had a coven of more than one, they'd outnumber me. I didn't have stealth training, either. Although it would be a struggle, sneaking the decoction into Alastor's food or drink was my only option. I prayed I wouldn't screw up and attract attention.

A coward's weapon, but so appropriate in this case. What was more cowardly than a man tormenting and raping a lone woman who wasn't his physical equal? He didn't deserve some masculine fantasy of a hero's death. Fuck him.

Magic wouldn't make my plan infallible, but it boosted my chances of success. After preparing my poison, I also enhanced one of my necklaces for a personal spell of protection and luck. Mama gave me a special pentagram when I graduated from high school, enchanting the small heart-shaped garnet at the center.

For you, my love. The pentagram symbolizes Balance, Wisdom, and Protection to purify the Spirit—everything I wish for you as an adult. In gem lore, the garnet represents the pomegranate. Did you know that? It will gift you with the fire of love, inspiration, and health. It's said to promote fertility, which you won't need yet, but it may help you access the power and mystique all women share. And if you journey far away, may it always bring you home to me.

Tears burned my eyes as I recalled the private moment before we drove to the graduation ceremony. I'd worn the necklace under my robes that day, but took it off right after. It seemed too special for everyday use. Such sacred magic was not to be wasted.

To refresh the spells set by Mama nearly three years ago, I filled a small silver bowl with angelica, rosemary, dried garlic, mugwort, and thistle. A spicy but earthy smell rose from the mini cauldron, cleansing the necklace. I prayed to any gods and goddesses who might've been listening, imploring them to bolster my mother's love and devotion. The cauldron sizzled as two tears dropped in—a bonus protection with the salt and additional fuel from my heartfelt emotions.

Please let this work. See the truth behind my actions. Revenge, yes, but also justice for my mother and any other woman that monster harmed with impunity.

It was time to end Alastor Colburn's reign.

***

"I need your help, but you have to swear to keep this a secret." I interrupted Monica's diatribe on corsets, a relevant discussion since both of us had bought one for our costumes.

"What are you talking about? When have I ever told on you?" She tossed her cell phone aside after taking a quick selfie.

"I'm not going with you tonight. Hayden's picking me up, and I'm spending the holiday with him. Don't tell Mama."

"Get it, girl!" Monica hugged me against the grossly inflated bosom of her new corset. "What time? I'm not even close to finished with your hair."

"This is important, Monica. Mama does *not* want me around any Colburns. She'd lose her mind if she found out." I winced when she pulled the flat iron too tight. "I won't get you in trouble. I'll be home just like if I went out with you, but I need you to drop me off on the way to your party."

"I was born for this. You got no idea! I'm the Gabrielle to your Xena, Etta Candy to your Wonder Woman... And I don't think she was anyone's sidekick, but I'm gonna grab Catwoman for myself. In the right light, I kinda look like Halle—don't you think?"

"Yes, you're a gorgeous badass, but will you please help me and keep this quiet?" I asked, exasperated by her glee. If she only knew... No way. That would make her an official accomplice. The responsibility for this had to fall solely on me.

"Only if you swear to give me all the nasty details afterwards," she said, suffocating us both with a cloud of hair spray. "I'm still waiting for more details from your first night with him. I told you all about me and Dany."

"And I learned more than enough, so thank you for the valuable info." I patted her hand, sharing a teasing smile through the mirror. "Will Dany be at your party tonight?"

"Yes. I cannot wait for some more of that—and don't tell *my* mama, if you don't mind. You know how she gets." Her saucy persona fluttered, then sagged on the last part.

Dora still struggled with Monica's fluctuating tastes in sexual partners, but she was getting better. Marcus helped with his steady defense of his sister and her choices. The world was changing, but some were slower to catch up—even if, by dragging their feet, they accidentally hurt those they loved the most.

"You think Dany's the one?" I reversed to a happier subject, enjoying the renewed spark in my friend as she further discussed her current infatuation.

"It's too soon to tell. Maybe after tonight we'll both find out if this is it. Or maybe we'll both head back to the drawing board."

"Tonight will definitely have some answers. But, no matter what happens, I'll always love you." I blinked back the swell of emotion before she caught on that something was very wrong.

"Awww Cori, I love you too! I don't know what I'd do without you."

Me either, I almost said aloud, basking while I could in my friend's unconditional support.

I fortified my armor and finished my costume. A stroke of luck for all this to occur on Halloween, particularly since the Colburn's party was a masquerade. These were deeds best executed under cover of a solid disguise.

Hayden wanted to skip the event, but that was too bad. He would not ruin my plans. All this preparation wasn't to look cute for a private date with him. I wanted to be unrecognizable, not that any of the Greenwich vipers knew me from Adam—just one more faceless servant, no one of consequence. I was counting on their dismissive attitudes, otherwise I might never escape their nest unscathed.

***

Monica offered to wait with me at the gastropub, but I told her to hurry and head out in case of traffic. Hayden wouldn't stand me up after his frequent texts over the past few days. I asked him not to come by my home again, and he agreed to meet at Fiore di Pergusa.

I had never entered the grand restaurant before. Like so many places on Greenwich Avenue, it was far above my price range. It astounded me— worth the trip, if only to admire the priceless art on the walls and the imported marble statues.

I scanned the menu, spotting several dishes and cocktails I wish I could've shown Mama. We loved trying new things, always seeking inspiration for our seasonal specials. She'd have blanched at the prices— frugal to her core—but would've tried one of everything if given the chance.

Someday, Mama. When you feel safe again, maybe we can see more of the world together.

"Holy hell, you look amazing."

Spinning on my barstool, my heart leapt at his sudden appearance. He'd coated his face in white pancake makeup, likely to match the fanged half-mask in his hand. The costume itself must've cost hundreds of dollars; an embroidered black velvet cape, vintage tuxedo, and a red silk cravat held in place with a gold wolf's head brooch.

"You don't look too shabby yourself, my lord Count." I stood, adjusting my cloak and gown to show him more.

I decided to go as a wicked witch, even if the irony was lost on everyone but me. The black slip clung to my curves, held together by a corset accented with scarlet ribbons, but the skirt was loose for ease of movement. I wore an elaborate bat-wing mask, topping the ensemble with a midnight cape intended for warmth and concealment. We wore similar colors but, unlike his fancier outfit, my costume was flimsy polyester and likely wouldn't survive one cycle in the washing machine. Monica thought my final idea was unnecessary but helped me, anyway. I dyed my dark hair with a temporary red rinse—a noticeable shade, but at least it hid my true appearance.

He reached for my pentagram necklace, the most authentic of my accessories, thumbing the polished garnet. "This is pretty, nicer than the stuff they usually have in the costume shops."

"Yeah, I must've lucked out." I shrugged off his hand. He didn't need to know the truth behind Mama's gift. Seeing him touch it raised my hackles.

Cool it. He's dumb, but not so much he won't sense your anger.

"What do you say we sneak off somewhere and have our own party?" Hayden leaned in for a kiss I hadn't planned on offering, but I played along. What was a kiss, anyway?

"And miss the biggest Halloween party on the East Coast? You owe me at least a couple of hours there before we run off." I slid one black fingernail down the front of his immaculate white shirt.

"Wait—what party are you talking about?"

"Your family's party." My vacuous smile spread as his bewildered expression shrank with chagrin. *Easy, gently...* "You're probably bored with it, but I've never been to such a fancy Halloween party. I was kinda hoping you'd take me there first."

"Cori, I..." he clasped my hand as it toyed with his collar. Too firm, his expression changed to accommodate a different type of mask. "You don't want to go there, trust me. It's just a bunch of evil old bastards, all congratulating each other on their latest business deal or betrayal. We can go anywhere else—even the city, if you want."

I took a deep breath, dramatically exhaling and stabbing my nails into my palms to squeeze a bead of moisture from my eyes. "Are you ashamed to be seen with me? Is that why you don't want me to go to your family's house?"

Boom! Dodge that, motherfucker.

A flush overrode the white makeup while his mouth worked, helpless to find the right words. His stunned eyes blinked before he rolled off on my manufactured guilt trip. I lowered my head, preparing to flee in shame. *One, two, th—*

"Cori, why would I ever think that? If anything, you're too good to be around them."

I swallowed a triumphant smile when he swept me into his arms, tucking me against his chest in an attempt to soothe my poor little feelings.

"Oh Hayden, you're sweet." I fluttered my lashes and kissed his cheek. *Eat your heart out, Scarlett O'Hara.* "Please, it would mean so much. We don't have to stay long."

"Fair enough. I'm happy with the chance to take you on an actual date." Hayden's guileless smile jabbed me, and I almost felt bad—almost. He seriously had no idea how much I hated him right now. I refused to regret anything he suffered while he lied right to my face. He was just a good actor, and I'd be damned if he beat me at my own game.

"When does the party start?"

"The invitation always says sundown, but people don't usually arrive until seven or eight. Why?"

"Maybe we could take our time, tour the grounds or something with a bottle of wine," I suggested archly, brushing imaginary lint off his cloak. "I'm a little nervous to be the first ones there. Don't want to draw too much attention to myself, you know?"

"They'll be fine, and Bronte promised to behave herself next time she saw you." He smiled, tugging one of the ribbons on my corset. "Let's go. I've got someplace special where we can hang before the party. Do you have to settle up here first?"

I laughed, placing my phone in the pouch at my waist, which held my tools for tonight. "Are you kidding? I didn't order anything. Have you seen these prices?"

"Good point. It probably isn't any better than what you could make, anyway." Hayden linked his arm through mine as we made our way to the door. "Speaking of prices, wait 'til you see what they'll serve at my family's house. It'd make the ancient Romans blush. But remember—that's my family, not me."

"Don't worry. I won't forget."

No...like my mama, I didn't forget anything—especially when a payment was owed.

CHAPTER TEN

After a quick stop at the package store, we drove to the edge of town along the coast road. The closer we got to his family home, the more memories popped in my mind like cheap fireworks—sparkles of colored light, there then gone. I hadn't been on this road in years. No reason to once we moved from Cypress Point—and thank God we did. If Mama stayed with the Colburns after what Alastor did, it would've undoubtedly destroyed the both of us.

A line of cars clogged the road, a sign we were close. "We won't have to wait. There's a back entrance for family."

"What's holding them all up?" I asked. With fifty acres, parking shouldn't have been an issue. "Isn't there a valet service to keep things moving?"

"Security check, first. My father's a little paranoid," Hayden replied, stony while mentioning the man himself.

"Seems excessive, unless he has actual enemies." I had to be careful while fishing for information, but a little prying was irresistible.

"Men like him always have actual enemies, usually for an excellent reason." After a sharp right turn, Hayden sneaked through a slender break between the thick trees. I would've missed it, as the dirt path was hardly wide enough for a single car. "Don't worry about my father. You won't see him often, if at all. None of us do."

"You don't get along with your father?"

"Let's talk about something more pleasant," he said, slowing as the path curved uphill. "What was your favorite Halloween experience as a kid?"

"Oh God, that's easy." I gazed at the rows of tall, pointed trees arching overhead—teeth in a gaping mouth, about to swallow us whole. *Happy thoughts, no panicking.* "I was eight, I think? Halloween fell on a Monday, which meant we could go out because Cornucopia was closed. I raced home from school, thrilled Mama was finally taking me trick-or-treating. I dressed as Hannah Montana, complete with a plastic microphone and a blonde wig. We stayed out for hours, hitting all the best houses with Monica and her family. Then we went home, watched cartoons, and shared my candy. It was awesome."

"I bet you were adorable." His hand moved from the stick shift to my thigh. "But what do the restaurant hours have to do with Halloween? Couldn't your mom take the night off?"

"And abandon her adoring public? Yeah, no." I casually scooted closer to the door—*oops, there goes his hand.* "Even if she wanted to, there was no one to cover. Her role is too important. Plus, we can't afford to take days off. I started working there the next summer, washing dishes until she trusted me to do more."

"You've been working since you were nine years old? That's illegal!"

"Not for a family business, so long as I didn't operate any dangerous equipment." Unable to stop myself, I added in a chilly reproach, "In the real world, sometimes kids have to work—even if it's just by helping their parents. We don't all have endless wealth as a safety net."

"I'm well aware the best parts of my life came from my family's money and name." The words were clipped with restraint as he swerved beyond the claustrophobic tree canopy toward a low-slung garage. "I had the privilege of the best schools. My basic needs were met and exceeded, and yes, my trust fund purchased my home and business. But I work my ass off every day, the same as you, in the trenches alongside my employees. Whatever success comes from Cypress Lounge, it's because of what me and my crew put into it."

I didn't know how to respond. What if his defense held some truth? That would imply Hayden had a measure of honor, endurance, and an honest work ethic. *He doesn't deserve my respect.*

"I guess everyone's path has its ups and downs." I unbuckled my seatbelt, reaching for the door.

"Hey, hold on." He grabbed my arm—firm enough to stop me, but not hard enough to hurt. "I know some people in this town, like my lovely sister and her friends, haven't always treated you well. We don't know a hell of a lot about each other, but I've only ever been decent toward you. Do you really believe I'm one of those entitled rich guys? A playboy or some generic douchebag? 'Cause if so, I can take you right back home. I wouldn't dream of offending your delicate sensibilities with my family's repugnant wealth."

Dammit, backpedal and fix this!

"I'm sorry. That was unfair." I laid my hand on his, offering a bashful smile. "Of course you're different, otherwise I wouldn't be here."

The pithy apology seemed to work, eroding his rocky eyes and grim slash of a mouth. "I'm sorry, too. I get a little defensive when people lump me in with those types—spoiled, out of touch, lazy. That's not me, Cori."

But he didn't move, stewing in the dissipating fumes from our brief clash. That wouldn't do. If his mood didn't improve, he might not take me to the party. I'd come too far to turn back now.

"Why don't you show me the special place you talked about, and we'll crack open that bottle of wine?" I leaned in, intending to give him a quick make-up kiss. The opening left him with other ideas.

His hands spanned my waist, pulling me close. The center console saved me from landing on his lap, but not from the hot mouth, which demanded more than he deserved. He cradled my back, each kiss hammering into my will. His free hand skidded over the oppressive corset before resting on my breasts. I clung to his shoulders for balance, then sank into his embrace. The sensual invasion stirred a rebellious reaction in my body despite the warnings screaming in my brain.

The cheap polyester scoured my hardened nipples, my discomfort worsening as his fingers plucked the tips. I shifted when the console bit into my buttocks, my left hand scrabbling for purchase, then landing on his throbbing erection. "Ouch! Sorry, but this isn't working for me."

"You sure?" Hayden murmured, his thumbnail tracing the sensitive skin through the thin cloth. "How is it you conveniently forget to wear bras in these fancy dresses? I can't even think straight, knowing you're bare as can be underneath."

"Can we just go? Show me the thing—er, place—whatever it is." I bit my lip, trapping the moan in my throat but losing after one final pinch.

"And those little noises...each one cracks that prissy exterior a bit more." His hand crept lower as he stole a kiss from my parted lips. Sweet as the Prince must've been to lure Snow White from her glass coffin—another entitled bastard, forcing her into a happily ever after. He saved her life, sure, but what if she had other plans for her future than simply being his wife? "Will you save some more of those for later? I'll be good, promise."

The hand on my belly inched the long skirt up my legs. Although it pained me to admit it, if he touched me like he did the other night, I'd give in. Sometimes clichés were spot on, like the whole thin line between love and hate. I'd love nothing more than to bash his head against the steering wheel. And while I'd never had "hate sex," tonight I understood the appeal. His touch might convince me to surrender physically, but I wouldn't be gracious about it. If he gained any further ground, I'd only despise him more and plot increasingly vicious attacks as punishment.

"It's too cramped in here. Let's go." Careful this time where I placed my hands, I escaped the car. So what if I stumbled a bit to find my footing? I adjusted my costume and patted my breastbone, admonishing my racing heart.

Mask in hand, purse and poison on my hip, I had what I needed. Now, I only had to survive the next hour with Hayden and his hormones, join the party crowd, and pray they ignored me.

***

"Not much farther," Hayden said, swigging from the wine bottle before passing it back to me. The flashlight illuminated our path after we walked beyond the garage's floodlights. "You okay? I didn't notice what kind of shoes you had."

"I'm good. No more heels for a while. Last week filled my annual quota." I showed off my ballet flats, deliberately chosen for ease of walking and absolute silence—assuming I didn't traipse through crackling leaves and twigs, like now.

He stopped without warning, spreading his arms like a ringmaster. "Here we are! My favorite place as a kid. You should be honored. Used to be no girls allowed."

"Wow... A random spot in the woods doesn't exactly scream special, but I'm sure there's more to the story." I sipped from the bottle, pretending to drink more than I did. "Can you ban girls from an entire forest? Pretty sure that would be against the law."

"It's my castle, my rules." He punctuated the comment with a fond slap to a massive oak tree.

I squinted, finally seeing what he meant. An off-kilter row of planks rose along the thick trunk, through the dense foliage, to a faded wooden house above. "Your home away from home? Because two dozen rooms didn't offer enough hiding spots." I grinned, handing him back the bottle.

"That was their space, this is mine. Come on up." He didn't wait for my reply, climbing the ladder with the lip of the bottle braced between his teeth and the flashlight peeking over his pocket.

"Be careful! It's dark, and you'll break a tooth if that bottle smacks anything." My hands flew over my own tooth-filled mouth, squeamish at such a foolish risk.

A beam of blinding white shot through the narrow hole in the treehouse floor, revealing a disembodied hand beckoning me onward. "Your turn. I'll help you."

"I don't know about this. Climbing trees in the dark... You've got a strange idea of fun." I strained to keep the sole-less ballet flats steady on the smooth slats of wood. Bare feet would've been best, but I didn't want to risk losing my shoes in the piles of dead leaves.

His hands slid up my forearms, lifting while I crawled up each ladder step. After much groaning and heavy breathing, his grip switched to my armpits, then to my waist. I sprawled in an undignified heap across the floor.

"I wasted time shaving my legs," I panted, refreshing myself with another sip of wine. "I think that entrance sliced the top layer of skin from the front of my thighs."

"Are you all right?" He chuckled, reaching out to touch me. I scooted back in time, but hit my head on a tree limb. "Damn, look around first before you flail all over the place."

The flashlight created a unique backdrop in the small but pleasant hut. Three windows surrounded us, each insulated by a thin pane of glass; a chair in the corner beside a pallet of mildewing blankets; but the best part was how the thick tree limbs wove through the tiny space, providing both extra structural support and bonus seating.

"My apologies for doubting you. This is awesome." I ran my hand along the center limb, curved like a lazy S. "I've never been in a treehouse, but I would've loved this as a kid."

"My parents offered to build some gigantic play castle on the main grounds, but this was what I wanted. Only enough room for me, I made them swear." He hopped and sat on the curved branch, which put us at eye level. "They'd just brought Bronte home, you see, and I wanted a place where no girls or babies could bother me—you included, come to think of it. Your crying often ruined my playtime with Tessa."

"I guess you broke your own rules." I flashed a grin, pulling my cloak closer when a swift cross-breeze passed.

"I'm all grown up now, and girls aren't as annoying—well, most of them." He tugged on my cloak until I stood between his legs. "You, though, have got to be the most annoying one of the bunch."

"What? I'm probably the least annoying girl you've ever met." I raised a hand, counting off the first qualities which popped to mind. "I eat and drink anything. I think fad diets are stupid. I'm low maintenance, rarely complain, and I don't waste money on stupid stuff like fake nails and eyelashes."

"That's quite a list, but what about the things you are guilty of?" With another tug and lift, I was half in his lap. "Rarely wearing bras, rolling your eyes all the damn time, and acting like the most insufferable snob to privileged but hard-working, small-business owners."

"Snob? How can I be a snob? You're the rich one." I reminded him, wiggling away from the arm snaking around my waist.

"Do you help your mama with the finances? Then you have a good idea what profits come from a small restaurant once expenses go out. That's what I live off of, too. The bulk of my trust fund is tied to the property, not liquid. I earn my living, same as you," he said, irritatingly practical as he brushed my hair back to kiss the pulse racing beneath my neck. "But you look down on me. You judge me for being born into something I didn't choose. That's a bit snobby, wouldn't you agree?"

"I think you're full of shit, trying to start another argument now that you've trapped me in this tree dungeon." Somehow I was in between his legs, leaning into the lips against my neck.

"I think I'm wondering if you forgot your panties at home with your bra."

His throaty challenge provoked another sarcastic remark but, before I could speak, he silenced me with a breathtaking kiss. My arm flew around his shoulder, bracing myself as his hand cupped my core through the thin skirt. His fingers rolled, stirring a flood of warmth within the hidden flesh. How easy it would be to yield. I almost did until panic flooded my veins, barking a series of orders to my treacherous body. Fight or flight—I'd take either option at the moment.

"Stop it!" I jumped down, wincing when bark scraped my elbow. "Dammit Hayden, what are you doing?"

"Relax, I won't hurt you." The wicked grin hinted otherwise. He sprang from his seat to follow me, hugging me when I turned my back.

"So you said already." I shook him off, resting beside the nearest window and glaring through the blurry glass.

"Hey, what's going on? You're so tense tonight." He leaned on the other side of the window, examining my face with a concerned frown. "If I pissed you off, then tell me. Is this about your mother ordering you to stay away from me?"

Fucking hell, my emotions were running away again, like when I screwed up in the kitchen. All because I couldn't keep a safe distance from him in this wonderful tree house where I could almost imagine... No, things couldn't be different.

Pull your shit together. He's on to you.

"Yeah—I mean, I don't know." I evaded his touch, pacing away.

My brain reeled, searching for a likely excuse before pushing out a story that rang a little too close to home. But the best lies sprouted from a grain of truth. "Mama, she can't let go. She's always paranoid that something will happen to me. All I do is work and stay close to home. When she found out I lied and spent the night with you, it freaked her out. She doesn't want to lose me like... It's stupid, not even the same. Daddy died. I just went on a date, for Christ's sake."

"She was a wreck when Felix passed. It was horrible," Hayden said, repentant. As if he cared. "I get her need to protect you. I'd probably feel the same way in her place." He paused, clearing his throat. "I'm sorry she's mad at me. I should talk to her. I respect the hell out of Tessa."

"No, leave it for now—please." I spun around, planting my hands on his chest so he'd keep his distance this time. "It's not a big deal."

"Not a big deal? Your mother's been through a lot. So have you. But you're a woman now, Cori. You're allowed to choose your path." He gazed at me with a sad, shy smile. "It's a big deal, your future. The more time I spend with you, I'd kind of like to see how it goes."

"How what goes?" I asked, entranced as the forgotten flashlight's beam reflected from his eyes.

"I—well, I wasn't sure if you'd be interested in something more, unless..."

"Unless what?"

It was his turn to pace away, hands stuffed in his pockets while he wrestled with whatever sat on his mind. I balled my fists, expecting anything other than what I received.

"Maybe Bronte was right. She swears you've still got a thing for Nolan. That you pursued me to piss her off and make him jealous." The dry chuckle didn't match the humorless gaze that reluctantly locked with mine.

"Are you fucking serious?"

My infuriated disbelief somehow relaxed the tension. Was my anger entertaining? But Hayden's crooked smile smoothed my ruffled feathers. I couldn't be mad he doubted my intentions. He'd correctly sensed an ulterior motive, but it certainly wasn't Nolan's dumb ass.

"You want the truth?" I challenged, planting my hands on my hips.

"Nolan broke my heart, and it took a while to heal. The worst part... He was one of my best friends, but he chose ambition over us—over our friendship. We started talking less and less. It hurt...a lot. I assure you I'm over it, and I absolutely do not want him back. He's a shallow little bitch, just like your sister. They deserve each other." I winced, quickly tacking on, "No offense."

Hayden released a burst of easy laughter. He returned to my side with a broad grin, infectious enough to make me return the sentiment. "Jesus, Cori, don't hold back on my account. Tell me how you really feel."

One last chance, almost there.

I slid my hands up his chest and twirled them behind his neck. "Okay, so I'm not a fan of your family or this surreal world you come from. But I... There's something between us, Hayden. I wouldn't be here otherwise."

"Cori..." he began thickly, swallowing whatever words hovered on his tongue. Instead, he gave me a tentative kiss that tasted like an apology.

Got him.

I balanced on my tiptoes to claim even more of his warm mouth, and an amused voice poked at me. *You sure about that?*

Everything wavered, protective veils falling to reveal people more akin to our purest selves—just a girl and a boy, both wounded and uncertain, working up the nerve to share their feelings. We moved again like we did that night at Inferno, a dance without music—or a music only we could hear.

Why did he have to lie to me? He'd been so perfect that night. Everything about him had felt so right, once. Even now, I'd almost believed he was ready to tell me about his father and Mama, then he stumped me with that bullshit about Bronte. He'd never planned on telling me the truth.

Would that change my mind if he confessed what he'd seen and done? Was it fair to be mad at him when his actions had ultimately saved her?

"Can I ask you something?" he whispered.

"Hmmm?" A lame response, but it was becoming hard to focus.

We swayed back and forth, so lightly even the floorboards stopped creaking. His lips rested on my forehead, one hand cupping the back of my head while the other held my hips to his. There, I heard it: the song from the club, playing right when I realized he was mine...at least for the night.

"Would you want to—"

"Hayden, are you up there?"

Goddammit! We froze like kids playing musical chairs, trapped in the open when the music screeched to a halt.

"Yeah, give me a second!"

"Is that...?" I whispered before his mouth seized mine. One last kiss before the outside world intruded to drag us back, a kiss filled with such passion and longing that my head spun. I flattened myself against his chest, balling my hands in his cloak to hold him as long as possible. Once I let go, the game would resume, and he'd become my enemy again.

"Hayden, Mother is looking for you! I thought you said you weren't coming tonight? Hurry or you'll make me late, too."

"Be right there—Christ!" Hayden broke first, trying to catch his breath.

He treated me to one last peek of that sweet boy and his trusting smile. Too quickly, his other persona clicked into place—privileged son, jaded business owner, Prince of Greenwich. What else had I expected? Maybe those were indicative of his true form, and I was the naïve one.

"Come on, Coralena. They found us."

CHAPTER ELEVEN

"You're kidding me, right? This is your date?"

"Bronte, be nice," Hayden admonished, not nearly as harsh as I would've liked.

"Happy Halloween." It was the only positive greeting which came to mind when faced with her open disgust and delusional costume. Glinda the Good? Give me a freaking break. But I had to admit, her fanciful gem-encrusted gown and bejeweled tiara were on point.

"Ugh, whatever. I brought the golf cart." Bronte flounced to the driver's seat in a cloud of tulle, cranking the vehicle. "They saw you sneak up here on the security cameras and thought you'd be in sooner. Mother made me come find you, and now Nolan is all alone with Daddy and his fossilized friends."

"What?" I perked up, fearing the worst. "We should hurry back."

"Let it be a test. See if the moron can handle himself," Hayden grumbled, staring straight ahead.

"I can take care of my own boyfriend, Cori, thanks." Bronte spun the wheel toward a row of lights looming ahead. "He's my concern now, not yours."

"Enough with Nolan, for fuck's sake!" Hayden snarled, kicking the dash.

"Calm down and stop acting like some juiced-up teenager." Bronte laughed, elbowing Hayden until he gently slapped her arm.

I stared at the passing scenery, losing interest in their antics. What a bunch of jackasses. Nolan was too gullible to be exposed to a bunch of crafty Satanists. And Hayden... What the hell happened in that treehouse? Was he trying to ask me to be his girlfriend—as fucking if! I almost believed him for a second, but how could he be different than the others? He'd been primed to turn into a raging asshole one day, just like his father. Maybe I'd make him a nice Tonic, too, and dampen that troublesome libido for good.

"Cori, look—there's the house you were born in," Hayden said, gesturing to the right.

The cottage was smaller than I remembered and the siding was different, a lighter color. The sight sent a pang through my heart. The small porch swing was still in front beside the rows of prickly bushes I once tried to hide in—only once. I cried for Daddy when they ripped my soft skin, teaching me a valuable lesson in blind exploration. Amazing, the things one recalled with the proper cue.

"Can we visit it later?" My voice cracked, and I cleared my throat. No way I'd appear vulnerable in front of Bronte.

"Some other time, sure," he replied, suspiciously evasive.

"Daddy stays there now, and it's off limits," Bronte clarified, bossy and bitchy until Hayden pinched her arm. "Ow—what, it's true!"

"It's fine. I wouldn't want to intrude." I filed away the tidbit for later—useful for a Plan B or C, depending on what I found at the party.

"Too late," Bronte muttered, but I pretended not to hear.

Cypress Point's main house emerged in all its glory; three stories, two slate-roofed towers on either end, and a widow's walk connecting them both. A miniature castle, lost in a private forest on the tip of Connecticut. If the sun were up, the crashing waves of the Long Island Sound would be visible beyond the endless lawn leading to an enclosed beach with its own marina.

Unreal, that one family owned this small and vital slice of land—nearly a full peninsula on some of the most valuable real estate in the country.

The party we'd soon enter probably cost enough to feed a starving village in Africa for a year, but that kind of extravagance wasn't enough to satisfy Alastor Colburn. No, he amused himself with black magic and torture, stealing the best of others to consolidate his power.

Clutching the small bag at my waist, I said a brief prayer. *Keep me strong, Mother. Shield me from harm on this night of long-overdue justice.*

***

I remembered walking through these doors before, even if the tented path was disorienting. The large party spread across the back patio. Black and orange awnings contained the warmth blaring from portable heaters. My skin tingled after the chilly ride over, numb fingertips adjusting my mask when I recognized some of the guests from town.

The costumes were lavish—every colorful variation of princess, queen, and goddess imaginable—decorated with jewels that sparkled with their own fire. A pair of ladies stood out from the pack, dapper and unique in specially tailored tuxedos and top hats. Even the men dressed up, disguised as characters ranging from Roman leaders, kings, knights in burnished armor, and furry animals with toothy masks.

Everyone appeared to be enjoying themselves, eating delicacies from china plates and sipping fruity cocktails and golden scotch. The night was young, and the elite were on their best behavior—for now. What might happen closer to midnight, after hours of carousing? Was that when Alastor and his cronies engaged in their depraved rites? Most Satanists weren't malicious, valuing pure hedonism over traditional religion. The stories I'd read on the internet about some truly dark cults, however, were not for the faint of heart.

How many of these seemingly innocent people were involved? Engaging in debauched rituals of blood and sex, calling upon malevolent forces for a further boost to their already significant power and wealth. Who dared stand against them, stopping them from hurting others? They had the clout to do whatever they wanted, to whomever they wanted, without fear of recrimination or punishment.

Maybe taking out Alastor would be a step toward ending their cavalier revelries. The vengeful act might damn my immortal soul—a consequence too esoteric for me to comprehend—but it would so be worth it to knock those complacent criminals down a few pegs.

"There's Nolan. I better go rescue him," Bronte said, kissing Hayden's cheek. "Mother's in the kitchen, I believe. Just stop in so she calms down. Tell her to have some fun, for once."

"We will. See you in a bit." His hand clasped mine as his gaze settled on the largest cluster of men across the room. A possessive gesture, but I didn't fight it. Better the others believed I was unavailable, or I'd be forced to inform them myself. If it came to that, I wouldn't do it nicely.

Nolan's bright head was easy to spot among the dark hoods and masks of that particular group. He wore some complex outfit of leather and fur—a reject from *Game of Thrones,* maybe. The men around him were a mixture of sorcerers, priests, and yet another vampire—an excuse for their matching cloaks, I'd wager.

But it was the man beside Nolan, wearing a cryptic smile within a neatly trimmed silver beard, who caught my full attention. Alastor Colburn—the one unmasked face among the bunch—wore a black and purple toga, crowned with horns and a gold laurel wreath. I guessed he was impersonating some powerful god, maybe Dionysius—of course that was how he saw himself, the creepy bastard. He clutched an expensive goblet in the base of his palm, gesturing with it while preaching to his rapt audience.

"When's the last time you saw my mother?" Hayden asked, dodging party guests while guiding me out the nearby door.

I flipped through vague snippets of my childhood memory, the images superimposed upon my current environment—recognizable even with the temporary party decorations. This hallway led from the solarium and living room, past the main entrance, then to the kitchen.

"A couple of years, maybe?" I jumped to avoid the first over-indulger of the night as he ran from the bathroom, bellowing a war cry before racing back to the party.

Here we go...

"I'm surprised to hear that. She loves your mother's cooking and teas. I thought she'd be a regular at your restaurant."

"Maybe she found someplace she liked better," I said quickly, unwilling to reveal my mother's secret correspondence with Aspasia. They didn't meet in person to avoid suspicion, and I wouldn't give them up to Hayden. "Wow, this is stunning."

We stood within the heart of the house: walls and columns rose for three stories, stopped only by a sizable stained-glass dome. A dual staircase dominated the space, unfurling to the second-floor landing. If I recalled, the gallery level was on the third floor, accessible by a narrow staircase in the library on the far side of the house. Polished mahogany gleamed, setting off the immaculate displays of colorful art and antique tapestries. More of a museum than a home, it was easily the most impressive place I'd ever been. A shame such beauty was wasted on a family like them.

"You and Bronte used to slide down those banisters, racing each other to the bottom. Your mother got so mad when she caught you." Hayden slung an arm over my shoulders. "She thought it was my idea, or at least blamed me for not stopping you. Both of you little crybabies looked so afraid of getting a spanking, so I kept your secret."

"Aren't you heroic?" I stepped away, running my hand along the banister. Yes, I remembered the wind in my face, the hardwood floor rushing up—cross-patterned wood that resembled an acrobat's net. Bronte and I as friends, playing, having fun... That part seemed more unreal than all the rest. How times had changed.

"I have my moments. I'm a sucker for a damsel in distress." He reclaimed my hand and tried to kiss it, but the fanged mask blocked most of his mouth.

"I hate to disappoint you, but my mama taught me how to take care of myself. I don't need a white knight." I sent him a pithy smile and continued walking toward the kitchen.

"You weren't that independent in my apartment." He caught up, pinching my ass until I spun around again. "I recall quite a bit of begging."

I sputtered while deciding on the best retort, realizing too late he backed me into the alcove beneath the staircase. Pinned, one of his arms on either side, his lips curled into a victorious smile.

"You begged plenty, too, so stop acting all superior." But the comeback wavered before those hypnotic eyes, pulling me in like a sci-fi tractor beam.

"Maybe we could—"

"Hayden, there you are," the gentle voice interrupted his sentence, and we turned toward the source. Small and tanned, brown hair shot with silver, she hid within a wealth of blue silk and peacock feathers. I sucked in my breath at the lovely woman watching us both without expression. "Introduce me to your friend."

"We were just coming to see you, Mother." Hayden nudged me forward. "You remember Theresa's daughter, Coralena?"

"My, haven't you grown." Aspasia's smile cracked like ice thawing above a frozen pond. "Not a little girl with pigtails anymore. What a beauty you've become, just like your mother. I hope she's well?"

"Yes, Mrs. Colburn. She's doing fine." My heart thumped beneath her frigid judgment. Was she really a friend of ours, like Mama said? She looked as if she'd just as soon toss me out the door...or off the side of a cliff.

"Hayden, there's a bar set up in the breakfast nook. Would you be a darling and grab us something to drink? I'd like to sit and chat for a moment with this pretty young lady. I've been on my feet for hours supervising the cooks." Her thin lips melted into a warm smile, tiny white teeth sparkling like the rhinestones on her blue and gold mask. "Come along, Coralena. Let's rest for a moment."

She stepped through the adjacent door, a small study tastefully decorated in ocean shades with a dainty antique desk and a pair of cozy armchairs. At her invitation, I sat in the chair opposite hers. She removed her mask, revealing small hooks like glasses—designed so as not to ruin her intricate hairstyle, perhaps? In contrast, the rubber bands on mine would tear out clumps of hair when I took it off later. Did their advantages ever end?

"Does your mother know where you are? I should call her this instant and send you away from here," Aspasia said, not a quiver of emotion upsetting her urbane persona. "Has she told you everything yet?"

"Yes, ma'am." I resisted the urge to clutch the vial of digitalis. If I drew attention to my pouch, she'd surely sniff it out. This woman was not some insipid socialite like the others. She saw more than people gave her credit for, I'd bet—including her own family.

"Has my son shared his part of the tale?"

"No, not yet." My fists clenched, but I recalled where I was and forced them flat against my knees.

"He's not like my husband." She tilted her head, dispassionately examining my face and form. "He suffered for saving your mother, more than he may be willing to discuss with someone he barely knows. And he's despised his father ever since.

"If you're here to hurt my boy, I'll be forced to do some unpleasant things. I may lack your mother's gifts, but I have no shortage of more prosaic resources. Do you understand?"

"Yes, ma'am," I said automatically, sensing the truth and danger in her warning. My pride swelled, unwilling to take orders from this woman, but aware I had to exercise caution.

"Your mother and I have this situation under control. My husband is punished every day from her spell. He's never caught on that I dose his food and beverages with her tonics. I intend to keep it that way. It's safest." She sat back, unfolding her arms like a queen on her throne. "Stay away from Alastor tonight. He's bound and neutered, but that doesn't mean he won't bite. Tell my son to take you home early. Once you're away, I never want to see you near my family again. Do you understand me, Coralena?"

"Yes, ma'am." My damp palms clutched my skirt as fresh tears stung my eyes. Chastised by this grand woman, shamed and threatened... It was infuriating.

Someone tapped on the door, and Aspasia reached over to turn the knob. Hayden entered with three glasses and an oblivious smile. "Ladies, here you are. What did I miss?"

"Sharing our recipes and beauty secrets, what else?" she said with a light laugh, clinking her glass against both of ours. "I'm pleased Theresa's child grew into such an accomplished and intelligent young lady. Children are a mother's greatest treasure."

"Thank you, Mrs. Colburn. I won't forget the kindness you've shown me." After another artificial smile, I finished my drink and set the glass on a polished end table. I hoped it left a ring behind.

"I must make my rounds. I'll see you both shortly." Aspasia allowed Hayden to help her stand, accepting a kiss on her cheek, then exited with enviable grace.

Hayden picked up my glass, giving me a funny look. "What did she say to you? You seem upset."

"Nothing. It's just been a while since I met someone's mother—a little nerve-wracking, but I'm okay." I breezed past, almost making it out of the room.

"Hey," he reached to stop me, stroking my bare arm beneath the cloak, "I hate these parties, too. That's why I skip whenever possible. Are you sure you want to stay?"

"No, it's great. Thanks again for inviting me." I freed myself from his grip, holding the door for him. "I can't wait for the real fun to begin."

CHAPTER TWELVE

Why couldn't there be just one moment where the pompous asshole wandered off? He never stopped sipping from that ridiculous goblet, laughing with his slimy friends, and accepting fealty from his toadies. How could I get close enough, unnoticed, to spike his drink?

He refilled his cup from a crystal decanter on a nearby table, blood-red wine he graciously shared among his friends. Some of them were probably as disgusting as him, and would've been improved by a swift death, but what if I was wrong? I couldn't just poison the decanter and risk killing the group.

If he'd only step away, even to the bathroom, he might set his cup down long enough for me to add my present. Surely after all those sips he had to pee?

This wouldn't work. I had to get to the cottage, away from so many curious eyes. Hayden's old friends chatted with him, dragging me into their lame conversations. Waiters and bodyguards stood in unobtrusive corners, watching over us all. The cottage would have food or drink in the fridge, maybe an open bottle of liquor. Hayden and Bronte said the place was off-limits, likely a private cave just for their beast of a father. It was my best shot.

"When are you going for a Michelin star? Your place kicks ass, bro," some idiot friend said, clapping Hayden on the back. They must've moved on from the yawn-worthy tales of their good old prep school days. Time to make an exit, or risk saying something they'd consider rude.

"Not for a while yet, man. Francisco and I are trying some new things, so we'll see," Hayden said, drumming his fingers against my hipbone.

"Do you get to the city often, Cori?" Idiot asked, his real name never registering in my distracted mind.

"Not that often, no." I jiggled my empty glass, then set it on the bar. "Excuse me, I need to run to the ladies' room."

"I hear you. The dam always breaks for me after the third drink," Idiot laughed, a sound only describable as a guffaw. Christ, he was dumber than his costume—an uninspired choice, even for a stockbroker. He wore a suit and a wolf mask, howling and beating his chest while proclaiming himself The Wolf of Wall Street. Too bad Leo wasn't here to smack him for us all.

"Do you want me to show you where it is?" Hayden asked.

"No—thanks, though. I remember the way." I ground my teeth beneath the sweet crust of my smile. "Be back in a minute."

I didn't turn around when Idiot howled once more, followed by a smacking sound like a high five. What a pack of animals, always thinking about one thing. I'd be wise to heed my mother and Aspasia, washing my hands of Hayden and his strange life as soon as possible.

We passed a bathroom on our way to the kitchen, but I didn't want to go in that direction. I hadn't seen Aspasia in a minute, but I wasn't keen on bumping into her again. The entire rear of the home was lined with French doors leading to the patio. There was bound to be another way out, less conspicuous than the tented enclosure connected to the living room.

"Is that you, Cori?"

God...damn...it.

"Hey, Nolan. Just heading to the bathroom." I spun from my spot by the staircase, reminding myself to keep smiling.

My quasi-friend and former love stumbled over, batting the plastic sword tied to his waist as it tried to trip him. "They're back there. Want me to take you?"

I stared, holding back a cutting retort before replying, "Thanks, but I'm good. You should get back to Bronte. She was looking for you."

"Okay, cool. I was talking to her dad earlier," he confided, spraying me with his high-octane breath. "He's one badass motherfucker, man! Like meeting the President or something. He said he might bring me in to visit with some of his club members. Isn't that awesome?"

"Nolan," I said, cursing myself for even caring, "it is *not* awesome. You need to stay away from them. They're dangerous."

He laughed, stepping back in astonishment. "Holy shit, Bronte's right. You're jealous. Are you really trying to get me back? I thought we were cool as friends."

"Get over yourself. That's the last thing I want, you dumbass." I waved him off, a waste of my time in more ways than one. "None of these people are what they seem. Don't say I didn't warn you."

"We weren't good together, Cori. You need to let it go." Nolan captured my hand, giving it a friendly squeeze. "I mean, I liked you as a friend, but as anything else? You never wanted to go out, you were always working— as if that place is a career—and you pushed me away all the time like I annoyed you. I hope, for Hayden's sake, you're more relaxed now."

Yanking my hand back, I slapped his cheek and stunned him to silence. "Go fuck yourself, Nolan."

"Yeah, walk away—frigid bitch. Nothing's worth your precious time, is it?"

I kept moving, more than done with him and the pointless conversation. I tried to wipe my eyes, but my fingers couldn't get around the stupid plastic ridges of the mask. Fuck him. He didn't deserve more of my tears. I gave him all I had, but I wasn't good enough—not when girls like Bronte Colburn started sniffing around.

Jealous, no way... You're only jealous when someone threatens to steal what you can't live without.

My life was fine without him. I knew whatever we'd shared would end, even before Yale. As kids, we always dreamed of different paths and goals.

What do you want to be when you grow up? I asked.

I don't know, whatever pays the most, he said, as if it were a joke.

I'd lost Nolan long before he ever left me to immature dreams of privilege and position, ambition for nothing more than power itself and the perks it offered. How could I have competed with that?

***

The night air nipped through my cloak, and I pulled it closer to shield myself. No one saw me leave through the dining room doors, I made sure. All the light and sound centered on the tents at the far end of the patio. With my hooded black cloak, padded ballet flats, and a wall of dwarfed cypresses, I was practically invisible.

Darting across the open lawn to the nearby trees, I glanced back and still saw nothing behind me. I continued along the tree line in the general direction of the cottage. There wasn't time to waste. Shouldn't be more than a five-minute walk each way, but I had to get in and out. Even ten minutes might be long enough to send Hayden searching, and what would I say?

Just thought I'd poke around alone. Hope you don't mind? Yeah, that wouldn't be weird.

A porch light cut through the foliage, guiding me toward the cottage. I studied the small house in the clearing, waiting to detect any guards or movement. Seemed empty. Must not have anything worth protecting beyond its dear master, and he was too busy dallying with his subjects.

I avoided the front entrance, heading straight for the back door leading to the kitchen. Amazing how much of this layout came back to me after only a couple of hours. I may not have lived here for long, but those were the best years our family had. It left a deeper impression than I realized.

The door was unlocked, not even beeping from a security alarm. I ducked in, carefully fitting the door into the jamb without a sound.

Disappointment welled as I scanned the small room. It'd been modernized and repainted—sterile, unlike the colorful and comfortable home my mother built for us. The only thing that remained the same was the enormous cast-iron stove—cold tonight, but flaring to life thanks to my memory: My mother, bent over those flames, calling out curses like a wild-haired Disney villain. That was an image I'd never forget as long as I lived.

I shuddered, turning to open the fridge. Someone kept it decently stocked with beverages and condiments, a few containers of sliced fruits and vegetables, but not much else. Maybe he still took meals with Aspasia at the main house or ate out? There wasn't time to ponder his dining habits.

One container stood out, etched blue glass half-filled with a juice blend. I set it on the counter, taking off the lid to sniff the contents—kale, apple, celery, tomato and various herbs. I dipped a finger in, rolling the taste across my tongue before spitting it out. Seemed normal, no sign of the tonics Mama sent to Aspasia. Good—I didn't want my actions traced back to her.

Some conscientious member of the kitchen staff labeled the contents, made today and expiring on November second. It was half gone; the old man must've loved this stuff. I had to go with my gut on this one.

I removed the vial from the inner pocket of the pouch, filled to the brim with murky water. I didn't dare try the foxglove decoction, given its virulence, but the herbal odor was mild. In such an array of scents and tastes, it should blend seamlessly with the juice.

I poured it in, exhaling with relief before dropping the empty vial into my pouch. I'd toss it somewhere later, a random Dumpster or the ocean. The lid was secure, label still in place, and the jug returned to the fridge. Time to get back.

My hand squeezed the knob to the back door when I heard a creak. Had I found a weak floorboard?

"Don't open that door."

I didn't wait to meet the giant with a rumbling bass voice lurking behind me. I kicked into motion. The door crashed open, screaming on its hinges as I ran into the dark yard. Maybe if I didn't stop I could make it, hide in the bushes, find the treehouse...

A zap to my lower back stunned me, toppling me against the coarse winter grass and into the black.

CHAPTER THIRTEEN

A hand stroked my cheek, so soothing that I leaned in for more. Mama's voice sang through my aching head, *Wake up, baby. It's a new day!*

"Coming, Mama." My thickened tongue stuck to the roof of my mouth. I blindly rolled toward my nightstand, thirsty for the water I always left there, but nothing wanted to work. Had I gotten tangled in the sheets?

"Yes, time to wake up," a male voice cooed. The genteel accent should've put me at ease, but I sensed something vicious beneath—dangerous as a rattle from a vigilant snake. "How lovely you are, an absolute angel! A fitting tribute to Theresa and Felix."

The overhead light burned my eyes, forcing them to shut again. A stranger sat beside me, his roving hand sliding up my arm. Two sets of zip ties gnawed at my wrists and ankles—*What?*

I flailed against the cushions, recalling that my attempt to flee had been thwarted. At least I was stuck on something soft, better than the hard ground I'd smacked into when someone zapped me unconscious.

Shit, shit, shit! I didn't have a plan for escaping capture.

My eyelids opened again, blinking at the man behind the posh voice and the uninvited touch. The black and purple toga, rosy cheeks, and silver beard beneath a golden crown of laurels—the last person I wanted to see, but the one I should've expected. We were in a comfortable living room with new furniture and wallpaper, but the former space whispered to me. This was the cottage's interior, my first home and maybe my final destination in a life I'd barely begun.

"Stay away from me." I skidded back, lifting my bound hands to ward him off—whatever good that would do.

"Presumptuous, aren't you? Making demands after you attempted to poison me." Alastor gave a delighted chuckle, his blue eyes sparkling—Hayden's eyes. Would he look the same as his father when he grew older, or even worse, would his personality change to resemble the smirking fiend now before me?

"I don't know what you're talking about." The denial sounded good to me, but I doubted he bought it.

"No matter. My men are shipping a sample to some friends as we speak. Once we were tipped off to your identity, I sent one of my guards to follow you. A brave attempt, but you're hardly as skilled as my staff. He watched as you emptied that little vial into my juice so there's no need to lie," he said amiably, as if we were old friends. "Then the most extraordinary thing happened. Sitting here while you were out cold, touching your beautiful face... It fixed something that's been broken for far too long."

"What are you talking about?" I cried out when the rattlesnake finally struck, grabbing my hands. Instead of hitting me, he dragged my unwilling fingertips to the space between his legs. "Ewww, gross—you nasty pig, let me go!"

Laughing again, he released the zip tie. I tucked my arms against my chest, as far from him as possible. "My dear, I haven't had an erection for fifteen years! And believe me, with my connections and money, there's been no shortage of attempts to remedy that. Something about you cured me, though. A legacy of your eminently talented mother, no doubt—fitting, as she was my last partner before I was struck with this inexplicable affliction."

A ragged breath sputtered from my lips as I scrubbed my eyes. How dare he speak of her with such casual ease? As if brutalizing my mother meant nothing to him. He didn't know or didn't care that she sacrificed the purest parts of herself to incite her dramatic revenge. A revenge that was null and void now, thanks to me.

Mama, I'm so sorry. I should've listened to you.

"I don't know what you're blabbering about," I gritted my teeth, trying to adjust my prone position, "but if you make me touch your dick again, I'll tear it out by the fucking roots."

Alastor undoubtedly planned something unspeakable, but if I had to go down, it would be with a fight. Carefully, though—I had to distract him enough so only I suffered. I couldn't allow him near my mother again.

I rocked against the cushions when his palm smacked my cheek. Swift and light, the unexpected assault stung my pride far more than my skin. I blinked back surprised tears and a wave of shame I hadn't earned.

"You will take care when you speak to me, young lady, or you'll learn to live without a tongue. Not that you'll need a tongue for what I have planned to finish our Samhain celebration."

Samhain, the old Celtic name for Halloween. Mama told me stories about the Irish pagan traditions—different from our own, but still a noble path to the gods. It'd been a day of sacrifice for several cultures, including the Celts, who sought to appease the gods before the Season of Death. They offered gifts and prayer, hoping to survive long enough to see the land reborn into abundant Spring.

Death for Life... Oh, fuck me.

"What are you going to do to me?"

"The party should wrap up soon, then our fun will begin." Alastor's self-satisfied grin spread like butter on toast. "My men will take you to our small island where you'll be prepared for the ritual. Also fitting, as it was the same ritual where I took your mother and broke *her* spirit. A fine night, even if there were some unexpected side effects, but now I don't need to worry about that."

"So you're going to rape me? Just you, or will your mindless cult friends join in?" I swallowed back an acidic burst of fear, attempting to appear braver than I felt. "Anyone ever tell you that literal Satanism is a joke? That it's not real?"

"How cute. Our Lord enjoys any opportunity to educate the ignorant." He patted my leg fondly. "Your mother tried the same argument, but she learned. In fact, our joining and her breaking allowed me to create a more visceral bond with our Lord. I'm eternally grateful to her for that, hence why I gave her such a lavish reward."

"You're crazy! And you won't break me, so don't waste your time," I scoffed, but quailed inside as he laughed again.

"What a precious thing you are! I must admit, the thought of you squirming beneath me arouses more excitement than I've felt in years. I may be unwilling to share such a treat, even with my dear brothers and sisters. But," his merry tone calmed into a good-natured warning, "if you're less enjoyable than I imagine, I won't hesitate to toss you to them. Be careful, they tend to grow frenzied when the spirit of our Lord is present."

A knock broke his concentration, allowing me time to compose myself. *Queen Hekate, protect me. Give me strength to face whatever's coming.*

"Sir, your wife was looking for you. Should we tell her you'll be delayed?" a tuxedo-clad meathead asked, tapping the wire at his ear.

"No, I'm heading back. Please escort my enchanting young friend to the island. No one is to harm or violate her before the ceremony. Is that understood? She's a bit feisty, so beware. Perhaps some duct tape over her mouth would be beneficial?"

"Understood, yes sir," the man said, retreating with a curt nod.

Who the hell are these people?

"All right, my dear. Forgive me, but I need to scoot the regular guests from my home. Only a little longer, then I'll rejoin you for the real party. I hope your enthusiasm grows. It wouldn't do to bore me." Alastor mocked me with a spry half-bow, adding one final tidbit. "And you should forget about my son coming to your rescue. That didn't work out so well for him with your mother. We simply told him you left, upset over your spat with my daughter's new boyfriend—Nolan, is it? Security confirmed he's driving through the neighborhood to find you. The poor, weak boy... He'll be gone for hours, but it's for the best. Once I offer to compare notes about your...finer qualities, he'll want nothing to do with you. Colburn men have their pride. We aren't known for sharing."

Gathering a final thread of courage, I threatened, "If you don't let me go, I have no problem killing you. I don't care what it does to my soul. Unlike your little cult, I have real magic to fight with."

He paused at the door, throwing me one last smile—moistened by a pink tongue racing across his thin lips. "That's what we're all counting on, my dear. Your soul is our Lord's prize, but we'll be more than satisfied with whatever's left. I'll see you shortly, Coralena."

***

I didn't fight against Meathead One and Two. Each wore a holster beneath their tuxedo jackets, armed with heavy guns in addition to their impossible muscles. Despite my bluff to Alastor, I'd never attempted offensive magic; I wasn't sure it was even possible. I refused to give up hope, but this wasn't the moment to test my potential capabilities. Mama never shared anything with me beyond approved spellwork. I'd have to dig deep to figure something out before the ritual began.

Rage, hatred, vengeance, a desire to inflict pain—those emotions would form the base. Thankfully, after spending some quality time with Alastor Colburn, I had plenty of negative emotions to turn into ammunition. There had to be a way to attack with magic, something more direct than time-released curses, otherwise the First Rule wouldn't be necessary.

The trip to the shore only took a few minutes in the golf cart. My captors cut the ties at my feet so I could walk. They didn't have to warn me not to run. I knew better. They helped me into the small speedboat, untethering us and driving toward the wooded island in the center of the small bay that opened into the Sound.

I closed my eyes, casting my mind back to that night. Mama in the kitchen before the stove, surrounded by flames and smoke from the herbs she tossed into her cauldron. So many Greek words my child's mind couldn't decipher eluded my adult memories. I knew bits and pieces of both my parents' native languages—Mama's Greek and Daddy's Spanish—but I was far from fluent in either. The only words I trained myself to memorize were pieces of spells or special prayers. Words of power, but would my will alone ignite them without any kindling from Nature?

Forget about my son...weak boy...out for hours, driving to find you.

Hayden believed I ran away. He wanted to find me. I shouldn't care. After accomplishing my mission, I planned on telling him off; but the way his father spoke about him, dripping with cold disdain, pricked my conscience. He resented Hayden for rescuing Mama. That was clear.

Aspasia said Alastor had punished him, too.

If he'd known where I was, maybe he would've fought for me. Hell, he hadn't even wanted to bring me here. Meanwhile, I only looked forward to hurting him. What if I'd been wrong, blaming him for something he tried to protect me from?

Stop thinking like that. Won't do any good. And you've got bigger problems than Hayden's feelings.

My thoughts cut off with the boat's engine. The island was close enough to touch. Balding trees and evergreen cypresses towered above the blasted mound of sand and rock. We drifted toward the small dock where another pair awaited. Hooded in black robes, they were faceless and shapeless except for a glimpse of white fingers folded against their stomachs.

"Up you go," Meathead One said, planting his legs to steady the narrow boat.

The pair on the docks were strong, holding each of my forearms and helping me up the ladder. "Tell Him we're all set here. Just standing by for the show."

Meathead Two nodded, cranking the engine before heading back to the mainland. Alone with a fresh pair of psychopaths, perfect. At the party, Alastor was surrounded by unsavory friends—many of whom I assumed were part of his cult. Two were here now, and more must've been on the way. How many enemies would I face during this ceremony?

"Let's go, and don't bother running," the one said—a man, by his deep voice and stubbled jaw. Most of his face was covered in a black half-mask beneath his hood.

"It'd be fun to catch her, though," a lighter voice said, feminine and sly behind a similar mask. She was taller than me, with shoulders as broad as her companion, super athletic and way beyond my league if it came to a physical altercation.

Don't panic. Pay attention to where they take you, and keep your eyes open for an escape.

The island wasn't huge, from what I could see in the poor light. Even with the mass of trees, water peeked through on all sides. A clearing lay toward the far end where another pair of robed figures chatted by a picnic table, working on a project by lantern light. Mixing something? Hard to see from this angle. Another pair continued to lay twigs and kindling at the base of an enormous pyre.

My feet tripped over my hem when I considered what else the pyre might burn, forcing my wardens to set me upright again. Rape was bad enough, a threat I refused to entertain because it might cripple my motivation. But what if I couldn't find a way out of this? After they used me, would I be tossed into the fire like one more log?

Burn the witch! A chorus of cries from some long-forgotten movie taunted me. Just one more persecuted witch in Connecticut, except there'd be no one to tell my tale or fight for justice on my behalf. No one knew where I was, stuck on a private island with a cult of delusional Satanists thirsting for their annual blood rite.

Mama, help me.

A tent lay on the outskirts of the morbid camp, our apparent destination. "Get in there," the man said, lifting the flap while the woman nudged me forward.

The tent smelled faintly of mildew, obviously not getting regular use. An army cot lay against one wall, while the other held a small table and chair. My prison cell for the next hour.

"Sit down and don't try anything funny. You're stuck here, so get used to it." The man removed more zip ties from a pocket of his robe, tying me to the chair.

"I don't see why we shouldn't test her out before he gets here. We had to leave the party early, barely any time to have some proper fun." The woman pouted beneath her half-mask. Her nail dragged lightly down my cheek.

I jerked back with a muffled curse, wishing the duct tape was off my mouth. I never wanted to spit on someone more than right now.

"You don't want to cross him, trust me. No piece of ass is worth that." The man tugged the ties over my upper my arms and ankles, testing their strength. With the zip ties already on my wrists, this new position was extra uncomfortable. My curled hands pressed against my heart, forcing my back into unnatural straightness. "Plus, it's more fun to have a go once they're broken in a bit."

"For you, maybe." The woman folded her arms over her chest while studying me. "Oh well, we can play once the ritual is underway. Don't worry, girl. I'll be sweet as pie as long as you mind your manners."

The duct tape blocked another string of curses, but it didn't matter. They just laughed, as if faced with a talking dog instead of a bound and scared woman. Unbelievable, that such people existed—true maniacs, in the flesh, not portrayed by actors on some television documentary or horror film.

"Leave her be. We have work to finish." The man waved in dismissal.

"Think happy thoughts." The woman gave a shrill laugh and pinched my cheek. "I'll be thinking them about you!"

The tent flap lowered behind them, a thin barrier against the fading chatter. A strange set of vibes filled the air, anticipation for a party balanced with solemnity for the upcoming ritual. They kept saying I had to stay unharmed and unsullied—ironic, given what they all hinted would happen to me in only an hour or so.

Time was running out. I needed to attempt a spell.

I searched the area, but the room was barren of anything useful. Even the lantern on the table was battery operated—not a true flame in sight. The floor of the tent was plastic, no access to the earth below. A cold night, but the tent's walls also kept out the fresh air. Blood, one of the most potent magical ingredients, wouldn't be an option unless I forced the zip ties to cut me. Or I could squeeze out some tears for salt and water.

Would it be enough, the blood and tears, even though I was gagged and my limbs restrained? I had no choice but to try.

Genuine tears filled my eyes after a minute or more of sawing my ankles and wrists against the bindings. Four slender rings of hot pain arose, but the stubborn skin refused to split open. Moving my wrists that much killed my shoulders and back. When I thought of Alastor's sick smile, the eager rod he forced into my hands, I sawed harder. This pain was nothing compared to what lay in store.

The tent flap raised again, stopping me cold while I sniffled back tears. I wouldn't cry in front of either of those lunatics. Especially that woman, who'd probably try to lick the water from my cheeks. Fuck the lot of them. I refused to feed their sickness with my fear.

But the stream soon overflowed when I saw him, the sliver of duct tape puffing over my shaky sobs. Hayden knelt before me, a finger to his lips and compassion beaming from his glorious eyes—almost as lovely as the small knife cutting away the zip ties. He worked quickly, focused on the task at hand instead of whatever psychic injuries pulsed from my face like a strobe light.

When my hands were free, they flew to my mouth and tore the duct tape away. Done with my feet, Hayden stood and helped me up. One set of whispered words stopped me from breaking into a run.

"Not a sound. Move when I move."

I nodded, not trusting myself to talk without screaming. All I could do was take his hand and follow.

We dove around the side of the tent, a move he must've judged safe from watchful eyes. Then we followed a path away from the camp, weaving through the ring of trees. My pulse galloped between my temples, down my neck and into my belly, every sense on high alert for enemy footsteps or voices. I glanced once, causing me to slam into Hayden's back. He squeezed my hand, a silent reproach for being careless. I didn't dare look back again.

After long minutes that stretched like days, we arrived on the other side of the island. Thank God it was only a blip of earth instead of some massive expanse. My unstable nerves couldn't handle a lengthy hike, ducking a team of black-clad Satanists in the dead of night.

Another speedboat awaited, tied to a nest of fallen branches. The icy seawater burned my feet and calves, raw from where I'd been bound. A moment of pain, then the healing liquid anesthetized my wounds. Hayden helped me into the boat, where I collapsed in a heap, then jumped in after untying the rope.

Both hands pressed to my mouth, hiding my anxious breaths. My trepidation grew, seasoned with a mad hope for freedom. We were almost away...so close. He rowed a few strokes, pointing us toward open waters, then powered up the motor. We sped for the opposite shore, away from the island and his family's home. Right hand steering the boat, eyes on the horizon, his left hand gave my shoulder a supportive squeeze.

Free, thank the gods. Maybe Hekate, Queen of the Night and Protector of Witches, heard my plea. Mama, I had to get home and warn her.

They'd be coming for us.

CHAPTER FOURTEEN

We docked at the town pier, abandoned at this time of night. Late autumn was too cold to be out on the water for pleasure, an activity which—even in the summer—seemed foolish and indulgent. Who had time to float on the sea for fun when there was work to be done?

"Hurry, Cori. We have to get on the road." Hayden pulled me up, nudging me toward the ladder. My numb legs rocked like stalks of uncooked spaghetti about to snap, but I forced them to obey.

"I need my mama." I struggled, climbing with icy hands that refused to fold properly.

He joined me on the dock, snatching my arms so quickly I cried out. "No. That's the first place they'll go, then she'll be in danger too. Give me your cell phone."

"Good idea. I'll call first and warn her." I fumbled with the pouch, finding the device and tapping the screen back to life.

Hayden grabbed the phone, smashing it against a nearby pole. Glass and plastic splintered, raining into the water until he tossed what was left. Red exploded across my field of vision, and I raised my fists to attack. I almost got him, but he easily blocked the strike.

"You motherfucker! What are you doing?" I wrestled away from his larger hands, kicking his shin instead. "I said I want my mother, now let me go!"

"Cori, we need to get you away from Greenwich. Stop fighting, goddammit." He winced at each blow, but stood firm. "Quiet down, and we can go somewhere safe."

"Safe? With you?" I laughed wildly. "You're one of them! That's your father who grabbed me and made me touch—"

"What? Did he... Jesus Christ." More hands crawled over my skin. His eyes narrowed to fierce laser points, searching for hidden wounds, as if he could've been as affronted as me. What the hell did he know?

"Stop touching me!" I pushed again, slapping his face hard enough to sting my hand. "He hurt my mama, not me. But you knew all about it, didn't you? You lied to me! I'm not going anywhere with you. Fuck off!"

Hayden flinched, though his jaw was locked in a cage of contracting muscles. His grip loosened, almost enough to let me go; he changed his mind, tightening even more. In a low, hard voice he ordered, "We can talk about this in the car, but let's get one thing straight: you're coming with me, right now. You will allow me to save you. If I have to knock your ass out and drag you along this fucking dock, I will. Don't test me, Cori."

Our feet thumped across the wood, a steady patter as we half-ran to the parking lot. The marina was only a mile or so from home. I'd walk if I had to. No way would I abandon my mother to Alastor Colburn and his goons.

The sleek sports car came into view, a modern-day chariot wrapped in shadows that dissipated when a click of his keychain turned on the lights. We walked around to the passenger side. He tugged on my wrists when I paused, ignoring how raw they were from his father's bindings. One last chance.

I kicked his kneecap, staggering him, then took off. I focused on the streetlights at the far end of the lot, refusing to look back. The adrenaline kept me from stumbling. I almost thought I'd escape, but he caught up thanks to those long legs. He pinned my arms to my sides, lifting me off the ground. He turned toward the car, steady even as I fought back with all my might.

"I don't want to hurt you, but you have to come with me. We don't have much time," he grunted, trying to force me into the passenger seat. "These people are powerful and crazy. You're not safe here. If you go to your mother, they'll take you both. Is that what you want?"

"I just want to go home, away from all of you!" The furious cry broke something in my chest. A series of ragged sobs followed, tumbling from my aching throat.

Hayden knelt, carefully buckling me into the seat. He wiped the stream of tears from my cheeks and said thickly, "I'll protect you. Trust me, please. Let me help you."

"Trust you?" I choked as a rush of cool air unbalanced the heat in my lungs. "I fucking hate you!"

He stiffened, taking a moment to consider what I said. He nodded crisply and stood. "Let's get out of here. We'll figure out a safe way for you to call your mother, I promise."

The door shut, sealing me in a bubble of silence. My mind body trembled with so many useless emotions—rage, fear, sadness. No way to go home, no way to fight back... I was useless. A witch who couldn't unlock her full powers, as castrated by ignorance as Alastor Colburn had been from Mama's spell until I somehow broke it.

They would hunt for me, I had no doubt. They'd go to Cornucopia first, tear the place apart... Or maybe not. Manpower, money, technology—who knew what they had available? I was just a girl with an unreliable ability to enhance food or beverages with magic, a step above some carnival fortune teller. I didn't stand a chance.

***

We didn't speak on the trip down I-95. There was nothing to say—at least, nothing that didn't involve more screaming. I silently dared him to speak so I could lash out again, but he only drove with that same rigid frown—as if he shared even a fraction of the anger burning through me.

I didn't expect him to pull over so soon. We hadn't even hit the border. A rest area sprawled ahead, crowded with lines of tractor trailers but few cars. He parked by the main building, turned off the engine, and took a deep breath.

"There are still some functioning pay phones in here. Call your mother, but make it quick. I don't know how long it takes to trace a phone call, but I assure you the people in that group have access to others who can track you that way," Hayden said with all the enthusiasm of a rusty robot. "Don't tell her anything about me, even though they'll probably come to my place after hers."

"Is this for real?" The rest area's floodlights unnerved me. I imagined hooded figures in the shadows, waiting to pounce once I left the security of the car.

"If you'll listen without screaming, I'll tell you whatever you want to know." He stared straight ahead, half-shrouded in darkness. "I didn't tell you the truth about your mother, but it wasn't my story to share. Maybe I shouldn't have." He faced me again, appearing weary, but I didn't have any sympathy to spare. "I never meant for all this to happen. If you give me a chance, Cori, I will help you fix it."

"Let's go, then." I cowered beneath my hooded cloak, striding toward the well-lit building. He caught up quickly, never touching me, but close enough I smelled the citrus in his aftershave.

Once inside, I made a beeline for the digital payphones by the bathrooms. Hayden handed me some bills, gesturing toward the travel store on our right. "That should be more than enough. I'll get a change of clothes and some other stuff. Stay close, and don't talk long."

He appeared older than twenty-nine under the unforgiving fluorescents. His white makeup had grown patchy. The once-dapper vampire suit was wrinkled and stained from the boat trip and crawl through the woods—a pitiful sight, though I couldn't have looked much better. I nodded, not trusting myself to speak where others might overhear. So many emotions continued to throb, aching for release, but I had to hold back. Until I figured out what to do, I couldn't afford to make this crisis worse.

I dialed Mama's cell phone from memory, the number she had for half of my life and insisted I memorize. A good thing, too, because this most definitely counted as an emergency.

After two rings, I bit back a fresh sob at the beloved but fearful voice. "Hello? Cori, is that you?"

"Oh, Mama," I blurted, terrified as the pressures of the night crashed over me once more, "I'm in trouble."

"Where are you? I'm leaving right now."

"You can't. They kidnapped me, the Col... I mean, the ones who hurt you before. I got away, though. I'm all right, for now." I glanced back toward the travel shop, but I didn't see Hayden anywhere. "I'll find a way to get back to you."

A pause, then she spoke—each word winding her voice into a tighter knot. "No, stay away. They may have begun the hunt, so you can't be here. Find a place to hide. Mail me a postcard in a few days, but don't tell me where you are. Or create a fake email address and only check it from someplace public, like the library. I'll contact you once I set them on another trail."

"I'm so scared," I confessed, leaning against the partition dividing each phone. "Why is this happening?"

"It's complicated, but it's our gift. It draws them, feeds whatever darkness fuels them. But you have to go now. Don't call again. No electronics, unless its public and away from wherever you're staying," she said, brisk as usual whenever catastrophe struck, but her last words swelled with sorrowful longing. "I love you, baby—more than anything. Stay safe for me."

"I love you, Mama." My lips continued to move, yearning to add so much more, but she hung up. I was left with a metallic dial tone, listening to the hum until it cut off.

Dammit. No, no, no!

I didn't get to tell her I was sorry, that whatever happened was my fault. I'd riled up a threat which had assaulted our family once but moved on. I should've left things alone, never made Hayden take me to that awful party, listened to Mama's wisdom when I had the chance.

With my idiotic plan for revenge, I'd doomed us all.

CHAPTER FIFTEEN

We were back on I-95, headed to New York City. At least, I assumed that was our destination. What better place to lose oneself than the most crowded city in the country?

"So what's the plan?" I asked, counting the mile markers flying past the window. At least I was fully warm again. Hayden had bought me an "I Love New York" sweatshirt and yoga pants from the travel shop, along with a bag full of snacks and toiletries. He told me to change in the bathroom and toss out my costume. Not a problem. I couldn't stand the sight of it.

"I've got some cash. We'll get you a hotel room for a few days," Hayden said evenly, focused on the widening freeway. "I'll think of an excuse once they pay me a visit. Something like I tried to find you, but you vanished."

"Mama said she'd point them in another direction, too." I tucked my fingers into the sweatshirt sleeves, trying to stop their continued drumming against my thighs. "She sounded like you, warning me away from technology and telling me to hide."

"She'll be fine. She knows how to handle them. If they hadn't worked out some kind of deal, she wouldn't have the restaurant...or still be alive."

"It'd take a lot more than that to keep *me* quiet," I muttered.

"Don't be stupid, Cori," Hayden snapped. "You think the restaurant was a reward for a job well done? Your mother took what they offered to protect you. If she didn't play nice, they wouldn't be able to trust her. Do you understand? They would've killed her—and maybe you, too, just as a precaution."

"So why the hell don't you do something? You could fight back instead of taking their trust fund and going to fancy parties like everything is normal." I could yell too. I relished the tightness of his lips and erratic bobbing of his Adam's apple. The leather steering wheel creaked beneath his fists. Anger, good—I wanted him hurt and scared. I shouldn't be the only one hanging onto sanity by a fraying thread. "You lied to me, acting all sweet and hitting on me. You *knew* what your father did to my mother, but you still pursued me. How dare you?"

"You have no idea what I've done, the things I've endured... You don't get to judge me." He finally faced me, unleashing an electric rage which paused my racing heart. "I didn't want to go to the goddamn party. You did, and why was that? If you knew what happened to your mother, why in the hell did you choose to stroll right into the lion's den?"

"I was going to kill him!" Even though it had failed spectacularly, sharing my plan felt empowering. Also, the sentiment spurring me on hadn't died; if anything, I was more pissed off than ever.

"Are you insane?" Hayden demanded, torn between outrage and amused disbelief. "Kill Alastor Colburn, in his own home, while he's surrounded by friends and security guards. How was that supposed to work? I didn't notice any weapons on you when we were...close."

Flushing at the memory, I went back to staring at my mile markers. "I made a poison."

"Poison? Fucking hell... Like no one would notice one of the few strangers at a crowded party acting suspicious—not to mention how easily they could trace it through forensics," he said, each word laced with derision. "Where'd you get such a dumb idea?"

"Look, I knew what I was doing—in theory." I fully turned my back, trying to ignore his ridicule. "You don't know anything about me. I'm not some helpless idiot."

"Oh no, of course not. That's why you got caught and dragged to a

Satanic ritual as the guest of fucking honor. You had it all under control, obviously."

"I swear to God, if you don't shut the fuck up—"

"You'll what? Poison me, too?" The scornful laughter snagged my attention, and I whirled around. I didn't care how fast we were going, I'd smack the shit out of him.

"I have gifts, okay? Mama and I both do. That's why they want us. As soon as I can, I'm going back to finish what I started."

"What gifts? Baker and coffee master, Sorceress Supreme of Spaghetti?"

"We're witches, you dickhead!" I smacked the dashboard. "Why do you think people love Cornucopia so much? We're no better than the other restaurants in town. We *spell* the food and the drinks. Mama's been doing it for years!"

His harsh laughter faded as the words sunk in, paling his ruddy skin and mocking smile. "Spelled food? Like the coffees you made me, those desserts and the pasta... Did you drug me, too?"

Blood rushed to my cheeks, as if whatever passion inflamed him transferred to me. Didn't last, though; it curdled with unexpected shame. "It wasn't like that."

"No? How was it, then?" He grew subdued, reminiscent of his icy mother. "Ever since that night with Bronte and Nolan, I couldn't get you out of my head. It was worse after I picked up the damned cake—which I offered to do because I stayed up half the night thinking about you. The way we danced at the club, then when you cooked for us, and later in my room... I've never felt so out of control, and it was all a lie. Just some spell you cast—for what, to hurt me?"

"No! That's not how the magic works," I protested, but my righteous fire died beneath his gust of justified rancor. I studied the limp hands in my lap, chilled by the realization of how he must've felt.

I had lied, just like him. *No, not like him.* But was it that different?

"My powers just started this week. I can't control them. Mama trained me for this my entire life, and I've been trying to hold back. The spells are suggestive, but not any kind of mind-control. The magic wears off once the food is gone. Your feelings...those were all you, just boosted a bit."

"Too bad," he replied, taking the exit into the city. "After hearing this,

I'd really love nothing more than to hate you, too. Maybe you can make me something to fix that?"

Swallowing back the hurt, I didn't say anything else. Soon, though. He owed me, and I wasn't done collecting.

***

We rode the elevator to the third floor. The hotel wasn't far from Hayden's restaurant, only a couple of blocks down St. Marks. It was plain, but at least everything was clean. The only noises were from the traffic, but even that was muted by the deafening weight of our mutual resentment and betrayals.

How would this arrangement work? He offered to help, but refused to look at me. I was too tired to fake it anymore, but I couldn't let him leave without more answers.

Once in the room, tinier than my snug bedroom in Greenwich, I finally spoke again. "You promised me an explanation."

"Yeah, but I'm a liar and an asshole, remember? Why would you listen?" He tossed the plastic room key on the narrow bureau already crowded by an old flat-screen TV.

"What is this cult all about, and what do they want?" I ignored his theatrics, sitting on the squeaky bed.

"My dad and his friends made it up. It's based on some old-English, Aleister Crowley shit—a hero of his, naturally. They both used sex and drugs in rituals, trying to communicate with their version of the gods, obsessed with the idea of magic as a tool and a weapon," Hayden began, trying to fit his tall frame in the dainty corner chair. "At least, that's what I found in my research."

"Research? You mean your dad didn't try to bring you in?" I asked with naked suspicion, recalling Nolan's laughing face with his hopes of some sort of recruitment. If they'd consider an ass like him, the initiation process couldn't be too rigorous.

"Maybe he would've once, but I ruined my chances after helping your mom." He shrugged, car keys clinking in his hand. "I was too late to save her from the worst, but I saw...stuff. I still have nightmares, even after all these years. Shit like that, no one should see. But I was only thirteen. I did the best I could. She cried when I sneaked into the tent, hugged me. After we took the boat back, she thanked me and apologized for causing any trouble."

The lifeless words punched my chest. I'd never heard such a recollection, a weary confession of unconscionable childhood trauma. He carried that weight alone for sixteen years. Mama had suffered. I felt it during her story. My recent experiences drove the worst parts of her tale home. But what if she wasn't the only victim that night?

"Dad rolled back the security footage, saw me helping your mother back to the cottage. He took me downstairs where we have a panic room. Lead-lined walls, air-tight, with only a couple of bunk beds and shelves." He took a deep breath, as if working up his nerve. "He tied me to the bed and beat the shit out of me. Then he locked the door. I spent a week like that, mostly in the dark and with no company. He only allowed my mother to bring me food and water. Maybe that was to punish her, too.

"When they let me out, my bags were packed. They sent me off to New Hampshire for prep school. Mother and Bronte visited for holidays. After a few months, I was permitted to join them at different vacation spots during school breaks. I barely saw my father after that, which was fine by me." He finally faced me once more, a fierce pride glinting behind his darkened gaze. "Then I was an adult. I had limited access to my trust fund, and I got accepted to NYU for business. I made my own choices. The first one was staying far away from Greenwich."

"Why did you come back?" I asked, unable to suppress my curiosity after the intense tale.

"My mother asked me to," he replied with a rueful smile. "Bronte's been struggling in school, partying too much. She's finally sowing her wild oats. Mom hoped I could talk some sense into her. She asked me to look out for her at the party, but we all know how *that* went. My sister's been the last thing on my mind since meeting you again."

The barb stung, but I pressed forward like a curious kid picking at a scab. "The cult...what else do you know about them?"

"*Lupus Filios*, Children of the Wolf," he replied, translating the Latin before I asked. "From what I caught of the ritual, the demon they worship is Mammon. Allegedly, he's some demon lord of greed—an ideal deity for these power-hungry captains of industry. They meet occasionally at one place or another around the world, but every Halloween there's a full ritual. Conspiracy theorists on the internet hint about sex rites and general debauchery, but it's all hearsay. No one credible ever spoke up, but what I saw wasn't too far off the mark."

"A ritual every year? So there were fifteen other victims after my mother?" I shuddered at the thought of more abused women, hiding like Mama—or worse, maybe they never found a way back from that godforsaken island.

"No, I don't think so." He shook his head, adamant. "I eventually worked up the nerve to ask my mother the summer before I went to NYU. She took me on a special trip to Athens to visit her cousins. She told me Dad hadn't been the same since that night. He was impotent and cut the sex from the rituals out of frustration. She has her sources among his friends, although she'd never tell me who. I didn't want to push her, but she wouldn't lie to me."

I envisioned the refined lady who'd warned me away from her son—imperious, but polite in her way—not what I expected. She hardly seemed a fitting match for her roguish husband. "Why would she stay with such a monster?"

"Where could she go if he didn't want her to leave?" Hayden spat, defending her and maybe angry at the position she was in. "These people in the cult, they're not regular rich people. They're CEOs, politicians, financiers—people with unlimited power and money who have friends everywhere. They can do what they want—rape, kill, it's all just covered up. If Mother tried to leave, unless my father allowed it, she'd have already met with some tragic accident. There's no divorce in this group."

I hadn't expected to sympathize with Aspasia. Despite her wealth, she wasn't much better off than my mother. Gifted with a comfortable life in exchange for silence, taking a despicable deal to protect the family she loved. How many other women were in the same boat, wives of those horrid men, blackmailed into compliance? And that nasty woman who taunted me, did she have a significant other who suspected what she was yet stayed by her side out of fear?

"That's terrible." I crossed my legs beneath me, huddling in a defensive pose. "Does Bronte know what you both have been through?"

"No, we tried our best to keep her out of it," he replied with renewed vigor. "She's aware we have a strained relationship with Dad, but not the specific details. Please don't tell her if you see her again. It's safer that way."

We sat in silence for a minute, each of us rebalancing our burdens after this long night of traumatic memories and exposed secrets. The sky peeked through the blinds; still dark, but it had to be nearing sunrise. Hard to believe only a few hours ago I'd snuggled against Hayden in his treehouse, our lips locked while we floated through our brief dance. I didn't even feel like the same youthful girl anymore. Tonight's close calls and bitter revelations drained me dry.

"So what's next?" I asked finally, raising my arms to stretch the kinks from my back. "Do I live here now, locked away in a hotel, waiting for you to bring me food? Never allowed to see my family and friends again? Or maybe your dad and his buddies will track me down and bust through the door to finish what they started."

"We'll figure something out. Hang tight for a couple of days." He left the chair, sitting instead at the opposite corner of the bed. His expression softened, absent of his earlier anger, but I sensed a wall rising between us—flinty as those chilled blue eyes, intent on keeping me out. "I'm sorry this happened, Cori. No one deserves to be terrorized. I'll help you and your mother. It's time to finally finish this."

"Are you leaving?" I asked, hating the whiny catch at the end of my question. I'd been so furious with Hayden, but after his story, I wasn't sure how to feel. Could I trust him? Did his multiple rescues and seemingly sincere desire to help override the evil acts committed by his father?

I knew one thing: I was scared to death. How could I find any peace stuck in a random hotel room in New York City, waiting for the wolves to sniff me out?

"I can go, if you'd rather be alone." When I shook my head, he nodded. "Okay, let's try to get some sleep. I'll lay on the floor, and you take the bed."

"It's cold, and the room is too small. Don't worry about it for now."

We settled in the lumpy queen-sized bed, but Hayden stayed above the covers—flat on his back, while I curled to face the wall. I listened to his breathing, deepening to soft snores once he fell asleep.

Awake, I counted the seconds that faded along with the last shreds of my freedom. I couldn't hide from my new enemies forever. This was their world; New York City, a sprawling domain built to accommodate a band of kings who made their own rules. Who was I to stand against such a force?

CHAPTER SIXTEEN

I couldn't fall back asleep after Hayden left. Instead, I replayed our last conversation.

He hadn't meant to wake me, but my nerves were so unsettled I bolted upward when the mattress shifted. Seemingly reluctant to leave, he apologized again for startling me. Kind of him, even though last night's argument left both of us unsure of how to handle each other.

My father might send people to the restaurant. I have to be there, or it'll be a dead giveaway. Go back to sleep, keep the door locked, and don't use the phone. I'll send someone to bring you food if I get stuck—Francisco, he's trustworthy.

How will I know it's him? I'd asked, clutching the blankets against my chest.

He's one of a kind, don't worry. Hayden had given me a fleeting smile, patting my foot as he gathered his coat and keys. *Picture a giant covered in tribal tattoos with hair like an Easter egg. He looks rough, but he's a big baby.*

Will your father hurt you? With my last question, I'd leapt to follow him to the door.

No, men like him never throw away their only son. I'm safe enough for now. He'd reached out, then changed his mind, stuffing his hands into his pockets. *Slide the bolt on and stay here. Please Cori, it's important.*

I punched his pillow, then held it to my chest. Diving beneath the covers again, all I wanted was to sleep until this whole mess passed us by.

***

I hated the room after only a few hours.

The water pressure was nonexistent, a lukewarm stream incapable of piercing my thick curls. The soap and shampoo smelled like vanilla cucumbers, a combination I didn't realize would've been gag-worthy. And I was starving. The snacks from the rest area were good enough for breakfast, but the processed treats didn't satisfy for long.

Hayden promised he wouldn't forget about me. I had to trust his word after what he risked in saving me last night...or did it count as morning, given when we finally settled in the hotel? Too confusing—my body wasn't used to these wild, late nights.

I missed Mama and Monica, everyone at the restaurant, and I hadn't even made it twenty-four hours. We were a family, bonded through love and years of shared memories. The ancient brown phone never rang, but I found my eyes drawn to it frequently. My end was safe, but what if Hayden was right and someone had tapped Mama's phone? I'd done all this in her honor, and it would be foolish to disregard that sacrifice and endanger her again. Best she didn't know where I was. If she was interrogated, she could answer honestly.

Another judge show rolled across the screen, and I buried my face in the pillow to hide a groan. How many of these shows were there? I hadn't watched daytime tv in years, always healthy and never one to skip school. Plus, Mama and I preferred streaming for our infrequent movie nights. Unbelievable that people watched crap like this on purpose.

A knock sounded at the door, and I rushed to mute the tv. Quiet now, not a noise from either side of the barrier. I tiptoed to check the peephole. The "Do Not Disturb" sign was out, so it couldn't be housekeeping. Was it Hayden, or maybe his friend? Had to be. No one else could've found me yet.

I flinched from the peephole after another round of knocks,

repositioning my eye and fingering the latch. That had to be Francisco, ducking to ensure I saw the head that would've otherwise been too tall for easy visibility. I doubted a hitman prowled the East Village with a cotton-candy pink mohawk.

I cracked the door. "Francisco?"

"Claro, who else were you expecting?" he trilled, impatiently busting through with a large plastic bag.

Hayden hadn't exaggerated his size. Francisco filled the room, nearly seven feet tall and built like a fortress. Thick, ropy muscles stressed the seams of a lime velour shirt which paired nicely with his buttery suede slacks. He was gorgeous, even with the outrageous hair; fierce, with vibrant tattoos peeking over the edges of his shirt like flowers climbing a living wall.

"You brought me lunch?" I sniffed over the bag like a starving dog.

"Espero que tengas hambre, porque hice un banquete!" he rattled off, too fast to follow, but I understood about half the words.

"Um... No hablo español. Lo siento." I flushed with embarrassment.

"What? No eres Latina? Girl, you look like mi prima." Francisco examined me, eyes narrowed with mistrust.

"Kinda, but not really. My dad was from Puerto Rico, but he died when I was five. He never had a chance to teach me much. I learned what I could in school, but it's not the same, you know?"

"Ah niña, mis condolenscias." He crushed me against him in an impulsive hug. "Me and my big mouth. Don't pay me no mind. My parents died when I was a kid, back in El Salvador. Mi tío y tía lived here in New York and brought me here after the funeral. They saved me. Yo tambien lo siento for all you've lost. Familia, heritage...it matters, niña. Food for the soul, no?"

"Mis condolenscias," I parroted, hoping my accent was passable. My Spanish had rusted after sophomore year when I wasn't required to take a language anymore. Maybe I should have; Francisco had a point about staying connected to our ancestral roots.

"Está bien, niña. I'll help you practice more once El Príncipe releases you from whatever type of prison this is," Francisco said, folding his arms over his chest and clucking at the tiny room. "He wouldn't even tell me your name, like it's some big secret."

"I guess it kind of is," I said, missing my mother even more after this barrage of well-intentioned concern. "Some nasty people are looking for me, so it might not be safe to share much."

"Niña, do I look like I scare easily?" He made an excellent point, and I shrugged helplessly. "So tell me! Or at least let me pick a cute nickname?"

"I'm Coralena, but you can call me Cori." I offered my hand for a proper shake, but he laughed and hugged me again. His tree-limb biceps squeezed every trace of oxygen from my lungs, but I didn't mind. Such a hug when one was scared felt pretty good.

"Ah, sí! You're La Cocinera Misteriosa, stealing all my herbs and whatever else for the midnight pasta party." He attempted to chastise me but, with such a wide smile, I couldn't take him seriously. "And no one even saved me a bowl, but it's okay. At least you cleaned up, more than El Príncipe ever does after his crazy snacks and private parties."

"Does he have lots of parties? Lots of ladies spending the night?" I prodded, offended by the thought of being one in a train of girls after his fiancée left. Young, handsome, rich—he probably swam in a sea of willing volunteers...that bastard.

"Oh no, Coralita, you won't get me in trouble with El Príncipe. I do not mess with other people's love lives. Unless you want to share some secrets?" One of his delicate eyebrows arched, then he waved in refusal. "No! Do not tempt me, querida. My imagination runs wild without help. Now, I must return before one of those burros burns my kitchen down."

"Thank you again, Francisco. It means a lot to me, the lunch and the risk you took bringing it here."

"De nada, Coralita, my pleasure." He patted my head, then opened the door to peek outside. "Next time, you cook for me. We'll break you out of this prisión de pesadilla. Buenas tardes, querida—stay strong!"

My cheeks tingled from the smile Francisco inspired, an invigorating change after hours of torturous anxiety and second-guessing. Bolting the door again, I sat cross-legged on the bed to pig out.

Soup, salad, and an array of roasted meats and vegetables awaited. Someone even packed fresh-baked rolls and herb butter. More than I could eat, even though my body seemed to want it all. Each scent and taste was a testament to quality ingredients prepared by a master. I wouldn't mind watching Francisco the Head Chef in action. Maybe he could teach me a thing or two.

At the bottom of the bag, I found a different container. Plain brown cardboard, maybe from another restaurant? A decadent slice of chocolate cake sat inside the box, and wrapped in a bit of tissue paper, a single purple iris.

I forgot my lunch for a moment, carefully removing the fragile hothouse bloom and sniffing the petals. This was a spring flower. Someone must've run to a florist and crossed their fingers to find this. A flower Mama used to inspire love, a frequent gift for my birthday since they were the flower for that month. One of her favorites, as well, when we studied botany together.

Wisdom, faith, and hope...all the things you wish upon someone you love, Mama had told me once, kissing my cheek and holding me so tight.

It was a kind gesture, a step toward a more respectful relationship... or friendship. Did Hayden know about flower meanings, or was this a coincidence? I'd never told him that story about me and Mama.

Grabbing one of my empty water bottles, I filled it from the bathroom sink and set it beside the flashing tv. Only one flower, but it brightened the dull room. My lunch tasted even better now with a sign of life so close, a well-wish lifting my spirits and calming my overstressed heart.

***

Another knock woke me from the thin nap I'd sunk into, each insistent tap a fishhook trawling across my battered brain. The yellow glow of the lamp saved me from tripping, and I eventually made it to the door. What time was it? A maw of black night expanded beyond the lone window. Always disorienting how the world grew dark so fast this time of year.

"Cori, it's me."

Ah, finally! Maybe he had news to share? I flung the door open, heartened by the bags in his hand and the bright eyes slicing through the room's gloom. He was safe and didn't seem as upset as last night.

"What time is it?" I asked, rubbing the grogginess from my face.

"I'm sorry, I tried to hurry. It's just after nine," Hayden said, setting the bags on the floor. He paused by the iris, standing straight and proud in the slim water bottle. "Francisco offered to cover for me since there's been a car parked out front most of the day with some goon in it. I sneaked out the back door and walked here. I left my phone in the office, turned on in case they track it with GPS."

"This is crazy." I watched as he unwound from his layers. A black knit cap concealed his blond hair, but he also wore a dark scarf, black wool coat, and matching gloves. It was a miracle he wasn't hit while crossing the street. "How long can we keep this up? I don't know how many more days I can stay locked in this cube."

"Try to hang on a little longer. I'll move you somewhere better once it's safe." He forced a smile, unpacking one of the bags. "Now let's eat. I'm starving, and Francisco packed us a mountain of pasta. He said something about letting the games begin. He's dying to have some sort of Latino cook-off with you. I told him you had secret Greek weapons, but he rolled his eyes and said that didn't matter."

"He was really nice. Thanks for sending him along." I sat beside Hayden, studying my bowl of homemade noodles filled with seared chunks of seafood and vegetables, all topped with a rosy cream sauce. After one bite, I moaned, "Oh my God, the gauntlet is definitely thrown. I don't think I can compete with this."

Hayden took a sizable bite, licking the extra sauce off his lips while he chewed with grave contemplation. "Yeah... I mean, it's awesome. That's why I hired him. The dude's a maniac in the kitchen, but the pasta you made for us was still the best dinner I've ever had."

"No, that's just the magic you remember. My actual cooking skills have nothing on Francisco's." I averted my eyes, stung again by the memory of our recent argument.

I'd love to hate you, too. Maybe you can make me something to fix that.

"Nah, I don't believe you." He gave my knee a companionable nudge with his. I drank in the genuine smile and compliments. "You learned from Tessa, first off, and she's the best chef I know. Your magic goes way beyond cooking. That's all you, Cori. No one else can touch that."

Staring into his encouraging face, illuminated by some inner light I'd never seen on anyone else, I felt suddenly blessed. This beautiful man, fearsome and angry the other night, was also capable of unsolicited empathy and sincere support—two things I needed more than ever. How could he do that with a string of ordinary, if kind, words?

"Thank you, Hayden." My mouth snapped shut before I gushed something that might embarrass us both.

"Don't thank me." He shook his head, poking at his dinner with a sudden lack of interest. "It's my fault you're in this mess now. I should've stayed away from you, let you live your life as your mother intended. Maybe then my fucked-up family wouldn't have interfered."

"Hey, I made a choice too." I set my dinner aside to grab his hand. "I didn't have to go with you that night. I'm glad I know the truth now, even if it landed me in this horrible place. My mama suffered enough for me. I want to help her. I don't care if it puts me in danger. I'd help you, too, if I could, for protecting me, hiding me... You came back for me. You didn't have to do any of that."

"Yes, I did. I couldn't live with myself if he hurt you. It's hard enough knowing what your mother went through, not to mention the nightmares I still have about who else he may've hurt over the years. I can't let him do this again. It's not right."

"You're a good man," I declared, blushing at the spontaneous statement.

I'd been wrong to hate Hayden, but he made such an easy target. Maybe I damaged us permanently with my outpouring of vitriol—or not; there might be hope for a reconciliation. He was still here, offering himself as a knight in my time of need.

"I don't know about that. My motivations aren't all unselfish, no matter what you choose to believe." He shook my hand off, gesturing toward my abandoned dinner. "Now, eat. You need to stay healthy."

What if he was right, and I only saw what I wanted? He made a perfect hero with his golden good looks, cool confidence, and natural sense of authority. Of course he had other reasons, less pure than simply doing what was right. He hated his father, possibly even more than I ever could.

And just maybe, something else motivated him—the waning glimmer of desire we'd once shared. Those previous encounters seemed like they occurred a lifetime ago. They lingered, though, filling me with evocative images and ardent emotions I'd never forget.

Maybe that tainted something in me, too. Despite our horrible argument, the dangers we faced, and the specific threat to my family, I couldn't help but want him still. Goddess, what a fool... I was glad my mother couldn't see me like this, forgoing common sense and caution to indulge in girlish fantasies about a guy. She'd raised me to be smarter than that.

CHAPTER SEVENTEEN

The next day followed the same pattern, as did the day after. Francisco brought me lunch and sat with me while I ate, cheering me with his natural exuberance, strange sense of humor, and tales of working with El Príncipe. By the way they both talked, Hayden and Francisco, it was clear they valued each other both as friends and co-workers.

"...and he wanted cauliflower, but I say no—asqueroso! I don't care how many gringos want it. Ay, I hate trends. So I made jicama frita instead, and it sells like crazy. I remind him soy un genio, and he's lucky I saved him again."

I laughed, finishing my portion of the delicious jicama fries while Francisco braided my damp hair. "I'm glad you stood your ground. This is amazing, by the way. My mama would love it."

My smile faded at the thought of Mama... Less than an hour away, but it felt like the other side of the world. I set my to-go box on the table, my appetite lost.

"No Coralita, don't be sad. El Príncipe may not be un genio like me, but he will find a way to help you." Francisco finished my braid, then hugged me tight. "I see how he cares for you. He was never like that with..."

"With who?" I prompted when his voice trailed off, already suspecting the who he meant.

"Oh no, you will not make un chismoso of me." He waved me away, gathering his coat and satchel. He paused by the door, cursed, then faced me. "Okay, so yes, he planned to marry another. And *that* cabrona estúpida...never mind. But that ended months ago! I will tell you one more thing, but that's it, chica curiosa: he never spoke of her the way he does of you."

My heart flipped at the switch in tone, exasperated to gentle, his dark eyes brimming with sympathy. "Thanks Francisco, but you know that doesn't matter. There isn't anything going on between Hayden and me."

Francisco's eyes bulged, then rolled back as booming laughs rumbled from his thick throat. "Coralita, eres divertidísima! You may be able to fool each other, pero veo la verdad. That's okay, I got a feeling you two will figure it out."

***

I poked at my dinner, still stuck on Francisco's frustrating hints and teasing laughter. Okay, so maybe I shouldn't have tried to fool him. Even after what we'd been through, a stubborn attraction lingered between Hayden and I, but that didn't mean anything. Whatever we may have felt that night couldn't survive what we'd been through, or the pain we'd caused each other.

"Cori, either spit out whatever's on your mind or eat," Hayden sighed, clicking off the latest cop drama and abandoning his own meal. "If something's bothering you—"

"Why would anything be bothering me? I've always begged Mama for a vacation, and look at me now—three days in fabulous New York City! Never mind that I'm hiding from demon-worshipping rapists and trapped in this dingy cubicle." I gestured at the tiny room with a sardonic grin, then threw my napkin over the delicious but unsatisfying meal.

"I know you're frustrated..."

"You have no idea what I'm going through." I stood to pace, stopping at the window and yanking back the curtain. The lights of the East Village twinkled in mockery, and I smacked the wall beside my only view of the world outside. "Frustrated? That barely scratches the fucking surface."

He gave me a moment to stew, then said with infuriating patience, "I spent a week locked in a panic room, mostly alone and in the dark. I understand more than you realize."

I rested my head against the cool glass, closing my eyes to avoid what his reminder conjured. A young boy, hurt and afraid, unsure what might follow his father's vicious punishment for defending my mother. "Dammit, I'm sorry. What you must've gone through... I hate being trapped and scared, that's all. I didn't mean to take it out on you."

"You don't have to apologize. I'm not upset—not at you, anyway." His voice grew closer as he moved to the other side of the window, but I couldn't look over. His kindness only made me feel worse.

"Can we talk about anything else? I think about this all day while I'm stuck in here. I can't do it right now."

"That's fine. We'll find something on tv—you pick. And I won't fight you over that last slice of cake, either."

His light banter inspired a weak chuckle as I rolled away from the glass for a glimpse of his reassuring smile. "Why are you doing this for me, Hayden? You don't have to, you know."

"I want to." Luminous eyes met mine, then slid away when he turned to dispose of our dinner. "Go ahead, see what you can find for us to watch. I'll run this to the trash."

I flopped on the bed, flipping through the scant amount of functioning channels but barely paying attention. Hayden seemed to be handling this far better than me, and it was hard not to lash out. He did have more experience with this madness. Still, I could tell he was struggling, too.

The isolation sucked, but even worse, I didn't know what might happen next. How hard were Alastor and his cronies searching? Was Mama all right? Did they bust down her door looking for me yet? I couldn't let my mind wander to worst-case scenarios, or imagine what my mother's screams sounded like.

I found on an old movie by the time Hayden returned—a comedy, at least. I doubted either of us would actually laugh, but it was better than continuing to sink into despair.

He tossed me the small box with the slice of cake, sitting in the chair by the bed and resting his feet on the mattress. We watched the movie while I nibbled on the cake, sneaking an occasional glance when he chuckled at something on the screen.

I supposed things could've been worse. At least I wasn't alone.

***

I rolled over again with a sigh, kicking my feet from under the covers. They'd gotten too warm. Maybe that was why I couldn't fall asleep.

"Stop it," Hayden mumbled from the far side of the bed.

"Sorry," I cringed, glancing over my shoulder.

"What time is it?"

"Just after two."

"Go to sleep."

"I can't." I rolled onto my back and stared at the shadows wavering along the ceiling. "Hayden?"

"Hmmm?"

"Why don't you ever talk about her?"

"Who?"

"You know who. Your fiancée."

He didn't reply, and I thought he'd fallen back asleep. It was a stupid question, anyway, and none of my business. But the conversation with Francisco stuck in my mind, stoking the curiosity Bronte initially sparked that night at Inferno.

"There's nothing to talk about." The firm statement lacked the fuzzy disorientation from moments ago, indicating plenty of stories existed about the woman he once loved.

"Bronte didn't seem to think so. Then again, she probably only wanted to piss me off." I chewed my lip, then rolled toward him. "You know, she talks a lot of shit. Because of her lies and exaggerations, you made me tell you about my broken heart. Don't I get to hear about yours?"

"My broken heart isn't a bedtime story. Go to sleep." He faced the wall, pretending to ignore me, but his back muscles flexed beneath my scrutiny.

Yet something prodded me, a mischievous nosiness brought on by boredom. Or maybe I simply had to know how I compared to her, the woman who'd preceded me in Hayden's affections. I couldn't let it go, even though in the grand scheme of things, it didn't matter. I doubted we'd ever meet. And who cared what she once meant to him? I wasn't Hayden's girlfriend, nor was that ever a likely conclusion to the unusual partnership we were building.

I blamed Francisco. His hint that Hayden cared about me—maybe more than a woman he'd planned to spend the rest of his life with—wouldn't quit its nagging.

"Was she the only woman you ever loved?"

"Goddammit, Cori, drop it." He flipped over, revealing a scowl that sent me scooting to the very edge of the mattress.

"I'm sor—"

"We were together for three years. I loved her, yes, but she hated the lounge. She complained I spent too much time there. She said I should reconcile with my dad, get a real career and stop playing around. We planned for a spring wedding, but she called it off this past July. She met some douchey lawyer and moved out. I haven't seen her since."

He didn't yell, and his expression remained unyielding despite the anger simmering beneath each curt sentence. Yet the story struck me, pressing on my old scars from Nolan. Had Hayden felt the same when I shared my story in the treehouse?

"Hayden, I'm so sorry. I shouldn't have..." I laid on my back, closing my eyes.

"It's fine," he sighed, sounding more like his normal self. "What happened, it was for the best. I love my job. I'm alive there. You know what it's like. The fast pace, constant adrenaline, working as one part of an inspired, kickass team. It's so satisfying when your dreams become reality, when you create something amazing that no one's ever tried before. There's nothing like it."

Each of his words conjured a vision of my life at Cornucopia. The exhilaration of our rushes, the epic wins and frustrating losses—hell, surviving even the worst shifts felt awesome in retrospect. The best times were cooking side by side with Mama, each of us debating ingredients or techniques and delighting in what we discovered. I'd never worked at any other job, but I had a hard time imagining being as fulfilled anywhere else.

"Nolan said all I did was work, too. That cooking wasn't a real career, even though the restaurant would be mine one day. I tried to explain that to him, but he didn't get it. That's what Mama wants, for me to carry on after her. Not just with Cornucopia, but with our magic." The words tumbled out, more than I'd intended to share. Maybe it was payment to balance the weight of Hayden's story.

"What do *you* want, Cori?"

The question stirred my mind, a solid oar through murky waters. A good question, one I'd never really considered beyond its sensible surface.

"All I ever wanted was to cast magic like Mama. I never really thought much beyond that, but... I love Cornucopia. Without it, where would I be able to practice everything she taught me?" And it helped, saying the words out loud; they clicked, pieces of a bigger puzzle sliding into place.

"Then you'll do it. This situation... We'll get through it, and you can go on with your life." Hayden's hand clasped mine across the empty expanse between us. After a moment, he added, "And fuck Nolan if he didn't care about what mattered to you."

For some reason, the statement drew a stream of laughter from me. I wiped my eyes, enjoying the release following that unexpected declaration.

"Yeah, fuck Nolan." Then I thought of something else. "What was her name?"

"Lana," he replied gruffly.

"Fuck Lana, too."

"Fuck them both." He joined in with a bark of laughter that didn't quite pair with mine. But it didn't matter—they didn't matter, not anymore.

A few minutes later, I yawned and closed my eyes again. I was sleepy at last. I drifted, hand in hand with Hayden, into a peaceful slumber—free of dreams about a past I couldn't change. No more regrets. It wasn't always tragic when certain things we used to want weren't meant to be.

CHAPTER EIGHTEEN

Seven days: I couldn't take it anymore.

I appreciated everything Hayden was doing, the risk he took in hiding me. He'd done his best to make it easy on me with gifts of books, music, and daily visits from him and Francisco, but I was cut off from everything I'd ever known—and I needed to update Mama.

If Hayden could sneak over, camouflaged in his layers, then I could sneak out.

"Can I borrow some money? I'm going to take a cab to the library," I stated, forceful and quick before he could interrupt.

"Absolutely not. Are you out of your mind?" Hayden said, packing the trash from last night's dinner to take on his way out. "They're still watching the restaurant, and my father texts me every day asking if I've heard from you. I think he's on to us."

"You don't know that." I hopped off the bed, blocking his path. "Mama's idea about an anonymous message was smart. I have to tell her I'm still okay. If she doesn't hear from me soon, she might retaliate. What if this time she doesn't get away with it?"

"I could drive there and find a way to talk with her."

"No! If you go up there—where she's most certainly being watched, too—it'll tip them off. What if that makes them act? They might hurt her until she had no choice but to talk." My fire fizzled at the thought of torture—a possibility I feared awaited us all—but if it came to that, I'd forgive her. She shouldn't have to experience any more pain on my behalf.

"I don't like this at all." He dropped the bag, holding me at arm's length. "It's too dangerous. I may not be able to save you again, Cori. They'd plan for it and stop me."

"Just one brief email from a random location won't lead them near me," I wheedled, resting my hand on his chest and gifting him with a hopeful smile. "They have to know I'm in New York City. It's the most obvious and convenient hiding spot—assuming they even discover the email. Are you sure they can tap into anything?"

"If you knew the men my father kept on the payroll, you wouldn't even ask that question." He closed his eyes, expelling a defeated sigh. "Give me a couple of hours. I'll find some sort of disguise, make an excuse to Francisco, and come back to get you. Just please, don't go anywhere alone. We'll do this together, okay?"

"It's a deal."

I threw my arms around him. He held me, squeezing once then backing away. The air stuck in my throat after his earnest reaction, which both comforted and disturbed me. Why couldn't I block how he made me feel?

We watched each other, awkward after the momentary contact. I nudged all the tender words which yearned to escape, but I waited too long. He picked up the trash bag, pained reluctance visible in his parting glance. Maybe he also wanted to say something, but didn't know where to begin.

"I better get going. Be ready when I return."

I didn't argue, following him and locking the latch. I'd made my point and gotten what I wanted, but it didn't feel like a victory. I leaned against the wooden frame, crossing my arms to smother a chill from his rational warnings. I only hoped it was paranoia, that Hayden had exaggerated the cult's capabilities.

Either way, it'd been too many days without contact. I had to reach out. Just maybe I'd get an email back, learning whether Mama was safe and praying for me still.

***

Hayden returned, as promised, shortly before noon and laden with shopping bags.

"It's not even Christmas yet," I said, happy to make him laugh.

"After what I've spent on you this week, there won't be anything left for Christmas." He handed me a silver plastic bag first. "Compliments of Francisco. He ran to the vintage clothing store while I went to the pawnshop, and he yelled at me again for locking you up in...whatever the pissed-off Spanish phrase was."

"Prisión de pesadilla?"

"That's it!"

"Yeah, prison of nightmares. He knows how to hit the nail on the head." I dug through the bag, exclaiming over the gifts from my new friend. "Oh, this might actually be kinda fun."

"He's so dramatic." Hayden tried to peek, but I snatched the bag back. "Hey, no fair!"

"Give me a few minutes." I darted through the bathroom door and locked it. I paused, changing my mind and reversing the latch. I didn't need to shut Hayden out. It seemed wrong after all he'd done to earn my trust.

The leather pants were almost impossible after being fattened over the past week with high-calorie fine dining and no physical activity. But the low-cut sequined top was perfect, and the coat would be extra warm with its faux-fur lining. I pulled my hair into a low, tight bun and slipped on the gaudy burgundy wig. Eyeliner, mascara, lipstick, and a glittery eyeshadow palette were the last items. I smeared the colors on without a care for proper blending. This character would be outrageous and a bit manic, the opposite of my usual self.

When I exited the bathroom, Hayden groaned. "For fuck's sake... You look like a Jersey housewife crossed with The Little Mermaid."

"I feel like I need some gum or a cigarette." I lowered the oversized sunglasses, giving my best attempt at a saucy wink.

Blushing, he shook his head and resumed filling the battered black backpack. "You better keep that move to yourself."

"Why? Didn't I do it right?" I rolled my hips, tossing the plasticine curls back.

"I don't know what your intention was, but it worked for me," Hayden said with a wry smile. The amusement faded, his expression darkening as it raked over my body. He shook his head, roughly adjusting the backpack straps. "Let's get a move on before I change my mind."

That look wasn't much different from others he'd shared during our most passionate moments. The feelings it spawned... I was half-tempted to consider other ways we might spend our afternoon.

I coughed lightly, dispelling the mood and waking from my brief daydream. "Yeah, sure. After you."

"Oh no—in those pants, you go first." He unfurled his arm toward the open door. "My early Christmas present."

I walked past, ducking so he didn't see the slight smile trying to escape. Maybe I should experiment with some proper catwalk moves since I had a captive audience.

***

The breeze sliced through our clothes, and I regretted leaving my ugly sweatshirt behind. Hayden rubbed between my shoulder blades as I shivered at the crosswalk, jamming my hands into the coat pockets. "Hang in there. It's not far."

"We're not going to the library? I've been dying to visit the big one in Midtown. It looks so cool in the movies."

"I'm sorry to spoil your sightseeing, but I don't want to stray too far. I found an alternative." He grabbed my hand as we jogged to the other side of the street.

"How far do we have to go? I'm freezing."

"We're almost there, and they'll have something to warm you up."

A few minutes of rapid walking down one more city block, then he stopped in front of a small café. "Ta da! Coffee and public wi-fi, can't get better than this."

"Are you sure it's safe so close to the hotel?" Not caring as much as

I should've for his answer, I raced into the snug and deliciously warm interior. The aroma of roasted coffee caressed my face, a pleasure strong enough to open my pores with a thirst for that lovely, restorative liquid.

"I did some research, and I believe this might work in small doses." He handed me the backpack, walking to the counter. "Go find a table. I'll get our drinks and the wi-fi password. Think about what you want to write."

"Already done," I confirmed, heading to a corner loveseat beside a hideous coffee table composed of several coarse logs and a scuffed glass top—an idea which must've sounded better than the ugly reality. At least the glass would prevent splinters.

Curious about the backpack's contents, I started digging. An older laptop, a cord, and a slender lithium battery, each piece kept separate—interesting. I set it up, plugged it into the floor strip, then slipped on the loveseat's velour fabric and knocked my forehead against the wall.

When I righted myself, huffing with irritation, I found Hayden watching—a coffee in each hand, and a smirk on his face. "What? Could've happened to anyone."

"Now you're just trolling me with those pants." He sat down, passing me a fragrant latte. "Password's starbuckssux—original, I know."

"Creatives can't succeed all the time." I took a careful sip, humming with pleasure. "This is tasty, though. They restored their cool points."

"Let's get this sent." He rapidly entered the password, waiting as the signal connected. "In theory, older devices can't be tracked once you turn the machine off and disconnect the battery. You can keep this in your room and take it down here for emergencies. Or use it any place with wi-fi. Just not too close to the hotel, okay?"

"Yeah, of course." I flexed my fingers, then searched for the email sign-up page. "That's kind of a brilliant idea. So who gave it to you?"

"Thanks, smartass. Technology isn't my thing, but apparently, my dishwasher is an amateur hacker. Shocked me, too, given what a raging pothead he is," Hayden said with a laugh. "What's your top-secret name gonna be?"

"You sort of inspired it without even knowing," I hinted while typing a fake profile, checked if the name was available. Yes, got it.

"IrisBaby_201? Nice. I'm glad you liked the flower. And what about the number?"

"It's the date for Imbolc, our favorite holiday and close to my birthday. She'll understand."

"Isn't that Groundhog Day?" Hayden pressed until I shushed him.

"Let me get this out. Don't distract me," I said, sharper than intended, but I flashed him an apologetic smile. I typed out the message I'd worked on all morning.

SAFE WITH BURNING COAL?
WHO'S WATCHING YOUR CHILDREN?
BOY AND GIRL PROTECT EACH OTHER, WITH YOUR HELP
GO GREEN, SEE OUR VILLAGES, EAST TO WEST—
SENDING LOVE TO MOTHER EARTH.
PRAY TODAY & SUPPORT THE CAUSE!

"That's a bit odd," he said, squinting. "Will it even make sense to her? Looks like some kooky spam mail."

"'SAFE,' because I am, and Burning Coal is Colburn. Children, Boy and Girl—that's us. We're protecting each other, but we need her help. Green, Village, and East are capitalized for my location. Obviously, the rest is sending my mother love and asking for her prayers and support...or even one of her spells, which goes back to protection."

"Not bad, assuming she gets your weird brain," he admitted, giving me a friendly nudge. "Good job. I don't know anyone who'd crack that shit without help."

I hit "Send," exhaling once the little envelope wrapped up and flew away. "Come on, Mama. You got this," I whispered.

"We can wait a couple of minutes, then it's best we shut it down. You can always come back and check tomorrow."

"Yeah, I suppose. Maybe we'll get lucky, and she'll be waiting for any email notification."

"Is there anything you need while we're out? I want to get back soon, but we could make a quick detour." Hayden rested his hand on my knee while sipping his coffee. The casual yet intimate touch caused sweat to bead beneath my stifling wig.

"Um, I don't know? What do you get the prisoner who already has everything?" I sat back, gripping my coffee with both hands.

"I hate keeping you locked away. If there were a better solution, I'd do anything to make you more comfortable."

I pictured his golden body sprawled across that black satin bed. His skin was even smoother than those sheets, except for the velvety patches of short blond curls on his chest and belly, trailing lower... Now, that would be comfort, lounging in his sinful nook again. I shifted against the cushions, aware of how constricting the leather pants had become. My movement knocked his hand away, causing him to mumble an apology.

"No, I'm sorry. My stupid leg fell asleep." I took his hand, holding it in the sliver of space between our thighs. While we waited, I leaned against him and his head rested against mine.

Ding! One message.

"Cori..."

"I'm on it." I dove forward, clicking the necessary buttons.

It was from Mama. I barely contained my squeal.

PRAYERS WORKING FOR CHILDREN OF GREEN EARTH.
KEEP TO VILLAGES, HOME GUARD WATCHES ALL.
STUDY, READ, LEARN—EDUCATION SAVES LIVES.
TAKE A TORCH IN SHADOWS, LOVE UNENDING.
MOTHER EARTH BREAKS COAL.
STAND BY FOR PEACE.

"The apple didn't fall far from the tree. So, what the hell does this mean?"

"Okay, so first line: she's praying for us, which is awesome since her prayers actually get things done. She wants us to stay here. Our home is being watched, too, which we already suspected. Study, read, learn—maybe find some spell books? I thought most of them were garbage, but all right. The Torch in Shadows is probably for Hekate, our Goddess. The torch is one of her sigils. And Love Unending... Well, she is my mom, but the last part—"

"Sounds ominous as hell," Hayden interrupted as I powered down the laptop. "You think she's planning an attack on my dad? Stand By for Peace, as in she'll give us some type of 'all clear' when it's safe?"

"Shit, I hope not. That last curse she put on him could've really wrecked her. We're supposed to 'do no harm.' It's the core of everything we believe for a reason."

"Let's get out of here," he said while packing up our belongings.

"Wait, I've got an idea." I took our empty cups to the bored barista, who polished the espresso machine with zero enthusiasm. "Excuse me, are there any bookstores nearby? Preferably used, maybe with some rare editions?"

"There's a good one a couple blocks south, back toward St. Mark's. Takes up a whole corner, you can't miss it." He waved vaguely toward the direction we'd come from.

"Thanks, and the coffee was awesome!" I tried not to skip back toward a curious Hayden, already poised by the door. "Come on—one more adventure, then you can lock me back in the tower."

CHAPTER NINETEEN

"I reiterate: no Christmas presents for you," Hayden said as we rushed from the cold back into the heated hotel lobby.

"I'll pay you back, jeez." I swung my sack of books in one hand and our takeout bag in the other. "I have money at home. Mama pays me plenty, probably more than I'm worth."

"I doubt that." He smiled, tapping the elevator buttons. "If she ever gets tired of you, you're welcome in my kitchen. Francisco needs someone to keep him in line."

"I appreciate the offer, but you don't want to rile Mama up—trust me. She seems sweet, but don't mess with her business."

"Or her daughter."

"Just so," I agreed, thinking of a way to change the subject. I couldn't even consider never returning to Cornucopia. Funny—I yearned for years to escape, but now I would've given anything to be stuck in that kitchen again. "Can you believe they had so many spell books? I can't wait to dive into these. And that Hekate one, I'm starting there. I read it years ago, but a refresher wouldn't hurt."

"Please, don't blow anything up. I can't afford a whole hotel."

"It's okay, I bet they're insured. You worry too much."

When we reached the room, I spun through the door. "Today was perfect. Hayden, thank you so much!"

"My pleasure." He tossed his coat onto the chair. "What should we watch on tv while we eat? And no more reality shows. Our brains will rot."

"I'm sure we can find something." I placed the bags on the table, laying my coat and wig in the chair. With swift fingers, I released my hair from its tight bun. I leaned over to shake my long curls loose, sighing at the luxurious sensation of the blood rushing back through my scalp.

When I flipped upright, Hayden sat on the edge of the bed, staring at me like a dehydrated desert wanderer who'd discovered a hidden spring. I checked my clothes—the skimpy top, in case something popped out, then my pants to ensure my zipper was up.

"What is it? I spared you another sight of my ass. Did I spill something on myself?" I walked toward him with my arms out.

His hands rose, fingers tracing the ring of faded bruises on my wrists from Halloween. Then lower, settling on my hips. "You're so beautiful, Cori. Sometimes it blindsides me."

"What are you talking about? Shaking out this sweaty mop?" I tried to joke, but it was difficult to get the words out. My trembling hands hovered on either side of his wind-chapped cheeks. Bright as apples against his creamy skin, all that tawny hair, and eyes like two portholes revealing an endless sapphire sea. Beautiful? He had no idea.

"Come here," he said, torn between a command and a plea. He hooked his fingers into the waistband of my pants, the leather creaking as he pulled me into his lap. I straddled him, and he cupped my buttocks, bracing me as we continued to gaze at each other.

I tossed my hair back, arching in leisurely invitation. The victories of the day lightened my heavy soul. His firm grip kindled my excitement, increasing when the member beneath me sprang to life. I clung to fistfuls of his sweater, rubbing against his hips with aching slowness. Our new dance began, pairing with the pounding in my head and torso, beating its rhythm along every awakening nerve.

His lips pressed against my bare breastbone, unmoving, as if receiving sustenance from my vigorous heartbeat. Fingers inched beneath my shirt, tickling along my lower back and ribs until I trembled in anticipation.

"Hayden—" I lifted his jaw, seizing his attention, but the words wouldn't come. Too many clustered together, waiting to be said—apologies, requests, endearments; each sounded way better in my head than they could've out loud.

"I can't fight against you, Coralena. I can't even think anymore without you hijacking my brain. I need you. I need more of whatever this is between us. Please...if you shut me out again, I'll lose my mind."

"I don't want to shut you out. Not anymore. I want—"

"What do you want?"

With another creak of leather, my legs spread so I could rest more securely in his lap. A move he appreciated, squeezing my backside in response. My mouth lowered, a flick of my tongue across his lower lip before I pulled back to admire his heightening desire. Goddess, it was indescribable to feel how much he wanted me; almost as intoxicating as revealing how much I wanted him.

I ran one hand down his chest, resting it against both of our centers. Stroking him through his pants, I whispered, "I want you inside of me."

In half a second, he flipped me on my back. My legs rode up, wrapping tight above the swell of his buttocks. He moved against me, frustrated as layers of useless clothes muted our friction. My nipples sprang to life after rubbing against the spangled shirt. I teased them higher while Hayden made a sound between a curse and a whimper.

"You're too much." He batted my hands, then tore at the flimsy fabric. "Get that shit off before I rip it to pieces."

Both of us fought against our tops, throwing them in the corner. We ground against each other, and he stumbled, stopping short of crushing me when his forearms landed on either side of my shoulders. I worked at his buttons and zipper while his tongue attacked my nipple, followed by his entire mouth. The suction wiped everything else from my mind.

"Hurry." I resumed my previous task, tugging on those pesky jeans. My hand pushed between the folds of fabric. I released a triumphant cry when I found his cock pushing for a way out.

"Don't! I'm gonna come if you touch me right now." He sank to his knees, unzipping my pants and yanking them down my legs, aggravated when my shoes halted his progress. "Touch yourself for me."

I backed toward the pillows while he removed his pants and shoes. My hands trailed over my breasts, then slid to other areas that screamed for service. I took off my panties, tossing them in his face.

Sinking into the soft bedding, I massaged the swollen bud between my thighs. Never before had this felt so good, enhanced by the man of my dreams being fixated to my every move. But he also entranced me with a magic that, in this moment, was as effective as my own. I moaned and sped up, certain that if I asked him to do anything, he'd say yes without a second thought.

"Get over here, now." I spread my legs wider, curling a finger to summon him.

"What do you want me to do?" he asked, advancing with a wicked grin but not touching one part of me.

"You know, your mouth..." I grew suddenly shy under that scorching gaze. "Put it down there."

"Down where?"

"On my..." I cried out when he cupped my core, gently squeezing "... pussy! Hayden, hurry."

His thumb dipped lower, teasing me. Each move was unhurried, even as my hips rose for more. His mouth and fingers worked together with an efficiency that had me climaxing in minutes.

My inner walls trembled as if struck by a massive quake. I cried out again when he thrust every inch of himself inside—pistoning half a dozen times or more. He bit his lip, struggling to contain himself, but I could tell he was losing.

He pulled out, laying back and gesturing forward. "Get on top, face the tv. I want to see that ass you punished me with all day."

Too excited to plan out the logistics, I did as he asked. His cock curved upward, trembling like a racehorse gnawing at the bit. I straightened it as best I could with my hand gripping the base. Curious, I rubbed it slowly around my entrance to see which of us would crack first.

"Cori—fucking quit that!" he groaned, and I half-turned to share an impish grin.

"Poor baby. Begging's no fun, is it?" I sheathed him in me, a perfect fit, sighing at the amplified sensation from this new position.

His hands latched on, clinging as I slowly rode him up and down. So good...delicious as ice cream on a summer day. I rose and sank, ever faster, cooperating as he guided me in a more circular path.

"Jesus Christ, you're killing me." He pushed me away, finishing with a ragged moan.

"What happened?" I frowned, crawling up from the corner of the bed.

"Forgot a condom," he exhaled, milking the last drops before his arm fell to his side. "Goddamn, that felt too good—a crime to stop."

"You didn't have to." I entered his waiting embrace, snuggling against his chest.

"You don't know what you're saying," he said brusquely, kissing my forehead. "Cori, it's too soon for all that. Don't you want to have a life, see the world...maybe find someone whose family isn't filled with Satanists?"

"Or maybe you want to find a girl who isn't, technically, a witch?" I asked sweetly, wiping a droplet from his belly and rubbing it between my fingertips. Human seed, rich and salty as the sea—the place where some believed all life began. One half of creation, the greatest magic and blessing bestowed on us by Nature herself. "You should be careful. All sorts of spells require a man's semen."

"I'm already yours. Save your energy for our enemies," he said in between gentle kisses along my neck, gasping when I reached down to stroke him again.

"Are you mine? I might need some more convincing."

"Greedy little witch." He rolled back on top, pinning my arms above my head. "Once more, and then you're going to eat dinner."

"Mmm, whatever you say." My eyelashes fluttered closed as my legs drew him closer. Melting together, joining with him in our private world... the most unpredictable and delightful place I'd ever been.

No one ever made me feel this way, but the unbridled emotions were both amazing and terrifying. He claimed I stole him, but he held me prisoner in more ways than one.

***

After a shower and an early dinner, I stretched across the remade bed with my books. Once again, Hayden began tidying up. I set my book to the side.

"You aren't leaving now, are you?" I pouted.

"I should make an appearance at the restaurant. Haven't been there all day and who knows what happened while I was gone," he said with regret, stuffing his wallet and keys in his pockets. "I'll be back after closing."

"I hate this, hiding and slinking around." I skipped over to follow him. "I could come, too. With my handy wig on, no one would know."

"We'll figure out something better soon." He offered a lingering kiss as an apology—carefully, as my mouth was a bit swollen from all the kissing earlier. "This has to end sometime, Cori. Then we can live a normal life, you'll see."

"If you say so." I hugged him tight, reaching up to plant a last kiss at the base of his neck. "Hurry back, okay? Or else I'll call and sic Francisco on you."

"I'd be in real trouble if both of you turned against me," Hayden said with a low chuckle. "Latch up behind me. Read your books and find us a way out of this mess."

"Aye aye, El Príncipe! I'll do my best," I said blithely, spanking him when he entered the hallway. "I'll wait up for you, so be polite and hurry."

"Where else would I want to be other than here with you?" he asked, warming me to the tips of my toes.

I hated saying goodbye, but it had to be done. He was right. The watchers would want a sighting of him today, and I had research to begin as Mama instructed. Not as fun as romping through the sheets, but we had real problems which needed a solution sooner rather than later.

We'd never have a truly happy existence separated from the people we loved. Even as I hid from my family and friends to protect them, he was also banished from his mother and sister. This room was both a refuge and a prison—a necessary evil forced on us by his rotten father.

For the people I loved, I'd endure it a while longer. But no one was meant to be a captive forever.

CHAPTER TWENTY

A frantic fist pounded, rattling the door on its hinges. Something was wrong.

I tossed my book to the side, stumbling over and fumbling with the latch. No, wait. I stared through the peephole like Hayden instructed. It wasn't him at the door, but the face was one we both trusted.

"Francisco, what—"

"Rapido, Coralita! Get your coat and shoes." He pushed past, scanning the room with wild eyes. "Don't worry about the rest. I'll come back later and pick it all up."

"Where's Hayden?" I pulled on a fresh pair of yoga pants beneath my "I Love New York" sweatshirt, stuffing my feet into the tired pair of ballet flats.

"Waiting for us and not doing so good, niña." He led me firmly from the room, shutting the door while I wiggled into the faux-fur jacket. "He said no hospital, no police, but he told me you could help."

"He's hurt?" I sprang forward, clutching his arm.

"Ay, hijos de puta... They worked him hard. He called, told me to protect you. He said you could fix him." Francisco squinted at me. "I thought you were a cocinera. What do you know about medicine?"

"Soy una bruja," I confessed, hoping he was open-minded enough not to flip out while we raced across the hotel lobby.

"Dios mío... I hope you're a good one and not a bad one."

We jogged toward the restaurant, hand in hand. White plumes steamed from my mouth, and I prayed in preparation for whatever new horrors awaited.

***

Francisco took us through the back entrance into the kitchen. He examined every shadow with paranoid diligence, but seemed satisfied. Everything was clean and quiet. The cooler and freezer hummed peacefully. The deceptive calm crumbled when we entered the dining room.

Hayden slumped over the bar, barely in the chair, with an open bottle of whiskey beside him. I wasn't sure if he was even conscious. My nails dug into Francisco's hand, fearing the worst until he grabbed the bottle—awkwardly, with his left hand curled against his chest.

"What happened?" I reined in a spike of angry fear before striding to his side. Hard to stop feeling altogether when the man you cared for smiled like that, his perfect face laying in pieces along his skull.

"Sorry, Cori. I fucked up," he said, dropping the whiskey bottle then falling while trying to catch it. Francisco caught both of them, averting any new disasters.

"Oh Hayden, who did this?" Silly to ask because I already knew. He'd been beaten last time when he rescued Mama. His dad must've repeated his abuse, a sick family tradition. My heart sank beneath a shroud of mourning, certain that whatever escape we planned was pointless. We couldn't run, there was no place to hide, and only more pain awaited.

"Dad came by with a message and some stupidly strong guys—a message for us." Hayden groaned as Francisco helped him stand.

"To the kitchen. We need light and supplies," Francisco interrupted, his crisp tone waking me up. I helped, lifting his free arm over my shoulders. Hayden screamed, revealing a grotesque injury which made me gag.

"Careful! His hand, it's... Oh hell. We need a hospital," I cried, moving faster to stay in line with Francisco but bumping against a table when

Hayden staggered.

"No hospital or police, or else he'll hurt her." Hayden—despite his earlier slurred speech—adamantly cut off my protest. "Theresa, they took her. He knows what she did...forced my mother to confess."

Tears suddenly burned my eyes, boiling water in a rattling pot. I couldn't help any of them. Everything had grown worse and worse. And now, what could I do for Hayden?

In the unforgiving light of the kitchen, his face oozed like a freshly butchered slab of meat—red from countless abrasions, a trickle of blood plinking from his mangled hand. We swayed together, stopping when we reached the massive prep table.

"Hold him up," I told Francisco while fumbling with Hayden's shirt buttons. "We have to see what they did."

As I undressed him, I bit my lip so hard coppery blood mingled with my saliva. A bit nauseating, but that grew worse when he mumbled, "Cori, I think he hurt my mother. She'd never give up Tessa, and she won't answer the phone. He's got both of them. Bait, he said..."

"Bait for what?" I fought against the snug trousers, forcing them down his splayed legs before tugging off his shoes. "Hayden! Stay awake, talk to me."

"He wants you for a ceremony on Yule...punished me. They saw the email."

"Lay him down." I grunted beneath the weight of his legs, even though Francisco managed the bulk. The prep table was almost big enough, but Hayden's socked feet dangled off the edge.

Darkening bruises blossomed from his gut, spreading across his chest—a chain that would turn truly ugly by morning. I rested his mangled left hand on his belly, but he screamed. A sound like broken glass grinding together sickened me more than the lumps poking from beneath the skin. I feared having to touch that swollen mess again. Moving closer to his face, my trembling fingers hovered over emerging bruises and nasty slices—one across his right eyebrow and cheekbone, a split lower lip, and a thin gash across the bridge of his too-wide nose. Not just broken, flattened.

"Well, what next? You lay on hands or something?" Francisco asked, impatient to regain my attention.

"I don't know." I scrubbed the back of my hand against my wet cheeks, covering my mouth before I screamed. "I need my mama. It's too much, impossible…"

"Detente y escúchame, Coralita." His massive hands squeezed, then shook me, forcing me to focus on his ferocious eyes. "Mama is not here right now, just you. Pensar! She taught you things, yes? Breathe, close your eyes."

Listen, think, breathe. In and out, over and over, until something murmured from behind the wall of my subconscious.

Mama shared so many lessons over the years, words still engraved in my memory. Her herb book, a grimoire more useful than the fluff I bought at the bookstore, had everything sorted by general function. Healing, love, prosperity, spell enhancement, divination—only positive aspects.

She always warned against curses; after all, she was the expert about what could go wrong. How many times over the years had she counseled me on magic's many consequences, yet ultimately kept me in the dark? Instead, she gradually unburdened her soul using our general lessons as a private pilgrimage toward absolution.

White for healing, candles and clean cloths, boiled water for purity— infuse it with what fits best, use what's available. Examine, feel with your hands. Rely on your eyes and nose, even your sense of taste. Let your instinct guide you, baby. That's where our power lives.

"Okay." I exhaled, looking only at Francisco. "I need boiling water, olive oil, sea salt, any fresh or dried herbs and flowers, clean cloths, white candles, and a lighter. Do you have a mortar and pestle?"

"Sí, todo de eso," he said with a tight grin. "Let's get started, bruja. Show me what you got!"

***

White tea candles sat on each corner of the steel prep table, hopefully far enough from Hayden that he wouldn't knock them off while I worked. The preparation helped center my riotous emotions, narrowing them into focus with each leafy chop of my blade and firm pound of the pestle. While the water boiled, filled with herbs and restoratives, I washed Hayden's wounds with salt water and thyme. A small bowl of olive oil also awaited, leaching the essence from the ingredients I'd broken down and stirred in.

He was quieter now, the whiskey combining with the spelled cup of chamomile tea I prepared. *Sleep, heal, no more pain...* Each word became a prayer as I swirled the tea bag back and forth. Not as effective as Mama's special loose-leaf blends, but it sufficed.

The hand was broken. We didn't need a doctor to see that. The middle finger wiggled like a loose tooth, and something below the knuckle sounded like nuts spinning in a food processor. I had never set a bone before. I wasn't even sure my idea would work, but he insisted on no hospitals. With our mothers being held hostage, even though it sickened me to hurt him, I had to do as he asked.

"Está listo, Coralita. Here are the cloths," Francisco said, filling a bowl and placing it on a mobile cart. Everything was laid out like a surgery, except I knew less about proper medicine than a nurse on a tv show.

"Stand at his shoulders and be ready to hold him down. This might get ugly, and I can't have his arms swinging."

"Will it hurt if I pray?" Francisco asked, a frightened child peeking from within his gigantic, technicolor body.

"No, it never hurts." I forced a smile. "Just keep your thoughts as positive as possible or you may harm the work. White light, that's all you need to focus on—okay?"

"Sí, bruja." He closed his eyes, spreading his wide hands across Hayden's shoulders.

The first cloth swirled in the light-brown water, releasing tufts of steam. Hot, but not enough to hurt my skin; it was safe for Hayden. White light, I painted it across my thoughts. I needed a blank canvas to start. Hazy images rose from the blinding page of my mind, an abstract watercolor taking shape.

Hayden, porcelain skin and magnetic blue eyes under a mop of golden hair; the smiles he shared with me—sly, smug, shy—each one reflecting a certain mood during iconic moments of our brief time together. His body radiated vitality when we glided on the dance floor, wrestled against the satin sheets...strong hands that pinned me down but never hurt. Passion that occasionally strayed too far, always held in check by the gentle soul peering from within his steady gaze.

Loosely wringing out the cloth, I laid it over his battered face—some of the lacerations still seeping blood. I placed three more cloths, spreading them over his bruised chest and belly. With each action, I held his unmarked face and form firmly in my mind, recalling how he made me feel in our best and most intimate moments. Happy, adored, treasured... I never allowed fear to drag my mind into a darker place. Those energies were not welcome here and could end up harming all of us.

The sense of peace in the air was palpable, sweet and airy as one of Mama's fabulous desserts, circulating beneath my skin like a sugar rush. Encouraged, I faced the biggest challenge with an open mind and heart.

Another set of cloths waited beside a bowl filled with a mash of avocado, agave nectar, and pumpkin puree. Cool, silky, and sticky, I rolled a handful through my fingers. Images set into the thick mixture like a comic on Silly Putty. Inflamed muscles, cracked white bones, overstretched joints—pulsating, then shrinking back to normal. I would burn away infection, and with the agave, glue his broken pieces back together. Each image blazed with clarity against the screen of my eyelids, encouraging me to dig deeper.

When my fingers massaged the charged mixture into his lumpy flesh, he finally rebelled. Writhing with a howl of agony, Francisco was forced to pin him down. Hayden fought me, despite the restraints, and my frantic mind overflowed with frustration.

"*Stamató!*" The Greek command shot out like a javelin, knocking Hayden back. Mama taught me the basics of her parents' language, a key to our shared magical heritage, but I didn't recognize the word. *Where did it come from?*

Hayden froze, muscles stiffening and binding themselves. The low, whining buzz hurt my heart—a scream, trapped in a throat which refused to release anything other than the most shallow breaths.

Quick, don't let him suffer. The memory of Mama's voice prodded me to act, no different from when she worked over my shoulder at Cornucopia.

I swallowed a shot of cool oxygen, my fingers on either side of the hidden break in his palm. A quick plea—to Hekate, to Mama, to anyone listening—and I pressed.

Fingers slid upward, coated with the special mix, and I guided the bone blindly into place. I stopped after an audible click. It appeared straighter. Maybe that was enough?

I wrung out a steaming towel before wrapping it around his hand. Hayden seemed to sink again, blanketed in an aura of peace. I lifted the cooling cloth from his face, performing the same spell on his nose while swallowing back a wave of hot vomit. How did people do this for a job, practicing medicine in all its gruesome glory, every day?

"Francisco, help me get on top of him."

"Madre nos salvan, what next?"

"Almost done, for now." I used Francisco's bent leg for a ladder. He braced my lower back, helping me straddle Hayden's hips. Secure, I stared at his bandaged face and chest, then took a deep breath. I had no idea if this would work, but it seemed appropriate.

I dipped my fingers into the olive oil infusion, rubbing my hands then resting them palm to palm. I closed my eyes to enhance the images I needed, struggling again to remain positive.

But the flush of power roused my anger, so vast it was nearly impossible to contain—no! I wanted happy thoughts, healing thoughts. I envisioned his skin against mine, whole and radiant with life. The mouth against my lips and neck, trailing lower, firm hands tenderly coaxing passion, lust, desire...love.

Maiden, Mother, Crone—Hekate, heal this man. Make him whole for me, your daughter, who—

Clapping my hands three times, each report summoned whatever energy swam through the surrounding aether.

"*Therapévo... Mitéra, ton agápo.*"

As the words translated in my mind, I realized their truth. I loved him.

An electric flash fused my hands to his chest. I screamed as waves of white light robbed me of sight, immolating every carefully crafted image. Instead, my mind reeled with agonizing darkness: Mama, bruised and weeping; Alastor's cruel grin; my father's face, flames gnawing his skin down to the bone; but mostly Hayden, broken and bleeding, depending on all my skills and magic to recover.

He needed me, here and now. I could save him, just as he tried to save me.

High-pitched wails erupted—from one or all of us—until my hearing disappeared with a faint pop. I fell through a tunnel of flashing light and fading sound, up and out of my spasming body. Gone, maybe never to be found.

Kóri, I am with you. Rest now.

Mother?

CHAPTER
TWENTY-ONE

My eyes opened to a sea of green and white beneath a dark canopy, a moonlit meadow where the grass was soft flannel instead of scratchy blades. A bed, endlessly sprawling, empty except for me.

But I wasn't alone. A figure slumped in the armchair beside me, snoring softly. He stirred when I touched his knee. The move stung my hand with invisible waves of pins and needles.

"Thank God." Hayden moved to the bed, hesitant as he examined me.

"How long was I asleep? Everything hurts." I yawned, yelping from the surprise breeze as he removed the down comforter.

"Almost twenty-four hours. You were beginning to worry me." His bright smile highlighted traces of bruising. Slender scabs decorated his eyebrow, cheek, and lip. His nose appeared normal again, if a bit swollen. Everything rushed back in a horrid flood of sewer water.

The fear, blood and pain, not knowing what to do...I recalled it all. Then I did something, which must've had a positive effect because Hayden looked much better. "Wow, I've never passed out like that. How are you? Your hand..."

"It's sore, but somehow you accelerated the healing process," he said, showing off a pressure bandage. "Francisco thought this might help keep the bone straight. How the hell did you set it? Everything looks normal. What did you do?"

"I don't know, but this is the worst hangover I ever had." I curled against his chest, weary from a pounding head and a sour, hollow stomach. "Is there water?"

"Yeah, here you go." He held the bottom of the bottle while I sipped slowly. I knew better than to go too fast during extreme thirst. "Are you hungry? Francisco left some soup in the fridge. He'll be back in the morning, or so he says. You scared the shit out of him."

"I'll apologize when I see him." I sat up, feebly pushing at the layers of bedding. "I've got to pee so bad...sorry."

"Here, let me help you. And," he said while guiding me along, "don't be scared when you look in the mirror."

"What?" I bolted, tripping over my feet like a toddler. The light shot off the marble, blinding me. When my vision normalized, I screamed.

"No, Cori, it's okay—a surprise, but it's not bad," he soothed, embracing me from behind and kissing the top of my head.

My curly black hair now sported a slender streak of white, rising from the center of my hairline and extending to the outermost tip. "What the fuck... When did this happen?"

"Francisco said it was right when you passed out," he explained calmly, turning me from the mirror to face him. "He caught you and watched all the color drain from that one piece of hair. He said the rest of you paled, too. He thought you died until he found your pulse. I woke up shortly after, and I was strong enough to help him get you upstairs."

"Can I have a minute, please?" I couldn't face his overwhelming sympathy right now.

After the door closed, I hunched over on the toilet, head in hands. Drained, more than physically, enough so a portion of my hair turned white. Mama had never gone into specifics of how magic might alter us, unless it was something really bad. Even then, she said the penalties varied depending on the spell and intent.

All magic came at a cost, of course. I'd never trained for spells beyond our normal blessings, harmless enchantments which were far from taxing.

This had been a massive work of healing, the backlash leaving me empty. I'd intended to only be a conduit for the Goddess, a vessel to channel her infinite power, but I must've messed up. Some of the energy came from me, or else I wouldn't be left in such a frail state.

After Mama cast her curse on Alastor Colburn, she'd seemed fine. That would've been a wicked spell, too, but maybe she was altered in a different way? Her mark of punishment could've been hidden anywhere, and because she'd been taken from me, I couldn't even ask. That would have to be remedied immediately.

One thing at a time. More water, food, regain some strength, get my head on straight, then I would save my mama. No way in hell I'd leave her with that asshole for a moment longer than necessary.

***

Francisco burst in, brighter than the rising sun. "Buenos días, Coralita! No, you stay there. I'll bring you breakfast soon, so no turning me into a toad."

"I don't turn people into toads," I sighed, sinking back into the bedding. "And I'm sorry for scaring you the other night. Nothing like that has ever happened to me."

"Está bien, you were amazing." He hugged me, then flipped the lock of white hair from my grainy eyes. "I only had one nightmare from it, but I lived. How do you feel?"

"I think I'll be okay." After a good night's sleep, I felt stronger, but something was off. Joints and muscles still ached, although less than before. Parts of me rang hollow, as if small holes had been left behind and awaited a refill. The spell took something from me. I just didn't know what or how much. "What happened before I passed out?"

"You almost gave me a heart attack," he said, dramatic but earnest. He reached for my necklace, shying away before touching it. "There was a light around you, luz blanca. Then that stone joined in, bouncing on your neck, red as fuego del infierno. You fell, and I caught you. Then everything went dark. You were gone—passed out like Sleeping Beauty until El Príncipe woke you. Where is he?"

"Showering, but he should be done soon."

"Ay veo! You must be feeling better, chica ardiente," Francisco giggled, rearranging my blankets. "I thought you rested, but I see how it is."

"We didn't do anything. Get your mind out of the gutter!" He dodged the pillow I tossed, pretending to ignore my protest before leaving to make a breakfast I wasn't sure I was ready to eat. Even the soup last night, although delicious, hadn't sat well.

"Mind in the gutter? Must be Francisco." Hayden stepped from the steaming bathroom with a towel swathed around his slim hips, a sight which had me groping for the water beside the bed. Silly of me; I'd seen far more of him than that.

"How are you?" He sat next to me, offering a tame kiss in greeting.

"I'm all right, but you're dripping. Speaking of, when did you change the bed?" Not that I was complaining—the leafy-green sheets and comforter were much nicer than the garish red and black satin. "All you need now is to ditch the black walls, then you'd have a pleasant sleeping area instead of a vampire's lair."

"Aren't you sassy this morning?" He shook more water in my face, causing me to duck under the covers. "If you must know, someone made fun of the décor their first night here. It might've pushed me to buy some new things."

"I'm sorry, but it was kinda sleazy. I like this better." I peeked, watching for flashes of naked limbs from the open closet. Long, lean muscles and smooth skin—toned but realistic, unlike Francisco's mind-boggling lumps of veiny sinew. Hayden was a sight I could happily wake up to every morning.

"If you play your cards right, we can make some other changes." He turned, catching me mid-ogle, then raced to jump on the bed. "And I see you staring. You'd better stop, or I'll give you a reason to be tired."

"Don't you dare, or I'll tell on you. Francisco's on my side."

"This may not be the right time, but if you want to make any changes here...we can." His playful demeanor grew serious, eyes searching mine for a sign. "We have a lot to work on, I know, but you can stay with me for as long as you want."

"You might regret saying that. I've only brought us trouble, and there will surely be more soon." I softened the ominous words with a quick kiss.

Part of me wished for more, but I was reluctant to start something my exhausted body might be unable to finish.

"No, this isn't all on you. My father is both of our problems, and if our mothers are in danger, then it's up to both of us to stop him. Maybe for good."

"As soon as I'm strong, I'll go back." I attempted to verbalize the plan already forming in my head. "Trade me for them. Maybe I can cause some damage. After the healing ritual, who knows what I'm capable of? I could be the perfect weapon."

"No, that's not an option." He gripped my arm, loosening when I grimaced in discomfort. "We'll beat him, but I won't allow you to endanger yourself. You need to recover. In the meantime, we'll think of something. Your mother would lose her shit if you surrendered."

"Mama risked herself to protect me," I argued, pushing him back. "Why can she do that—put her body and soul on the line for me—but I can't do the same for her?"

"You're her daughter, and that's what a good parent does—not the other way around," he said with a sad half-smile. "At least that's what I think good parents do. It's what I would do."

"Your mother loves you," I murmured, wishing I could make all of our burdens vanish. "She wanted me to stay away, probably to avoid exactly the situation we're in. I should go before I get you hurt again."

"You're not going anywhere," Hayden insisted, imperious and unrelenting as his nickname from Francisco. The Prince, cunning and implacable—Machiavellian in his own mind, anyway—but I'd seen his true nature and wasn't scared off. "My father has to know you're here. He's baiting his trap with people we love. This is just one more sick game. He won't waste his fun on a simple capture. He wants us to go to him and grovel for mercy. I won't lose you, Cori."

"Am I supposed to let you take another beating? No way. I'm the one he wants, so trade me," I said stubbornly. "We're in this together, which means we share the heat. You aren't allowed to hide me away forever, risking yourself and our mothers. I'll wait until I heal, but I'm not out of the game. Not by a long shot. Do you understand?"

"We'll talk about this after you've rested. Drop it for now." His hardened features relaxed as he gave me one last kiss. "I've got to get dressed for work."

I rolled beneath the covers, clutching the necklace my mother gave me. I stared at the harmless garnet heart, trying to imagine it flaring to life. Hellfire, Francisco had said... Didn't seem right for a healing spell, but maybe it was only because the stone was red? Another question to save if—when—I could speak with Mama again.

Was she safe in a nice room, or locked in a makeshift cell? Were they feeding her, letting her bathe? I prayed they weren't abusing her as they had before.

Hayden was right, but I didn't care. It was customary for a parent to give their life for their child. Custom be damned, though; I'd do what it took to save my mama. I didn't want to die when I sensed a viable future with Hayden, but any future we shared would become a wasteland if I held back my potential, hiding instead of fighting for the wonderful woman I loved above all else.

***

My next nap broke off a few hours later, and my stomach roared back to life. I hadn't eaten much for breakfast. Francisco threw his hands in the air, proclaiming he had to go to his real job, where people paid for his glorious cooking instead of picking at it. Maybe my body was ready to catch up now.

In the kitchen, I turned into a starved beast. The scents wafting from the restaurant below only made it worse. I tore every bit of food from the fridge to set up a buffet for myself. Soup, salad, hard-boiled eggs, fruit... Nothing appealed, even though I took a bite of them all.

The prize awaited in a plastic container, a massive slab of steak marinating in a delightful mix of olive oil, garlic, herbs, and a dash of red wine. Saliva flooded my mouth, urging me to tear the raw meat with my teeth. I wanted it, needed the fresh meat and blood, but I wasn't a goddamn savage.

It only took a few minutes to heat the copper sauté pan, and another minute on each side to sear the steak and seal in its juices. Juices, not blood, because that was too gruesome. *It's okay. It's what you need to heal, what you crave*—Shut up!

The tender cut melted in my mouth. Delicate herbs and bracing spices warmed my tongue, sending my senses into overdrive. Culinary magic, not at Mama's level, but Francisco definitely had brujo potential—or I was just hungry. Hard to say.

The elevator dinged, startling me from my binge. My chaotic mess mortified me—what would Hayden think? If I'd known he planned to check on me, I might've controlled myself. Not the sexiest look in a new relationship, attempting to devour the contents of his fridge when left alone for five minutes.

"I fucking knew it!"

Determined heels clicked across the hardwood. I fumbled with a handful of containers as that angry, familiar voice struck again.

"He lied to me. You *have* been here, hiding like a fucking coward! How dare you?"

"Bronte, you don't know what you're talking about." I tried to summon a sense of calm, conserving my barely restored energy. I wouldn't win this fight today, but that grating tone, combined with everything that had happened... Oh, how I relished a future opportunity to smack her bitch-ass down.

"Don't play with me. I know everything—finally. My mother told me. She begged me to call Hayden, but he kept ignoring me." She spat the words, tossing her handbag on the counter. Her lovely face frowned when she saw my half-eaten meal, oozing its crimson juices across the plate. "Gross, what is this? Some post-Halloween, Rosemary-fucking-Woodhouse cosplay? Oh my God... Are you pregnant?"

"Will you shut the fuck up?" I smacked the counter, but a new ding from the elevator distracted me.

"I told you to leave, then the servers said you sneaked up here." Hayden stormed in to confront his sister. She turned her back on me without a thought, impatient to dig her claws into the real object of her ire. "Now what are you going to do? Call Dad? I love you, Bronte, but I'm warning you—"

"What? You won't be my brother anymore? I don't even care." She shoved a small hand against his chest, then began jabbing with her pointer finger. "Mother told me everything, and you're going to let her sit there—a prisoner in her own home—instead of giving up this stupid slut?"

"Don't you call her that, or you'll have to worry about more than disowning me." Hayden loomed over his fearless sister. I didn't believe he'd have done anything worse—even though Bronte deserved a slap—but enough was enough.

"Both of you, quit it!"

The kitchen light bulb popped, sprinkling a murderous layer of glass to ruin my glorious steak. Hayden and Bronte stared at me, mouths open, identical blue eyes wide and innocent as cherubs.

At least I have their attention. I swooned, passing out when I hit the tile.

CHAPTER TWENTY-TWO

"...never tell me anything. I'm not a baby anymore!"

"Mother wanted you safe, dumbass. You don't know what happened—"

"And I won't unless you tell me!"

Groggy and lost in my fog, their rising voices drilled into my throbbing forehead like corkscrews through a stubborn wine bottle. At times, I'd wished for a sibling—someone to play with, a companion to share secrets from our parents. Listening to the Colburn children, especially today, I thanked Mama for only having me.

"Can you guys just not?" I asked weakly, sitting up and losing the cold cloth Hayden must've placed on my forehead. "Isn't there a way to discuss this without shouting?"

"Yes, we can absolutely handle this better," Hayden said, perched beside me on the sofa arm. "Tay, come on. Let's sit like civilized adults and clear the air."

"Fine." She sank into an armchair with a petulant pout. "You keep a leash on Carrie over there. I don't need to catch fire just because I'm not all gooey over the thought of you two in love and ruining our entire family."

"Bronte, I'm sorry, but we've got way bigger problems than you may realize." I scooted so Hayden had room to sit. He held me, his warm scent and soothing presence calming the ache in my head—hopefully long enough I didn't light that bitch up just for fun.

"So tell me, why is Mother not allowed to leave the estate? Why have the guards doubled around the cottage? And where the hell is Theresa? Cornucopia's been closed for three days, which is unacceptable."

"You said Mother told you everything, so those questions should already be answered," Hayden retorted. I pinched him for the smart-ass reply.

"Mother said you and that...Cori—fine, whatever—pissed Daddy off. Then you both ran away with something important to him. Mother said only I could help fix this, so here I am—sacrificing my time and energy. You're welcome." She primly folded her hands in her lap, condescending as hell but the picture of ladylike restraint.

Hayden stiffened, his anger nearly enough to ignite my own. I sent him a stern glance before facing Bronte. "There's no easy way to say this. It has to stay a secret, of course, but...my mama and I are witches. Also, your dad is a Satanist who wants to use us in his cult's dark ritual."

Silent as a grave, but better than the screeching I'd feared. Maybe the earlier tension prepared her somewhat for this news. Whatever Aspasia said to force this trip to the city must've been upsetting.

Bronte didn't move from her perfect pose, barely blinking. I waited to see if the overloaded circuits in her poor Barbie brain would spark and catch fire. But she surprised me, speaking calmly. "Okay. So basically, my dad is a cult leader. Mother knew but stayed with him, anyway. And you and Theresa are intended as some sort of sacrifice? Also, my own brother has known about this for years but never told me."

"Tay, I know it sounds—" Hayden said, but she cut him off with a voice that sheared like a frozen scythe.

"Fuck all of you. I'm done."

Hayden leaped to stop her, calling her name in a way that pained my heart. No love was lost between Bronte and me, especially after her birthday debacle with Nolan, but the thought of Hayden losing his only sister because of me was unacceptable.

"Bronte, wait," I called out, following the pair but keeping my distance. "I know you care about my mother, and she's only ever said good things about you. Right now, your father is keeping both of our mothers hostage to make me turn myself in. Which I have every intention of doing to protect them. Please, if you're here to help...then help."

"You're not turning—" Hayden strode over, cheeks reddening, but I raised a hand in warning.

Bronte watched us both, her thick lashes sparkling with tears of anger or fear, maybe sorrow. They never fell, even when she daintily sat again.

"I'll listen, but I won't promise anything," she said coolly, resuming her model's pose. Her own type of coping mechanism, maybe—the consummate debutante, armored with dignity and propriety.

She didn't flinch once as I continued my tale, making me consider a wild possibility: I might learn to respect Bronte Colburn. Pampered and spoiled, but she contained plenty of steel beneath her outer fluff. Maybe she'd become another ally in this mess.

***

After our talk, Bronte excused herself to rest in the spare bedroom. Only an hour or so of conversation, but it took a toll. The sassy princess shrank into a solemn child, struggling with the hardest truth of adolescence—finally, at this late age—that our parents weren't perfect. And, in her father's case, sometimes parents could love us yet commit evil acts against others. I couldn't imagine how hurtful that was, a betrayal of all she believed about the comfortable life she cherished.

At least Hayden found out at a young age what kind of man his father was. He even received physical punishment, beaten by a man who should've been driven to shield him from all harm. Alastor's image didn't have so far to fall for Hayden, as he had years to adjust. Maybe that helped—or should've—but he didn't appear grateful for the difference.

"Back to bed, and don't you argue with me." Hayden guided me to the room, tucking me into the cheerful bedding bought just for me. Back when I was innocent to him—not a witch, only a girl who'd lost her father but was fortunate to have a mostly positive youth thanks to a brave boy who made his own stand against darkness.

He had sacrificed his innocence and peace of mind by rescuing my mother, a woman we both loved. How could I consider throwing that away, volunteering to be the next sacrificial lamb and bowing to the wolves?

"I will, I promise. No more raiding the fridge, except...could you ask Francisco to make me something high in protein for dinner?"

"Of course, but he'll bitch about that steak all day. That was supposed to be your dinner." He kissed my forehead, then stood and straightened his suit. "Once tonight's covers are settled, I'll be back. It looks like it might be a slower night, for now. I'll talk again with Bronte, make sure she's okay."

"None of us should be okay, Hayden. Give her time." My eyelids drooped as the cocoon swallowed me again.

I didn't hear him leave, lost to that gray realm again—a purgatory between reality and dreams. But which was Heaven and which was Hell? Lately, the distinction was harder to make.

A nudge on my shoulder parted the filmy curtain, impatiently summoning me back to the real world. Definitely more of a hell at the moment.

Bronte sat on the edge of the bed. Her childlike features hardened, reminding me of her mother at the Halloween party. This was the first glimpse, perhaps, of the woman she'd become. Just as the new lock of white hair reflected my own changes—one of many which would eventually turn me into my mama, whose hair was full of similar silvery threads.

"Hey Cori, wake up! You can't be that tired. It's early."

"You don't even know," I sighed, running a hand over my eyes. We'd told her of Hayden's attack, but not explicitly how I healed him. It was enough to generalize about why her father was drawn to me and Mama, but I didn't want her to know what happened to ramp up my magic into an incalculable—and somewhat frightening—force.

"We only have a little time before Hayden's back." Her nudges were unrelenting until I sat up against the pillows. "You said you'd turn yourself over to save our mothers. Did you really mean that or was it all talk to impress my brother?"

"Of course I meant it. I don't lie...not about stuff like that." I shied from a full declaration of who I'd already lied to and why. Again, she didn't need to know everything. "My mama means everything to me, and I'd do anything to help Hayden. He loves your mother just as much as you do."

"Then what are we waiting for?" She leaned closer, blue eyes unyielding as icebergs. "Fuck my dad for what he did and what he's doing now. I want my mother out of there, and your mother doesn't deserve any more pain. My car is parked in the lot, ready to go."

"But Hayden..." I hesitated, picturing the look on his face. One more betrayal, the peril increasing as someone he cared for gambled their life. Someone more than a friend, even if we hadn't exactly worked out what we meant to each other.

"He won't like it, but how can he not understand? He stood up to Dad twice, rescuing women who weren't even his family. Why would he think you'd do any less for your own mother?" she reasoned. Her words were laced with cool logic, but she didn't need to win me over. I was onboard when I offered to go in the first place.

A new rite, the reason I was being blackmailed. Maybe a repeated attempt at some sort of ritualistic rape, or worse? *Never see Hayden again...*

"Give me tonight, Bronte. We can leave first thing in the morning." I held out my hand, firm with resolve—on the outside, at least.

She laughed and grabbed it. "We should've spit first to seal the pact."

"Maybe next time. My throat's a little dry right now," I said, half-joking but already wary of this new bargain. A stroll back into the lion's den, laying myself belly-up to the larger predators in an act of submission.

Sacrifice. Didn't true love depend on such unselfish acts? More than a fair trade, myself for two beloved mothers. I could live with that—if they let me live long enough to confirm the trade was truly worth it.

***

"I can't believe your appetite. I'm sort of scared to take your plate without bringing more first." Hayden lounged at my feet while I devoured the platter of meats, ignoring the salad and bread beside it. "I may have to buy new sheets after this frenzy."

"I didn't spill anything, don't worry," I said through a mouthful of food, licking my fingers before remembering to use a napkin. "Is Francisco still here? I want to say thank you."

"He cut out early, too, after dinner service. You've worn him out, and he needs his beauty sleep." His fingertip danced over my toes, light as a feather, sending a series of shivers up my body.

"Stop it, you're such a pain. Is there any more steak left?" I asked hopefully, setting the tray aside after dutifully wiping the grease from my hands and mouth.

"There's no way you have room left," he laughed, moving up to stretch beside me. "A 12-ounce bloody ribeye, two short-ribs, a baby filet, and carnitas is more than enough for anyone. Please don't make me watch all that come back up."

"I'll just go get it myself later," I said primly. "You aren't the boss of me or my belly."

"Don't I know it. You rarely let me forget," he replied, amused, until those bright eyes narrowed while studying my face. "Are you sure you're feeling better, Cori? Is this type of recharge normal—all this sleep and food? If you need a doctor—"

"No, I don't need anything but what I already have," I insisted, kissing him firmly enough to dispel doubt. "Hayden, I—"

"You need your mother, though. We'll work on that issue tomorrow, since you're feeling better," he interrupted, misjudging what I wanted to say—words which might mean everything in our last moments together. Even if Alastor and his cult didn't kill me, Hayden wouldn't want me after I'd been used by them. "I may not have Dad's clout, but I have friends too. Maybe some who can help us get in there and break up a possible stand-off. They'd be witnesses to his crimes. He won't risk his name and reputation just for some ritual, not when he's worked his whole life to get this far."

"What kind of friends do you have? The Avengers or The Justice League? 'Cause, honestly, my vote is for Thor and whoever he feels like inviting." I stroked Hayden's blond hair, admiring his similarities to the Asgardian heartthrob.

"Who needs superheroes when I have my own, real-life witch?" Hayden's lips grazed mine while his finger ran along my collarbone, then rested against the hollow of my throat. "Mmm, pulse seems a bit rapid. I don't think you'll be able to leave this bed anytime soon. I've watched a lot of doctor shows. I'm practically an expert."

"I don't want to leave," I admitted, wrapping myself around him. "There's nowhere I'd rather be than here, the two of us alone and away from everything. But..."

"No." The refusal was punctuated with a kiss, a languorous claiming of my mouth with his own. Velvety soft, banishing the chill in my heart—for now. Until the wee morning hours when I'd skulk away from his light and love. "It doesn't have to change, Coralena. You can stay here as long as you need. Forever, if you want."

"Promise me, no matter what happens, you'll always mean those words. That you won't turn away or forget about me—about us—in this moment." I grew suddenly desperate for a vow I feared would mean nothing in the end, but I asked anyway, halting beneath his determined lips. "Hayden, I couldn't bear it if... Goddammit, will you listen to me? I'm falling in love with you."

"Finally." His eyes gleamed from their crinkled beds—a smile, relieved but haunted by something darker. Maybe remorse for the rocky path that led to this moment. "I'm pretty sure I loved you from that first night at Cornucopia. Your annoyed glare when we stumbled in, late and drunk. Then you gave us a big, fake smile and came over, anyway. And after the club... I'll never forget that night, either. Every little sound, your smile, how you tasted like spring flowers and sunshine, even after a night of dancing and drinking." He parted the folds of my bathrobe, whispering against my neck, "You could never lose me, Coralena."

I gave in one last time, merging with that magnificent man and his incandescent soul. A heart so full, but with room enough to welcome me in. A girl he half-remembered and a woman he barely knew. He gifted me with a love I never imagined I'd find. Our differences didn't matter—age, background, status. Nothing mattered but us, moving as one in the dimly lit room to create something new—brilliant together, if only for a moment.

Perfect, until it was gone. Nothing lasted forever, not even true love. My parents learned that the hard way; maybe his did, too. All we had was now. It wasn't nearly enough time to learn about each other and see where this relationship would head, but with Hayden, I suspected even eternity wouldn't have been enough. Something so good wasn't intended to survive this brutal world.

CHAPTER TWENTY-THREE

We didn't speak until crossing into Connecticut. The silent escape from New York occupied my thoughts. Unshed tears filled my eyes and regret gnawed at my heart as I pined for the man I abandoned.

Coward. Leaving him, lying to him... How could you?

With just the clothes on my back and the necklace my mother gave me, I slinked away before the sun rose. I debated taking more—some sort of weapon, man-made or natural, but opted against the desperate idea. The villain awaited my arrival in a private, impenetrable compound. He suspected my capabilities, and my mother was his hostage. I wasn't skilled enough to plan an offensive sneak-attack, but I hadn't given up all hope of finding a helpful tool.

"I need to stop by Cornucopia before we go to your house." I broke the silence once my nerves steadied and the moisture in my eyes reabsorbed.

"For what?" she asked, maybe irritated to be distracted from her own musings.

"I need something. It won't be long, and no one else should be there." I picked my cuticles, feigning a casual attitude. "Don't worry, I'm committed to this plan. I won't trick you."

Committed, a good word—that's what they did to the mentally ill, offering professional care at secured locations so they couldn't hurt themselves or others. And wasn't that proving to be the rising star of my skill set? How many more people would I hurt? Not to mention, what dangers did I open myself up to with this latest hasty decision?

Goddamn, what was wrong with me—leaving a man like Hayden in bed without a word or a final kiss. A man I might've spent a lifetime with, happily ever after, if only the rest of this mess didn't exist.

"All right, but nothing funny. I don't want anything to happen to them because you decided to twitch your nose or something," Bronte giggled—a sweet sound failing to hide the resentment souring beneath the sugar coating. On her own, she was incapable of rescuing her mother and mine—a woman she considered a friend. She was forced to ask me, a rival, for assistance. After all, it was me her demented father wanted. Must've been a bitter pill to swallow for a spoiled princess and lifelong daddy's girl.

"I won't endanger them." I meant every word, even if I didn't care enough to assuage her wounded pride further.

Mama was my top priority; but for Hayden, I'd fight to protect the mother he loved—even if she wasn't my biggest fan. Worst-case scenario, if I only freed Mama, that would be more than enough. She was armed with a wealth of tools and knowledge I could only guess at. I wouldn't even have to speak up or fight back; as long as she knew where I was, she would save us all. Together, we'd make everything right.

Mama will be free. Then they better watch out. Everything will be all right. Yes, a solid alternative if I couldn't find a way out on my own. *Don't try to rescue me, Hayden. He might not let you off with just a beating this time.* Bronte might help, too. She loved her brother, and she would want to protect him as much as I did.

Forgive me, Hayden. I love you.

***

The atmosphere in the apartment was claustrophobic as a coffin, stained by the spectral scent of burned herbs. The reason sat before me: an altar, set up in the living room but mostly knocked over. A sign of a struggle, the contents of the cauldron scattered across the multihued tablecloth and carpet. At least the fallen candles were extinguished before anything caught fire.

Candles, clumps of used herbs, shattered glass containers, a broken obsidian athamé, and crushed flowers. Monkshood, those purple blossoms were too unique to be anything else. What were the dried green leaves among the broken glass? There, on the bottle's bottom—whole, despite the jagged top—wormwood. Energy redirection, psychic protection, divination and summoning. What had she been doing?

Another symbol winked from the wreckage, a silver medal half-obscured by the overturned cauldron. I recognized the iconic carving of a three-headed woman armed with torch and blade, one of many Mama used for decoration or rituals. Hekate...and monkshood, or aconite, was sacred to her.

Summoning—she called upon Hekate before being taken. Someone interrupted her spell, otherwise she wouldn't have left such a mess behind. Our sacred goddess and patroness, called by Mama in our time of need. Had she made contact? There wasn't any way of knowing unless I spoke with her—if they allowed us a moment to speak.

After a brief search of the living room, transformed into a makeshift ritual space, there was no sign of Mama's grimoire. Maybe they'd taken it, too? And with it, my hope of finding something—anything—helpful vanished.

"How much longer will you be?" Bronte stepped in, uninvited.

"I asked you to wait in the car," I said, gazing helplessly at my broken home.

"Well, I was bored. Let's get a move on," she said with definite impatience, holding the door open. "There's nothing here for you."

"No, I suppose not." Everything I wanted was held prisoner by Bronte's father, and it was time to move on. I had to trust in my growing—if still unpredictable—skills, Mama's inestimable talents, Hekate's protection, and Hayden's love. Nothing else would aid me in this battle.

***

Cypress Point awaited. The palace had been built by a madman to house his family, but it remained a mystery how they ended up relatively normal under his poisonous reign. His evil also failed to taint the house's appearance. Lit up against the last of the darkness, it reflected the blushing dawn which bled over the horizon. The roof and towers glowed, a halo against the backdrop of dark-green cypress and fiery maple trees. Festive, magnificent, but a place where I'd meet my ruin...maybe even my death. This was the prettiest prison I'd been in yet, more lovely than the famed Pearly Gates or the hallowed Fields of Elysium.

When we entered the home, a half-dozen guards stood inside. Dark suits and ties, white shirts, earpieces, and blank expressions; a beefy wall of uniformed clones, armed to the teeth and devoid of any trace of humanity.

"All this for me? I'm so flattered." I crossed my arms to appear tough, but the move just held my shaking nerves together. Why had I believed this was a good idea?

Another set of guests joined us from the living area to the left, the mismatched trio wearing a strange display of opposing emotions. Alastor grinned, polished as a silver coin, his bearded face as cheery as Santa on Christmas Eve. Aspasia's gaze rested on me before flitting away, still the implacable ice queen. And the one I needed to see the most...Mama. White streaks shot through her black curls like comets in the night sky. Her sweet brown eyes brimmed with disappointed tears.

"At least one of my children is obedient," Alastor observed, opening his arms for Bronte. She ran to his embrace—a child, eager to please and seeking her reward. My slice of optimism descended in a ball of flames as I watched them kiss, hug, and share murmured words. What a touching reunion. I should've known—maybe I *did* know—but I believed her love for her mother was as strong as mine. What a gross misjudgment.

"He doesn't know yet, but please, can I be the one who calls him?" Bronte said to her father, tossing me a smirk. "It's worse than we thought. The idiot is totally in love with her. It's the magic, right? Because honestly, I don't get the appeal. I mean, look at her?"

A light slap shut her up, almost too quick for the naked eye to register. Alastor's mirth faded to derision. "Now darling, envy is unbecoming of a Colburn. She is lovely, otherwise my son would not have been bewitched. And our Lord would never offer me a gift unworthy of my station."

A laugh tripped from my mouth, a manic reaction to the fear inspired by Alastor's unsettling certainty and the delight in witnessing Bronte's humiliation. "Money can't buy happiness, I guess, or sanity. You're all fucking crazy."

"Coralena, *siopí*!" Mama stepped forward, almost reaching me until a pair of goons stopped her.

"Mama, I'm sorry." I ran to her, uncaring if anyone tried to stop me. The tears, threatening since we left New York, compromised my vision. "Tell Hayden—"

"Get her out of here," Alastor barked. Pairs of hands dragged me away before I might touch my mother, who also wept and reached for me.

"You promised not to hurt her. Let her go!" I fought, even though it was useless, but it felt more right than giving in meekly.

"She'll be fine. We're sending her home, where she'll be free to continue her life—safe, as long as she doesn't interfere." Alastor ran a proprietary finger down the back of her hair. Mama shuddered but otherwise didn't move, fixing her gaze firmly on mine.

"*Boreí na sas kathodigísei o fakós tis Mitéras!*" Her last words before they dragged me away, part of the prayer we shared for years during our practice sessions and actual castings. *May the torch of the Mother guide you...*a reference to Hekate—a prayer, a clue, a blessing—before my mama disappeared from my sight and maybe my future.

Down the stairs and into a narrow hallway, we passed an unlit but spotless wine cellar, then entered a metal door into a barren room with narrow bunk beds and empty shelves. The panic room; an apt choice as my anxiety was off the charts, blaring its alarm against the walls of my mind. The place where a young Hayden had received his punishment, beaten and locked away for a week, a child of thirteen who'd only wanted to do the right thing. A theft of innocence, the act leaving scars he'd carry on his body and in his soul for life.

My prison for tonight, maybe until Yule. Five weeks alone in this windowless hell, left to imagine whatever horrors waited in the shadows down the road.

ACT III
GERÁMATA

"O what will she do, a soul bitten into with wrong?"

—Euripides, *Medea*

CHAPTER
TWENTY-FOUR

They made me wait for hours, long after I paced across the room and searched for anything which might help. Nothing—the room was impenetrable, empty of anything useful except blankets and pillows on the three cots. Plenty of spots to rest, but I couldn't fathom the thought until someone told me what to expect next.

Hayden must've discovered I was missing. Maybe he was already here, demanding my release, receiving another punishment I couldn't heal this time. Maybe the deal I made was a lie, and Mama was being hurt right alongside him. No way to know.

A series of beeps from outside unlocked the door. I rose, stopping at the sight of a grim bodyguard carrying a meal tray, followed by Alastor and another man. This one was small, plump, and bald; his beady eyes probed my appearance with clinical interest. I, on the other hand, was only interested in what hid within his black leather bag.

"There she is, our guest of honor." Alastor spread his arms, as if expecting a hug. *Sure, when Hell freezes over.* "Did you rest, my dear?"

"Don't play like you're some gracious host when I'm stuck here behind feet of steel and concrete." I snatched the tray from the bodyguard, slamming it onto the table. "What's the plan? I won't fight you idiots, but I deserve to know what's coming."

"Moderate your tone, or you'll begin fasting—your choice, young lady," Alastor snapped, the hospitable veneer cracking before settling in that same oily smile. "Meet a friend and loyal soldier for our Lord, Dr. Max Kaplan. He's here to monitor your health until the ceremony. We must have you in tip-top shape, untouched and clean. A pity my fool son spoiled you, but there's time to remedy that."

"You leave him out of this," I warned, glancing to Dr. Kaplan, who bent over one of the beds and dug through his bag. "I want Mama and Hayden left alone, or I won't be very cooperative."

"I'm curious: Bronte said he appeared healthy besides some light bruising." Alastor leaned casually against the steel door. "My men did quite a thorough job. I watched with my own eyes. How were you able to heal him so fast? Does it have anything to do with your striking new hair accent?"

"I don't know what you're talking about." Sweat pricked my clenched palms, both from Alastor's insinuation and the empty syringe in Dr. Kaplan's hand. "What's that for?"

"Blood tests first, then we'll do a physical exam later," Dr. Kaplan replied crisply, gesturing for me to sit. "Just relax. Only a pinch, and it'll be over."

Alastor continued his conversation once Dr. Kaplan poked, drawing his tubes of blood with near-painless competency. "Coralena, you don't need to conceal your power from me. I'm well-aware of your mother's gifts. I know they passed to you, one in a line of *pharmakis* experts, stretching back to your mother's homeland. But those wise Greeks had another word, a better word—*mágissa*, isn't that right?"

"Healers and herbalists, sure, but witch is a bit dramatic." I winced when the bloodletting finished and the syringe slipped out. "As for my hair, Mama went gray early, too. Must be genetics."

"We'll see, my dear," he said, making way for the doctor and bodyguard to exit. "Eat and rest up. Your exam will prove enjoyable, at least for us. You'll need your strength."

The door slammed, another set of beeps sliding the bolts back into place. I glanced at the silver-domed tray, turned my back, and laid across the bed. After days of ravenous hunger, my appetite vanished along with my momentary surge of bravado.

***

Black and red silk faded in place of soft green cotton, a setting he favored me in which also brought out the gold in his skin and hair. Mouth against mine, his touch caused faint threads of electricity to crackle across my skin as we moved together beneath our verdant hideaway.

Love you, beautiful...want you.

Stay, Coralena... Forever, promise me.

I sank into the bottomless bedding, opening myself and unable to stop because it was never enough. The scenery swirled as his lips pressed against my neck, climbing upward until hot words blew through my ear canal like a desert wind.

Touch yourself. I won't hurt you, Cori.

Help me. I need you...

A dry chuckle before he joined me as promised, bringing us toward the same peak until—

Four loud beeps and a click, then the cultured voices and sharp footsteps returned to banish the sweet dream. Pushing aside the fading images of Hayden, I ducked beneath the thin blanket, retreating until I hit the concrete wall.

"Oh my dearest, you've made me so happy." Alastor sank to his knees beside my cot, nimble despite his age. He gazed at me, Hayden's eyes sparkling in a monster's face. The sight forced me deeper beneath the blanket to snatch whatever warmth I could from the pure memory of my love. "This is better than we could've hoped for. You're an absolute treasure, Coralena."

"What are you talking about?" I jerked away from his avaricious hand, disgusted but fearful of anything that made him so happy.

"Come along, darling. We won't keep you in this hole. You're far too precious for such rude treatment."

His solicitous manner sent a flip-flop through my stomach. My skin prickled as he helped me rise, gallant as an Arthurian knight. The blood test... Something had happened. Whatever it was, it couldn't be good news for me. We strolled through the dim basement again, ascending into the light of the main hall.

"What did I do for the upgrade in accommodations? 'Cause I damn sure didn't mean it. Don't count on me paying you back for the favor."

"No, you'll give us what we need when the time is right," Alastor said with creepy ease, ushering me through the patio doors to a goon-chauffeured golf cart. I hadn't spotted anyone else as we walked, but my skin crawled as if countless eyes watched from their protective nooks.

"Maybe if you tell me more about this ceremony, I can offer some insight." I decided to appear reasonable, hoping to lull him into revealing anything useful. I had nothing but time, so might as well begin plotting some sort of sabotage. "Hayden already told me about your lord and the order. Got a thing for wolves, eh?"

"More like our Lord is the Great Wolf, an Alpha we cannot deny. Nor would I dream of turning him away now. Fair is fair, after the life he's given me. It's an honor and a privilege to be his High Priest."

"What more could he possibly give you?" I waved at the grandeur passing us by. "Who wouldn't be satisfied with all this?"

"There's always room for more power, darling. Additional boundaries to push beyond, mysteries to explore." Alastor patted my knee, his paternal fondness more offensive than if he'd spit in my face. "And eternal life is possible to the most faithful."

"So this is how the zombie apocalypse begins. Good to know." I scooted away, clinging to the pole beside me.

His fingers dug into my arm, one squeeze then he regained control of himself. No marks. I recalled the same command from the last time he kidnapped me. "This won't be some zombie transformation, girl. A rotted corpse without sentience, shambling in its own decomposing filth. Blood purchases youth and vitality—a life for a life, one might say."

"Whose life?" I stood to face him once we reached the cottage, quailing at the crooked grin cutting through his web of laugh lines.

"Not yours, darling—never fear." He gestured magnanimously toward the cottage door our good driver held open. "You're far too valuable now, a vessel for eternal life and magic. I wouldn't dream of casting you aside after one use."

"What use am I then? I refuse to be your whore, by the way."

"That mouth..." Alastor snapped his fingers. The goon stomped forward, raising a paw the size of a shovel. "No, don't hurt her. Bring her to the room. Lock her in. I won't have my grandson harmed...yet."

Greenery from the cypress trees blended with the autumn leaves, the rustling canopy spinning as I swooned against a fleshy mountain of prison guard. Stumbling, but not fainting. Not this time. But that word...

"That's impossible," I gasped, picked up like a sack of groceries and carried by the uncomplaining guard into my old home.

Alastor's laugh followed us down the narrow hallway, along with his dubious blessing. "We'll talk more later about your interesting blood test. Sleep well, dearest."

Pregnant? No way. It had barely been a month since I met Hayden, and we only had one slip without a condom. Calculations whirled through my brain, so blindingly fast I didn't notice being sat on a bed behind another locked door. A room I recognized, my childhood bedroom with the picture window.

Redone with fresh paint and new furniture, it was a woman's bedroom now—white, gray, and blue like the sky before a rainstorm.

A storm, like my life right now—our life, if Alastor spoke true. A fertilized egg floated in my womb, a place that might seem like infinite space to the microscopic interloper. Not a baby, yet; only a clump of dividing cells, following an ancient design and impetus even modern science hadn't unlocked. Women's magic, the miracle of life happening right now without my knowledge or consent.

Magic...the slip with Hayden, right before the crazed ritual that saved his life, but that had been only days ago! Too soon for fertilization, never mind test results. Did I unleash something to kick-start the process? Was such a thing possible? How would the fountain of power pouring in and through me that night affect an unborn child?

What have I done?

CHAPTER
TWENTY-FIVE

He didn't return. The day passed with only two food trays, lunch and dinner, delivered by another stone-faced bodyguard. Expertly prepared and healthy, I didn't detect any funny scents. Despite my inclination towards suspicion, I doubted they'd hurt me yet. I survived lunch with no side effects, so I ate dinner. I planned to examine every meal carefully, but I couldn't starve myself. I needed my strength.

For the baby—Hayden's baby—whom neither of us intended to create. *It's too soon... Don't you want to have a life, see the world.*

My future, yeah right; that didn't matter anymore. All I'd seen since Halloween was the inside of various prison cells. *Stop it! Mama will think of something*. But my hope dimmed when another day passed with no further information or visits from my captor.

My spoon swirled a lazy pattern in the congealing bowl of squash soup as I stared at the drizzle spraying the foliage beyond the glass. The same window I sat at as a child, waiting for Daddy to come home from the big house. Memories of clinging to frizzy-headed dolls, faces smeared with Mama's makeup...foolish to put oil-based products on plastic, but I didn't know anything then.

Not exactly a genius now, either, a voice snickered.

"Shush." I'd begun talking out loud because why not? Who would hear me or care? The voices occasionally argued about possible solutions, but they were all just me—divided, confused, angry, but ultimately too apathetic to act.

There was nothing to be done.

If I escaped, somehow—through a cadre of high-level security guards just waiting for me to be dumb enough to try—where would I go? To Mama? Maybe, but that was the first place they'd look. And if I went anywhere else—to Monica or Hayden—then a different set of loved ones would be scooped up and used as bait.

Also, it wasn't just me now. Someone was growing in me; a baby I never asked for, but apparently my wishes didn't matter. An accident or a fluke—or a miracle, some might say—boosted to grow faster than normal. Mutating...but maybe it wasn't so bad. I'd only released the one massive surge of magic. One time wouldn't be enough to hurt the baby, right?

My body hadn't changed, although my period appeared to have taken a vacation. My breasts ached, no worse than normal PMS symptoms. No morning sickness, although it might be too early—at least, from what I recalled of Cristina's pregnancies.

The dreams, though...

Big-screen events premiered every night and filled every boredom-induced nap, exquisitely detailed images from early childhood through adolescence. Colorful settings, crisp sounds, and a wealth of scents anchoring me even more to the visions. Lucid dreams, of a sort; I watched, conscious and fully aware, but I couldn't control the body I was in. A passenger, staring through the eyes of a child who didn't know what was coming for her.

Daddy, so tall and brown from the sun, his black hair and moustache tickling my cheek and neck when he kissed me. He took me out on my first Halloween, carrying me most of the way through the expensive Greenwich neighborhoods, demanding I share my candy with him. Or how he and Mama danced in the living room, salsa music blasting as they spun like tops before swooping me up to join them. Storytime at night, where Mama and Daddy took turns reading from small books as I clutched my stuffed lion—Leona, my favorite. She was still at home on my bed, waiting. I missed her.

What kind of family might we have become? Mama and I survived, bolstered by our genuine love—barring a few minor rebellions over the years. There were times her mood snapped, nights she cried herself to sleep. Usually, those happened on Mondays; without work to occupy her, she often stayed in bed all day. We would've been happier with him—maybe never perfect, but stronger—whole.

Dormir, mi cielo. Papá siempre está aquí.

Yes, Daddy, I'll sleep...but don't lie. You weren't always there, even if that was your intention.

But I'd be here for my baby, for whatever priceless span of time they would grant us. They'd have to kill me, too. Blood relatives or no, the Colburns would not get my baby. Over my dead body.

(Be careful what you wish for)

"I'll be careful."

Mama, come get me soon—please!

A lone tear trickled down my cheek, plinking into my soup bowl. *I'm losing my mind.*

***

Four days of solitude, three meals a day. My mind clouded with what had been, what was, and a low-key panic for what awaited. Until Alastor and Dr. Kaplan returned with smug smiles and a soft bathrobe. Then my panic yawned and awakened, bright-eyed and bushy-tailed, ready for the next hellish adventure.

"Time for another exam, my dear. We'll be waiting for you in the living room." Alastor tossed the robe on the bed, not bothering to make it an order. I'd say yes just to be somewhere else for a while. I might learn more about the baby from my unsolicited doctor.

The living room was transformed into a temporary exam room—drawn curtains, extra light from a set of spotlights, and furniture removed to make room for a padded table and several pieces of equipment I didn't recognize. One held a monitor—dark, for now, but chirping steadily in standby mode—an ultrasound, I'd bet. But again, it was too soon for that to be effective...wasn't it?

"Allow me to help." Alastor extended a hand, which I ignored.

"I can manage, thanks," I said sourly, boosting myself onto the table.

Dr. Kaplan extended the stirrups on either end, motioning me forward. "You've had one of these exams before, I hope?"

"Duh, I'm twenty-one. Do you think I've never had the benefit of modern medical care?" After firmly crossing my arms and legs, I added, "And you are seriously deluded to think I'll allow you to poke around inside of me."

"We're all adults here, only curious about the health of your child. Nothing more," Alastor said, his old-man breath tickling my cheek. "If you're reluctant to cooperate, I could also ask my men to hold you down."

"No," I said hastily, glancing between the pair. "I'll do it, just... No funny business."

"Darling, would I do that to you?" He stroked my cheek, his fingers hovering above the pendant at my neck—drawn to the stone, but pulling back as if repelled. "Charming, a garnet. How apropos for our young mother."

"What do you know about gem lore?" I asked, laying back. Dr. Kaplan placed each leg in the stirrups before gently guiding my hips forward. At least he had the decency to cover me with a sheet once the robe drifted open.

"Everyone has a hobby, and mine has always been the occult." Alastor stroked my hair absently, staring past me to the hidden doctor. "Without knowledge and will, I would never have been able to summon our Lord and make my initial bargain."

"I'll start with some samples, so lie still," Dr. Kaplan said, beginning the probing that drew a hiss between my clenched teeth. "Speculum is going in. Take a deep breath."

"You're glowing with health and life, dearest," Alastor said dreamily, his finger moving back to my cheek and down my neck in a slow, nauseating trail. "Toasted sugar, like the top of a crème brûlée. Did my son find you as sweet?"

"I told you, shut your mouth about Hayden. And don't compare my skin to food, or I'll talk about your skin—and it won't be pretty or tasty."

I gritted my teeth, trying to breathe despite the increasing pressure below. A few quick plunges were followed by a careful prodding from something more slender. Uncomfortable, but I had to give it to the twisted doctor. He seemed to be trying not to hurt me.

"The boy begged to see you, abasing himself like some pathetic cretin. Unwashed, unshaven...a complete disgrace." The fingers toyed with the edges of the robe until I slapped his hand away. His hand clamped down, squashing the insults roaring up my throat. "I warned you to be nice, did I not?"

"Get your fucking hands off me," I squeaked through constricted vocal cords, clawing his wrist.

"My Lord, she mustn't be marred—your own orders, remember?" Dr. Kaplan said, peeking from beneath the sheet with the clipped but nonthreatening reminder. Brave little toady. Who would've guessed he had that in him?

"For now, only until Yule," he amended, relaxing his grip.

"And then what? You kill me like you wanted to kill my mother?"

"Lovely girl, whatever gave you that idea?" Alastor laughed, chucking my chin. "I never dreamed of killing your mother. The act we shared unlocked her body, drawing forth her magic. Together, we opened a door into this world and welcomed our Lord among us."

I shook my head to rid myself of the graphic vision he conjured. "Bullshit."

"When I open you, I can't wait to see the wonders that emerge." He smiled, bending to kiss my forehead.

He resumed parting my robe, cupping a breast which trembled from the sobs I fought to hold in. The rod in his pants prodded my shoulder, excited despite the tears streaming from my eyes. I bit my bottom lip to keep from screaming, hard enough to draw blood. Maybe my distress excited him more, the pervert.

"My Lord, please..." Dr. Kaplan said, faintly pained, as if struggling to contain a bit of gas. He was forced to stand up for me again, even if he feared defying Alastor. Or he feared whatever consequences would be doled out by the mysterious demon lord who made such explicit rules for his rituals.

"Quite right, Max," Alastor sighed, reluctantly backing up and leaving me be. "Please, continue."

"A moment, sir," Dr. Kaplan said, dropping a series of long swabs into plastic bags. "Coralena, you may relax now. Please bare your stomach for me."

Sending a furtive glance toward Alastor, who kept his distance even though he continued to watch me, I carefully adjusted the robe—stomach only. I refused to grant him another viewing of the rest...for as long as I could, anyway. A small rebellion which caused his lips to twitch, much the same as Hayden when he was amused.

Stop seeing their facial similarities! They're nothing alike.
(nothing alike, nothing alike, no way are they anything alike!)

The goop on my belly was warm but slimy, a faintly distasteful sensation. Dr. Kaplan hummed, a tune that sounded more like a dirge, but he never lost his smile while sliding the sensor across my currently flat stomach.

"Oh my... This can't be right." Dr. Kaplan clicked a keyboard with one hand while angling the sensor. "Who was the last man you were with before Hayden? Someone in the first week of September, perhaps?"

"It's none of your damn business," I snapped.

"Coralena, language!" Alastor took a step closer, raising a hand as if to strike me but containing himself—barely. "You will answer Dr. Kaplan's question. Do not lie, girl, or I will personally ensure you regret it."

I slammed my eyes shut to block out these men I never imagined sharing such personal details with. "Hayden is the father. We...shared relations at the end of October. I've only been with one other man, my first. We broke up nearly two years ago. I have no reason to lie."

"This is madness! I'd swear this fetus was nearly six weeks along, but that's impossible according to her information. Marvelous," Dr. Kaplan murmured, cleaning my belly but talking as if I weren't present. "The exam is fine, my Lord. I'll take these samples and head out, if you don't mind."

"Go ahead. Call me as soon as you know something." Alastor's smile revealed his incisors, twinkling thanks to the spotlights. "I'll take care of our expectant mother. Come along, my dear."

"I can take care of myself." I hopped off the table, cinched my robe, and walked to the room—trying not to run from his disturbing chuckles. I shut the door, unable to lock it from my end but leaning against it, using my body as a barrier between this space and whatever plans festered in his revolting mind.

This wouldn't do for another five weeks. I needed help.

I sat on the carpet, crossing my legs and resting my arms along my thighs. *Mitéra na me voithísei... Mother help me, hear me, shine your torch to light a path through the darkness.*

The Greek failed me midway, but I knew enough to begin. And to repeat, over and over, the words thumping a measured beat in my slowly emptying mind. Eyes closed, a shield of white light emerged from my head, heart, and belly. Merging, a veil of holy calm cloaked my frazzled and violated body.

Hekate, I need you. Please don't forsake me.

Nails dug into my palms, hard but painless, like squeezing a big marshmallow. I dug deeper, sucking in my breath before opening my eyes. The light was still there, not just in my mind, but blazing through the room to outshine the afternoon sun. The conjured light grew into a physical shield, fortified by Blood—iron, salt, water, minerals—symbols of life and power, chock full of whatever magic sped through my system under the rising pressure of this new threat.

He wouldn't hurt me, couldn't touch me. My spiritual Mother would protect me. Her shield merged with mine, pulsing alongside my heartbeat.

Sleep, child. Hide within and stay with me. No harm will come to you.

Blinding white fire flared, painless against my widened eyes—now dry and rolling back in an ecstasy which rattled the flesh from my bones. She was here, bringing the scent of summer flowers—exotic and overwhelming, potent enough to taste as the aroma flooded my nostrils. My mouth opened wide, releasing a triumphant cry for all to hear.

"Mitéra me sósei!"

They pounded on the door, each shove pushing it and me forward. I rolled, sinking without a sound—a stone tossed into a bottomless lake and swallowed up.

She arrived—here, at last, to save me...

CHAPTER TWENTY-SIX

I awoke to the sound of barking dogs. My eyes popped open with alarm but failed to spot anything. Four paths jutted out, over and beyond the slate-gray hills rolling beneath a sooty crimson sky. Not a hint of greenery, no calming blue, only the faint lick of flames the color of autumn leaves. The place was a wasteland, but vibrant and humming with energy—not alive, but far from dead.

Kóri, me akoúei.

Daughter, hear me... She'd used the original form of my name, transforming it into both a title and a command. Her presence answered the last words that had flown across my lips, a hasty but desperate prayer for help.

"Mama," I said, choked with tears. I turned in circles, but she wasn't there. A terrible dream, to taunt me with her voice; the promise of her presence when I needed her most, except I was given nothing but death and fire.

Wait—there she was. Where did she come from? I'd spun past that spot at least three times.

A hooded figure waited, hulking and shapeless, with a long, gnarled torch gripped in one elderly claw. Not my mama, but still a Mother.

Mitéra Hekate, akoúo. Mother, I listen.

She continued, her words all hard consonants and guttural vowels—no longer the Greek, but something different...older. Somehow, even though the sounds made no sense, the words tapped across my brain like letters on a screen.

Four paths. A life, a future...each different. Your choice, alone.

Mitéra, Polyagapiménos, Paidí, Psychí.

Mother, Beloved, Child, Self.

Save one, lose one of the others.

Decide, Kóri-daughter. Once a maiden, now a woman.

"But how do I know? What if I choose wrong? I don't want to lose any of them." I reached toward the hooded figure, but She stayed just out of reach. "I don't want to die. Is that wrong?"

Mitéra, Polyagapiménos, Paidí, Psychí. Each path had a sign, names scrawled across the faded wood with barely visible ink. What was the right choice, the choice I could live with?

Mama wouldn't want to lose me or my child. Neither would Hayden. And the baby, didn't it deserve a chance? But could it even live without me—how did that make sense?

If I chose myself, would it save me and the baby since we were linked right now? But who could I travel through the years without—Mama? No way. But I also understood what life was like without a father. Could I do that to my unborn child? Hayden and I had only been together for a few weeks, but could I sacrifice one of the only people who kept me sane during this nightmare?

"*Mitéra* Hekate, I can't do it. I won't risk them. Take me, *psychí*. I couldn't live with myself if my choice killed any of them."

She lifted her torch high, illuminating the head beneath the hood—no, heads; one turned left, one turned right, and one stared straight ahead. Maiden, Mother, Crone—a head for each, hard as marble, alternating between exquisite beauty and chalky horror. Black voids swirled in each eye socket, portals to infinite mysteries and madness. The central visage gaped my way—the Crone, framed in ivory desiccation. Those terrible eyes fixed on my face, and something within broke.

Two red lips, slashes in a swath of bloodless skin, split to release a howl that slaughtered my ears. My knees cracked against the hard ground, hands squeezing my agonized head. The figure scurried forward, shuffling like dead leaves snatched by a sudden whirlwind. One bony hand stretched to swipe at my hands, forcing me to acknowledge the nightmarish vision.

Nothing should move that fast.

"Then let the Fates decide. *Thanátou!*"

The torch swung in an arc overhead. Her body quaked with raucous laughter, colorless robes flapping to release a miasma of musty flowers and decomposition. Three screaming faces, white hair standing on end and crackling with purple veins of electricity, six black holes where Their eyes should've been, speckled with stars...or witch-fire.

Take me, not them. Mother, show mercy. Take me, please.

***

When I awoke, I wasn't alone. I recognized the woman beside the bed, graying brown hair unbound alongside skin far too smooth for a woman in her fifties. Brittle eyes fixed on mine, fracturing beneath a burden that didn't seem to lighten when I turned toward her.

"Welcome back," Aspasia said, uncrossing her legs to lean closer. "Whatever you did to yourself worked. I've never seen my husband frightened, enough that he agreed to transfer you to my care. You're lucky, young lady, because I will protect you. I may not be one of them, but I still retain some rights and rank in this family. Although if it wasn't for my grandchild in your belly, I'd let him take you for all the trouble you've caused."

The harsh words battered me, limbs heavy with sleep even as my nerves screamed themselves awake. "It's not my fault. I didn't ask for this."

"I told you to stay away, and you did not. Who else is to blame for where we are?" Aspasia asked grimly. "Now, my grandchild is in danger. My daughter and my son are with their father instead of me, volunteering to join that demented cult. I may lose my family, all because of you."

"Hayden did what? No, that's not possible." I tried to sit up, but my muscles failed. "How long was I out?"

"Nearly a week, thanks to your magical light show. Dr. Kaplan has kept a close watch on you, assuring us you were stable. My son refused to be kept away, offering himself in exchange to be with you." She sat back, a grimace smeared over her cool façade. "Alastor got what he always wanted, his son to agree to join in this lunacy. He'll be initiated on the new moon, as will my Bronte. Then on Yule, they'll stretch you across the altar with my only grandchild in your belly."

"Please, let me see him." I struggled to escape but only tangled myself further in a nest of wires. "I'll make him leave. He can't do this."

"He already has. He's forsaken you and the rest of us. My son made his choice, as has my baby girl. Alastor won, and I'm alone—a prisoner in this madhouse, just like you." She stood, smoothing her designer pantsuit and heading toward the door. "I managed to contact Tessa. She sent over a special tea. I'll brew a pot for you. Another innocent woman, beside herself with worry—just so you know. She's determined to save you, but I don't have the heart to stop her. A mother has a right to choose, after all. It's done. He has you now."

"But he doesn't have power like my mama. She'll put a stop to this. Satanism, demons—it's all a Christian myth. My mama, her power is real," I proclaimed, desperate to convince Aspasia and maybe myself.

She shared a pitiful smile. "The darkness is real, too, Coralena. If you haven't learned that by now, you'll never make it out of here alive."

***

Aspasia and Dr. Kaplan were my only visitors in the days that followed. They kept their own counsel yet assured me the baby appeared healthy despite the growth spurts. No other news, but at least there wasn't an immediate threat from Alastor. Somehow the pair kept me safe, even if only for selfish reasons. Aspasia swore to protect her grandchild, and Dr. Kaplan wanted a pure vessel for Yule—hardly altruistic, but I'd take it for now.

Finally, a new visitor arrived with my daily tea. She bounced in, exuberant and sporty, wearing expensive yoga clothes. A picture of perfection to some, but I knew better.

"Aren't you so cute when you wake up? All that crazy hair and the drool on your cheek. Adorable," Bronte cooed, setting down the tray and pouring a steaming portion of tea into an expensive china cup. "I can almost see where Hayden would be drawn to you, sort of like some shaggy stray on those ASPCA commercials."

"We've had our issues, but you can't be serious about joining with your dad," I said, refusing to acknowledge her insult. "After New York, I thought you were on our side. If there's a plan, then let me in on it. This isn't you! You may be a bitch, but you're not evil."

"Thank you, Cori." She sat on the edge of the bed, gesturing for me to drink. "I feel like, after all these years, you never took me seriously. And I wouldn't say I'm evil. Is it wrong to want to find a place in the world? To follow in my father's footsteps, when I've always admired him? He's finally seeing me. He was so proud I brought you here. Now he's treating me like an adult—an ally, instead of a decorative little girl. I truly appreciate your help."

"You're bullshitting me."

"No," she said with a condescending smile. "And I thought my mother sheltered us. Your mother may have shown you magic, but she locked you away from the world. How do you think power is obtained—hard work, a dab of elbow grease, or giving it the good ole college try? Sacrifice, the real kind, comes from blood and offerings to something bigger than yourself. Something bigger than you could ever imagine. Daddy showed me a piece, but I'll see more tonight at the Dark Moon Ritual. Now don't be jealous. Your big moment at Yule is only a month away—yay!" She clapped cheerily. "So drink your mama's tea and be a good girl."

"You're insane." A lame comeback, but I couldn't cobble together anything more eloquent. There wasn't time, anyway. She was finished, serving both her bizarre message and the wholesome tea. Chores complete—now she was off to start her day, perhaps with a shopping trip or a mani-pedi with her friends at the local spa.

"No, honey. I'm right on track, and it's an awesome feeling." Bronte waved, skipping to the door. "See you tonight!"

Dark Moon Ritual... Could they be any more unhinged? *Hekate, give me strength.*

CHAPTER TWENTY-SEVEN

At least I wasn't alone in the tent this time. Aspasia sat beside me, bundled in a winter coat and hat, sipping on a mug of hot tea as was I. Mama's tea was the preferred beverage of the fine ladies of Greenwich, a refined pastime for the wives of confirmed Satanists. Did they know where their husbands were tonight?

Would they care so long as their extravagant lifestyles were maintained?

"Have you seen one of these before?" I asked, my nerves fraying to the point I no longer cared about annoying my one ally here. An alliance only made for her unborn grandchild, but I trusted she'd keep me safe while I was his human incubator.

"The Dark Moon Ritual? Yes, once." Aspasia avoided my gaze, swirling the steam in her cup as if it were a cauldron filled with past scenes best forgotten. "It was back when Alastor cared what I thought. He attempted to draw me into his hobby. I watched one which, like this, was an initiation. That was the moment our relationship changed forever."

"Why did you never leave? How could you stay with someone so evil?" The question had burned for weeks now, my mind unable to reconcile this stately woman choosing someone so unhinged as her mate.

"I tried to leave. Once," she admitted, her impeccable posture slumping; the years of dejection must've caught up with her. "I packed up the children shortly after Bronte was born, rented an apartment in New York. We lived there for only one day. Alastor came with his bodyguards, some NYPD friends, and coven members. Security at the building didn't stop them. They put ritual knives against Bronte's throat, and she cried for me. My poor little baby, so scared and helpless..."

"No one would help you? Honest police, lawyers, anyone?" I pressed, unwilling to believe the coven's influence ran so deep.

"Enough power was on his side, so I didn't dare risk searching for allies." Her casual shrug didn't diminish the rigid tension in her back and arms. "He told me he only needed a son to follow him, that a daughter was expendable. He swore he'd kill her without a second thought, smiling as I begged and wept. Thank God we never had more children, a bonus blessing from your mother's curse. I couldn't bear the thought of any more innocents in danger."

"But doesn't he love you? Doesn't that matter to him?"

"Alastor loves power," Aspasia corrected. "I like to think he loved me once. He certainly wanted me before we were married. He was different then, dashing and confident, undeniable. Sometimes I saw that side after Hayden was born, but the man I fell in love with disappeared more each year, worse after every ritual. I don't believe he can love any of us now, but—in his mind—we belong to him. And he's never been one to surrender what's his. He'll destroy anyone who tries to take from him."

"If you get me out of here, Mama and I can find a way to stop him." I impulsively grabbed her hand. She frowned and shook me off.

"I have no doubt you and Tessa could find some way to cripple him again, but that won't be enough. Don't you see? Alastor won't quit. He's too far gone, and I will not risk losing my family." Her voice lowered, even as her eyes flared. "I promise you this, as I told your mother: once the baby is born, I'll help you find a way out. That's the most I'm willing to do. But if I sense you try to leave before that, I'll turn you in myself."

I didn't know what to say, sagging into the chair. After a fortifying sip from my cooling tea, I stated with quiet dignity, "I'm someone's daughter, too."

"Yes, but you're not mine."

She jumped to her feet when the tent flap moved. A cloaked figure entered, shadowed features materializing as he turned toward me. Icy eyes softened, the tight lines of his mouth relaxing even as my heart lurched to see him again at last. "Give us a moment please, Mother."

"Don't do anything stupid." Aspasia glanced between us before resting a hand on his shoulder. "It's too late for heroics now, love."

"It's fine. Dad said I could speak with her before we start. Nothing to worry about."

"I'll be right outside." A final, unspoken warning hung in the air, sweet as rotting fruit. No sooner than the flap lowered, I was up and in Hayden's arms.

"We have to get out of here. They're planning something awful for me and the baby. Our baby, but I don't know how... We'll figure it out once we escape, okay?" I said in between frantic kisses, my heart tripping over itself with relief. He was here, succeeding at his subterfuge. He found me. And, like before, he could save me.

"Cori, we can't—stop!" He grabbed my wrists, prying us apart. His tortured gaze locked to mine, throat muscles working as he fought himself. "The tent is surrounded. He's not taking any chances tonight, even though I agreed to give him what he's always wanted. We won't make it out of here."

"No! Hayden, he scares me. I think I know what he wants. He made that clear. He...touched me. Don't leave me here. I can't do this." The whine in my voice shamed me, as did the tears I couldn't hold back. I hated myself for weakening, wanting to hate him for not automatically whisking me away. "I love you. Please, don't do this."

"And I love you," Hayden said, voice cracking as his eyes fell to my belly. He released my hands to rest his on my abdomen, stroking the fleshy cradle beneath my clothes. "Cori, I don't have a choice. If I join, I can stay close and defend you. Maybe a better opportunity will come later, but right now this is the only option we've got. They'll initiate me and Bronte tonight. I have to do this. If I get them to trust me, I might find some weapon to use against them."

"What weapon?" I slapped his hands, then hid my wet face. "This is all bullshit! There isn't a Satan or a Hell, but evil fucking people exist. You can't become one of them. How could you?"

"You said belief makes things real. These people believe. I've seen what they're capable of. I have to act." He gently forced me to meet his anguished, but unrelenting, face. "I believe in *you*, Coralena. I'm doing this for you... for us. It's just a game, right? Join their little club, gain a rank, then I'll have power like my father. I'll use every bit of it to protect you and crush him."

"Hayden, no..." I took a deep breath, pouring out my love in one last, naked plea. "Go to Mama, I beg you. She must have a plan. We can find a way to fight! And if we can't fight, we can run—somewhere, anywhere. If they make you do something evil, you'll change. You could lose your soul, be ruined forever. Don't you understand?"

"I don't believe that." His thumbs wiped my eyes, trailing down my cheekbones and resting on my jaw. He held me still for his sweet kiss—a promise of devotion, but I could taste the failure and regret. "Nothing can be evil if it's meant to save those we love. I'd give up everything—my mind, my body, my soul—for you and the baby we created together. They can't ruin us, Cori. I won't let them."

"You may not have a choice." I sank into my chair, knees buckling after his foolish vow. "If you do this, step down a path toward darkness, there won't be anything left to save."

"Trust me as I trust you. I won't let them hurt you or the baby." He knelt beside me, holding my hands and kissing my fingertips before letting them go. "Stay with Mother and know that whatever happens, I'm always yours."

Another rustle of the tent flap interrupted us, revealing a masked woman whose voice I couldn't forget. "Well, if it isn't the one who got away. Come along, Princess, time for the show to begin. Don't worry, I'll take excellent care of your prince tonight. Maybe we can compare notes later?"

I leapt without a second thought, snarling, "Keep your fucking hands to yourself, or I'll—"

"Cori, stop!" Hayden's sharp command was tougher than his wounded gaze, hard as if armoring himself against the woman and her vulgar laughter.

Aspasia reentered with a squat figure in a black robe and mask lined with red leather. Different from the others, maybe he was a higher-ranking member. "It's time. Enough of the dramatics. Our Lord awaits."

The pair guided Hayden from the tent, his face now hidden behind a mask he removed from his pocket. Aspasia's hands rested on my shoulders, holding me in the chair, but she didn't need to bother. The fight faded from me, along with the hope of this nightmare ever ending.

***

The bonfire blazed in the clearing, high and bright in the moonless night. The only light, but more than enough to reveal the two rows of twelve cultists—hooded and masked, linking hands and singing in Latin before a lone pair. Hayden and Bronte stood in silhouette, holding hands beside a pair of iron spikes planted in the earth.

The tone of the song began calmly enough, even though the words meant nothing to me. Aspasia stood beside me, physically close but as emotionally distant as a spirit from the Otherworld. We were witnesses tonight, not participants, ringed by a trio of impassive bodyguards. As if we could've run, locked on this small island—a captive audience for whatever show Alastor and his friends planned.

"Lupus Filios, we gather to summon our Lord Mammon on this Dark Moon Ritual," Alastor's voice rang from behind a gold mask. He exited the group to stand before his children. "Bless this Rite of Initiation and strike down the supplicants if they fail to please you."

Aspasia clutched my hand, a gesture I didn't mind despite her earlier snub. Anchoring myself to her calmed the tempest in my soul as we waited for the show to reach its terrible climax.

A slow beat began from within the crowd. Cultists shifted to reveal a trio on the end, tapping a pair of hide drums strapped to their chests. The Latin resumed, a deceptively dull whisper barely audible over the crackling bonfire.

The chant rose when two bodyguards emerged, dragging a pair of goats. The innocent animals were tied to the spikes beside Hayden and Bronte, abandoned to their fate.

"What are they doing?" I asked Aspasia, grunting when a bodyguard poked me with some kind of stick.

"Silence."

Aspasia's wide eyes flowered with dread, but she shook her head and moved even closer. The bleating goats recaptured my attention, my stomach lurching when I spotted the glimmer of steel in Hayden and Bronte's hands. *No, they can't...*

The chanting increased, louder and faster to match the speeding drums, urging the participants onward like an audience surrounding a boxing ring. Hayden and Bronte stood above each goat, one light and one dark, their hooves rapidly shuffling the dirt as if the poor things sensed what was coming.

Alastor raised his hands, the Latin commands flying too fast from his lips to make sense. The cruel female cultist and the squat male took position beside Hayden and Bronte, the four of them shedding their robes to reveal their nakedness.

"We have to stop this," I hissed in Aspasia's ear, low enough to evade our handlers' notice. "Help me!"

"They chose this. We can't..." she whimpered, forgetting herself and receiving her own sharp poke from the scowling guard.

"Mammon, Our Dark Lord and General of Hell, welcome these children if they are worthy. Smite them if not, for only the strongest wolves may join the Brotherhood." Alastor lowered his arms, barking an incoherent command. The light of the bonfire cast terrifying shadows across his countenance. More dusky, jagged shapes hovered above the small group encircling the now-bucking goats.

Still masked, naked bodies reddened by the swirling hell-light, they stalked toward their animals with knives raised. This couldn't be happening. Impossible, that a girl I'd spent my entire school career with and the man I loved would kill blameless animals. Goddess knew what they'd do with the blood and organs. The siblings readied themselves, stark naked as a crowd of chanting maniacs summoned their one true lord to judge the performance.

"Hayden, don't!" I screamed, breaking free from Aspasia but falling to my knees after a mild jolt from the guard's prod.

The figures looked up momentarily, a tableau of impending horror. The gleaming blades sliced through the night, silencing the frantic goats forever.

Gouts of blood pumped forth as the pair of animals swayed, stumbled, and fell. The Latin chant shrieked with exultation. The pair beside Hayden and Bronte dipped their hands into the spreading puddles. They drew ominous symbols on the initiates with swift fingers, including a large pentagram on their chests. The reverse of the pentagram on my necklace, representing the Five Elements of Nature; a symbol sacred to the gods, inverted into an abomination...a mark of evil.

I turned just in time, vomiting into the dirt instead of down the front of my robe.

"Don't hurt her, idiots," Aspasia snapped at the guards. She knelt, her arms gathering me against her trembling chest. Her voice buzzed in my ear, far harsher than how she'd spoken to the guards. "Stop it, Coralena! You'll spoil their chance. Don't look if you can't control yourself."

She was right. If he stopped now, the fanatics would tear him to pieces; but surely the worst was over?

I rolled over, trying to see, but the darkness pressed in from all directions, clashing with the bonfire. The light and heat overwhelmed me, my pores shrinking tight as new leather even as I shivered from the late November breeze.

Alastor called the group forward, drumbeat speeding up as the bodies closed around the two couples. The cult members pawed Hayden and Bronte, both still naked and smeared with goat's blood. Their handlers forced the pair into the dirt, then mounted them.

No... Hayden, fight back! What are you doing?

The woman who tormented me on Halloween laughed and rode Hayden, who laid in a submissive position. Her friends drew bloody symbols across her lean frame. I heard her grunts even from a distance, louder with each wild gyration of her hips. She sucked blood from the fingers of the surrounding cultists while blithely stealing the vital essence of the man I loved. And he allowed it, martyring himself to complete the ceremony.

Bronte cried out, ecstatic during her initiation. She ran her hands along her breasts, tossing her head with wild abandon as random hands pinched and stroked her. Never caring that her mother crouched beside me in the dirt, weeping and tearing her hair, unable to stop the disgraceful display.

Struggling to my feet, I faced their repulsive ritual with newly dried eyes. Threads of power flickered over my arms and crackled between my fingertips. Was this electricity connected to the shock from the guard's prod, inspiring a natural response in my overtaxed body and screeching brain?

Mitéra Hekate, Queen of the Night, Protector of Witches, Guardian of Young Mothers, imbue me with the strength to stop them, hurt them, end this...

"NA STAMATÍSEI!"

Power rose from the earth and shot toward the sky, returning as a lightning bolt to demolish a nearby tree. That got their attention, stopping the sacrilegious orgy in its tracks. All eyes were on me—good. I hoped they enjoyed the show before I torched them.

A roar from the bonfire stopped my progress, the flames rising and curling like a hand raised in greeting. The golden center of the blaze, more brilliant than the rest, revealed a pair of ruby eyes and a sooty mouth filled with scorched teeth. A snarl snapped from the inferno's core—*did it call my name?*—followed by a wolf's howl, shattering the night. I flinched, shaking my head at a new voice; a dusty, wicked chuckle in my ear, sizzling over my fried nerves in an uninvited caress.

What the fuck was that?

Multiple shocks bit through my robes, fanning throughout my lower back. Before I hit the ground, a weight thudded into my skull and toppled me into unconsciousness.

CHAPTER TWENTY-EIGHT

The smell of fresh herbs, garlic, and a tangy splash of lemon brightened my bedroom. I snuggled closer to Mama and her scent, listening to the rest of her story even as I fought against fatigue's allure.

"...and they lived happily ever after, ruling the kingdom built anew thanks to their love."

"Tell me another, Mama." I smothered a yawn with small hands. Tiny as a doll, which didn't make sense...

(*shhh, nopey nope*)

"It's time to sleep, my love. Your big day is coming soon," Mama said, her hair wild as midnight without a trace of silvery gray. Young, both of us, before the rest— What had just happened? I couldn't quite remember.

(*no 'member. Just be here now, happy.*)

"Don't wanna go. Can't I stay with you forever? I can help cook. You said I cut the herbs nice and neat." I sweetened my words, intending to persuade her.

"It's time to grow up, my love, and learn who you really are," she explained firmly, but the kiss she brushed against my forehead was gentle. "Cori, you know we have powers. The women in our family have always served mankind, helped others, shining a light into the darkness. If you want to help me, you have to learn all you can—both from the world and from me."

"But what if none of the kids like me?" I feared reentering the frightfully expensive building of glass and stone. All the kids in their beautiful clothes with expensive phones and laptops. They'd laugh at me, with my pencils and cheap notebooks, wearing my plain clothes from the superstore.

"You're beautiful, smart, funny, and brave. Who wouldn't want to be your friend? Don't be silly, baby. And if they don't want you, I'll always be your friend."

"I love you, Mama. You'll be my best friend forever."

"A mother always is." Her rich voice faded beneath the palpable vibrance of her beaming smile. "I'll never stop taking your side as long as I'm here. You're my good girl."

(come back, mama, let me try again)

She's burning up.

Sedate her, quick! Blood pressure's too high.

The background murmurs annoyed me, causing Mama's form to pulse and disappear—returning, but with difficulty. I could barely see her. The colorless smoke shaped itself into a faint outline, teasing me with the idea she might be with me...if only.

"Mama, come back! One more story, okay? I'll be good again."

Wake up, baby. Open your eyes for me.

(hurts... Don't wanna see no more.)

I know. Come home to me—my love, agápi mou. There's still time, never fear.

***

Music tinkled through my ears, soothing my senses along with the fresh rosemary and something spicy-sweet. "Mama?"

"I'm here, Cori." A cool hand smoothed the hair from my brow, her melodious voice a salve for my wounded soul.

Leaning into that touch, I opened my mouth to speak, but only coughed. My throat was dry, each swallow like razor blades rubbing together. "Can't—"

"Take a sip. It's okay," she said, placing a straw between my lips. As wave after wave of restorative water streamed down my throat, the scene above me cleared. Her skin remained unlined, resembling an older sister rather than my middle-aged mother; she grew ever prettier as her weary eyes brightened above a beatific smile.

"Your hair... What did you do?" I reached toward the new white streaks, no longer a random thread here or there. She must've been busy working with forces at a level we'd always avoided.

"I see yours is getting as bad as mine," Mama said, a gentle reproof causing a light flush along my cheeks. "What's done is done, but you cannot let yourself go again. The baby can't take anymore, love."

"What do you mean?" Panicked hands flew around the fine web of lines snaking from my chest and arm. I croaked in surprise when I found the bump between my hips. "No freaking way! How... It's too big, isn't it?"

"The doctor says he's fine, but what you did at the ritual caused another growth spurt." She covered my hand, and we both held my belly to calm the restless child swimming in my womb. It tickled inside me, like a fish fighting against an ever-shrinking net. "Another surge of power might be too much for him. Do you understand, Cori?"

"Him?" Not at all an expert about babies, I tried to recall the only pregnant woman I'd spent any time with. My cousin, Cristina—what had she said about her gender reveal? How many months? Second trimester, for sure. "How do you know it's a 'he?'"

"You pushed him, and yourself, too much during the ritual," she explained, the memory of that night ratcheting my fear again. "Aspasia said you were glowing. The bonfire rose and lashed out at the cult members. No one was killed, but several were burned enough to require medical attention. Their security guards knocked you out, but by then you were spotting from the exertion. You might have lost him."

"How long have I been like this?" I lifted the arm sporting an IV, patting my chest to find various pads stuck to my unwashed skin, tacky from dried sweat.

"A week, but you were much worse before I arrived." She lifted the cup and straw, urging me to drink more. "Aspasia gained permission to call me. She was desperate to stabilize you and the baby. It was quite the job, a full night of prayers and healing spells which took a toll on me."

"I'm sorry."

"No, never be sorry for needing me. I'm here for you, always." Mama pressed a button so my bed rose to a sitting position. "But now that you're awake, our time will be limited. I need you to listen and do as I say. Don't speak, just nod."

I nodded, holding the cup as her hands rested on either side of my face.

"The ritual will begin on the 21st, a perversion of the Yule ceremony. I promise I will rescue you, but you cannot give them a reason to suspect anything. Do what they say, do not fight back, do not use magic. You must eat and drink to stay strong. Aspasia has the new batch of tea I made. Drink a cup, three times a day, to restore your health and spirit. They may try to sedate you. Let them. She'll get the tea in you somehow." She pressed on my cheeks, as if afraid words weren't enough to impress the seriousness of our predicament. "On Yule, be brave and ready to run. Trust no one—not even Aspasia. She believes the tea will only benefit the baby, which is why she's cooperating. I didn't tell her my plan. She will choose her children above you, never forget."

"Thank you, Mama. I promise I'll listen this time." I sniffed back the swell of emotion inspired by the sparkle of tears in her sweet brown eyes.

"I know you will, baby. I'm sorry this had to happen, but we'll make it right." She kissed my cheek and laid her head against my shoulder—an awkward embrace thanks to the tubes and other equipment.

"What's happening to me? These powers, I've never felt anything like it," I whispered in case they could hear us. But it must've been safe, otherwise Mama wouldn't have told me her plan. "Somehow I healed Hayden. It drained me, but not as bad as this. All I remember of the other night was rage. I wanted to destroy them all. I should've been scared, but I wanted it—the power, their fear...their deaths. Is something wrong with me?"

"There's a dark side to every power, you know that." Her words were encouraging, but carried a warning that made me shiver beneath the blankets. "All the women in our line have the power to heal. Our small spells at the restaurant, they're slivers of that larger restorative gift. But the same force can easily turn toward its opposite—destruction and death. We're all vulnerable to our emotions, which fuel our power along with Nature. You must fight back, baby. Darkness doesn't have to be evil. We all carry it in our hearts. But if you give in, allow the shadows to overtake the light, you'll be worse than dead."

"Hayden, he gave in. Is he—"

"Stay away from him, Cori, I beg you." Mama squeezed my hand as steps approached the closed door. "Even if he meant well, the choice he made corrupted him forever. Both children, they're lost now."

Aspasia entered—composed and lovely again, unlike the other night— carrying a covered bowl. "You're awake. I'll ring for another lunch. You must be famished."

"That's unnecessary." Mama gave me a final kiss, then stood, helping me settle against the pillows. "I should head home. She's stable now. I won't violate our bargain."

"I'm glad to hear it. Thank you for coming," Aspasia replied, setting the bowl on the side table.

Blinking at the pair of them, I struggled to contain my rising emotions—disbelief, disgust, and a growing fury. "How can you talk like this is some tea party that went on for a little too long? You're holding me prisoner, forcing my mother to care for me, then throwing her out to start the hostage routine again. What the fuck is wrong with you all?"

"Cori! Calm yourself, for the baby's sake." Mama's voice cracked through the room. She stilled, drawing her dignity around her like a cloak against Aspasia's scrutiny. "She'll obey. I calmed her down. If anything happens, I'm only a phone call away."

"Thank you again, Theresa," Aspasia gestured toward the door. "Come, I'll walk you out. Coralena, eat your soup. I'll bring some tea before Dr. Kaplan's visit."

"Remember what I said," Mama pleaded, her face half-shadowed by the closing door. "Cooperate, and we can leave this all behind soon enough. I love you, my baby."

"Love you, Mama."

I clenched my fists as the pair left me alone in the opulent but empty room. The little man moved, poking me from the inside. Maybe he was excited by the earthy richness wafting from the nearby bowl.

I began the lunch I had no appetite for, but what I wanted didn't matter now. I was a mother and—with my own as an example—I began to understand what sacrifice meant.

***

I spent another night hooked to the array of monitors which, Dr. Kaplan happily informed me, were all linked by Wi-Fi to his phone. As if I gave a shit. This meant he'd know if anything went wrong before it was too late. *You and the baby will be even safer, isn't that nice?*

Yes, right before you murder us... But I kept that part in, like Mama ordered.

The window next to my bed revealed a row of treetops beneath a waxing moon and, in the distance, the faint lights of Greenwich. No ocean view for the holiday sacrifice; after all, I was only a step above the help. Anger simmered with every letter I carved into the crossword book Aspasia left for me—a surprise present to keep my mind active, she claimed. I hated puzzles, but at this moment any distraction was better than stewing in useless despair.

A creak sounded from behind me, but I didn't care to see who it was. "Can I help you? Not that I have a choice."

"Cori."

I sucked in my breath and tucked the pencil into my fist, leaving the point poking out. A weapon, even if it was far from ideal, and wouldn't I love to stab it somewhere soft on him.

"Go away, Hayden."

"I brought you a present."

"The only present I need is for your whole fucking family to disappear from the face of the earth." I struggled to face him with my mutant belly, nearly stabbing myself with the pencil.

Hayden, still handsome even as exhaustion stained his features and repentance burdened his proud shoulders. He maintained his distance beside the closed door, carrying a small stack of books. A man I'd stupidly fallen in love with—I even told him as much. Not that it mattered. He'd betrayed me, instigating a toxic burst of magic that nearly killed both me and our baby. Now he dared to bring me gifts?

"I know you don't agree with my methods, but I only want the best for—"

"You want the best for me?" I threw the paper crossword book, which he dodged easily before moving closer. "I begged you to get us out of here, to stay away from that fucking ritual. Now, you're an animal murderer and a... I can't even believe you and that psychopath did *that* right in front of me—in front of your mother. Jesus Christ! I hope you enjoyed yourself."

"How can you say that?" He slammed the stack of books on the side table, leaning over the bed rail to grab my hand and take the pencil before I stabbed. "I joined this cult to save you, and yes, a psychopath assaulted me. I didn't fight because they'd have killed me. I did it for you! Then you tried to set us all on fire—the most terrifying fucking thing I've ever seen, by the way. Black magic coming from the woman I love, who's carrying our child..." he sputtered, running low on gas before croaking, "You think I enjoyed any of that?"

"I hate you." I wrestled against his hands until the monitors started beeping in a frenzy. "Back the fuck up before the doctor comes in to mess with me again."

"Hate me if you want." Hayden dropped my hands, slamming the pencil on the nightstand and kicking it so the books jumped. "You're alive, the both of you, and I'm going to keep it that way—no matter who I have to kill or fuck. You and I *not* done, Cori."

"Yes, we are. Now get out," I said, attempting to regulate my breathing until the monitors slowed. I turned my back, disgusted by his wounded expression. "I'm sorry I don't remember the fire. I'm more sorry I didn't burn your ass up first."

"Don't do me any favors. Maybe you'll get a better chance on Yule." I heard him retreat, or so I assumed. I damn sure wasn't going to watch him go. "Anyway, the books are to help with the boredom. I recommend *A Tale of Two Cities.*"

"Oh, great choice. I hate to burst your bubble, but you're a far cry from Sidney Carton," I scoffed, stabbing my nails into my palm—hard as I could stand, but not breaking the skin.

"Maybe so. But I'll still save you, even if it ends up killing me."

The door shut, a quiet click instead of a slam, but it still made me flinch. Books—what did he care if I was bored?—and classics, to boot. Did he think I wasn't as smart as him, that I needed to expand my knowledge base? I might not have gone to a fancy prep school or college, but I was just as smart after a lifetime of Greenwich public schools.

Distraction, something to ease the boredom…and maybe the fear.

"For fuck's sake," I muttered, grabbing the dark blue, leather-bound edition of *A Tale of Two Cities*. Bigger than the others, maybe it was some ultra-rare first edition. Knowing this family's connections, it was probably signed with a heart and a kiss from Dickens himself.

Flipping back the cover and the title page, I stopped and let it fall into my lap. This wasn't Dickens. This was Mama's grimoire, her book of magic built up over decades. Spells, prayers, recipes, and more—she'd never let me read through it on my own.

The book I'd searched for after fleeing New York. I had assumed Alastor's goons took it, but here it was—rebound in another cover so no one would've looked twice.

I hate you…burn your ass up. Fucking hell! How'd he always find a way to make me feel like the asshole?

I huddled over the book to read, ready to shut it if anyone else came by to bother me. My gift, the best thing Hayden could've given me; a way out, maybe a way to fight, but I needed to find a way without magic. Yule would arrive in a couple of weeks, which would have to be enough time. The chance I needed, brought to me by the man I wanted to hate even if—

Don't you go there, not again.

But that was easier said than done, as always, when it came to Hayden.

CHAPTER TWENTY-NINE

Over the next two weeks, I studied every day. Aspasia brought my meals and tea, but she never stayed long. Dr. Kaplan visited a couple of times a week, and my body normalized. My good behavior proved I wasn't a flight risk. They removed my tethers to the medical equipment, allowing me the freedom of the spacious bedroom.

Bronte and Alastor kept their distance, a mercy likely orchestrated by Aspasia. Although, I admitted to being interested in how Bronte was coping after the Dark Moon Ritual. Did she feel different after joining her father's cult? Validated, powerful...loved and noticed? Had it been worth the total surrender of self? Maybe not much of a hardship for a girl who always adhered to others' wishes, fulfilling the expectations outlined by society and her idiot father.

Hayden didn't visit again, but that was for the best. I didn't need to shoulder his guilt along with my own. I certainly didn't want to hear more useless proclamations of love. He'd made his choice, agreeing to crimes I'd begged him not to commit. How much could I have really mattered to him?

Mama never visited, but according to Aspasia, there was no need. My health was steady, better than ever with Mama's recommended diet and her tea. Strength, fortitude, protection, and maybe more; every bite and sip sent loving tendrils of her magic through my body. Even at a distance, she helped me prepare for the coming ceremony and our eventual escape from the Colburns. I trusted she knew what she was doing. She had never let me down before.

Although she was absent, I spoke with her on every page of the grimoire. I memorized recipes for a variety of beverages and meals combatting every infirmity imaginable—physical ailments, mental illness, and spiritual attack. Potions for love, luck, divination, protection against evil, but I found nothing of the curse she constructed against Alastor.

Maybe that was on purpose. A curse lay as heavy on the caster as the recipient, sending a punishment three times as strong for breaking the First Law. She must've wanted no evidence of the night she retaliated against a man who hurt her, the night she fell from grace. That was one step she didn't want me to follow her in. I understood her decision, yet I still craved the knowledge.

I'd have my vengeance soon, and at this point, I didn't care what parts of myself I lost in the process.

***

On the night before the Yule ceremony, Aspasia entered the room with a lovely green silk bathrobe over her arm. An odd accessory, clashing with her expensive blue evening gown.

"I've come to escort you to dinner," she said, tossing the robe across the bed. "My husband asked me to collect you, against my wishes, so here we are. Please wear the robe as I have nothing suitable to fit you."

"What if I don't want to go to dinner?" I asked, already knowing the answer.

"Why should it matter what you want? Get used to disappointment with the men in this family." She extended her hands to help me from the armchair.

My stomach ballooned under the nightgown, far larger than it should've been for a month of pregnancy. Dr. Kaplan likened the baby to a cantaloupe. A healthy boy, or so they assured me, but I hadn't been shown any ultrasound photos nor informed beyond the basics.

I agreed with the healthy part, enduring every kick and change of position with the occasional grunt. Felix, that was what I called him—my father's name, and a decision I shared with no one.

My baby, my only friend in this hellhole.

"You say that as if I'll be joining this family." I pulled the robe on, punctuating my statement by tying a snug knot under my breasts. "Sorry to break your heart, but it'll never happen."

Aspasia shook her head, opening the door for me. "That ship has already sailed, dear. You're one of us now, regardless of what you might choose. Come along."

I hadn't been in the formal dining room since my Halloween stealth mission, and I'd never seen it decorated for a holiday dinner. An extravagant display sprawled before me—crystal and gold fixtures, muted rose and charcoal walls, polished dark chairs, and a fabulously overdone centerpiece of flowers and fruits. No holly or mistletoe, too bad. I would've enjoyed another chance to spike Alastor's food or drink.

He sat at the head of the table with Bronte at one side. An empty seat awaited me on his immediate left, with Hayden on my other side. Aspasia sat at the opposite end of the table, her sharp eyes sending me one last warning. The other dozen seats were filled with elegant men and two women, smiling in hungry anticipation—unmasked, key members of Lupus Filios.

"There's our precious girl." Alastor stood and waved me toward the seat he saved, smiling as if I were a treasured friend or family member. Not the unwilling guest of honor at tomorrow's sacrilegious ritual. "What radiance! Motherhood becomes you, darling."

I didn't trust myself to speak, lumbering to my spot between the two men I despised most in the world. Hayden's eyes continued to avoid mine, focused on the empty plate, but I noticed the balled fists in his lap. Stubborn idiot; he didn't have to be a prisoner here. He was free to leave if he pleased, unlike me.

"Please, let us enjoy this holiday meal as a family before the festivities begin tomorrow." Alastor raised his same goblet from Halloween, gesturing to every beaming face like a king among his thankful courtiers. "*Lupus*

Filios, Mors in Victoria!"

The group repeated the euphoric toast, raising their glasses and drinking—everyone but me. I had no interest in partaking of anything related to my upcoming doom.

"Victory over death," Hayden murmured in my ear, low enough the group would've missed it as they clinked glasses and talked amongst themselves.

"I don't need a translator," I hissed back, even though I kind of did when it came to Latin.

Aspasia rang a small bell, and servants entered with trays of food—a variety of delicacies, amuse bouche, and soup. The richness of the food sent my stomach spinning, but I tried to force down a few bites.

"Not hungry? For shame, I thought your people were too thrifty to waste food," Bronte said from across the table, popping a festive starter between her rosy lips.

The laugh of the woman beside her chilled my blood, a sound which rang through my nightmares. It was her, the masked female cult member from Halloween and the Dark Moon Ritual—the one who'd threatened me and assaulted Hayden. Muscular and slender as an eel, her overlarge teeth reflected the candlelight, which set off her tanned skin and bleached crop of curls. Formidable, but less scary now that I could put a face to the voice.

"She's pacing herself for tomorrow, obviously," the woman said, lifting a bony hand to pinch Bronte's cheek. "I'd try to do the same, but I'm terrible with willpower on my vacations."

"I suggest you try, Mindy, for your own sake," Alastor said, fork scraping across the china in warning. "There's always room for additional volunteers on the Yule altar."

"Of course, Lord." Mindy dipped her head but tossed me an irreverent wink. "Mustn't let our...appetites get the best of us until the time is right."

"Get used to going without because you won't be touching her tomorrow," Hayden said, expelling a low growl which raised the hairs on my neck.

"Whatever you say, boy. We all get the gift we deserve on Yule," Mindy laughed, leaning into Bronte, who shook with a string of giggles—red-faced from her wine and whatever the older woman whispered into her ear. A private joke or a promise of something more later, which didn't seem to bother Bronte. She nuzzled the older woman's neck with her glossy lips.

"Bronte, I didn't realize you found a new toy so soon. Nolan wasn't enough?" I asked, making room to receive a new plate of broiled fish and vegetables.

"No, Daddy was right. He wasn't quite good enough for us. I'm keeping my options open, for now," she replied with a pleasant smile. "Unlike my brother, I know my worth and keep away from the slums."

"At least one of us got away from you crazy bastards before it was too late." I stabbed my fish, but Bronte snickered some more.

"Yes, lucky for both of us that he bored me. I cut my losses before creating any little mongrels, but Hayden always had a soft spot for strays." Her laughter cut off when Alastor slammed his cup on the table.

"Careful, daughter."

Flushed with anger, the symptoms of another magical outburst rising, I stood from the table and slapped Hayden's hand away. "My baby can't be that much of a mongrel if you all want him so badly."

"He'll satisfy Our Lord, but neither of you will ever be a part of this family—just fodder." Bronte sneered until her head rollicked back, receiving a vicious slap from her father.

"Fodder?"

"Come, my dear, you should rest," Dr. Kaplan said hurriedly, both him and Aspasia striding toward me.

"Wait a minute... What are you all saying?" I demanded, fighting as Hayden restrained me from choking the life out of Bronte.

"Take Coralena to her room. Your sister has had a bit too much to drink," Alastor ordered, gripping his daughter's arm until she cried out.

"What are you bastards planning to do to my baby?" My clawed hands stretched toward Alastor as I wiggled against Hayden's smothering embrace.

"Nothing, go rest. Hayden! Take her away."

"Sleep well, Cori! Can't wait until tomorrow." Bronte blew me a kiss, recovered from her punishment and leaning against Mindy's shoulder.

"If you hurt my baby, I'll fucking kill you all." The warning steamed with frustration, low at first, but finishing in a yelp when Hayden's arms constricted. He pulled off a combination of lifting then dragging me from the room.

"Control yourself," he warned, breathing hard when he set me before the main staircase. "Any magic and you'll—"

"I know, goddammit! Leave me alone."

"Let's go to your room." He took my hand, tugging with mulish insistence.

"Are you going to let them threaten our baby, call him a mongrel...like he's nothing?" I choked out, finally free and pushing ahead without him. By the time I reached the top of the stairs, I was out of breath thanks to over a month of being locked in one room or tied to a bed. "How do you people live with yourselves, torturing anyone who's different? It's repulsive, and you should be ashamed."

"Hey, I don't think like that," He protested. "Will you slow down before you hurt yourself?"

"What do you care? I'm one step closer to unlocking the next level of demonic lunacy. Then I'll burn this entire place to the ground. Now fuck off!"

"Get in this room, now, and lay down." Hayden blocked my path, so I had no choice. He shut the door, hovering until I complied and sat on the bed.

"You better tell me what's supposed to happen tomorrow," I warned, unable to relax even though my anger subsided with the absence of the demented cult members. "And don't lie to me, Hayden. If you care about me or the baby at all, then tell me the truth."

"All right, but keep it quiet in case someone checks on us." He sat on the edge of the bed, rolling his eyes when I scooted further away. "Jesus, Cori, can you be an adult for one goddamn minute?"

"Tell me!" I chewed through clenched teeth, privately willing to admit a quieter conversation was probably in our best interest.

"I overheard my dad and his lieutenants talking. They will use the baby, but not in the way you think," he said tersely. "There's something different about you, unusual genetic markers. I didn't understand the science, sorry. They plan on inviting Mammon to possess the baby."

"Like hell they will!" I blustered, then bit my lip and glanced at my melon belly. Sleeping now, safe in my body... *And that's how you'll stay, my Felix.*

"I agree. That's why I stole back your mother's grimoire from Dad's study. Can't you use one of those protection spells or will it hurt the baby, too?"

"I don't know. Mama said not to cast anything," I replied, cursing myself for mentioning her at all when our talk was supposed to be a secret. "I can't use magic, Hayden. If I lose control of my emotions, it'll be ugly."

"What do you need me to do?" He reached toward my belly, pausing when I flinched.

"I need a distraction, but I won't know when. We have to wait for Mama. If you want to help, then that's the best way." I lifted a hand when he tried to speak. "Just shut up. No more useless promises. If you want to be a part of our lives, you have to choose us over them. I'm tired of words. I need action—something more clever than a clumsy, half-assed infiltration of a cult."

"You may think it was unnecessary, but it's allowed me to watch over you for the past few weeks." He walked to the windows, staring through the bleak night. "I took a leave of absence, left Francisco in charge of my business...my life. I've sacrificed everything for you, Cori. I'll give even more if it helps." After a few moments of silence, he leaned his head against the glass and closed his eyes. "I really wish we'd never met. You'd be happier. Me too, maybe—hard to say because I'd still be stuck with this fucked-up family."

My throat thickened with unshed tears at the unexpected statement. I batted away a bead of guilt, which poked up like a groundhog. We might've been better off if we'd never met or reconnected. I wouldn't have some overlarge baby fighting for space in my womb; but now that Felix was here, did I really want him to disappear? And the loving moments Hayden and I shared, would my life have been happier without them?

The door opened, and Aspasia stepped in, her lips twisting with annoyance. "Sure, now you're spending quality time together. Better late than never, I suppose. They're drinking and celebrating downstairs. I'm off to bed to avoid them. You should stay here, Hayden. Some of them may start wandering for...entertainment."

"I don't want—" I began, but he cut me off with an impatient wave.

"Yes, Mother. I'll stay here. You should get some rest. And lock your door."

"He won't bother me tonight, hasn't for years," she said, embracing her son. "You worry too much, love. I'm perfectly safe, essential for keeping up appearances."

"I love you, Mother."

"And I love you." She gave him a kiss, ruffled his hair, then turned to me without revealing a scrap of the tenderness she showed her son. "Rest up, Coralena. You have a big day tomorrow. Take care of my grandson."

"Of course," I said, unwilling to add anything more personal. For what? None of this was my fault, nothing I ever asked for. She would never like me or welcome me into her heart. Why bother trying to kiss her ass?

"I think she's warming up to you," he said, forcing a smile which disappeared at my skeptical snort.

"Doubt it. She wants a pampered little debutante for her baby prince, not a working-class *mágissa*."

"I thought you were a bruja?" The sparkle returned to his eyes for a moment, forcing me to turn away from that expression I used to adore.

"Close enough." I rolled beneath the covers, sliding to the edge of the bed. "Doesn't matter, anyway. It wasn't meant to be."

"Don't say that. We could still make it out of this." The bed sank as he laid beside me. He kept his hands to himself, but his body heat warmed mine through the blanket.

"I won't deny my son access to his father, but there will be nothing between us again, Hayden." I bit the inside of my cheek once the sentence slithered from my wounded heart to the light, expecting his angry rebuttal or another impassioned plea.

Instead, after a pensive pause, I only received, "Whatever you want. Go to sleep, Cori."

The lids drooped over my eyes, a voluntary shuttering to hide from the oppressive presence at my back, but I didn't sleep. Impossible with him beside me, likely just as awake and filled with doubt. Both of us were lost to our private fears and increasingly hopeless prayers to avoid a grim future that loomed closer than ever.

CHAPTER THIRTY

Hayden was gone when I awoke; instead, I was greeted by Aspasia and my morning tea. Quiet and ladylike, she poured the cup with precision while ignoring me the whole time. But I was irritable this morning, more than usual, and interrupted her efficient routine.

"Will you still pour me this helpful prenatal tea once they stuff the soul of their demon lord into my child? Or will you get the servants to take care of that since I won't be of any use to you anymore?"

"Do you have faith in anything, Coralena?" Aspasia asked, passing me the cup with her customary steadiness. "Were you always this negative, or have the past weeks run you down into such a hateful wretch?"

"I have faith in Mama and our goddess, that's about it," I shot back, sipping the tea too soon and burning my tongue. "I damn sure don't see much good anywhere else in this world."

"You're a fool, then," she stated, heading toward the door then stopping. "He loves you, and you know it, but you gave up so easily. Why did you reject such a wonderful man? You don't care for his family? You're loyal to your mother? Do you even know why now?"

"When we spoke at Halloween, you told me to stay away from him.

You don't think I'm good enough for him, so why aren't you happy about this?" I wished she'd look at me, but she only showed me her unbowed back.

"You're not good enough for him, but it's not because of your social status, foolish girl." She turned, offering a pitying smile. "You're reckless and quick to judge, stained by darkness and hate. And Hayden...he's always been the most loving boy I've known. For you, he'll sabotage the best parts of himself, but there's nothing I can do. He's my son, and I love him. I can only watch this all unfold and offer my support when every dream he has crumbles to dust."

"You could've done more years ago, but you were a coward. I'll never be like you, staying with the wrong man because it's easy," I said as the sweet tea soured in my mouth. "I'll fight for the people I love instead of giving in to my enemies."

"And when you've decimated all of your enemies, alienating those who love you in favor of satisfying your obsession with revenge, who will be left? Who will love you then, Coralena?"

I didn't have a response, nor was she compelled to belabor her point. When she left, I gazed at the naked branches tapping on my window.

Faith, the belief in something one couldn't see, a powerful and positive lure—but also an anesthetic for the weak. I'd seen my mama's power, been touched by Great Hekate, and unleashed fire on my enemies. A miracle child grew in my belly; maybe not the easiest or most normal pregnancy, but he would be fully mine. What more did I need?

***

A maid arrived with a packet of salted herbs and another pot of tea, instructing via Aspasia that I was to bathe and dress for the evening. She'd also sent a loose robe of plain red silk, pretty but impractical given the plummeting temperature.

That was the least of my worries, though. Yule, another ceremony without the pure protection of the moon, the night of sacrifice. My son's soul on the altar this time, along with my body and mind... They'd have neither of us.

Don't worry, Felix. Yaya is coming.

Aspasia didn't know what she was talking about. These past few weeks had been a test of my faith, and it'd never shaken once in my mama. Mother—now Yaya to my son—was the one person in this world I'd always been able to count on. She'd save us. Nothing to worry about.

I didn't fight against their instructions, bathing with water that smelled of Mama's magic. I submerged myself and imagined it soaking through my pores to revive my dimming spirit. White light blended with the blaze of Hekate's torch, reinforcing the stout walls built on the foundation of my mothers' love—Mama and Mitéra.

*Bless and protect us tonight, guard us from the evil of men...a*nd the face I recalled from the flames at the Dark Moon Ritual. Maybe it hadn't been real—a product of a panicked mind, breaking when I watched the man I once loved sell his soul.

Satan wasn't real, nor were his devils—all were products of Christian superstition. That's what Mama had always said, but the darkness was real. Her and Aspasia's warnings were crystal clear. I had to admit, they might've been on to something.

None of that could defeat me, though, unless I let it. My light was my own, and vengeance could be righteous. As long as I kept my shields up, we'd make it through—Felix, Mama, me...even Hayden.

Keep telling yourself that. I squashed the snickering voice, sneaking up on me more often to undermine my fragile certainty. No room for doubt when everything that mattered most dangled on a fraying rope above a fiery pit.

Faith: I'd show them all what it really meant.

***

The chanting began, same as the Dark Moon Ritual, with sonorous Latin words filling the night air. Ominous, but this time I had an inkling of what to expect. Or so I hoped.

Trust, faith, light over dark. Cradling the space beneath my rounded belly, I sent a bolt of love to the little bundle resting within. *I love you, Felix. Don't be scared, Mama has you.*

Of course, Hayden was the one sent to fetch me from the tent this time. He was pale, his sleepless face carrying a pair of purplish bags that obscured his eyes. He looked like death warmed over, a phrase I heard often from my mother when I was sick. Sad... Only two months ago, when I met this man, he was dazzling and irresistible.

Did I do this to him? No, he made his own choices. I was only responsible for myself.

When I took his outstretched hand, I gave it a slight squeeze and pressed mine against his chest. My lips to his ear, I whispered the reminder of what we discussed last night, hidden from our enemies. "Remember the distraction. Wait for her signal."

"I won't let you down," Hayden said, pulling back to bathe me in the light of those troubled blue eyes. When he kissed me, I didn't fight. I surrendered, indulging in a taste of the steadfast love he carried even after everything. "Coralena, I love you. Stay strong. We'll get out of this—okay?"

I nodded, unable to speak. I stood on tiptoes and kissed him once more. A chaste kiss to extend the light I envisioned, spreading its wings to wrap him up, too. For Felix, who needed his father, and for me. Even after everything, the thought of irreversible harm befalling Hayden threatened to send my newly bolstered confidence into a disastrous freefall.

Time to hurt the actual villains. The rest of us had suffered long enough.

Another bonfire awaited—larger than the Dark Moon Ritual, but not as big as the pile for Halloween. They gathered round the altar, a rough-hewn slab with leather straps at its four corners. Made sense—with my limbs spread like that, I'd resemble a five-pointed star. Depending on one's perspective, it might be the witches' symbol of protection or the Satanists' attempt to pervert our ancient beliefs. Clinging to my trusty pentagram, blessed by my mother, I walked toward whatever fate awaited.

Hooded and masked figures swayed in a line, arms down and palms stretched open as if sucking energy from the earth itself. The opposite for witches, who raised their palms to the heavens and absorbed the clean light of the Goddess's moon. How did they expect anything to come through in their favor...idiots. Any wickedness born tonight would come straight from their black hearts.

The heat from the bonfire kept the worst of the chill at bay. Connecticut in December was brutal, but at least there hadn't been snow for over a week. Anticipation tap danced along my spine once those drums changed, the meticulous tempo steadily increasing. They were waiting, but for what? Something more than me. They watched from the moment I left the tent, but their tone remained the same—expectant.

Closer to the altar, my eyes caught a glint of steel from an adjacent table. Sharpened blades, some straight and some curved as a fiend's smile— bright tools for a dark purpose. Painful cutting, slicing, but on who...me?

Countless hands suddenly grabbed my arms. I fought, but they only tightened and dragged me along. My feet scrabbled over the frozen earth while my eyes raked across the group of faceless cultists. I needed a way out—now, before it was too late.

Where was Hayden? Where was Mama with her promise of rescue? Maybe they caught her, and we were done for—me and Felix, victims of whatever massacre this was doomed to become.

"Calmly now, darling, or you'll get blood on your hands," Alastor said. He was unmasked but camouflaged, the hooded robe burying his face in thick shadows untouched by the dancing firelight. "Knives are at their throats, even now. Make no mistake, they'll die if you attempt to fight back."

I followed the length of his arm to a pair beside the altar, an armed cultist on either side. Aspasia and Hayden were safe from the knives, for now, but both faces were rigid with a mounting fear. Worse for Aspasia, a proud woman dragged to this low point after years of poor choices made with the best of intentions. Tears glimmered in her eyes as she clutched her son's hand for solace, desperate for comfort, but there was none to be had. No, as she recently chided me, that ship had sailed.

But I couldn't stop. I wouldn't let it end like this. Making one last rally, I cried, "You won't do it—you can't! Not your wife and your son. People would find out. How could you hide it?"

"What do I need a wife for, where I'm going? Especially not a wife who conspired with my enemies for years, robbing me of my virility." Alastor smiled, his musty breath rolling over my now-clammy skin. "I've prayed on it, and our Lord has relented. He's offered me a gift for my years of diligent service. He will allow me to live again. No need for a son when I'll be reborn inside of you. It's been promised, and our Lord has never forsaken me."

"What? That doesn't even make sense." My frantic mind pieced together his new plan, examining those vacant, madman's eyes while pulling once more against my captors. "You can't just hop into a baby and take him over, you goddamn lunatic!"

"No? It has happened before. Our Lord assured me. An infant's soul is delicate, unattached, so easy to push out. You'll become everything to me, Coralena—my lover tonight, then my mother and protector. You'll feel the child grow within, never knowing if it's really me. Nurturing me, gazing into that innocent little face, wondering who's staring back at you." His grin widened, eyes snapping with humor and fanaticism as flecks of spittle showered me. "Blindfold and gag her in case she tries anything. Strip her, bind her to the altar. It's time to begin."

"Hayden!" I fought against the ruthless hands, trying to reach him, but the knives pressed harder against their throats. His face flattened with enraged dread, torn between my call and his mother's strangled sob. It was the last thing I saw before the cloth bound my eyeballs in their sockets.

As the red silk tore from my frame, I was spared the sight of Hayden's face but quailed at his shouted curses. My cries were cut off by a strip of cloth, digging into my cheeks and flattening my tongue—an attempt to stop my magic, in case I couldn't control myself.

Would it work? I had no idea, far from an expert in what was possible. So much of my power was based on instinct, but the crippling restraints might prove effective if I couldn't see or talk.

As I stumbled forward, mystery hands danced across my naked body. The shrill voices chanted even louder. I tasted something alkaline at the back of my throat—undistilled fear, maybe. The smell of scorched wood clogged the air, burning a path down my flaring nostrils until I coughed and fought for clean oxygen.

Smoke inhalation, a raging fire beside me... Was this how my father felt before he died?

My stomach flipped, acid tickling the back of my throat when they raised, then laid me on the icy stone. *Don't puke, you'll choke! Hold it in and wait for Mama.*

But it was hard to stay calm as leather straps bit into my wrists and ankles. My limbs spread wide, straining my lower back with the awkward angle. Stretched like a victim on the rack, I couldn't fight the fingertips that smeared something warm and sticky over my belly and breasts. Aching nipples tightened to piercing points in the frosty air. My skin pebbled and hardened in a natural attempt at armor, but none of it would keep my enemies out.

I choked again as another round of oily smoke from the bonfire blew across my face. I tried to scream and breathe through the gags, anxious at the lack of fresh air, but something was different. The smoke now carried a subtle fragrance. A greener type of wood or some sort of herbs? It itched my dripping nasal passages until I sneezed violently.

Mama...

Waves of sensation rolled from my head and down my limbs, plucking a languorous song from my taut nerves as the tainted smoke coursed through my body. *Fight it, don't breathe in too much.* The cautions were sensible but impossible in that dense air. I sensed she was close, maybe using her strength—like I had—to sway the bonfire's flames. The herbs... Someone must've placed them in the logs or the fire itself, waiting for them to catch.

The chanting broke off, voices murmuring in confusion. The drumbeat staggered, unsteady, until it trickled to a stop.

Then the screams began.

The altered smoke infected me, scratching the inside of my skull like a rabid animal seeking escape. I sobbed and fought against my bindings. I'd die here, prepped and ready for a blasphemous ritual, while whatever was out there attacked them. My mind imagined a supernatural slasher movie in big-screen, cinematic glory: massive, molten demonic forms leaping from the flames, talons slicing through every squishy human body. Pools of blood and stinking heaps of guts, pulverized skulls, organs sputtering with their last flicker of life...

When the blindfold was torn from my face, I kept my eyes shut. Couldn't stand to look, to see what had happened; I wouldn't lose my mind like the rest of them.

"Cori, come on. We've got to go."

Hayden stood above, bleeding from a gash down his face, urgent eyes cutting through the smoke. A swath of cloth was tied across his nose and mouth, which his hands hurried to duplicate for me after repurposing my blindfold. The gag was out, and my hands and feet were freed by someone else. Aspasia—nasal passages protected by a cloth—sliced the other bindings, head down to avoid an accidental peek at the surrounding chaos.

Cultists tripped over each other, wailing and slashing at the air or prostrating themselves before the bonfire, which seemed to double in size—a fiery fist punching the moonless canopy above.

The multihued flames flared as twisted, horrific figures danced to a beat all their own in celebration of the mayhem. Understandable, with such a display, how ancient people worshipped fire as a living entity. Even I was awed and spooked, rubbing my eyes in disbelief. It didn't matter whether the vision was brought on by hallucinogenic herbs or a literal crack in the Gates of Hell. My mind accepted each figure as undeniably present, cheerful devils popping up to say hello before melting to join their fellows in the heart of the inferno.

Out of the smoke, striding through the tree line, another cloaked figure approached the frenzied circle. The diminutive newcomer paused, angry eyes hard and unforgiving while taking in the scene. A savior swathed in shadows, studying her handiwork before getting too close.

Mama, she'd come for me.

"Hayden, hurry. She's here," I said, my arms tangling in the sleeves of the red robe he helped me reenter. The thin silk didn't help my shivers, but it was better than full-on nudity. The wintry air filled with either white snowflakes or ashes—maybe some of both.

"We're not done here, children," Alastor cried. I spun at his voice and a nearby feminine shriek. Hayden and I bumped into each other—him moving forward, me taking a step back. "Blood will flow tonight. It's up to you to decide whose it will be."

Aspasia didn't fight her captor, terrified eyes pulsing with a mute appeal. Her trembling lips opened and closed, flapping to shape the words: *run, go.* Cut off when Hayden sped forward to help, but he stopped abruptly when the knife in his father's hand dimpled his mother's slender throat.

"Leave her alone," Hayden barked, flinching when I stepped forward to take his hand.

"Stop this! No one needs to die tonight," Mama said, hands out as she approached. Her steady expression never changed, even when Alastor laughed in delight.

"And there she is, my lovely witch." Alastor offered each of us a game show host's glittery smile. "But you're wrong, darling. Someone always needs to die. Our Lord demands it, and who am I to deny Him?"

"That's not true. No one died when you took Mama," I said, even as Mama hissed a warning. "Do what you want with me. Just please, don't hurt anyone else."

Alastor nodded, still arrogant but somewhat relieved, pressing a kiss to Aspasia's cheek. He crooned to her, "It's been a pleasure, my love. Quite a life you've given us, and at least one worthy child, which is better than none."

"Father, what...? No!" Bronte appeared, red-eyed and maskless, blotches erupting on her skin from the oppressive smoke. Hayden grabbed her, but she fought him and tumbled into the dirt with childlike confusion.

Alastor giggled, arms constricting like tentacles until Aspasia cried out again. Sharing a conspiratorial wink with Mama, he said, "We'll both be single now. Funny how that works out. I wonder if Felix would've wept and begged if he'd been conscious? My wife was strong once, but listen to her blubbering now. Maybe you had the better spouse, after all, my Tessa."

"What are you saying?" I asked, still woozy but rousing when that monster spoke my father's name.

"Cori, don't..." Mama reached out, stopping when Aspasia cried again from the pressure of the knife.

"I didn't want any interference at the ceremony with your mother, so I made sure to take care of Felix. He went down with barely a fight, disappointing really," Alastor said, summoning me with a pert tilt of his head. "Come along now, Coralena. Be a good girl, like your mother used to boast."

"Hayden, grab her!"

Mama's command flitted through my ears but never registered. Anger overwhelmed me—spiking, then sinking beneath a mind-numbing shroud. Alastor's revelation thumped, cracking through the barrier like a bird fighting its way from a shattered shell. Hands attempted to restrain me, but I shrugged them off—blew them off, more like. The slight gesture, boosted by the power sweeping across my vibrating muscles and bones, knocked Hayden several feet away. He landed at Mama's feet, stunned but unhurt. I returned my gaze to Alastor.

My target: the man who killed my father and raped my mother, destroying my family for his sick delusions—a search for a mythological demon, a selfish dream of immortality. As if the most important people in my life were merely pawns on his narcissistic quest.

Purple and blue lines veined the white ball of light around my hands—a second skin. I stared at the pair of them with detached interest. The surrounding noises—the bonfire, howling cultists, pleading loved ones—dulled as if I were submerged underwater.

The world shrank as I steadily sank then vanished. Falling into the abyss of myself, swimming through to the darkest corner of my spirit. What might I find in a place so deep the light couldn't reach?

Alastor's mouth snapped and quaked, releasing words I didn't hear, but the meaning was clear: *stay back or else.*

I paused to gaze at Aspasia's striking face, but her pride broke at the sight of me. Her lips overflowed with a stream of prayers for her beloved children. She gently shook her head, then smiled. A fellow woman, one more mother who had protected me for the child in my womb, if not for myself. Either way, I wouldn't see her hurt. We'd lost too many good people to Alastor Colburn.

But Alastor's hand sliced anyway, opening her throat like a creamy-white envelope. A crimson gush stained the front of her coat, splashing onto the dirt with a roar that hit my ears like a tidal wave. He laughed and discarded the body of his wife—a woman he'd spent thirty years with—raising his dripping blade to the heavens. A madman, a menace—and again—a murderer.

I inhaled the night air. It smelled cleaner now. The hallucinogens must've burned off. A torch approached from the periphery, held by a gnarled hand. Two swirling pits of blackness swayed within the bubble of firelight, portals to another realm—a place ruled by vengeance and madness. A place that, for me, felt like another type of home.

I sighed as the pressure released, my overfilled mind draining at last...

and the flames shot forth.

The gibbering panic on Alastor's blood-speckled face ignited with the power blasting from me—channeled through my mind, heart, body, and spirit. A slow-motion char rolled across his pasty flesh. He shrieked, a combination of laughter and terror, even as he roasted to the bone.

You've made your choice, Kóri. Come with me, agápi mou.

My vision blacked out in a swirl of Hekate's cloak, whisking me from the gruesome spectacle my vindictive soul yearned to witness. I relented to her coercion, allowing my senses to be overtaken and shut down for my own good.

She was my mother, too, and mothers always knew best.

CHAPTER THIRTY-ONE

The familiar setting sprawled before me: the sunlit dining area and rows of immaculate tables decorated with bud vases of spring flowers. The counter stretched along the back wall, expanding into an immaculate display case filled with tempting baked goods. The kitchen doors swung open, revealing the woman who'd blessed me with life.

Identical in shape and coloring, wearing her customary rosy smile, but something was off. The eyes belonged to another. When she sat across from me, setting a small plate between us, I couldn't tear my gaze away. Instead of pools of melted caramel, these eyes were all-black and swirling with a spray of light—embers from a bonfire, or suicidal stars diving through a midnight sky.

"We need to talk."

"Why am I here?" I asked the woman masquerading as my mother—a stranger, but not. I suspected she was much more than a figure in a dream, a Mother even greater than my earthly one.

"You made a choice, *Kóri*, and there's no turning back now," the woman said, ruby lips twisting in a halfhearted smile beneath her dispassionate alien gaze.

"What does that mean? Am I...?" I didn't want to finish my sentence or thought, but she divined the meaning, anyway.

"You're alive, for now, but blood has been spilled. Lives lost, from the most wicked to the most precious. One pays for the other, but the choice will cause you great suffering," the woman said, patting my lifeless hand. "You descend from powerful women, *Mágissa*, but you've unleashed something they could not. The use of such wild magic demands a price. Next time, you may not escape the ultimate payment. Do you understand, *Kóri*?"

"Is my magic gone, then?" I grieved the possible loss of a part of me I only recently discovered and misused. I wasn't a fit vessel for my ancestors' gifts.

"No, it's a part of you. Same as your flesh and spirit." The woman's voice thickened with the echoes of others—long-dead women whose noble love and sacrifices guided me to this moment. "But you will suffer from this choice, a payment for a crime you committed not only against the universe but also yourself. One more act of vengeance, and you will die, *Kóri*. And worse, your immortal soul will be lost forever—damned. Do you understand?"

"Yes, *Mitéra*."

She slid the plate closer. I examined the delicate pastry on the white porcelain. My favorite, Mama's springtime baklava with pistachios and pomegranate reduction. Lifting the slender fork, I began to eat. Each flaky bite melted against my tongue—the sugary tartness and earthy nuts fed more than my body, sending an energetic buzz to awaken my sedated soul. Each piece I swallowed chipped away the dream realm, ferrying me from the in-between back home.

"*Alítheia, sympónia, sofía*—never forget, my *Kóri*."

Truth, compassion, wisdom... No, Mitéra, I won't forget. I'll try, I promise.

***

Only one light kept the darkness from smothering the room, cramped with the scent of damp earth and the wet rot of hidden roots. Something else...a whiff of copper bound it together, a wayward drop of blood zig-zagging through my groggy senses.

Someone died. That *smell*...it overwhelmed the crushing atmosphere, vivid as burning toast or scorched garlic. And something else assaulted me, an ache as my ravaged heart lurched in my hollow chest—remorse.

A scuffling sound followed by a sharp sob, then she was on her knees and by my side. Her long hair was whiter than ever—streaked with darkness instead of the reverse. Mama, drained but happy, grateful... Her wan skin stretched too thin over her skull, a woman aged far before her time. Drenched in sorrow, yet a lively glimmer of hope flickered among the wreckage.

"Thank the Goddess," she whispered through cracked lips, laying a sandpapery kiss against my forehead. "Oh baby, I thought I'd lost you."

"Mama—she was here, I think..." my vocal cords seized, constricting from fatigue and thirst. Like swallowing broken glass, I tried to work up some spit to make it easier. The dream faded, a fish flopping through my fingertips to race beneath the waves of my subconscious. "Warned me, paid a price..."

"I'm so sorry, my love. I tried to stop you, but it was so quick. Your strength, it was unlike anything I'd ever seen. You killed Alastor...a horrible man, but a fellow human." Mama buried her face against my neck. She laid beside me on the dirt, thin arms tight to contain our broken pieces. "We have to leave as soon as you can travel."

I patted her arm, then ran my fingers lower to the dull howl throbbing between my hips. Cramps, slow at first but now snapping with a renewed strength.

Oh no! Please, no...

"The baby?"

"We lost him, Cori. Your body, it couldn't take the power. I did everything I could, but it was too much." Her words disintegrated into tears, lost in the nest of my hair. Yet, she held on—tighter as my body shook with helpless sobs more akin to dry heaves. I curled into myself, hiding from her words and their meaning. I hugged my empty womb as new spasms rocked my lower body. Empty, each cramp a wail for what was lost—another death on my hands.

"Hayden... Where is he?" The dirt puffed beneath my cheek, and my nails clawed the unforgiving earth. I swallowed a cry as the pain escalated—

worse when she continued.

"He's with his sister. You won't see him again," Mama said. Cold as the blizzard I dimly recalled, unleashed during our first steps of flight from the bonfire massacre.

"No, he wouldn't…" Sitting up, holding the pain beneath one shaking hand, I searched for a way out of this dank hole. A cellar, with a naked bulb dangling overhead and a set of stairs to a wooden door only a few feet away.

"He would, and he did." She guided me back to the ground. I was too weak to fight. "Don't move, I'll get help. You're not healed enough to walk unassisted."

I noticed the space around me, a circle of white candles and a steaming cauldron on a battery-powered hot plate. A jumble of roots and herbs scattered across a wooden cutting board beside a bucket of bloody water, pink rags bobbing on the surface. She worked on me in this pit beneath the earth, maybe for hours or days… Giving of herself to save me, once again.

"What did you do?"

"I did what needed to be done, Cori. That's all you need to know. Now wait here, I'll get help." She brushed herself off before heading to the stairs, stiff as a woman twenty years older. I'd done this to her. Could any amount of recuperation help her become the mama I knew and loved?

And Hayden… No, he wouldn't abandon me. She was angry. Maybe she told him to leave. I recalled our moment in the tent, his touch and kiss. All those earlier promises. He loved me. He said he did.

You killed his child, his parents… Are you sure?

Swiping the thought away, I stretched across the dirt. Hot eyes blinked, readying for tears which didn't come. The spasms calmed as a fresh wave of numbness enveloped me, a merciful cloak from my other Mother. Maybe she was here, too, in this dank room—an antechamber to Hell. I suffered for my misuse of magic, as She'd warned, an action rippling with consequences I couldn't bear to think about right now.

My baby boy… Felix, I'm so very sorry. I didn't mean it. Mama loves you, sweetheart.

Each word rapped across the blank walls of my empty mind, quieter than the heavy feet rushing down the steps. The help Mama left to find. I wouldn't turn them away, but I didn't deserve to be saved. Damned, alone, shattered—vengeance didn't seem worth it now, but it was too late. The price had been paid.

***

I sat with Papou in his first-floor room, uninterested in the family discussion in the kitchen. Cristina, Dora, Monica, Marcus—the whole crew was here, planning the next move. Cristina's husband, Adam, was out with his cousin setting up a temporary hideaway. It was important to Mama, finding a way to keep us both safe. But I wasn't sure I had any interest in more plans. Sitting with Papou in his silent sea of lost memories was far more comfortable.

The old television in his room played a VHS, a relic from Mama's childhood. The scratchy video showed a series of family parties—wild '80s hair and clothes, infectious music from a band of distant friends or relatives, and my grandparents entertaining everyone with tables full of marvelous food.

Papou and Yaya had been parents of an adult daughter, settled until Mama's birth surprised them in their early forties. And there she was: running around with her cousins, pestering her older sister, and stopped often by both of her parents for hugs and kisses. She was so tiny, with a mane of curly dark hair and impish eyes, beloved by everyone she encountered.

Too much time had passed, the older generation taking their traditions when they fled the earth. We never had family parties anymore. The restaurant was too demanding, and so many family members had died over the years or moved on to bigger and better lives around the world.

Family, a cornerstone of my mother's childhood but mostly absent from my own. I had Cristina and her family, but the losses of my grandparents and my father left a hole. Maybe if Yaya lived, Papou could've hung on to be present with us. If Daddy lived, I could've had a whole other family to spend important events and holidays with. Plenty of them lived in Puerto Rico, but I'd never met them as an adult.

Time and tragedy stole them all away. I'd never experienced being a member of a large extended group—a tribe. With my child lost, I couldn't fathom building a new family. What was the use, all of those idealized plans and unrewarded struggles, when life was ultimately ephemeral?

Our reflection in the mirror caught my eye, a sight which spooked me until I made sense of the image. Papou, small and withered in his wheelchair, and a strange woman sitting beside him with a lush head of pure-white hair. A ghost—was it Yaya, returned from the dead? No, just me; the last bit of rich ebony faded from my curls forever.

I couldn't bear what the mirror revealed, weeping when I first saw it; now, I forced myself to accept the change. Whatever magic I'd unleashed to kill Alastor—a pillar of flame from the nearby fire, Mama said—it leached both the color from my hair and the vitality from my spirit. Weak and tired, I shuffled through the house to find a sanctuary away from them all. Had any twenty-one-year-old ever felt so ancient? A sign of the end, maybe, but I couldn't muster enough anxiety to care. Death would be a rest, an endlessly peaceful sleep away from the devastating pains of this world.

Monica entered with a cup of tea, wary and red-eyed, forcing a smile. "Hey girl, your mama said you should drink this. Can I get you a snack or anything?"

"No, thanks." I broke away from the renewed round of middle-aged dancing on the screen to accept the cup and saucer. My hands trembled, pale and bloodless things, absent of their customary bronze glow. My strength was gone, maybe never to return. Just like my poor baby.

"They're sending you both away." Monica sat beside me on the bed, smoothing my colorless hair. Only a few strokes before she pulled back, maybe still scared by such a rapid and inexplicable change. "We'll keep the restaurant going, hold it down until you can come back."

I nodded, sipping the hot tea and closing my eyes. A small tingle followed the steaming liquid as it streamed down my throat, spreading through my vacant belly. A security blanket, like the one I had as a child, warming me from the inside out.

"Cori, I'm here if you need to talk," she said—cautious, but bravely forcing the offer out. "I don't know what happened, but I guess I'm not too surprised. There's always been something about you two, especially your Mama, but magic... It's crazy, right?"

"Crazy," I agreed, never taking my eyes from the screen. Someone brought out a massive cake on a rolling cart, covered with candles. A birthday party, interesting. Never saw that plot twist coming.

"Do you want me to talk to him... Hayden? I know how you felt—"

"No, don't." The words clattered like the cup against the saucer when I spun toward my friend.

"His family sucks, hell yes, but didn't you fall for him? I know he felt the same. He must be going out of his mind worrying about you."

"Doesn't matter. It's better we're apart after—" I covered my mouth, suppressing the words which longed for release. Or the screams. Dark feelings twisted within, wrangling at the thought of Hayden appearing here, seeing me like this. How could I face him again? "Monica, don't talk to him. He needs to forget me and move on. How could he love me after... Look at me!"

"I'm looking, don't worry." She wrapped me in her sturdy arms, laying a kiss on my forehead and cheek. "Cori, you're still beautiful and good. What happened, it was an accident. You panicked. It could've happened to anyone."

"He deserves a chance to be happy, and that won't be with me."

"Don't you deserve to be happy?"

"No," I said, before the last word left her mouth. "What I deserve is... Shit, I don't even know why I'm still here."

"I love you—do you hear me? It will get better, just please don't give up. We'll make this right." Her words shook with tears I couldn't see—didn't need to see—as she rocked me. A proper friend would've hugged her back, promised to keep fighting, vowed to stay strong—even if it was all bullshit. I couldn't muster the energy for a lie, even if it might comfort her.

This wasn't supposed to be my life. I didn't want this. If Hekate returned for me, I wouldn't fight. No, I'd welcome the chance to leave it all behind. Let my friends and family enjoy life again without their happiness spoiled by the divine retribution that surely headed my way.

"Monica, Ma needs you," Marcus said, filling the doorway but glancing away when I looked up. So unlike him, the most un-shy boy I'd ever met. He was frightened by whatever tale Mama spun in their far-off kitchen meeting.

"I'll be back," Monica promised. She left for now, but I believed she meant every bit of her support. I only wished I was worthy of such a true friend.

Papou shifted in the chair, staring at me with empty black eyes. His toothless mouth twitched, sliding over gums that trapped a wealth of words he'd never speak again. A hand struggled to rise, flopping awkwardly against the arm of his wheelchair until it rested palm-up in a wordless invitation. I took it, cradling the paper-thin skin, sucking in my breath at the faint squeeze I received.

"Go home," he wheezed, thick and rusty, with a voice that hadn't been used for over a decade. "This not your place, *korítsi fántasma*."

Ghost girl—apt, given my current appearance. I tried to hold his hand, but he wriggled free. Settling into himself, he turned back to the television and resumed his former catatonic state. Or maybe I finally became invisible, a ghost for real, trapped in a world which no longer held any future.

She sent me back for a purpose, *Mitéra* Hekate, or I'd simply misunderstood the dream. I couldn't quite remember. Life might return, energy refilling my depleted heart and soul... Some sort of new beginning was possible, but only if I left behind everything I'd ever known.

I couldn't think about that now. Mama would know what to do. She'd find a way for us to move forward, just as when we lost Daddy.

This was my first time coming back from the brutal edge of darkness, sliding away from the allure of Forgetting and the mercy of Death. I'd learn how to make it. Mama never failed before to teach me what I needed to survive. After everything, I couldn't fail her again...or myself.

Women know all about suffering, but that doesn't mean we'll be denied happiness. Cherish life's precious moments. Fill your heart and spirit with love. Always fight, Cori. Don't give up. You were meant to live, my love. Never forget.

I won't forget, Mama.

EPILOGUE

...THERE'S FIRE

Wall Street Journal
December 25, 20—

Global financier, Alastor Colburn, and his wife, Aspasia, died in a boating accident off the coast of their Greenwich, CT compound, Cypress Point. The Coast Guard and FBI forensics believe the accident was caused by a faulty fuel line in the family yacht, igniting a fire which sank the ship.

The bodies were recovered two days ago. Funeral rites are being organized by their children and heirs, Hayden and Bronte.

Mindy Packer, CFO of Cypress Group—the massive Colburn hedge fund—offered a brief statement after a shareholders' meeting. "Bronte Colburn is still young but nearly done with her economics degree at Yale. She will take over the Cypress Group, as her father intended. In the meantime, the Board will maintain standard operating protocol in her absence."

The Colburn children could not be reached for comment, but they appear to be supporting each other in the wake of this unexpected double loss. Ms. Colburn is the future of her family's business, an inheritance worth billions. Hayden, her older brother and a restauranteur in the East Village, remains uninvolved with the Colburn Group and its associated organizations.

"The family values its privacy in this dark time, but statements will be made at a later date when the children are ready to speak," Mindy Packer stated, wrapping up her speech. "Alastor's legacy lives on. It will endure, undoubtedly thriving under his children's inspired leadership. The future is bright for Cypress Group, never fear. All of us on the board are thrilled for what lies ahead in the next chapter of this indomitable family's saga."

ACKNOWLEDGMENTS

I wrote this book in one of my most crazed writing binges yet. It was a week into November, and NaNoWriMo (National Novel Writing Month) had already begun. I'd intended on participating, but I got caught up with edits on my previous novel. Still, I decided three weeks was enough to make something.

85k words later...

I'm honestly not trying to brag. But, the story tore itself out of my mind and didn't give me a chance to say no. Hell, one day I broke a personal record and wrote 10k. Is it a wonderful book? I guess that's up to you to decide. But I love it, and I'm damn proud of it.

Thank you to Cori, Hayden, Tessa, Aspasia, Bronte, Monica, and the crew—yes, even nasty old Alastor (that bastard!). And thank you Mitéra Hekate, for waving the torch and guiding me whenever I lost my way.

As always, I thank my family—my parents, Mary and Paul; my amazing sisters, Sarah and Cheryl; my step-parents, Cliff and Jose; my fabulous in-laws; and my unstoppable legion of brilliant nieces and nephews (extra thanks to Alannagh and Jazmin, who patiently suffered through a verbal retelling of the rough draft on our trip to North Carolina, but said: Wow

Auntie, that sounds cool!).

For my besties: Leanne, setting the world on fire in LV; to Las Chicas Fabulosas of LF/1.0—Becca, Brenda, Cynthia, Katie, Lindsay, and Paulina—our girls' nights saved me this year; Justin, my brother from another mother, keep fighting; and Shanna, your support and our various conversations over the year has meant the world to me. You're all amazing!

To my alpha/beta/ARC readers, I'm beyond grateful you offered your time to read this story. Your feedback is valuable and always welcome.

Guinness, I didn't forget: You're my furry, plump baby forever. I love you!

And last but not least, Stephen, you've been right by my side through this all. It hasn't been an easy year, filled with obstacles—each more daunting and unbelievable than the last. But, you've handled it all with aplomb. I'm so proud to share a life with you, se agapó.

Thank you, everyone, for traveling this road with me. I cherish you all.

Jennifer Soucy (July, 2020)

ABOUT THE AUTHOR

Jennifer Soucy is a quintessential New England girl, born and raised in Connecticut. A wanderer by nature, she moved to the Atlanta area with her family when she was nineteen and delights in being called a "Damn Yankee." She also spent nearly two years in Las Vegas, her home away from home. Back in Georgia now, she started writing again to fulfill her childhood dreams. This writer, assistant editor, and professional bartender is also a proud nerd who enjoys anything involving horror and fantasy.

Her debut novel, DEMON IN ME, is available on Amazon. THE MOTHER WE SHARE is coming in 2021 from Rhetoric Askew Publishing. And Book 2 of The Eleusinian Chronicles is also coming in 2021.

She hopes to continue publishing books that occasionally make people sleep with the light on.

Learn More about Jennifer at her website:

https://www.jenniferlsoucy.com

Author's Photo courtesy of Solia Digital Media LLC

https://www.soliamedia.com/

IF YOU LIKED THIS BOOK . . .

Please leave a review on Amazon, Goodreads, or anywhere you'd like. Your ratings and support mean the world to indie authors, boosting exposure, sales, and morale.

We craft our tales for you as much as for ourselves.

Thank you so much for reading

THE NIGHT SHE FELL

Stay Tuned for the Shocking Sequel

SHE WHO DESTROYS

Coming February 2022

www.ingramcontent.com/pod-product-compliance
Lightning Source LLC
Chambersburg PA
CBHW020315200626
46814CB00006BA/2248